To Gin[...]
Brothe[...]
I love you both.
Blessings on you
& your house

[signature]

K. R. Schultz

THE SONG OF THE DEFILER

By
K. R. Schultz

K. R. Schultz

ISBN-13: 9781461059707
ISBN-10: 1461059704
Printed in the United States of America

DEDICATION

To Patricia, my wife and proofreader, and to my family who waited many years to see this book in print.

To Verna King, my beta reader, for her help and insight. She boldly waded through an unfamiliar genre novel with great dedication.

Without them, this book would never have come this far, and to all the friends who encouraged me along the way.

Thank-you everyone!

K. R. Schultz

THE ISLAND OF KHEL BRAAH.

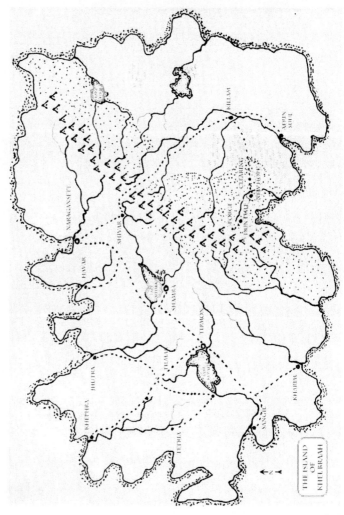

K. R. Schultz

PROLOGUE

Along the sharp spine of the ridge, the trunks of the trees leaned into the wind, to brace themselves against its force. Their coats of twigs and leaves streamed behind them in the moonlight, as if struggling to keep up with the branches that bore them. It was a trick of the light and the wind, but the trees appeared to race toward a destination somewhere in the shadows of the valley below. There was real movement as well; a lone figure picked his way through the forest at the base of the ridge. The figure, alone in the dark, had a name and a destiny. He was Laakea. The name meant 'light' in the ancient tongue.

The night wind was all sharp corners and jagged edges that pierced his clothing. The wind slashed at his face and ears, and his heart pumped warmth from his exposed flesh with every beat. He began to shiver and pulled his cloak tighter around himself. He tucked his numb fingers inside the cloak, next to his body, to warm them. The soft white light of the moon certainly gave off no heat.

In its pale light, he could just make out the dark lines of the trunks and branches ahead. The dim light cloaked everything in shades of gray and silver, ghostly shapes, insubstantial, and colorless in the darkness. The wind in the trees drowned out other sounds. His footsteps went unheard, as he picked his way among them. Occasionally he glanced up to the trees silhouetted along the ridge, to maintain his bearings. It had been easy enough to lose his way in daylight, but now he was disoriented. The game trail he had been following was now nowhere in sight.

Laakea had known that he was hopelessly lost after the first night. He had been walking day and night with only short naps and an occasional stop to drink the water he found in forest pools and hollow tree stumps. It was his fifth night of walking away from the mountain valley that had been his home. It was a hell of a night. A hell of a night to be out, far from shelter with no sure welcome at the end of this night's journey. A hell of a night to have no destination, just walking — endlessly — away.

"At least it's not raining," he thought.

His father had driven him from the comfort of hearth and home with no opportunity to return. He had little desire to reflect on that portion of his young life right now. There were more pressing problems tonight. The most pressing of all being survival.

Laakea knew that he should have reached the village of Dun Dale days ago. His stomach was empty and his legs were beginning to feel heavy. Although his earlier bouts of shivering from the damp spring air had subsided, he could feel the effects of hunger, exertion and cold combining to numb his mind and body. He needed rest in a warm place. Sleep called him, caressed his thoughts, and pulled at his tired limbs like a lover.

"It must be near freezing," he thought.

Each step was quickly becoming a battle. Every obstacle in his path grew taller and more ominously challenging with every stride. The forest began to close in. Wet branches stung his cold skin, slapping at him abusively, yet calling out seductively at the same time.

"Stop fighting — come — sleep — rest — stay. We will be your bower, your bed. You will find peace in our embrace."

Laakea heard another voice as well. He had no idea where it came from, but it urged him onward. If voices could have a color, this one was golden. It was brilliant. It was musical. It urged him to continue with its bright melodic power. The sound of the voice triggered memories of his mother.

Laakea's mind wandered replaying events from his distant past. The warm glow of those memories kept him from succumbing to the forest's cold embrace. He remembered hot summer days in the garden with his mother, weeding the vegetables, in the humid air. He missed her chattering and singing while they worked together. He remembered a similar golden power in Shelhera's songs before the shadows overtook her. She had weakened, and grown more frail and sickly with each passing month.

He remembered the winters in the forge with his father and the cool summer evenings of sword practice. He reminisced fondly about supper at the kitchen table where they laughed, joked, sang, and played together before turning in for the night. The memories kept him going even though those days were gone forever. He tripped over a root and it jarred him out of his reverie.

Laakea picked himself up, and brushed off the detritus and leaf mould as well as he could. His clothing was damp and dirty, from contact with the forest floor. He carried on, stumbling from tree to tree. By strength of will, the youngster fought to stay alert and upright. He forced his feet to keep moving forward in the darkness. The light disappeared and darkness fully enveloped him. Laakea had no idea how long he had been walking, but it seemed endless. He had hoped for dawn soon, but the night was now as black as soot. At first, he wasn't certain if his mind had just stopped working, because of fatigue and cold, or if something had suddenly blotted out the light from the moon and stars. He looked up.

There were clouds.

It started to rain.

He pulled his hat down as tight as he could, wrapped his cloak closer to his body and struggled on. The rain was not heavy, but it still quickly worked its way through his garments and the soles of his boots. It eventually carried the chilling wind through his clothing all the way to his bones.

What was that? A light — no — it was gone, a trick of the imagination. Laakea dragged himself forward, growing weaker with each step.

There it was again, a yellow glow that winked on and off with an irregular rhythm.

"Damn, my mind's going fuzzy. It's just brush or tree trunks blocking it as I move. It may be a lantern or perhaps a campfire," he thought.

His father had told him about the rough men, who preyed on weak and helpless people, like wolves devouring sheep. Would he find the warmth and welcome, he desperately needed in front of those flames, or would someone waiting there snuff out the faint glimmer of life remaining in him? If the fire belonged to the strange, tattooed men, who supposedly lurked in these woods, they would probably gut him like a fish. That firelight could lure him to his death, as surely as a moth, drawn to a candle's glow, perished in its flame.

He knew that the combat lessons his father had drilled into him would not do help him in his present condition. He would not be able to put up much of a fight, as cold and tired as he was, especially when his only weapon was the dagger he carried in his belt. He had never used it for anything more than a table knife. If he had been thinking at all when he fled, he would have at least brought his bow and the short sword his father made him practice with every day.

Laakea hadn't seen the point of the relentless schedule of practice at the time. Why would he need to know how to use weapons for defense? The Abrhaani who lived around them were simple farmers, gentle people of the land who steered clear of him and his family. Even their children avoided him, although he never truly understood why.

He knew his parents were different from the people in Dun Dale. Laakea's parents were bigger than their neighbors were. His whole family was as blonde as the bleached straw in the thatched roof of their house. He was like them, different from all the other green-eyed, dark-haired, green-skinned children around him. Though he was only thirteen summers, he towered above the other youngsters who were his own age. In fact, he was taller by a hand span than most of the men from the village.

Of course, there was the occasional bully among the older children, like the Sawyers three sons. They were nearly full-grown. The three bullies did not live in Dun Dale, but in the town of New Hope. They habitually caused trouble whenever they showed up in the village, but Laakea was big for his age and he could usually settle those disputes with enough bluster. Occasionally he had to resort to throwing a punch, but usually the worst that happened was a little scuffling and rolling in the dirt, until they sorted things out one way or another. Even when all three of them came at once, Laakea had not needed weapons, let alone weapons training. His father never asked him about the bruises and scrapes that had resulted from those encounters.

Laakea had questioned his father about why and how they were different from their neighbors, especially after his mother died, but Aelfric would tell him little of his heritage or origins. Aelfric had become a man of few words, saying little about his life before he and the boy's mother came to live on the island.

Shelhera, his mother, on the other hand, had taught him much. She taught him how to behave well, good manners she called it. She told him stories and legends about their gods. She taught him to garden. Her parents had been bowyers and fletchers for generations, and she had faithfully passed on those skills to him as they had been passed to her. Shelhera explained that they lived on an island called Kel Braah, in the sea of Syn Gersuul. Laakea's parents had never allowed him far enough from the farm and the forge to see much of anything. He supposed that their oversight contributed to his undoing tonight.

Laakea had never seen the sea; in fact, he had never been farther than the village. Shelhera, not his father, gave him bits of information about their people, the Eniila. Aelfric was more forthcoming with facts about the Abrhaani, the people who lived nearby. Aelfric rarely spoke of his lineage or his people, and always looked displeased whenever he caught her telling Laakea about them. In spite of those looks of disapproval, he never said anything to reprimand Shelhera, at least not when Laakea was there to hear it. Now that she was gone, Laakea had no outlet for his curiosity about the larger world and his mysterious heritage. The need to find answers to his questions drove him to risk his father's rages, because he knew that his mother had not told him everything she could. She was gone too quickly for that.

Since his mother's death, life around the forge had become increasingly unbearable. Laakea remembered the old days, when his father used to take him on his broad strong shoulders and run with him around the yard. They ran so fast that the wind blew his hair back. As they ran, they both laughed hard. He helped his father in the forge sorting nails and bits of iron at first, then, when he was strong enough, by fetching water and working the bellows. Those were golden sunny days, but then a shadow had fallen. His mother sickened and wasted away, and things changed.

Shelhera was the only one who had grown weaker, but it looked as if both his parents were ill. His father never showed any sign of physical illness, but Shelhera's illness seemed to drain the life out of Aelfric, like a bleeding wound, that would not heal. The first thing to go was the light in his eyes, and then laughter disappeared. Finally sullen, silence replaced speech. Aelfric looked the same outwardly, but the man inside was gone. He was like a garden plant, grown without sun, spindly and pale, and barely clinging to life. When she died, only shadows of the man he had been remained.

Laakea caught a momentary glimpse of his real father, when they stood together with torches, watching Shelhera's pyre brighten the night with flame. The breeze had freshened and blown sparks into the night sky, like a swarm of fireflies rushing toward the stars, until the darkness swallowed them, one by one. They had stood side by side facing the flames, and Aelfric had put his large hand on his son's shoulder, as if to comfort him. The next morning that comfort had disappeared, like the sparks that had flown into the previous night's sky.

After they had surrendered her body to the flames of the funeral pyre, his father's long silences had become even more brooding and sullen, punctuated by outbursts of rage. The best the boy could expect of him lately was a single word answer to a question. At worst, he would get a tongue-lashing that would blister the daub off the walls of their house. He could never please the man, no matter how hard he tried, and he was tired of trying. That was what had precipitated his departure. His

15

own anger had boiled hot within, until he had finally stood up to his father, and the older man had told him to get out.

"Get out and never come back. I never want to see you again. I wish you had never been born, so I wouldn't have to see your face and be reminded of her." Aelfric could not bring himself to speak her name.

Laakea had shouted hurtful, hating words back at his father, before he left. They were words that he could never take back, words for which there could be no remedy other than bloodshed. He had cursed his father; or rather, he cursed the man his father had become. He called down the wrath of all the gods he could name on his father's head.

All Laakea had intended to do was defend himself. He had only wanted his father's belligerence to stop, but his own anger had betrayed him. He had committed an unpardonable offense in cursing Aelfric. That transgression had provoked his father to threaten him with violence. It was a *Blood Debt*. A *Blood Debt* required blood for repayment, and his father could collect it at any time.

He could never go home again. No — that was not true; he could never go home again and survive, unless he could best his father in single combat. If he could defeat his father, it would be a sign that the god's had judged his case and granted him victory. He knew in his heart, that he was guilty, so the gods would never support him.

Shame branded his words of wrath indelibly into his memory. He had been so angry, that only when his father had brandished a piece of firewood like a club, had he realized the seriousness of his offense. His life was in danger. Afraid that his father would claim his life as payment for his dishonorable act, Laakea had fled into the night. He had taken only his cloak and hat from the peg by the door. He rushed out into the darkening forest leaving behind everything he had ever known.

So be it. He would face the world alone, shamed and unloved. He missed his mother.

He hated his father. He finally admitted it. It was the worst thing he could think of doing, but he hated him anyway. He was an outcast now. If his father had died with his mother, and been burned alongside her on the pyre he could be no more alone, no more orphaned than he was now.

Laakea wished that his father had died. If Aelfric had died he would not now be guilty of dishonoring his father, but his father still lived and Laakea had cursed him to his face. Had that been the worst that life had given him he could cope, but worse than that, he had dishonored himself and he had dishonored the memory of his mother as well.

In that moment of hatred, he had embodied all the worst character failings he saw in his father, and multiplied them fourfold. He had become what he hated, and he couldn't face it. Though he ran from his father, because he feared for his life, he also ran because he was afraid of himself. He feared the man he might become. Both fears, in almost equal measure, had driven him out into the wilderness alone. A small part of him wanted to quit, in case this was not the worst he could or would become.

"I was stupid. I should have stopped to collect provisions and a bedroll," he thought.

Laakea's fear of impending death had given him no chance to prepare or plan for this journey, and now it was too late for either preparation or planning. Once he had put some distance between himself and his father, he had planned to make for the village. Unfortunately, he had quickly lost the trail in the dark, so that plan too was unattainable. Now, because of his fear, and haste, his life was in grave danger.

He realized that his mind had begun to wander again, as it often did before he drifted off to sleep. He roused himself, realizing if he allowed this to continue he was done for. It was no use thinking about what he should have done. He needed warmth and rest immediately. He was too cold and desperate to care anymore. To stay where he was, or to continue in his present condition, promised certain death. The fire ahead at least held the possibility of keeping him alive. It was his best option. He faced the possibility of death with any of the choices he had left to him. He set his course by the light, forcing his way through wet undergrowth.

Hope, once nearly extinguished, grew within him as the light grew brighter. In a pitched battle with this hope, the cold rain trickled down his neck, squelched inside his boots, and drew away the last of his body's precious warmth. Each step demanded a payment of willpower and energy drawn from an account within. The balance plummeted to nearly nothing. He tried to call out, and shout for aid, but little more than a groan issued past his lips. He found it difficult to get his jaw and his lips to move. They were as numb and unresponsive from the cold as his arms and legs were becoming.

It was a race now. Could he reach the light, before strength and consciousness abandoned him? Time became elastic, measured in paces instead of minutes, one prolonged, sodden footstep at a time. Seconds stretched and became hours. His limbs belonged to someone else. By sheer force of will, he commanded them to cooperate with his mind and they grudgingly obeyed, for now. His will drove his recalcitrant arms and legs to do his bidding, like the whip of the drover forced unruly draft animals to obey.

Although he knew he was drawing closer to the light, it seemed to grow dimmer with each step. His eyelids grew heavy. His consciousness drifted, like the clouds in the wind overhead. He no longer felt anything except the need to sleep. Dreamlike memories seduced him again. What little he could still see in the darkness blurred, obscured by the fog that crept into his mind. His knees finally buckled and he dropped onto the soggy litter of the forest floor and fell forward onto his face, his outstretched hands barely slowed his fall.

"It is not over." He heard the golden voice speak again as blackness swallowed him in a single gulp.

CHAPTER 1: THE HERETIC

Rehaak had awakened with a nagging headache over his right eye and the feeling that he had forgotten something important from his dreams. It was morning. The sun outlined everything in gold. As daylight approached, it shredded the remains of the night and cast long shrinking shadows. Tatters of darkness clung in, isolated patches, where it still hid from the light. There might be an omen in this observation but he was too tired to care.

Though the day was fine and fair, he felt rough and foul. He was working for the cause again, instead of wasting his energy in debauchery and carousing, however he still felt dissolute. He had spoken, cajoled, and outright threatened the citizens of Narragansett, until he was exhausted. He had little to show for the great effort that he had expended so far. No one heeded his ominous tidings. He was a failure — again.

Perhaps he had finally sunk too far into rebellion. He had broken most of his God's laws. Perhaps God had finally forsaken him. In spite of his renewed efforts to complete The Creator's mission, his conscience plagued him this morning. Hope suffocated in the darkness of his heart, in spite of the bright new day being born around him.

"I've had enough. I'm sick of this life. I need to find something else to do," he said, feeling trapped.

He knew well enough that there was nothing else he could do for now. The Creator had caught him like a fish in a net. There was no chance of escape. Based on the last few days experience of rejection and derision, he was equally certain there was no hope for success.

Rehaak had come to the city of Narragansett, full of optimism. The scriptorium in the city was the center of all learning and knowledge in Kel Braah. If he could find the Aetheriad at all, this was the place to find it. The elusive ancient text had been the center of his quest and the center of his existence for most of his thirty odd years. He still suspected that it held the answer to his questions and that it would provide critical information to save his people from impending doom. The search had been long — long and fruitless thus far.

He vaguely remembered the hope that had flooded him when he entered Narragansett across the causeway seven years ago. That hope had slowly drained away, leaving him as dry as the sunlit dust on his windowsill this morning. Twelve years of ineffective searching through dusty books and forgotten ruins had taken their toll on his optimism and confidence.

He still had the resources of the scriptorium at hand, but the sheer volume of the material now intimidated him. He had lost the will to go on. He did not know where to continue his search, through the mountain of parchments and scrolls. Instead, he had turned aside from his quest and spent his time and his money on his own pleasures and desires, using and abusing others at his whim, in direct disobedience to the laws of decency and the laws of God.

His dedication and devotion to his lengthy studies had earned him the reputation of a scholar. No one knew more of what lay in the most ancient texts than he. No one knew the arcane writings better. None of the Ecclesiarches could match his wit in debate, however none of his impressive knowledge had led him any closer to the legendary volume that he sought. He had found clues and hints among the writings of long dead scholars, prophets and priests, but the clues were cryptic and contradictory. He had lost hope. He had given up and turned aside from the true path.

It had begun innocently; one person of influence sought him out for his advice, then another, and another. Then dozens had come to him for counsel and prophetic insight. People sought him out for his prophecies and they had paid him well for his advice. In the beginning, he told people what he believed The Creator wanted them to hear, but eventually he found better commerce in telling his customers only what pleased them. He had squandered his credibility filling their ears, and their hearts with soft sweet words devoid of real insight or worth.

He felt powerful on the one hand — trapped and helpless on the other. People who had valued his words gave him honor and wealth, but he knew how hollow his words had become. Their expectations on him mounted daily and engulfed him in an ever-deepening morass of deception. Each phrase sank him deeper into a mire of lies and deceit that he could never hope to escape.

God knew he had tried to escape. The courtesans had provided a distraction for a time and the drinking had numbed the pain, but it was only temporary relief. He still awoke the following day knowing that he had failed in his quest, and worse, that he was now not only a failure, but a degenerate as well.

Business had been good. The rich and bored paid well, even if they eventually came to consider him a charlatan. His words were creative, even poetic on the good days, when he was not too hung over. He entertained them. He charmed them and gave them what they wanted and they had rewarded him for it, in the same way that they would have rewarded a performing animal.

Before he had come to the city, he had gotten by on very little, without a home, without funds, without friends. What was the harm of taking a little recompense he had reasoned? His efforts deserved a reward, did they not? He tried to justify his actions by convincing himself that his words hurt no one. Unfortunately, his creative talents did not extend to self-deception. He eventually had to admit that they hurt someone — they hurt him. His deceitful words ate at his soul like acid. He felt cheap, dirty, defiled, used, and burned out. After compromising on so many things, the irony was that The Creator had chosen him to speak His words to the Abrhaani people and they left a bitter taste in his mouth.

The latest turn in the road of his life had surprised him. He was debating some points of interpretation of a manuscript, when he suddenly had the feeling that there was an unseen presence there with him. Without warning, it enveloped him like warm oil.

His theophany had finally occurred. Until that moment, he had only been intellectually convinced of the reality of the Creator. He fell to the ground entranced, as the presence of The Creator overcame him in broad daylight. As he lay on the steps outside the halls of learning, the Faithful One revealed himself to Rehaak. His convictions were no longer merely intellectual. They were hard experience. He had discovered lately just how hard experience could become.

The Faithfull One had shown Rehaak the future; a vision of blackened lands; a waking nightmare of destruction. In the vision, he felt dark, malevolent beings suck the life from the land as if it were happening to his own flesh. He suffered with the land, weakening, dying, and mourning for itself, as its life began to fade. Dark and deformed figures reared up from the ground, seeking to devour everything in their path. They were blacker than a moonless night in a mineshaft. They stank of death and disease. The vision forced him to relive his childhood nightmares and magnified those horrific images in his mind.

The Dark Ones, as he came to call them, had advanced into the city, draining the life from everything as they came, in a relentless orgy of devastation. The Dark Ones stripped life from people, livestock, gardens, and even the stones of the city itself. Nothing remained except dried husks and barren, blackened stone. He had never imagined that rock was capable of life until then, but when he felt the stones die, he understood by life's absence that they had once contained life. With each morsel of life the hellish creatures consumed they grew larger and more powerful. The land would never recover. Nothing would ever live or grow, in that barren wasteland, for all eternity.

His God had given him a message to relay to the people of Narragansett.

"Tell the people of this great city, that what you have seen this day will surely come to pass, unless they turn to me and follow me as they did before the Sundering of Brothers. It is your task, to warn them and to unite them with their brothers again. Tell them about me. Warn them of the fate of the blackened lands and of the battle yet to come. You have sought me and found me, and you are not alone."

He did not pretend to understand all that The Creator had said to him. He suspected the nightmare creatures were the Nethera, who he had read about in the works of the ancient sage, Ziade of Tensel. No one had seen or heard much of the ancient evil ones in the centuries since the Battle of Three Kings, on the battle plain in Baradon. Nowadays, the Nethera lived on only in tales to frighten unruly children into obedience.

"The Nethera will get you if you don't —," fill in the blanks to make the message appropriate. The saying had fallen into disuse, perhaps not even the children believed it anymore. Unfortunately, he now found himself saying essentially the same thing to adults with similar reactions.

He was not certain what "The Sundering of Brothers" meant, but he thought it might be a reference to the "Rending of the Clans of Men" in the "Histories of Nations" by Radomir the Historian. Until then, the three races of humankind had lived together in varying degrees of harmony. The Abrhaani, the Eniila, and the Sokai were very different peoples, but they managed to get along until this point in history.

There was little explanation for why war had happened, but it had been long and bloody. It had lasted for over five hundred years. In the end, the Eniila and the Abrhaani had agreed to inhabit different parts of the world. Their leaders felt, that if they had less contact with each other, there would be less opportunity for strife. By the time the Eniila and the Abrhaani overcame their madness long enough to notice such things, the Sokai had vanished, and no one was certain why, or how it had happened.

The "Rending" had attempted to preserve a remnant of humankind. There would have been nothing left but the wind, howling through ancient ruins and half-buried monuments if it had it failed. The Abrhaani traded with the Eniila nowadays, but when they had recently tried to build trading cities on Eniila land, it precipitated another war that had only ended when the Abrhaani had withdrawn to Kel Braah. The Abrhaani knew the Eniila were warlike and combative, even with

K. R. Schultz

each other. They knew it from centuries of painful experience. The Abrhaani had a saying that summed up their view of the other race. "They are about as likely to get along as two Eniila in a small room."

No one had heard of the Sokai for uncounted centuries. They were as much creatures of legend and myth, as the Nethera, and their bright counterparts, the Aethera.

Many centuries of war had had cost millions of lives. Much learning and knowledge was irrevocably lost. Humankind had paid an enormous price for millennia of conflict. Rehaak was certain that humankind was still paying the cost of that catastrophe, in many ways.

Although the Creator had told Rehaak that he was not alone, he had seen no evidence that anyone else was with him. No one else had taken up the cause of the Faithful One. He stood alone and unheeded, in a city of tens of thousands, so he assumed "you are not alone" was merely a divine euphemism for The Creator's presence in his life. Lately, he had begun to suspect divine indifference, rather than divine influence over his life.

None of the Abrhaani's other gods were particularly good at keeping their promises either. With nothing to convince the people, other than his words and his damaged reputation, Rehaak had warned, and pleaded with the people. When that failed, he begged and ranted, but to no avail.

Rehaak was certain that he needed the hard evidence of the Aetheriad. Without it to confirm his words all he had accomplished, was to make everyone despise him. They made no distinction between his Faithful One and the multitude of other deities, demigods, and spirits of nature that they held dear. The Abrhaani were a religious people at heart.

Animism held sway for so long that it was hard to convince them that the spirits of the plants, the animals, the rivers and the mountains could not hear or help them. The Abrhaani had been placating those spirits with elaborate rituals for so long, that any other belief system seemed bizarre to some, and outright deviant to others.

The people of the city wavered between several opinions and engaged in a three-sided debate concerning him. One side believed Rehaak was crazy and dangerous, another group thought he was crazy and harmless, and the final group was certain that Rehaak was crazy, but they didn't care. At least he had unified them in that much. They all thought he was crazy. They only disagreed on what to do about it.

The citizens of Narragansett either felt that they had so many gods to worship that they had no room for one more, or they felt that his Creator was just one of many, no more deserving of obedience than the rest. If he was brutally honest, after the recent and prolonged silence of his God, he was beginning to suspect the same thing. It was a hopeless task without the book for proof.

For a time, he had begun to search the scriptorium again, going daily to sift through the mountain of writings, while praying that The Creator would guide his hands to the right location, but the answer he sought still eluded him. This morning, he had lost hope again.

In spite of all his efforts, not one person had responded to his warnings. Rehaak's regular customers had stopped coming to seek his advice. Their absence was the only discernable result of his dire and disturbing warnings. He wanted to forsake the entire city, and its citizens, who murmured about his sanity, and were deaf to his warnings.

Rehaak had done all he could. If the people chose wrongly, after all his efforts, then it was not his fault if they perished. It bothered him somewhat that the people of Narragansett would perish, but what bothered Rehaak more was, that he feared that he would expire with them. In his vision, the destruction was complete. Nothing would survive. There would be no life left, not just in the city, but also in the whole of Aarda. Now that they had spurned his message, he wanted nothing more than to find a dark, safe corner to hide in, until it all passed over, if such a place existed.

Inarguably, there were other reasons they would not listen. His character was suspect. He had fed them sweet lies for so long that they would no longer tolerate bitter truth. He felt guilty about that. He had spoken so many worthless words and powerless prophecies, that when he finally spoke the truth they would no longer listen.

When Rehaak had first sought The Creator, he had been full of fervor. He had accomplished much good, and gained much knowledge, but over the years, he had given in to temptation. He had lost hope before and lost his way, as well. Now he was on the verge of losing both again.

The fire that had driven him had become embers again. He had known that eventually his words and deeds would come back to haunt him but he had not expected it to happen so soon, or with such dire consequences for people around him. He wished he had not forsaken the truth. He wished that he could unravel his past, like an old woman's knitting, but wishing would not change anything.

It was too easy for them to believe that he was mistaken or mad; after all, he was the only one who had seen the vision and heard the voice of The Creator. No one else would confirm what he saw. They all claimed they heard nothing and saw nothing except him standing entranced, before falling to the ground, unconscious. They were certain that he had passed out from too much wine. Everyone knew that he drank to excess.

Rehaak was angry with The Creator for not giving him at least one witness. Maybe he was as crazy as everyone believed after all. Wasn't it crazy to believe in something without corroboration?

Unfortunately, he was incapable of such self-deception. If anything, he knew that he was more rational now than ever. He knew he had all the proof he needed — he just didn't have all the evidence that everyone else needed.

He could not go forward because no one would listen, but he could not go back to his old life because he knew the truth. He found himself ensnared in a divine trap. He could never be happy while knowing that darkness and destruction loomed over all of Aarda. All the things that the people of the city held dear were doomed. If he were ignorant, he could be happy as they were — as he had tried in vain to be, but knowing what he knew, doomed him to misery.

When The Faithful One had spoken to him, it was as if liquid fire had replaced his blood. The experience rekindled his passion for the truth and for The Creator. He thought that surely he had rediscovered his purpose. He could begin his life anew, reborn out of the decaying corpse that his life had become. Unfortunately, that rush of enthusiasm had worn off, when no one responded to his message. — No, that wasn't true, they had responded, just not positively. It was costing him his reputation as a seer as well as his livelihood. He was disappointed and disillusioned. His head hurt, and he was tired.

A loud knock on the door interrupted his reverie.

"Rehaak! Open in the name of the king!"

"What now?" Rehaak thought. His predicament disgusted him, more than the interruption.

He walked to the door and opened it. Two of the King's guardsmen, bearing their short pikes and shields, stood outside his door, in the hallway of the inn. A herald, who held a parchment in his hand, accompanied them.

"You are Rehaak the scholar?" the herald asked?

"Yes, I am he. What do you want?"

The herald began to read the scroll that he held officiously in front of him.

"By order of the King and the Ecclesia you are forbidden from fomenting further fear and unrest among the people.

"Fear and unrest in people who won't even listen to me? Highly unlikely —" he heckled.

The herald continued in spite of the interruption, as if he no longer existed.

"You are hereby banished from Narragansett unless you recant your teaching regarding The Creator as well as the nonsense about the Blackened Lands. You are not to return to this city under any circumstances. If the city guard finds you within the city walls, you will be arrested, thrown into the dungeon and executed as soon as it can be conveniently arranged."

"You are hereby commanded to gather your belongings and leave before midnight this day, or face immediate imprisonment and death." The Herald paused to lend more weight to his final proclamation. He looked at Rehaak sternly.

"You are declared a heretic."

Rehaak began to laugh. The three men were confused by his laughter.

"Now I really seem crazy to them," he thought, but he couldn't help it.

How strange, how hilariously humorous — after everything he had done wrong, that something he had tried to do right should get him banished and threatened with death.

He had wanted out. Mere moments before the knock on the door, he was trying to think of a way to avoid fulfilling the hopeless task The Creator had set before him. Now they were about to forcibly eject him from a role he didn't want in the first place. The King and the Ecclesia had just granted his unspoken request. The Ecclesiarches who could never agree on anything had declared him a heretic.

The members of the — "He's crazy and dangerous faction," must have finally won the debate.

"Very well," he replied. "I shall pack my belongings and leave as soon as possible."

He wanted to add, "To hell with all of you." Looking at the burly guardsmen with their pikes in hand, he thought better of it and did not press the issue.

After they marched pompously away, he packed light, taking one change of travelling clothes, his water skin, some cheeses, and the bread he had gathered for his breakfast. He strapped on his money belt and dagger and slipped his red embroidered robe over his tunic.

"Thanks for nothing Faithful One," he mumbled sarcastically, as he finished packing.

"You gave me an impossible task! You didn't give me enough to work with! These bone headed people won't listen unless you come down from the clouds yourself! Although, if you do decide to come down, you'd best throw a few bolts of lightning their way, just to get their attention before you speak."

He snatched up his staff and slammed the door hard enough that it almost came off the hinges. The innkeeper watched in uncomfortable silence as he stomped down the hallway away from his room in the

K. R. Schultz

inn. He took the stairs two at a time until he reached the ground floor.

The innkeeper had liked having him there, because he was good for business. People used to eat and drink at the tables downstairs, while they waited to speak with him upstairs, but his popularity with the man had waned in direct proportion to his dwindling flow of clients.

Once outside, he glared at the sky and vowed, "See it couldn't be done — not by me! I am done with you oh great and mighty Creator! I am done with everything even remotely involving you! No one wants to follow you, including me! I'll look after myself from now on, thank you just the same. Go find another dupe to do your impossible and thankless work."

He picked his way through the tangled narrow streets, taking in the familiar sights one last time. The noise of human commerce, and the smells of the city, washed over him like a wave, as he made his way to the market place. It was still many hours to sundown. He considered lingering in the streets, waiting to buy some more provisions and some decent gear in case he encountered difficulty along the way. He changed his mind as he walked through the market square. He wouldn't buy anything from these stupid people. He would only take what he carried, nothing more.

He had originally contemplated buying a pack beast, but the cost would cut too deeply into his reserves of gold. He had never had much luck with pack animals, or any animals for that matter. It was a strange thing for the son of a farmer to say about himself. Besides, a lone pedestrian was less likely to attract the attention of bandits, than a man with a loaded pack animal was. It was probably better if he looked as if he were not worth bothering.

In the end, he only stopped briefly, to buy some hard cheese and some traveler's bread. He filled his water skin at the fountain in the square and walked slowly to the edge of the city. As he passed into the countryside, he sensed that somewhere a page had just turned; a chill ran down his spine and made him shiver, as a cloud passed over the sun.

Once outside the city he paused to consider his options. Should he go back the way he had come? Should he return to the land where he was born? There was nothing for him there, no good reason to go back. Why should he revisit places he had already seen? He felt a strange sense of freedom.

He knew that he should feel shame over the way they had exiled him, but in spite of the disgrace, he felt wonderfully free inside for the first time in many seasons. He had no reason to continue being the man he was. He could leave his past behind and start over if he wished. It was exhilarating. He felt alive again, for the first time in years.

His old life was over. He was on his own, writing in fresh ink upon empty pages in his life's book. Turning back was not an option. He would not plead for forgiveness. Although it was impossible to win redemption by his own efforts, it might yet overtake him along the road. He could not rewrite the narrative of his old life. He had already written those lines in ugly black ink. He could not expunge them, but he could write a new narrative in the pages that lay empty before him.

His only hope for the future lay in transformation; he must become new. He must become as different from his old self, as the butterfly was from the caterpillar that spun a cocoon, in hope of emerging transformed later. He needed to find a space where he could weave his own cocoon, to awaken one day, as a drastically different creature than he was now. He did not know what he would be, but he would be different. He was certain of it, even though he did not know the source of the feeling, nor did he have indisputable proof of its fulfillment. He refused to think about the problems standing in the way of this transformation.

He decided, for no reason, other than it felt right, to go southeast. The eastern slopes did not hold much history for his people. The settlements there were recent, so he had no reason to look there for clues from the ancient past.

Rehaak knew no one, who lived in that direction. That was reason enough in itself. He had never been east of the mountains before. Perhaps that was why he wanted to go. There he would be anonymous. He would find a place to live. His gold would last for quite a while. When that ran out, he would make his own way as best he could. It was the way he had spent his wandering years before he settled in Narragansett. He knew how to live on very little if necessary.

Rehaak had heard that the king occasionally granted land to the poor in the southern wilderness. He granted them enough supplies to get started and to get on their feet if all went well. If it did not go well — they were no longer the King's problem.

It was a way to rid Narragansett of the less desirable elements of the population. If they managed to make a life for themselves in the wilderness, then they contributed by paying taxes instead of living on the dole. Many died, because they did not have the skills they needed to forge a life from the wilderness. It was a harsh reality, but didn't matter to the King. Either they survived or they perished. They ceased to be a problem for the crown either way.

The cities' poor knew the harshness of wilderness life, but they went in spite of the knowledge, because they had nothing else. In Narragansett, they had no chance at all except to beg or to become some rich man's bondservant. Bondservants worked without pay for seven years, but at least their master would feed and house them during that time. At the end of the seven years, they would find themselves no further ahead than before. Unless they were young when they became bondsmen, their age prevented them from serving another term. Very few lived long enough to serve a second term of bondage. No one survived a third term, especially if the labor was hard or the master was difficult. It was a dead end, no pun intended.

In the south, beyond the mountains, they at least had hope. So Rehaak headed south, as so many people before him had. He would find one of the new settlements, and there he would find some hope to call his own. In the meantime, he reasoned, he still remembered how to live on very little.

CHAPTER 2: LIVING ON VERY LITTLE

It had taken him the better part of three tendays to make his way southeastward through the pass. The journey had been uneventful. It consisted of long days of tramping down the dusty road, followed by fitful sleep in whatever hovel disguised as an inn, he could find. He experienced a shift in attitude as he got further from Narragansett. He began to resent his exile, because the further he got from the city, the less people worked at disguising their hovels as inns.

The city was never his home, but he had been comfortable there. He had a life and a business, even if he based that business on deceit and fakery. Rehaak had lived well in Narragansett and had everything he thought he wanted, but now he had nothing but his clothing, and the things he carried with him. He was free to go where the wind blew him, free from the relentless expectations and demands of others, but his freedom had a bitter edge to it.

At first, it was intoxicating to be so free, but it wasn't long before the ugly underbelly of freedom began to reintroduce itself to him. He was free to starve to death, free to be savaged and devoured by wild animals, or free to be beaten by robbers. He noticed that he wasn't feeling particularly positive about his freedom lately.

The sense of elation that Rehaak had felt, just after leaving Narragansett, had fallen away with the miles. The plentiful ruins that marked the other side of the mountains were absent here. This place had no history and it left him feeling somehow disconnected.

The daily grind of tramping up and down hills lost its luster after the first day or two. The road on either side looked much the same today, as it did the day before, or the day before that. Some days he had almost wished robbers would set upon him. An attack would, at least have broken the monotony of the endless plodding along in the dust. Rehaak knew he had grown mentally unstable when he started looking for patterns in the swirls of dust raised by his stamping feet. He took to humming quietly or singing aloud so that he would not have to be alone with his thoughts. Unfortunately, he discovered that he could sing and still think at the same time.

He saw the occasional cart or wagon heading towards the city, but the road saw little use at this time of year. Trade with the city mostly came from the fertile plains to the southwest. The southeast was relatively unpopulated, and the road was virtually deserted at this time of year. Once the crops were ready and harvested, there would be abundant wagonloads of produce heading for the city to feed the residents of Narragansett. It was early spring and the farmers had just started their planting. It would be months before harvest time.

If there were no village or town within a day's walk there would be a mansio. The mansios were simple shelters for travelers, not much more than a roof and walls to keep out the wind and the rain. He was tired of sleeping in smelly, vermin-infested inns or crowded, equally smelly mansios. Those however, were the good nights. There were other nights too, long nights, when he alternately slept, and shivered, under the stars, if the inn or the mansio was full. He discovered that although he still remembered how to live on very little, living on very little was harder than it used to be, or perhaps just harder than he remembered.

In the town of Killaam, the better part of two days back, he had considered himself very lucky to find a decent inn. It was a small town along the banks of the Stone Song River. The river rushed over a rocky bed, winding downward from the great mountains. The road had more or less paralleled the river's course ever since he had come through the pass heading south. All along the road were many small villages spaced a day, or two day's walk apart.

Though villages were frequent, towns were rare, and rarer still were decent inns. He had taken the opportunity to have a hot bath at the bathhouse in the town, another rarity along the road. Once he was properly soaked and scrubbed, he sat with the locals to share gossip and some brew in the evening. From what he could remember, of the preceding evening, he had followed the drinking with a good night's sleep on a real bed. At least he had awakened in a decent bed — how he got there remained a mystery to him.

The people were friendly folk, eager for news of Narragansett and the wider world. He had regaled them with stories of his travels, and they in turn had given him the lay of the land nearby. He had drunk a lot of the local brew, much to his regret the following day, when the diarrhea had started. He wished he had brought his herbs to deal with such situations, but he had left the city too quickly for that. He made a mental note to locate some medicinal herbs at his first opportunity.

After he crossed the bridge south of town, the road had turned westward and away from the stream that it had followed. It had led out into a grassy plain, where it became little more than a rutted trail through the neck high grass. Rehaak had filled his water skin before setting out into the ocean of green plant life that rustled and undulated in the wind. He missed the sound of rushing water, but he missed the opportunity to fill his water skin more.

Last night Rehaak had slept under the stars again, if you could call it sleeping. There was no mansio, because there was so little traffic using this road. There were no building materials nearby, nor was there any source of water. He surmised that all three were contributing factors to the lack of accommodation.

There was just the broad expanse of sharp bladed grass that stretched for miles in all directions. Rehaak wondered how they had cut the trail across the plain. The green and growing blades of the grass were stiff and sharp as flint, sharp enough to cut through skin and clothing. The dry dead undergrowth was less nasty. It appeared that death blunted the edges of the vicious greenery. The fibers that remained after the grass had weathered to a pale brown were fine and flexible, although tough as iron. He knew it would make excellent rope and cordage.

There was no wood for a fire, just the abundant grass. He suspected that the matted dead undergrowth would burn well, very likely too well. He would have had to stay up all night hacking through the tough fibers with his dagger, and throwing armloads of it into a fire. He would also have a long night trying to keep the sparks from lighting the grass nearby, setting the entire countryside ablaze. For all his faults, he was not a pyromaniac. He also had no wish for the next person on the trail to discover his charred remains, which was more than likely, if he fell asleep with a fire blazing.

He decided against expending the effort required to make fire. He opted for sleep in a cold camp instead, piling the dry grasses under his bedroll for a passable mattress. He piled more grass over himself to keep the dampness and the chill of the night air from penetrating his bedroll, and the nocturnal biting insects from penetrating his sensitive skin.

He had risen before the sun, not by choice and not happily. He had tried to stretch away the stiffness he felt in all his joints and met with limited success. After a crude breakfast, he set out again. At mid-morning, he stopped to consider his options and to take a rest break. He was able to ignore his thirst for a while. The sun was warm and pleasant on his aching back. It was a beautiful day. The sky looked like someone hollowed it out of a perfect blue sapphire, lighter blue at the horizon. The dome of the sky contained only a few smudges of cloud, which looked like they had been dabbed onto its surface with a god-sized paintbrush. He considered turning back to Killaam, but he could see trees ahead in the distance, and that usually meant water was nearby. Since it was farther to go back than to go on, he decided to continue along the way, rationing his water as best he could.

With nothing to do but walk, he found his mind wandering again. He ran over his past like a merchant taking inventory. He had left home as a lad to in his quest for truth. He had wandered the length of Kel Braah, visiting every library or scriptorium he could find along the way. His search had led him to Narragansett, where he had run out of initiative and integrity almost simultaneously. He concluded that it was easy to remain moral in the absence of temptation.

The city had seduced him with all its beauty and wealth. The easy lifestyle and lax morals had claimed his honor and integrity as another casualty. Life in the city had changed him in ways that he could never have imagined. He was not proud of what he had become. He supposed that Narragansett was a beast that could accommodate a host of small parasites like him. He had found his niche in the patterns of its life and used the resources it provided, to make a comfortable life. In the end, Narragansett had excreted him like an intestinal roundworm when he had become too much of an irritant, for it to tolerate.

By early afternoon, his feet hurt and his mouth felt like he had chewed on a good-sized chunk of the trail behind him. His water had run out in spite of his careful rationing and it was still a long way to the tree line. How much farther it was to water he could not estimate.

The people at the inn in Killaam said that settlers had established the free town less than twenty years earlier. They told him that if he followed the trail he would soon get to it, but they were vague about the distance. He now suspected their vagueness was their idea of a joke. They also said that the townsfolk were looking for more people to help prepare the land for crops or to work in the forest as loggers. Maybe that was a joke too.

The people who lived in the free town called it New Hope, but the people at the inn had called the town No Hope. They made endless jokes about the name, as they disparaged the town, calling it Faint Hope, No Hope, Not a Hope in Hell, on and on it went. They had little respect for the poor, stupid city folk and their chances for success. He had joined in their laughter, but now he wondered if they were laughing at him instead of laughing with him.

When he had first set out, he felt that New Hope was a good name for a destination, a name full of portents of prosperity and fulfillment. Now, the better part of two long warm days and one interminably cold night later, he had changed his mind.

K. R. Schultz

"At least I'll find shade under the trees," he said aloud, just to hear the sound of his own voice. There was no silence to break. The sounds of life were abundant. Hoppers chirped, birds called to each other, and the grass rustled continuously, but the grassland felt desolate and silent in spite of it. As the sun-drenched plain continued to warm, the promise of shade in the forest beckoned him onward.

As his thirst and weariness grew, he changed his mind about the name of his destination. He was definitely on the road to No Hope, tired and thirsty every step of the way. He could clearly see the edge of the forest in front of him now. He plodded on weary to the bone.

Rumbling and creaking noises coming from behind him on the trail roused him from his reverie. He turned to investigate and saw a large freight wagon pulled by four gigantic mithun, moving slowly up the trail towards him. The people at the inn hadn't bothered to tell him there was a freight service. He was starting to resent their country humor. If they had told him, how far it was to New Hope and that there was freight service out here; he would have booked a ride.

Though the wagon's progress was relatively slow, they were still gaining on him. He decided to sit down beside the trail and wait for them to catch up. Perhaps the drover would have some water to spare. He marinated in a mixture of equal parts of sweat and anger, while the team approached. He had plenty of time to observe the team and their drover as they approached at a steady walk.

The mithun were huge ox-like animals, between six and seven feet tall at the shoulder hump. Their dense dark brown coats faded to light tan around the hocks. Nose to tail they must have been at least twelve feet long. The dewlap under the chin extended between the front legs. The drover had fastened the yoke to the three-foot long, wickedly curved horns. Their large ears flicked intermittently as insects tried to land on them.

The drover, who walked beside the wagon, probably had little to fear from wolves and other wild predators, because these four huge beasts would surely provide enough deterrent from attack. The team obviously knew their way, as they plodded along in the tracks that previous journeys had carved into the soil and the tall grass. The gigantic wagon they pulled was a small burden for such massive, powerful creatures. Dust rose and roiled in lazy clouds with each step of their cloven hooves, before it settled onto the earth once more. A cloud of flies circled above them and in their wake.

"Damn those people at the inn," he muttered.

This was obviously a regular freight route. The people at the inn were probably laughing their heads off at him, another stupid city dweller, while they swilled their wretched brew. They knew he would tramp for days in the hot sun and shiver through the cold nights, while swarms of biting insects feasted on his blood. He was just another uppity city boy too dumb to know any better. They had taken him down a peg.

When the team got within hailing range, Rehaak stood up, waved a greeting, and called out to the dark skinned figure with the wide-brimmed grass hat. The deep shadow under the hat brim hid the drover's face. His clothes were more dusty and worn, than Rehaak's own. He, like Rehaak, carried a stout staff that probably did double duty, both as a tool to herd the beasts and as a weapon. Rehaak wanted no misunderstandings. It would not do for the drover to suspect him as a bandit. The fellow had a hard and rugged look to him.

Rehaak smiled broadly and waved his greeting again. He made no moves towards the wagon. He patiently waited for them to draw nearer. The person

43

under the hat had still not responded, so Rehaak held his place in a calculated attempt to appear non-threatening. When they were no more than ten paces apart, the team stopped on the trail. Their tails flicked in lazy irritation at the flies attempting to take advantage of the pause in movement. The man accompanying the beasts had obviously seen him, but had not seen fit to issue a greeting in response until now.

"Hallo," croaked the stranger, in a voice as cracked as parched earth, and an accent as thick as the soil from which he could have sprung.

"If yuh be intent on mischief, I shall warn yuh now, dat dere ain't naught worth havin on dis wagon. Duh lazy beasts pullin it won't move lessn' I go with em, and dis wagon be mighty heavy tuh be tryin tuh pull by yerself. As tuh me, you mightn't find me an easy nut tuh crack with dat staff o yourn." He spat into the dust.

"I am a traveler not a bandit, good sir, headed for the village of New Hope, where I plan, God willing, to make my new home."

The man drew closer. Rehaak could see the man's dark eyes shining with mirth under the shadow of the hat. The bastard was grinning. It wasn't a pleasant grin. He was missing some teeth — no — many teeth.

"Ah," the fellow intoned sagely. "Another pilgrim from duh city den, come tuh seek fame and forchin in duh free town. Anudder lost soul on duh road to No Hope." A chuckle issued from the shadowed face. "Duh folk at duh inn warned me I might find such as yerself on duh road. A paying customer dey says. If duh wolves ain't et 'im, dey says or if he ain't froze to death dey says. Thought it right funny too, dey did."

To say that Rehaak was furious would have been an understatement of cosmic proportions, but he would be damned if he let this bumpkin make him the butt of their country humor. He bit back his rage and simply smiled back at the man as he held out his hand in greeting and said.

"I thought it was a pleasant day for a stroll, and I needed to air out my clothes to rid myself of the stench, of that nasty pigsty that calls itself a town back yonder." He said it all mildly, still smiling, still holding out his hand.

Laughter erupted from under the wide brimmed hat. The man laughed until he had to hold his sides and tears ran down his cheeks. He snorted and gasped trying to catch his breath.

"Do you need aid? I have some skill as a healer," Rehaak said, calmly raising one eyebrow. "When you have calmed yourself, I would be happy to accompany you the rest of the way to the free town. Do these fits overtake you often sir?"

By this time, the man was nearly helpless with mirth. Rehaak walked over and patted him consolingly on the shoulder. The fellow was wheezing now and Rehaak was becoming genuinely concerned. It looked as if he was having trouble getting enough air. The man began to cough and hack violently and finally the laughter stopped.

They stood looking at each other for a moment, while the drover struggled to regain his composure. Finally, the fellow spoke.

"Yuh have some metal in yuh I warrant. I did'n expect yuh tuh be so far this mornin."

"Let's just say I got an early start."

Rehaak looked on without comment as the man went to the wagon, and pulled up one of the dusty tarps at the back. He produced a large wooden tankard from a pile of stuff inside the wagon bed. He turned the tankard upside down, smacked it with the palm of his hand to knock the dust out of it, and then blew out the remainder of the dust. He proceeded to fill it with water from a

45

barrel in the back of the wagon bed. He downed the water quickly then turned to Rehaak.

"It be usual tuh git payment fer water stranger, but in yer case I'll be askin fer naught from yuh, 'cept duh entertainment yuh done given me already," he said, still smiling. He filled the cup again and held it out to Rehaak.

"I dare not refuse your generous offer and offend your hospitality good sir. For the sake of politeness, if for no other reason, I accept your hospitality," Rehaak smiled back and bowed with a flourish.

This started the man giggling again, as he handed Rehaak the cup. Rehaak took it quickly, afraid that he would spill it if he started laughing again. He drank it slowly and savored it. It was tepid and tasted woody. To Rehaak, it was better than the finest wines Narragansett had offered, as it carved a deliciously wet channel down his parched throat all the way to his gullet.

"Dere be no room on duh wagon, but we kin walk tugedder if yuh likes. I 'spect yuh'll be more entertainin dan most of duh people I gets tuh meet."

"No offense sir, but if that last statement is true you need a wider circle of acquaintances," Rehaak said, smiling.

"None taken," the man said, and smiled back. "But I ain't no sir."

"How shall I address you then, my good fellow?"

Another fit of laughter ensued, followed by more coughing. "Yuh sure talk funny. I ain't yer good fellow either. In fact I ain't no fellow a'tall," he said, followed by a short struggle with another bout of giggling.

"What do you mean?" Rehaak looked quizzically at the drover.

"I be a woman, stranger, but don't go gittin no funny ideas. I knows how tuh handle mithun; and men ain't dat much different. A good whack up duh side of duh head'll usually put either one right in a hurry. Course, y'are kinda cute and all."

She smiled at Rehaak in what she apparently believed was a seductive manner. It really only served to highlight the obvious effects of rampant tooth decay and the sun damage to her leathery, dirt encrusted visage. He stared in slack-jawed astonishment until he recovered his composure.

He studied her for a moment with a new understanding. She was probably only forty but didn't look a day over sixty. She was as rugged and weather-beaten as the mountain pines he had passed less than two ten days ago. It frightened him to think that she might well be the standard of feminine beauty in these parts.

"I would never dream of rejecting your gracious offer or of sullying your good name madam," he said, bowing with another flourish, "My name is Rehaak and I beg your pardon for assuming that you were anything other than the — fair flower of femininity, I now see revealed before me. Today's bright sunlight must have blinded me to your beauty, but how did one as lovely as yourself become a drover of mithun? Being a drover is traditionally a man's occupation is it not?"

"I swear lad, yuh've missed yer callin. Yuh can shovel shit better'n any stable hand I ever seen, without even enterin duh barn. I bin entertained enough fer now. We best git movin; otherwise, it'll be dark afore we reach duh mansio. Lessn we want a romantic evenin snuggled up tugedder under duh stars."

She paused and held out a callused, weathered hand. He looked at her and the extended hand wondering at her intent. She appeared oblivious to his hesitation. He finally decided it was a simple greeting gesture. He extended his own and took her callused, leathery hand in his.

"People calls me Lucky, but muh real name is Isilakari. My folks called me Isil or Isi most of duh time doh."

She smiled her seductive smile again, and chills ran down his spine. It was not a good feeling. He looked her over appraisingly again, but still came to the same conclusion. It had been a long time since he had been with a woman, but not *that* long. The townsfolk might call her Lucky, but she probably didn't get lucky often, and she was definitely not going to get lucky with him. He found it perversely reassuring to find that he was not the only object of the townsfolk's twisted senses of humor.

"Well, I shall also call you Isil if that is acceptable to you." He watched as she nodded her agreement.

"Let's be off then shall we?" he said cheerily, breaking free from the grip of her weathered hand. "I don't relish another night out in the open, wolves, and all that."

He turned and headed off toward the edge of the forest. He set a reasonable pace that she and the team could match. He thought the look in her eye might have been disappointment, but he decided he was better off not knowing for sure.

CHAPTER 3: THE ROAD GOES ON

It was almost nightfall, when they finally reached the mansio. From where Rehaak stood, it looked like no more than a three-walled shed, open on one side for the animals. There was a haystack, a corral, and a well.

While Isil unhooked the mithun from the wagon drew water for them. Once she got them unyoked and inside the enclosure, they were eager to drink. He poured water into the wooden drinking trough, using heavy wooden buckets that he found beside the well.

They nearly crushed Rehaak between their huge bodies, as they jostled each other for better position at the trough. When they had finished drinking, they ambled over to the haystack and ate huge mouthfuls of dry grass from the pile. He was exhausted from lugging the heavy buckets to the trough, while he tried to keep from either spilling the water, or being crushed between their enormous bodies.

He had lost sight of Isil while he was busy, and it was almost completely dark before he was finished. He had seen her walk around the corner of the shed, so he went the same direction to find her. He was curious and more than a little nervous about the sleeping arrangements for the night. Once he got around the corner, he could see a little cottage behind the shed. The two structures shared a common wall, but the shelter for the animals was much larger, to accommodate their huge bulks. Isil had started a fire in the hearth and he could smell the food before he got to the door. Rehaak opened the door cautiously and looked inside.

Isil was stirring a large kettle hanging over the fire. She had cleaned herself up and put on cleaner, less masculine apparel. When she heard the door open, she turned to look at him. Without the road grime clinging to her face, she looked far less aged, and with the feminine clothing; he began to see more hints of womanliness. Her skin had the verdigris tinge that all Abrhaani developed in bright sunshine, and without the coating of grime, it looked far less leathery. He found himself warming to her until the moment she smiled.

"Well, at least it smells as if she can cook," he muttered under his breath.

"Git yerself washed up a bit n' we'll eat. Dere's a basin on duh stand an a towel fer dryin." she gestured in the direction of the items.

The floor of the cottage was packed earth, covered in straw. The single room contained a table, with a long bench next to it. To his distinct relief, there were three beds along one wall and there were blankets strung on ropes between them, to provide at least a measure of privacy. He felt relieved that they would not have to share a bed, as he poured water into the basin and washed his face and hands.

When he was done, he took the basin to the door and emptied it outside. Stew steamed in wooden bowls on the table before he had finished cleaning up. Isil sat on the bench while she waited for him. Before he sat down to join her, he lifted his hands in his normal ritual blessing of the food.

When he first began serving The Creator, it seemed right to thank Him for the food. He still did it even though he had sworn off the service of his god. It still was the right thing to do. He usually felt empowered by the song, and perhaps that was why he kept the practice. He had been trying to break the habit in the city, but lately he had felt compelled to continue the practice. He sang his song of thanksgiving for the meal.

After he finished his song, he looked down. Isil was looking up at him. Her eyes were brimming with tears.

"What?" he said. Looking at her in bewilderment, "My singing can not be that bad."

"I did'n' know," she paused, collecting herself. "I did'n' know dere wuz no others."

"What are you talking about?"

"I did'n' know dere wuz other people who believe in Duh Faithful One, Duh Creator! Dere's not many left who keeps to duh ol' path and follows duh true teachins. Not many even remembers em nowadays."

"I never suspected, that you — were a follower of — The Creator," he stammered, completely nonplussed.

They both sat for a long time in silence and stared at each other.

"This is a twist," he said. "How do you know about —?"

"I always knew, my parents knew, dere parents before em knew. Forever. Dey all be dead and gone now, and I ain't got no one to tell after me, and if'n I tries to tell others dey jus laugh and call me crazy ol' Lucky." She paused for a moment, then asked, "How'd yuh know den? Yer folks?"

"I learned from studying ancient books and scrolls."

"Yuh read duh Aetheriad? What was written by Naom'han the Aethera scribe his self?" she asked in stunned amazement.

It was his turn to be stunned. How was it possible that this bumpkin from the backside of nowhere knew as much as he did after all his years of study and research? Had he wasted twelve years seeking answers in ancient ruins and dusty libraries, only to discover his hard-earned knowledge was commonplace here? It rankled that she knew more than he did after all his efforts, at far less cost.

"You know of the book?" It still exists?" he asked.

"I reckon it does, but I ain't ever seen it. But, muh Pa used tuh tell me about it. Yuh never seen it either den?"

"No, but I discovered clues to its existence in many of the oldest manuscripts. I believe it holds important information for our time.

"So yuh bin lookin fer it den?

"Yes I have devoted my life to acquiring it."

He hoped, finally, with a living representative of the faith, he would have a real guide to the book he had sought for so long.

"Dat's wonderful and all — but yuh still ain't found it?"

"No, but I am still looking. Do you know where it is?" he said hopefully.

"Nope."

His hope splattered on the floor like an egg dropped from a rooftop. He screamed inwardly in frustration and repeated his vow forswearing The Creator. It was cruel of her to present him with fresh hope only to tear it away and reveal another dead-end! It was hopeless!

He ate in sullen despair. Isil shrugged and started to eat as well. The food was good but he hardly noticed. She tried to make conversation but he ignored her attempts. Finally, she finished eating and went to bed. He turned, blew out the lamp, and laid his tired body on one of the remaining empty beds, while staring angrily at the underside of the roof thatch. His heart ached like frostbitten fingers, like a lump of ice within his chest.

He could hear the sound of her breathing above the crackling of the fire in the hearth.

"At least she doesn't snore. A point in her favor," he thought as he drifted off to sleep.

When morning light stole in through the open door, he realized Isil had already gone. He supposed he couldn't blame her. He had been obnoxious last night. He was rude and ungrateful, and he didn't deserve to be around decent people. She had done nothing wrong, but perhaps she thought that she had. He stepped outside and walked around the cottage, to the shed. The wagon and the mithun were gone and so was Isil.

When Rehaak returned to the cottage, he stuffed the bread and jerky she had left for him, in his pack. He filled his water skin, gathered his belongings, and carefully latched the door on his way out. He decided that he would continue to follow the trail to New Hope regardless of the outcome. He was more than willing to avoid her, but he suspected that he would meet her either in town or on the trail.

"Fair enough, I'll deal with it as it comes." He thought.

As he began to follow the trail, a growing sense of unease assailed him. What if something happened to her along the way? Rehaak tried to convince himself that she had taken this trail often and she had never encountered any problems before. No matter how hard he tried, he could not shake the feeling that he needed to catch up to her quickly, before something bad happened. Besides, it would be the right thing to do. He needed to apologize for his behavior of the preceding night.

If he traveled fast enough, he could catch up to her along the way. The mithun and wagon could only make eight to ten miles a day. Loaded lightly as he was, he could easily cover twice that distance if he pushed himself. By his estimate, she could only have two or three hour's head start. He could catch her by midday at best, or at worst sometime around mid afternoon. He would apologize to her then. The sense of urgency appeared to increase, not decrease, once he had made up his mind to intercept her.

Rehaak hurried along the rutted wagon track, cursing himself for being such an idiot. She had been kind to him and he had returned the favor by being insufferable. He had treated her with contempt, because she couldn't answer his question. He had chased the Aetheriad for over a decade now.

If he couldn't find it after all that time, what right did he have to expect her to know where it was? Unlike him, she apparently had a life to live, and lived it. His face flushed with shame when he remembered how she had tried to reopen a conversation with him several times last night. Each time he rebuffed those attempts with obstinate, angry silence.

There was probably much more he could have learned from her, if only he had allowed her the opportunity to tell him. There was always more information buried in one's mind than one knew. There were things that she knew, things that her ancestors told her, that she didn't realize were important. Rehaak fought off this notion. He knew that she owed him nothing, and that he deserved nothing except her contempt. He needed to apologize to her not because of what he could get out of her, but because of his own rudeness. It was her choice, once he apologized, if she chose to extend k'harsa to him.

As he hurried along, the sense of urgency to his mission grew larger than his need to make restitution. He set a pace that devoured the distance between them. Life on the road had toughened him to the point that he could walk all day without a rest, if needed. He felt he needed to do exactly that, so he kept up a rapid walk.

He was breathing heavily from his exertion. The sun shone dimly through the overhead canopy of leaves and branches. There was very little wind at ground level, but the treetops swayed and danced in the breeze. Rehaak had been walking for about two hours, and he had stopped only long enough to sip some water and relieve himself. Something drove him to push on, and to push harder. He needed to catch up to the wagon — quickly.

Rehaak had a knot in his stomach that had nothing to do with his exertion or anything else that he could name. He suspected that if he didn't catch up to her soon, it would be too late. He surrendered to his sense of urgency and began to lope along. Rehaak heard no sounds but the rustling of branches, the thuds of his heart in his chest, and the thuds of his feet on the hard packed earth. Sweat stung his eyes and washed gullies in the dust on his face.

The wagon trail twisted through the forest avoiding boulders and large trees. He was making good time. As he rounded one of the many bends, he caught sight of the wagon with Isil plodding along beside it. She was fine. The wagon was fine. The mithun were fine. He was disgusted.

Why had he pushed himself for nothing? He slowed to a walk and hailed her with what breath he had left. She walked on, pretending not to hear him. Her stride never changed as she walked silently, footsteps hitting the ground in counterpoint to her staff. Finally, when he was close enough, he reached for her arm and gently called her name.

When she turned to look at him, he saw the tears running down her cheeks and he felt doubly ashamed of himself. She stopped and looked into his eyes for a moment, before looking down at the ground. He could not bear to look in her eyes for long either. He stared at his feet and blurted out his apology. In spite of his skill with words, this speech did not come easily. He struggled and stammered, the words caught in his throat, but he finally managed to get through it. Only when he was finished did he dare to look up at her again.

She smiled gently. "Alright den, yuh ken finish makin amends by helpin me water duh beasts, since its midday, and time tuh stop. Dere's a bucket in duh back, and yuh know where duh barrels is."

Rehaak had nothing more he could say. He nodded and walked to the tail end of the long wagon, and got the bucket. He leaned his staff against the side of the wagon and climbed up on the wagon bed. Just as he was about to fill the wooden pail, he saw movement in the trees. He paused as his feeling of dread returned stronger than ever. Isil was checking the harness and did not notice anything unusual. He abandoned the bucket quickly in the water barrel, leapt down from the wagon, and grabbed his staff.

"Isil, beware!" he shouted as he ran around the wagon towards her.

"Wa's wrong," she said, as she grabbed her own staff, from where it rested on the wagon tongue.

"I'm not sure. Something is moving in the trees to the left." He pointed toward the forest. "I have a bad feeling."

"Bes to pay attention to doze feelins when dey comes." She looked warily in the direction he had indicated. "Dey usually comes from duh Faithful One."

As the words were leaving her mouth, four scruffy looking men emerged from the trees; all armed with long strange looking knives. The men approached cautiously. The largest of the four, an unkempt man, with a dark wild looking beard, spoke.

"If yuh be givin us what we wants, dere be no trouble in it for yuh."

What is it yuh be wantin den?" said Isil grimly.

Whatever coin the two o' yuh be carryin, will be fine enough, but we takes supplies just as well, if yuh got no gold."

"Ain't nuthin on dis wagon dat be mine for duh givin, or yours for duh takin, I be thinkin."

"Den you got a bit of a problem," the man snarled.

"I think you are mistaken my good fellow. It is you who have the problem," Rehaak responded.

The darker man smiled at his cronies. "We got us a city fella here, judgin by duh accent and a right genteel one at dat. Never seen a prissy city boy yet as could hold his water, when things got messy."

"Yuh gonna try talkin us to death or yuh gonna do something," growled Isil. "We got places tuh be and people what is waitin on us. So either have at it or be off with yuh. Don't let nothin but fear and common sense stay yer hand."

The four of them fanned out, trying to surround Rehaak and Isil. They couldn't get around behind the two travelers because the four mithun stood like a solid wall of flesh and bone at their backs. They would have to settle for a frontal assault. It was not what they would have preferred, for though they outnumbered the pair, the staffs that Rehaak and Isil held gave them the advantage of reach.

The men picked their targets and began to move in on Isil and Rehaak. Before they got within knife range, Isil moved with surprising speed and agility, swinging her staff at the first of her attackers. The bandit had misjudged her reach. She stepped forward and with a powerful overhand stroke of her staff, struck the forearm of the man's knife hand. The bone shattered with a snap and he dropped his knife, yowling in pain. Isil smiled her legendary smile at the other man, who now watched her with somewhat more respect. Rehaak glanced over as he waited for his own opening. He was not sure what frightened the man more, her smile, or her obvious ability with the staff.

The smaller of the two men facing Rehaak thought he saw his chance and made a lunge at him, but Rehaak was fast enough to sidestep his lunge. As his attacker's momentum carried him past where he stood, he swung his staff, soundly striking the man on the back. The added momentum of the blow carried the man forward, smacking his face into the muscular flank of one of the mithun.

As he fell to his knees stunned, the beast looked back, as if deeply offended by the man's impudence in touching him. The mithun lashed out with a cloven rear hoof the size of a dinner plate, striking the man in the right side of his chest. The kick lifted the brigand off the ground and deposited him at least three paces away. Dust puffed up and settled again around his silent form. The odds were now more or less even, if you discounted the mithun.

The leader of the brigands looked at his remaining uninjured henchman, either to gauge his resolve, or to encourage some. He feinted at Rehaak a few times to see if he could get him to make a mistake, but Rehaak remained unruffled, holding his staff low in both hands. Finally, the man lunged again trying to reach Rehaak over his guard but Rehaak stepped forward closing the distance, and at the same time lifting his staff.

This forced the man's knife hand up and out of the way. As Rehaak stepped forward, he aimed a kick at the man's groin. The attacker twisted and managed to avoid the kick, but while Rehaak engaged him, the fellow did not notice that his compatriot had backed off, allowing Isil time to swing at his head, with a vicious roundhouse. Her staff connected solidly, making a snapping, crunching sound as it did. Rehaak sidestepped the body as it fell twitching at his feet.

The two remaining thieves, who were still on their feet, appeared to lose their will to continue. The uninjured brigand helped his friend to his feet and they began backing away, warily, until they reached the cover of the trees. Once they reached cover, they turned and ran off into the dark shadows among the trees. Rehaak turned to look at the mithun. They had barely moved since the fighting started.

"I toll' yuh dey wouldn' move lessen I goes with em. Let's see if dese two still have life in em or no," rasped Isil, as she rolled the leader over onto his back. She checked his breathing. "Dis one's done for."

"Same here," Rehaak called out. "His chest is caved in where the mithun kicked him."

"Hort's always bin kinda touchy about who gets tuh touch im, gives the blacksmith's fits he does, when dey tries tuh shoe him."

"Uhm — shouldn't you have warned me about that before I started watering them last night?"

"Naw. I could tell he was right partial to yuh, right from duh get go. Wouldn't a given yuh no more'n a love tap at worst. Hardly even raise a bruise I should

59

say." She smiled at him again, as she picked up the thieves weapons, and handed them to Rehaak. "Dey won't be needin dese no more. Mebbe yuh could get summat fer em in town."

"No, why don't you keep them."

"Naw — I got no use fer em."

Finally, she acceded to his wishes, though she was still reluctant to accept the blades or even touch them.

"Awright, she said and stowed the long knives in the wagon alongside her cargo." But dey gives me duh shivers touchin em."

Rehaak felt much the same about the weapons. It was unusual for Abrhaani to use edged weapons, but he did not dwell on the thought. While she watered the mithun, he dragged the bodies off into the forest and covered them with deadfall to keep the scavengers away. He did it in spite of thinking they deserved to become food for the crows. Once both tasks were complete, they started toward New Hope again.

"Thanks fer duh help," she said.

"You're welcome."

They walked on together in silence until the shadows began to lengthen. Evening came early under the canopy of branches. Rehaak assumed they would either camp for the night or push on in the dark to reach town, because of the delay caused by their altercation with the brigands.

"What is your plan now?" he asked.

"Dere's an abandoned farmstead about half a mile from duh trail. Just round duh next bend. An empty house too. Folks what built it died a while back and nobody claimed it yet. Dere's a crick where the mithun can get water. We best make fer it I reckon. Not much else we can do. Too far now to make town afore midnight. Too risky in duh dark. Not much light under dese trees at night. Could break a wheel or a neck more'n likely if we goes on."

"How much farther to the farm then?"

"Less'n an hour at dis speed. Be just about full dark by den."

"Very well, lead on milady."

CHAPTER 4: NEW HOME

When they arrived at the abandoned farmstead, there was still some silver left in the sky. Through the gathering darkness, Rehaak could see a hut with a lean-to shed for firewood storage. Another smaller structure surrounded by a fence had probably held chickens or other small livestock. The hut looked sturdy, but the builders had wasted very little effort on the smaller shed. They had thrown it together in haste. It was beginning to sag and collapse under the weight of moss and debris on the roof.

The hut looked like a single roomed structure, made of daub and wattle between posts and beams. The roof thatch was sound, as far as Rehaak could tell, in the remaining light. The door was off its hinges, lying in the weeds beside the hut. The lone window was a dark, empty hole in the wall.

Since Isil knew the way down to the stream, she had unhitched the mithun and taken them to the water. Rehaak decided to get a fire going before it was too dark to see. He scrounged up some dry wood from inside the shed.

It was odd that this fine little place stood abandoned, but he knew that people were often reluctant to stay in a building where misfortune had fallen, especially in cases of disease. They were afraid of falling ill themselves. He supposed that this made sense, especially where the illness had been fatal. Since Isil had stopped here before, and had suffered no ill effects, he was certain that no contagion lingered.

By the time Rehaak got into the hut, it was almost completely dark inside. He paused to let his eyes adjust. There were several shadowy objects scattered inside. He picked his way over to the fireplace and set down the wood. The hearth was solidly built of river rock. He started the fire without much difficulty. The fireplace smoked a bit as they sometimes did until the flue heated.

Once he had the fire properly started, he rescued the front door from the weeds to see if he could hang it again. He discovered the hinges were broken, but he could lean it against one of the jambs to cover most of the doorway and keep the heat in. It was well aware that it got cold at night. He covered the window opening with a spare tarp taken from the wagon, and stood back to admire his handiwork.

Firelight now revealed the shadowy objects to be a table and a bench that lay tipped over in the middle of the room were the only remaining furnishings. Rehaak and Isil would sleep on the hard packed earthen floor tonight, but it was better than being outside. Any shelter was better than no shelter at all. Outside they would be at the mercy of the elements and a feast for bugs.

Bread and cheese would provide a meager supper, but they had a roof over their heads and walls to protect them and keep them warm. Rehaak counted his blessings.

Although the floor and walls were still cool and smelled of damp earth, the chill was already lessening, when Isil finally arrived at the door of the hut. They sat at the table and chatted while eating their meal. Rehaak questioned her about her family and their history at length. He was not surprised when her knowledge confirmed his belief that faith in The Creator predated the animism of modern Abrhaani society.

Belief in The Creator had been endemic among Isil's forbears and their neighbors. Time had passed them by, as had the changing fashions of Abrhaani religion. They lived in near isolation on the eastern slopes and cared very little for the trends of the rest of society. The situation they lived in and the attitudes they held, had protected them from the shift in religion, which had occurred elsewhere on Khel Braah.

As he listened to her talk, he began to wonder how the shift in belief systems had occurred. Was it a natural progression or had it been engineered by someone, or some group? If it was a conspiracy, who was behind it? What could anyone hope to gain from the changes? His mind worried at the edges of the problem but provided him with little insight. His frustration intensified; once again, he had more questions than answers.

It occurred to him that the Nethera were the only possible beneficiaries of the shift. Mankind could only lose, so why would men accede to this change?

Although he learned much about her family their customs and traditions, he gleaned nothing about the location of the Aetheriad. In spite of years of frustration, this legendary volume still drew him as a lodestone drew iron filings. He sometimes wondered why it still held such appeal for him. He could not seem to shake his compulsion to find it.

Rehaak had an overwhelming sense, that it held significance greater than mere proof that The Creator was real, and that the ancient legends were true. He suspected that secrets recorded there, held information essential to humankind's survival. When the Dark Ones arose in their full power, his people would need every scrap of knowledge from the ancient manuscript, to survive the onslaught.

Through the course of the evening's conversation, he also learned that he had underestimated Isil. She was neither coarse nor unintelligent. She had a sharp wit and a gentle disposition hidden under the rough exterior. He found, to his surprise, that he genuinely enjoyed her company. They could be friends.

He found himself at peace, here, with her, in spite of his failure to turn the city around, or to find the book he sought. It was ironic that he felt calm, and at peace in a house that had held only tragedy for its previous occupants. Was it the location, or the company? He had no way of knowing with certainty, but Isil's smile no longer held any terror for him.

Though she told him many tales about her life as a drover, he held his own secrets tightly. He focused on telling her outrageous stories that made her laugh. Her gravelly voice was not pleasing to listen to, but her laughter pared away the crusty exterior, and years of hard living. Eventually, they ran out of things to talk about, and sat on the bench in front of the fire, staring silently at the flames, — alone, but together. When they could no longer keep their eyes open, they unrolled their bedrolls and settled down to sleep in front of the fire.

***

Rehaak rose early, and stepped outside, because he loved to see the sunlit world stretching and yawning, taking its first breath of day. Because of the deepening twilight the previous evening, Rehaak had not seen much of the clearing, but now he stood enraptured by what he saw and felt. The world looked fresh and new in the pale yellow dawn. The world had not changed at all. He simply had new eyes with which to see it. He looked at the forest and the glade where he stood. It was a natural clearing large enough to support a decent sized farm.

The hut's builders had found this place, and tried to take advantage of the natural wonder. There was no discernable reason for the clearing to exist, but here it was just the same. The buildings were the only human intrusion into the primeval landscape. Huge trees hemmed it in on all sides like great green sentinels watching over the sleeping glade. This place spoke to him, in a language that his heart could understand. Rehaak saw and understood things here that he would not have ordinarily comprehended.

In his vision, the trees became tall old men with green beards and coats of moss. They stood their silent vigil over the clearing, guarding it with persistence not possible for lesser beings. He knew they had stood unmoved and undisturbed for longer than men had walked here. He knew with certainty that they would continue to do so long after mankind was a forgotten memory. Their strength defied time. They stood, ageless and ancient, in their verdant coats of moss and lichens. They were the sacred guardians of this place.

Today was moist, green, and full of life, full of the smells of both decay and growth. The decay fed the giant trees just as it nourished the lesser children of the forest floor, the ferns, ivies, flowers and mosses. The air seemed thick enough to chew and swallow, giving life to anyone or anything scuffling through the leaves and flowers.

The light shone through the foliage. It lent a green glow to everything so that even the air was green and growing, resonant with the sheer joy of creation. The mosses and ferns appeared to spring fully formed out of nothing. The clearing was a place of wonder, magical, vibrant with life, rich and diverse. Rehaak felt a rush of energy and ecstasy as he walked through the glade, a sensation he had felt nowhere else. The clearing was a large and lovely tributary in a rushing river of life, the antithesis of his revelation of blackened lands. He could feel the vitality and vigor of this place all the way to his bones. He wept silent tears of joy because of its splendor.

The forest subdued sound as if reverential awe were not merely required, but rigidly enforced. He always had so many questions, but at this moment, he knew one thing with absolute certainty. He wanted to stay here and forget his questions, his obstacles, and everything else. He made his decision in the time between heartbeats. This was his home, the refuge he had sought.

He needed to stay here; in spite of everything that he still needed to do. A divine charisma called and captured him. He felt reborn, and revitalized, just as he had when The Creator spoke to him on the steps of the Scriptorium. Peace, too enchanting to resist, enveloped him. He danced and sang through the clearing, like a drunken man, as the vibrant joy of the moment pulsed like a second heartbeat within him. He would have stripped off all his clothes and danced naked among the sunbeams, except for the chance that Isil might arise at any moment and discover him.

Smoke coming from the chimney signaled that Isil was not only awake, but had started a fire to prepare breakfast. When he saw it, he stopped his celebrations. Any other day he might have regretted his time alone with the forest, but the joy he had received was too intoxicating to allow him to feel guilty. He had wanted to cook for her this morning He considered himself an accomplished cook. The years of pouring over dusty tomes had given him many practical skills and cooking was one of them.

K. R. Schultz

By the time he had entered the door of the hut, Isil was already preparing porridge for their breakfast. "Good morning," he said, rather sheepishly.

"Did yuh have a nice time cavorting among the posies?' she asked with a wry grin.

"Yes it was rather nice. Did you say no one has yet laid claim to this building and farm?"

"Yup. I thinks dey be afeared o' catchin what kilt duh last batch dat lived here. Never worried about it muhself. Figured everyone's gotta go sometime. Nothin in particular holdin me tuh dis life anyway."

"Well then, meet the new owner," he smiled, "Unless of course you want to claim it for your own?"

"Naw, go ahead and take it fer yerself. I ain't much fer settlin, but I would take it as an honor, if'n yuh lets me stay once't in a while, as I comes by with muh freight."

"Consider it done. You shall have perpetual free room and board for you and your team at the house of Rehaak."

"The house of Rehaak" — it had a nice sound to it, he thought.

"Fair 'nough."

They shared another meal and more conversation, but in spite of the joy within him, Rehaak still held himself apart from her. When they finished, they hitched the mithun to the wagon together, and then she was on her way to the village once more, while Rehaak stayed behind to begin a new life.

Once he had gathered enough firewood for the evening, Rehaak cataloged the work necessary to get the place in livable condition. He wandered about the clearing, taking inventory. He salvaged whatever he could use to make the hut both habitable and comfortable. When that was complete, he gathered enough dried grasses from the matted undergrowth in the clearing, for a passable mattress to sleep on, and afterward worked hard to reattach the door to its opening. It would not seem like a real house to him unless it had a door.

It had been a very busy day. His new life had begun. For the first time in recent memory, the possibilities life offered excited him.

CHAPTER 5: NEW LIFE

In his typical style Rehaak accomplished a lot in the first few weeks after his arrival, however, the excitement and enthusiasm abated during the long months of hard work that followed.

Each day, he grew stronger and tougher, from many hours of manual labor. Once he had made the hut livable, he settled into a slightly easier routine. He explored the area around the hut during the day and when night came, he worked on projects like furniture for his hut. He only used wood from trees that had already died.

The Abrhaani held the belief that all life was sacred, their credo condemned needless or careless sacrifice of any life. They believed that the spirits within must be placated by appropriate offerings when they needed to take any life. He did not share the beliefs of his forebears, but there was an abundance of material, in the forest. He only needed to haul it, and shape it to his needs. There was no need to cut fresh timber.

He had gone to New Hope a few times to trade. On his first trips, he had bought some necessities, like tools and cookware with gold, but now preferred not to use the gold, lest he engender feelings of resentment from the villagers. Many of them barely had enough to survive. In his experience, envy was a powerful motivator for evil actions. While foraging about the clearing, he had found many medicinal herbs, from which he had made distillations and tinctures that he traded in town, so his gold stayed safely stashed.

With all the manual labor the townsfolk did, they were grateful for any pain relief medications and other remedies they could get. It took considerable time, but once he had gained their trust. He became the town's unofficial healer. Some welcomed him openly while others only grudgingly accepted him. Pockets of people who did not like or trust him remained even after almost two years, but he could take it all in stride, since most tolerated his presence. He was content and did not crave better treatment.

Raamya, the sawyer and his sons were exceptions to that acceptance. They despised him, though not his healing treatments. Rehaak suspected that Raamya, the sawyer, had wanted the forest hut for his son, but Rehaak had pre-empted his claim.

Raamya was not typical of the other folk who had come from the city. He was a man of considerable resources, who had come to the area after the town was beginning to take root. He came to take advantage of the fallen timber that the forest provided, and the ready labor force already settled there. He presumed that he was better than other townsfolk were. He acted like a duke. He was domineering and abusive to New Hope's other inhabitants, especially to the poorest who made up his labor force. His three sons had also adopted their father's attitudes.

Burly Radik, surly Ogun, and sly Mato, were always at the center of any trouble in the town. Radik, Raamya's firstborn and heir, was old enough to marry. By Abrhaani custom, a young man must first build a house for himself before he could wed. Once the house was complete, he could then start a family, if he could find a girl that would have him. It would have made sense for the lad to claim the hut so that he could begin married life, without expending the effort to build his own house.

Perhaps out of fear of contagion, they had waited too long. Rehaak's arrival and tenancy claim on the hut had effectively thwarted that plan. Rehaak had no way of knowing about the situation. So, to his dismay, Rehaak found that he had made enemies for himself even before his first visit to New Hope. Raamya would have to build a house for his boy. It would take time and divert energy from his other business endeavors. Raamya's only other option would be to convince Rehaak to move out and then claim the property for himself. Rehaak was not ready to abandon the new home that he had worked so many hard months to restore.

Some townsfolk looked like the got perverse pleasure from seeing the arrogant sawyer and his unruly brood bested by a newcomer. Although few people liked Raamya, they all deferred to him, because of his power and influence in the community.

Latonia, his wife was the polar opposite to her husband, always kind and generous with her neighbors. She was always the first to respond to any emergency, the first to give aid in any crisis. She was tender hearted and kind to everyone. Plump and pleasant, was how they all described her. She provided the necessary counterpoint to her husband that made living conditions tolerable for many in the town. There was a lot of speculation about why she had married the boorish sawyer in the first place, and even more, about why she would stay with a man who was so thoroughly unpleasant.

In spite of the dislike that most bore for Raamya, a few tried to curry favor with the lout, those few made life difficult for Rehaak whenever he was trading in town. No one caused any problems for him at his home. Everyone seemed eager to avoid the glade where he lived. There were rumors that glade was fey and Rehaak was loath to dissuade them, since that belief fostered his own status in the community. Perhaps they imagined that that he too was fey, since he lived there happily unmolested by its mysterious forces. He had never had anyone from the village visit him there in the last two years.

Since he mostly stayed in his forest glade, the animosity of a few people in town was a minor annoyance, not a major problem. For his part, he stayed out of the fabric of village life. He preferred the solitude of his wilderness home. Isil punctuated that solitude with her visits, as she passed by on her way to and from Narragansett. She was the only person who was unaffected by the general superstition about the place where he lived.

He rose early every morning and began each day by fetching water from the nearby stream. He still loved the way the light played across the leaves of the forest plants. He loved the smell of wet earth in his nostrils, birdsong in his ears, the solitude and the freedom, to do as he pleased, but this morning was different from most. Dawn came, slowly burning its way through the overcast sky, leaving heavy mists that hovered along the ground. The mist did not bother him. He had experienced many dreary days of rain and mist, but today was different. Perhaps the villagers' superstitions were finally having an effect on him. Something felt wrong.

He attempted to shrug off the feeling, as he gathered his water bucket and headed out the door. He intended to take the winding trail to the stream, but the feeling intensified, like a raw and nagging toothache of dread. There was danger somewhere in the mist this morning. His heart began to beat faster and a chill ran down the back of his neck and spread to his arms.

Scanning the area with his eyes, he stepped backward toward the door of his hut and reached for his staff, which he kept just inside the door. As he did, he sensed movement in the brush along the path to the stream. There was something or someone out there.

"Show yourself, whoever you are!" he challenged, and received no response.

"Have the villagers in league with Raamya decided to escalate things?" he wondered.

"I'm not in the mood for games this morning, so be on your way, or make your intentions known." There was still no response.

He grasped his staff in his free hand and set the bucket on the ground, preparing himself for the worst. A familiar fear closed in on him. As he did so, he noticed movement again, this time in several directions at once. Out of the corner of his eye, he imagined that he saw the mist begin to coalesce and darken to his left. The fear was so strong now that he was physically nauseated. He felt like retching. Suddenly, three men stepped out of the bracken and the mist.

Their abrupt appearance distracted him from the movement that had initially caught his attention. The men all carried clubs and knives like the ones the thugs had used to attack him and Isil at the wagon. As they advanced toward him together, he realized that he did not recognize any of them. They were not from New Hope.

Rehaak swiftly considered his options. If he tried to run, they would catch him before he got very far. If he barricaded himself in the hut, he was only delaying the inevitable. Eventually they would break down the door, or they may even set fire to the hut to burn him out. His best option was to make a stand. If he stood just inside the open doorway of the hut, he might be able to lure them into attacking him one at a time. They could wear him down eventually but perhaps he could even the odds a bit first.

"What do you want?" he asked hoping for a response that would shed some light on their purposes.

They continued their inexorable progress toward him without answering. They had a fierce and feral look about them. Sharp talons of fear raked at his insides, as his heart silently called out a prayer for aid. He was just about to step back to the doorway when he noticed more movement in the mist behind the men.

"Great," he muttered. "They brought more reinforcements."

The shapes that emerged from the underbrush were not more men at all, but three great shaggy wolves with yellow eyes and fearsome fangs. They glided along silently, as they fanned out behind the men, with fangs bared. They stood almost as tall as his hip, looking lean and powerful.

"Wonderful, after you kill me you feed me to your pets — is that your plan?" he vocalized, trying to calm his nerves.

Rehaak's three assailants were close enough now that he could see their faces clearly. They stopped, and looked puzzled by his comment. Noticing where he was looking, the man to Rehaak's left turned his head to see what had attracted Rehaak's attention. He cursed and snarled a warning, when he saw the animals slinking up behind them.

Before his companions could turn, the wolves began their charge. For a second or two, Rehaak watched in stunned silence. The wolves stopped short, in a semi-circle flanking the three men. They stood facing them, growling ominously, as they began to maneuver, and look for an opening to attack. The men had formed up, back to back, facing the beasts with their weapons at the ready. Both sides had forgotten about Rehaak, as he watched the scene from the doorway of his hut.

Just when he was certain this battle would end in a stale mate, one of the wolves saw his chance. Lunging for the brigand nearest him, the big grey animal locked his teeth on the man's knife arm and the battle began in earnest. The other two men dared not take their eyes off the other wolves to help their beleaguered companion. Rehaak knew that the man should be shrieking in pain from the sharp teeth buried in his flesh. He appeared oblivious to the pain and never uttered a sound, as he swung his club repeatedly at the beast. Rehaak saw that eventually he would succeed in bashing in the animal's skull with his club. He instinctively decided to take his chances and side with the animals. It was time for him to act.

Howling like a maniac, Rehaak threw caution aside and entered the fray, swinging his staff over his head. His yell distracted all the opponents for a second. The wolves were quickest to recover and pressed the attack to the other two men. This left Rehaak free to pick his targets. He began aiming at the heads of the men with wild two-handed swings, while dodging the moving bodies of the combatants. He flailed about until he eventually landed a blow that felled one of the men. It was not picture perfect combat, but it was effective nonetheless.

As the man hit the ground, the wolf he was battling pinned him down. Rehaak landed a second blow to his temple and the man twitched and became still. Rehaak pressed in again and another man went down under his attack, blood oozed from his ears and nose. As if on cue, the wolves broke off their attack, leaving the last man to face the four of them. The bleeding man looked around, his eyes glazed and vacant.

"What is it that you want?" Rehaak asked again

The man did not reply but smiled oddly. His face twisted in hatred, mingled with mad amusement. He turned to look at the wolves. He yowled, hissed and spat at them in frustration and anger like an alley cat in a fight for its life. He turned back to look at Rehaak, raised the knife to his neck and cut his own throat. As blood jetted from the wound, something in his eyes changed. He looked surprised at the blood spurting from his wound. He fell backward and began to twitch wildly.

The wolf cocked his head in perplexity as he watched this new turn of events. The man's knife hand began to stab and hack at his own torso, inflicting deep wounds wherever the blade touched his flesh, but there was no blood from the new wounds. The fellow was already dead. He was a marionette moved by an invisible force, which caused him to mutilate himself, long after death should have rendered him incapable of such actions.

Rehaak recovered enough to try to stop him and knocked the knife from his attacker's hand with his staff. The minute the knife flew from his grasp the man's corpse became motionless and limp. A dark mist formed around his body. Suddenly it thickened and surged upwards. The wolves reacted by snarling and snapping at the insubstantial shape before it dissolved into the air.

Rehaak stood in stunned silence as he stared at the body of the last of his attackers. Finally, he overcame his astonishment. He bent down and picked up the man as best he could. Rehaak stood still, for a moment, holding the man's bloodied, lifeless form. He realized that he was alone. The wolves had vanished.

They had left him with three graves to dig and no idea why these three men had wanted him dead, no idea how a dead man could mutilate his own body.

Equally perplexing questions surrounded the appearance of the wolves. Why had the wolves appeared out of nowhere to help him? Where had they gone? Would they return? It was maddening. The more he searched for answers, the more questions he found. He reminded himself that questions were the beginning of all knowledge. That statement of truth was the only plank he could grasp, to keep from drowning in the flood of uncertainty.

Isil would be here soon. He would have to ask her what she thought about all of this. He gathered up his attacker's belongings, as he began to prepare them for burial. He left the weapons lying on the ground, reluctant to touch the knives at first. Finally, he overcame his feelings of dread enough to clean them and wrap them in a cloth before he stashed them in the niche of his hearth

He buried the three men on the edge of the forest clearing, as far away from the hut as possible. He noticed the tattoos they bore on their backs. The designs were peculiar but he did not dwell on the idea. He sang over them as he covered their bodies with forest loam. The song was unfamiliar to him. He watched and listened from outside himself as it flowed up out of his heart. He did not understand the words and as soon as he had sung it, he barely remembered the act of singing.

He knew it was a song of grief and loss but it was also a song of anger. He supposed it flowed up, out of his own heart, because he had taken three lives. Only then did he realize that the wolves had not killed any of the men, they had merely kept the men busy while Rehaak did the actual killing. His conscience plagued him. He felt sickened that he had been more vicious than wild beasts. He felt the weight of guilt like a mithun yoke fastened on his neck.

CHAPTER 6: THE PLOT

Isil arrived in the late afternoon, two days after Rehaak's battle in the clearing. He pressured her to stay the night, because he wanted her input on the events of the last few days. After protesting that she needed to head on to New Hope, he overcame her reluctance with the offer of a fine meal of rabbit stew. Once they had finished the meal, he drew up the old bench beside his new chair, in front of the fire. She listened somberly to his story, nodding now and then.

"Well — what do you think?" he asked when he had finished his story.

"I think yuh landed yerself in a mess fer sure."

"Obviously, but what did they want?"

"More'n likely dey wanted yuh dead, I reckon, but we don't know who sent 'em."

"You think they were sent — hired by someone?"

"Yup."

"Do you think it was Raamya trying to get rid of me?"

"Nope."

"I think it is entirely possible, the man positively detests me."

"Nope."

"Are you sure?"

"Yup."

"How was a dead man able to mutilate his own body like that?"

"Dunno."

"That's what I like most about you, you know, your garrulous conversation. What do you think about these knives then?" He held one out to her. "Are they the same as the ones from the brigands that attacked us on the road when we first met?"

"Yup." She looked thoughtful, but said no more.

"Do you know how to answer a question in words of more than one syllable?"

"Yup."

"Well?" He stopped talking, while he rewrapped the three blades in oiled skin. He set them back in the small space he had discovered earlier built into the side of the fireplace. The previous owners had covered the spot with a loose stone. It was a good place to hide valuables and store the blades, dry and safe from rust. He was not sure why he kept them, since they gave him, in Isil's words, the "shivers" every time he handled them.

"Not Raamya," Isil finally replied. "Dis has duh feelin o' somethin more serious to it. Duh wolves comin tuh help yuh and all duh rest o' dis — dat tells me dis be somethin bigger dan a squabble over land 'n such."

"Do you have any ideas about what it could be about?

"Lemme think on it a stretch."

He had learned that it was pointless to continue talking once she got like this. He suggested they turn in for the night. It felt good to have her company again, especially since he was still nervous about another attack. He insisted that she take his newly constructed bed with its straw ticking while he unrolled his old bedroll in front of the hearth. Without any further conversation, they drifted off to sleep.

***

The next morning was as fine a day as any he had seen, but he was obsessed with thoughts that Raamya had hired assassins to kill him, in order to take possession of the hut.

After pondering the problem over night, Isil assured him that since the whole town had acknowledged his claim to the hut, Raamya would not interfere with him. The townsfolk would not tolerate it, and neither would she.

She held a crown monopoly on freight transportation both into and out of New Hope. Since Rehaak had her support, no one would meddle with him on his own property, not without risking her censure. She could refuse Raamya access to the supplies she brought monthly, for him and others. Raamya would not trifle with her, because she could also refuse to haul his lumber and logs to the city, and that would devastate his business. The hut would simply not be worth the risk, or the cost.

"But how do we know for certain that he's not involved," Rehaak asked.

Remember duh feeling yuh had afore we was attacked on duh trail?"

"Yes."

"Was it duh same as dis time?"

"Yes."

"Well, dat happened long before Raamya even knew about yuh. He had no grudge with me, den or now. In both attacks, *you* were duh only one dere at both o' dem, Rehaak. It appears tuh me dat dose guys with duh

K. R. Schultz

fancy pig stickers was after *you,* not me, even back den. Trus' me it's somethin else dat's got dem all riled up."

"Oh,"

Rehaak could no longer argue the point. Her reasoning was sound.

She smiled slyly at him and said, "Can yuh reply in words of more dan one syllable?"

He grimaced back at her, acknowledging that she was using his own words against him. They ate a breakfast of porridge and fresh berries, while exchanging gossip about the village and the city. When they had finished, they hitched the mithun and she was quickly on her way to New Hope.

Her final words to him were, "Methinks yuh should be lookin fer duh hand of duh Creator in dis mess yuh be in, and if'n he be in it, he'll be findin a way out fer yuh too. By duh way I buried dem other pig stickers in a safe place if'n yuh wants tuh start a collection."

"No thank you, I have enough already."

Rehaak knew in his heart that she was probably right. In spite of her homespun appearance and speech, she had wisdom that he could not match, and she had none of the doubts and fears that plagued him when it came to The Faithful One. He supposed generations of forebears believing as they did, and teaching her to do the same had that effect. He on the other hand had come to his beliefs alone and unassisted. He had no heritage of belief as she did.

It was also in his nature to be doubtful, always questioning, always looking for proof of things that she simply trusted as truth. He supposed it was a character flaw though he was not sure if the flaw was hers or his. He had never been capable of blind faith. He always needed proof for everything.

82

After she left, he settled back into the daily routine of caring for himself. He continued fishing or trapping small animals for food, cooking and cleaning. In those daily tasks, and in preparing herbs and potions to heal others, he found his own healing in the peaceful power of the forest glade. The fear that followed the attack eventually faded, but it never completely disappeared.

Although, outwardly, life returned to normal, Rehaak reduced the frequency of his visits to the village. It was his attempt to keep from entanglements in the wheels and cogs of village life. In spite of the logic of Isil's assurances, he was still suspicious that Raamya had something to do with his attack. His fear gave him a heightened sense of the underlying hostility between factions in the community. They had heard of the attempt on his life and were forming their own opinions about the source of his problem. Some were for him and some against, but he wanted no part of being a source of contention between the villagers.

He had always hated the political wrangling that came from living in communities. In many ways, his new home was no different from any other he had known. There was always someone with an agenda trying to take advantage of whatever situation arose. In spite of the undercurrent of politics, and in spite of this unknown new threat, his new life ran smoothly. His excellent recall of all that he had studied, prepared him well for his new life of small town sage and healer.

Rehaak considered getting some livestock to supplement his resources, but finally rejected the idea. He didn't want the responsibility of caring for anyone but himself, so he opted for snaring rabbits, or fishing in the stream, when he felt the need to supplement his diet. The days passed quietly.

Occasionally he was sure that he caught a glimpse of the wolves watching from the undergrowth, but he was never positive that it wasn't his imagination. They had helped him in a dangerous situation. They had risked their lives for him. The notion that they might be watching, brought him comfort. Occasionally when Rehaak trapped more than he could use, he would leave the meat as an offering for the animals in case they were still about. The carcasses always disappeared but he never found wolf tracks anywhere near his offerings to them.

Another year passed. He had shelter and food. He had powerful and mysterious guardians watching over him. Life would have been wonderful had it not been for the dreams that began to haunt his sleep.

CHAPTER 7: EXPOSURE

He dreamed dreams of nakedness and flight, and did not understand their meanings. Similar dreams had repeated themselves so many times in the last year that he had lost count. They appeared to be increasing in frequency lately. They were always variations on the theme. This time he walked naked, down unfamiliar streets. The town was gray and unremarkable in its leaden uniformity. Even the light had a quality of grayness to it, as if it were perpetually twilight in this place. It was twilight without a sundown. There were no splashes of color, no golden orb sliding slowly below the horizon, no blaze of red or yellow on the clouds, no real clouds. It was grayer than overcast. The gray was a spiritual quality that affected everything, including the light.

He stood, in the middle of the gray street, in the shadowless gray light, terrified, knowing that inevitably, the doors of the houses would open; someone would walk out, and see him exposed. He looked frantically for somewhere to hide. There was scant cover anywhere. The picket fences had pickets spaced too far apart and boards too narrow to hide him. Small shrubs provided the only other option for concealment. While he was still deciding on a direction to flee, the inevitable happened. All the doors began to open. People began to stream out of the houses and out into the gray street. Most of them had a similar quality of grayness, not that they were gray, but the muted and dulled colors, of both the people and their clothing, looked like they had been washed too often. The vibrancy of color was gone, not eradicated, just damped down, and subdued, to the point where it was almost, but not quite gray.

In growing panic he began to move, scuttling, hunched over, trying his best to cover himself. He presented a pathetic picture of shame and fear, scrambling from one shrub to the next. Each time he found a place that afforded him a small chance of avoiding exposure, someone new would walk out a door, or someone would move to a position that would allow him or her to witness his state of undress. People were everywhere.

Every new person presented a fresh opportunity to see that him, naked — and fundamentally wrong. He was in the wrong location, he had the wrong clothing, or rather, he was wrong because of his lack of clothing. He had no business being here. He was so frantic to cover himself that he didn't recognize, that no one took notice of him. Shame and fear of exposure, drove him on, while the faded people around him, went on with their dull gray lives, in their washed out world.

The realization, when it finally came, that they either didn't see him, or didn't care that he was there, and unclothed, gave him no comfort. He knew that he was naked, in a world that was clothed, even if they didn't know it. Besides, any one of them, at any time might suddenly become aware of his nakedness and alert the faded masses to both his presence, and his lack of covering. On he went, in his harried attempts to find shelter, crouching, creeping, and crawling in the gray-green grass. He ran in terror, from one inadequate hiding place to the next, his private parts flapping, obscenely exposed, with every jolting step.

Before long, he realized he was nearing the outskirts of the gray town. Just ahead, lay an equally washed out forest. The possibility of escape into its cover lent strength to his limbs, if not hope to his heart. He sprinted for the welcoming cover of the forest in a wild rush, hoping to a least limit the duration of exposure. He desperately hoped that no one would see him as he streaked towards the dark wall of trees. No one noticed; no one at all.

Once inside the cover of the forest, he observed several things. First, it was even darker and grayer than the town. Second, the trees, though larger than the shrubs in town, were actually quite far apart, affording him even less cover than before. Third, that under the canopy of the branches high overhead, there was no other vegetation growing there. The branches were too high for him to reach, eliminating the possibility of climbing up and hiding in the foliage. The fourth problem and by far the worst, in his mind, was that he was not alone. The gray people were here too. Not as numerous as they were in town, but still in numbers large enough to make exposure a very real threat.

He went on, still trying to cover himself, while scrambling from one hiding place to the next. At last, inside the center of the forest he saw a large storehouse, a building of gray limestone blocks. In desperation, he fought down his fear and ran for the building, in the faint hope that this structure would finally provide the hiding place, he so desperately wanted.

Once inside he discovered the portion of the building that he was in seemed empty. It was darker inside the storehouse than in the forest, on the same order of magnitude, than the forest was darker than the town. Disturbingly, the darkness hid nothing, just as the darkness in the forest had hidden nothing. It was an unusual darkness, unsympathetic and unwelcoming. He became aware that here too, he was not alone. Other rooms in this place had more of the dull colored people, who could enter where he stood, and see him. Imminent exposure still threatened, and there was nowhere else to run.

The building that he had pinned his frantic, flagging hopes on was no better than the street, or the forest. Fear and frustration engulfed him, like an ocean wave. It lifted him, smothered him, and subsequently smashed him, with brutal crushing force onto the rocky shore of despair. He woke, sweating, and breathless, in cold damp sheets.

"What does it mean?" he shouted into the darkness. "Why can't I just get a decent night's rest for once? Leave me alone — Damn it —."

Throwing his blanket to one side, he rose and stuffed his body into his clothes as he reflected on how his life had changed again. His hut and clearing had been a safe haven when he had first arrived here, but now his refuge was becoming a prison.

"It is not going to be a good day, not by a long shot," he sulked.

Rehaak got out of bed and fed the fire in the hearth. He felt very cold tonight. His anger rose and boiled over, as he paced in front of the fire. He kicked the door open leaving the door swinging wide. He stood in the doorway with his back to the blaze from his hearth. Once his eyes adjusted to the darkness outside, he headed for the privy. Even if it had been a fine day, this black fog of frustration would hold him hostage. It was neither fine nor day. It was dark. It was wet. The night was cold, and the wind was as jagged as broken pottery.

"It must be nearing dawn."

He hated these nights awake and alone with the brutal attacks of doubt and despair. Although he relieved his bladder, he could get no equivalent relief for his mind.

Rehaak remembered the man who had begun to hack at his own body after he was already dead. He feared that he would become like him, dead but still capable of inflicting injury to himself and others. He loathed the dull dead thing he was becoming. How was it possible that he had failed to attain the promise of his early days?

More important, was there still time left for him to change the course he was on? Did he still have the fortitude to turn and walk all the way back to where he had left the path? Rehaak had planned to become a better person when he left Narragansett, but now the walls of his own character hemmed him in again. He could never run far enough to escape himself.

How had he arrived at this condition? Well, that was an easy question to answer. It wasn't any one thing, there wasn't one day he could point to and say, "Here, here is where I left the road to truth and wandered away from the true path.

The right way was narrow and precarious to travel. That was true enough, but behind him, stretched a string of broken promises and tiny compromises that looked unimportant at the time. When piled one upon the other they rose like a monument of rebellion. His choices had led him by small steps to where he now stood as naked and ashamed in real life as he was in his dreams. He had come to this place to find refuge. The attempt had been successful for almost two years, but now his place of healing and peace had become a prison of fear.

They had ejected him from Narragansett, but a deeper problem had surfaced, since he had been living here in exile. His relationship with The Creator was the issue. True, he had obeyed when he felt it was important, and that had cost him his comfortable life in the city. However, he had lived here in safety, while the threat of extinction still hovered over his people. He knew it had been years since he had abandoned his commission to warn his people of the threat. He suspected that he no longer knew how to follow and obey his Creator, since he had lived in petty rebellion for so long.

He felt desperate and defeated. He had become isolated and withdrawn since the dreams started. He believed that he had nothing left to give anyone; hell, he had nothing left for himself, let alone for others. He was as hollow as a pumpkin lantern; a smiling face, carved with precision, but without the customary candle inside to give light to the smile.

None of this mattered. He still had to go on living and find his way from here. He had run far, and hidden well, only to find himself still ensnared in the divine trap. The walls of his prison had been wide indeed, but lately they pressed him hard on all sides.

The Dark Ones were still coming and the Abrhaani were still not ready to meet them. He knew that he had to warn them. He had to leave this place to do it, but he had nowhere to go where they would listen to his warning. His abandoned mission began to haunt his thoughts, like a vengeful spirit. He had learned much in the forest's quiet embrace. He had reached his thirtieth fifth summer, but he did not feel any wiser than the boy he had been on the day he left home. He was further from true peace than he had been when he first arrived here.

How could he be at peace knowing the appalling truth; The Dark Ones were coming. Destruction followed in their wake and he had done nothing about it, because he felt as powerless as ever. He still had no real evidence to offer his race as proof of his claims. His jaw clenched in frustration and his shoulders were tight and tense with anger, as he finished what he was doing. He turned toward his hut in silence.

Only the sound of the rain on the new spring leaves and the wind in the trees kept him company. He missed *The Boys*. He had given that name to the three wolves. When they had appeared out of the mists to help him defeat three knife-wielding attackers it had scared the hell out of him, but since then, they had become friends of a sort.

It was more of a cautious respect on his part. He would not hazard a guess as to their feelings on the matter. He saw them infrequently. They never stole from his snares; they never showed any fear of him and they never let him approach them. Lately it seemed they too had deserted him. They had provided negligible company but it was better than no companionship at all. Now even that comfort was gone.

In the three summers since he had taken over the abandoned dwelling and repaired it, he had spent most of his time alone. He didn't want company from anyone who could place demands on him. Alone in the forest, no one asked anything of him. Isil had become the only exception to his seclusion, but she never made demands, and as far as he knew, she had no expectations of him. He trusted her, more than he trusted anyone, but he still found it impossible to share the deep fears of his life with her. He tolerated her company, and even valued it, but their friendship did not go much deeper than that. When she passed by with her freight wagon, she still stopped to see how he was. Her visits were the only times he felt at peace with another human being. He was not sure why she should be the exception, but she was.

In the beginning, he had needed time to heal his emotional wounds, but now it was more of a habit of solitude that he had adopted. It was so different than the busy life he had lead in the city and the freedom was glorious for a time. As time had gone on, he began to long for company, yet at the same time, he feared having people around.

He hardly ever ventured into the town anymore. It was only a few hours walk, but when he arrived, he found that he felt uncomfortable with the bustle of village life. There were so many people, and so much emotional flotsam. His sense of their emotional states had heightened to the point that it was almost more than he could bear. It was like being able to see into their hearts and souls. He decided it was a feeling he could happily do without. The Dark Ones were coming. They would all perish, he had done nothing about it and he did not want to get to know the townsfolk only to feel more guilty, because of their friendships with him.

He came when they called him to tend their sick and he went to trade for the things he needed. There were only a few handfuls of residents in the village proper and only a few score more on market day, but it was too much for him all the same.

He sighed inwardly and for the first time in years, he spoke to his God. He was tired of running without getting anywhere. He had nowhere to hide from the darkness that was building like a tidal wave still far out at sea. No one could see it, until it reached the shallows, where it would tower over the land. By that time, it would be too late to escape its horrific power. He begged The Creator for one more chance, not fully believing that He would hear his prayer, much less answer it.

The light from his hearth glowed through the open door of the hut, ruining his night vision, while at the same time guiding his way. There was little other light, because of the heavy overcast and the drizzle. It was typical of early spring in the south. The lack of moonlight made it difficult to see the trail ahead, but the path was as familiar as the dirt on the floor of his hut. He started to walk back to the hut.

He heard noises in the bracken, ahead and to the right of the path, then a groan, followed by the sound of something heavy hitting the forest floor. He stopped; and listened for more sounds, but could hear nothing above the patter of the rain on the leaves. He began to move again, cautiously, but before he had gone more than a few steps, his foot caught on unexpected obstacle in the path. He sprawled headlong onto the muddy trail, collecting a mouthful of dirt and debris in the process. He spit it out and rubbed the muck off his face and lips with the back of his hand. Looking away from the light, back along the path, his night vision returned after a few seconds.

A heap of wet cloth lay across the path. He approached cautiously. There was a man lying on his face on the wet soil under the clothing. He turned him over so his face was up but it was too dark to make out much detail. The man was big and he was still breathing, but the breaths were shallow and labored. Two choices presented themselves. Leave him here on the ground to die and deal with the corpse in the morning; there wasn't much life left in him anyway; or drag him into the hut and try to revive him. He suspected that he would probably regret the decision in years to come but he chose option two.

It was hard to drag the limp, sodden bulk of the stranger's body the rest of the way to the hut. Rehaak slipped in the mud and fell down more than once. He had to stop to untangle the stranger's cloak from the underbrush along the turns in the trail a few times, but he finally made it to his door. He dragged the body by the wrists; it was the best way to get a good grip. When the stranger's feet finally bumped across his threshold, he released his grip and walked around to close the door.

"Let's see what we have here," he said, and began to untangle the clothes.

If the stranger had a hat, it was lost somewhere back along the trail where he had been skidded. His hair was long and if it were drier, and less muddy, Rehaak might have been able to distinguish a color, but it looked paler than normal. His face, especially around the eyes and lips, was blue. His fair skin looked pale, not the usual green-bronze of an Abrhaani complexion. Though the frame was that of a man, the face was that of a gangly youth not even old enough to grow a beard. The fellow was at least half a span taller than Rehaak himself.

"Well now, we have a puzzle. Where did you come from young bucko and what are you doing out here alone? I have never seen anyone so large and yet so young before. Let's get you dry and warm first. If you make it through the night, then we'll have to hear your tale."

Rehaak removed the boy's belt, set the dagger to the side. Next the peasant boots and homespun garments, which he hung on the cord he used to dry his own clothes beside the fire. Once he had the boy undressed, he rolled him closer to the hearth, hoping the warmth radiating from the stone would revive him. He checked the boy over to make sure there were no injuries. Apart from some small cuts and scrapes, there were no wounds on his tall frame. Most were minor bruises and abrasions on his legs. A walk through the dark forest could easily explain those. What the injuries could not explain was his presence here.

It was obvious that he was a lad and just about to enter manhood, although he was lean and muscled like someone used to hard labor.

Rehaak covered him with his only spare blanket. He lit his pipe, inhaled deeply and he blew smoke rings at the ceiling, as he placed his chair facing the hearth with the boy's supine body between him and the fire,. At least he had something else to occupy his thoughts until morning came.

What puzzled him was the way the boy looked. All the Abrhaani, especially the villagers in this area, were dark like Rehaak. All of them looked relatively similar, cut from the same cloth as it were. The boy didn't look anything like any of them; in fact, he didn't look like anyone Rehaak had ever seen before. He wondered if he was even from the island.

If that were true, he would have a very difficult time finding the youngster's kin. He had heard of the Eniila from the books he had studied and from stories of traders. This man-child looked like what the books and the stories had described. Until now, he had ignored the rumors about the Eniila smith who lived near the nearby village of Dun Dale. He had never been to that village. New Hope contained more than enough people for him. Villagers said the smith had crossed the sea from Baradon to Kel Braah, but this lad was far too young to be that man. There could be only one answer. He must be one of their offspring, but why had he come here, at night and alone?

After the wars they had fought against each other, it was strange, that people of that hard, violent race would have wanted to come and live among the Abrhaani. It had been decades since the Eniila drove the Abrhaani from their cities along the coast of Baradon, but both races had long memories when it came to conflict. The Eniila and the Abrhaani could never be friends. At best, they were uneasy neighbors with the Syn Gersuul keeping them separated and at peace. The Eniila were not sailors. From what Rehaak knew, they stayed well away from the water. If the Eniila ever developed a navy, that might well change.

Trade had sprung up between the former enemies. These days the Abrhaani traded from their ships, instead of the cities that they had built along the coast. They docked in ports, which had once been theirs.

The Eniila warlords now held those ports and cities. The only Abrhaani left on the continent were slaves, who worked in the mines and did other hard labor for their Eniila masters. Relations were relatively peaceful now, but no one knew when violence could erupt again. So how had this youngster gotten all the way to his doorstep? What drove him to leave the comfort of his own home to wander in the forest at night? Rehaak sat, smoked, and pondered his options.

When morning did come, it caught him by surprise. He had fallen asleep in the chair, his pipe had gone out, and the fire was only embers in the hearth. Rehaak hated falling asleep sitting up, because he was invariably stiff and his back hurt for days afterward. Today was no different. He could feel the pain in his joints as he rose.

The boy was lying exactly where he had left him. It didn't look like he had moved at all during the night. Bending over the youngster's recumbent form, he could see that his color had improved and that his breathing was much better. Now that his hair was dry, it was easy to see that he was as blonde as ripe grain. The lines and curves of his young face, though relaxed in sleep, hinted at the strong masculine features of the man that he would become. Rehaak put more wood on the fire, and went to fetch some water from the stream for herb tea. He would need it to ease the pain in his back. The youngster would also probably welcome the chance to wash in warm water, once he awoke.

When the boy was awake, he would take him to the village and send him back where he belonged. Rehaak didn't know the folk in Dun Dale at all and had never cared to involve himself in their village life. They were typical country folk he supposed, leery of the unknown. He suspected that if they knew of him at all, he looked mysterious and aloof. He had kept to himself and only traded in New Hope, ensuring that it remained that way. Now he wished he had more information. Surely, they knew more than he did about this youngster. He was suddenly in the unenviable position of needing their help. He didn't know where to else to turn.

Rehaak had built an insular wall around himself, but if he had wanted to join their community, he might still have found it difficult. It was different in Narragansett. Everyone in the city wanted to know everyone else's business, but people out here tried to escape their pasts. They wanted no one to know who or what they had been, before coming to New Hope. It was their method of protection as well as his own. Information was power. It gave other people an advantage over them that made them vulnerable.

In Narragansett, for a time, he had been the center of attention; here he was forever on the outside looking in. Most days that was exactly how he wanted it. He felt safer with it that way. The only exception to that rule was when someone needed healing. Most people treated Rehaak with respect; some treated him with indifference and a few with hostility. He was an outsider from the start, odd and untouchable, even in this place, where odd or untouchable was the norm. The last year had only intensified his separation from society. They valued his skills, not his company. He felt the difference keenly but it did not wound him at all. It was the way things were nothing more. Now it looked as if he had made a serious error by excluding himself from the social aspects of the communities around him.

They may know more in the village. That was where he needed to go eventually. It bothered him to have to ask for help from the villagers, but right now,

K. R. Schultz

Rehaak had more immediate concerns. He gathered up his water pot and his smoking things, slipped into his robe, and left the hut, careful to latch the door behind him. Once outside, he took the right hand branch of the trail that snaked through the trees and down the hill to the stream. His footsteps squelched, in the soft mud of the trail as he walked, breaking the soft stillness of the morning.

CHAPTER 8: NEW FRIENDS

Consciousness slowly returned. Laakea woke, warm and alone, the familiar sound of logs crackling and popping in the hearth. The last thing he remembered from the night before was the lure of firelight that drew him forward with its promise of warmth. All else was blackness, until he woke here on the packed earth floor, in front of this fire. He looked around to try to orient himself. He knew that it was daytime by the pale light that filtered through the lone window. He could not guess the time of day or see anything outside. The oiled skin of the window let the light in, but was too opaque to see through. The dim light from the window at one end of the building, and the fire in the hearth at the other provided enough light to see the interior of the hut clearly.

Besides the lone window, the hut had a single door, and a river rock fireplace. A straw tick on a rough bed-frame stood in the corner near the hearth. A table, a single chair and a bench created from branches and planks sat along a wall in the room. The planks of both the bench and the table had been worn smooth on the upper sides from long usage. The chair looked like a newer addition. He got up off the floor, keeping the blanket for a covering, and began to look for his clothing and belongings.

There were two copper pots of different sizes and smaller utensils for cooking and eating placed near the hearth. The lack of accumulated possessions gave evidence of a single occupant. Laakea found his clothes hung from a crude rope strung from two pegs that protruded about a foot from the daub and wattle walls, on the other side of the hearth. He estimated the hut's size at four paces long and three paces wide. It was not a lot of room, but big enough to be livable. The house where he had been born and raised was similar, although slightly larger, having had three rooms. It had one room this size, and two smaller ones for sleeping, but his parents had laid flagstones on the floor with packed clay between the gaps, rather than the dirt floor in this hut.

There were shelves along the opposite wall that consisted of planks resting on pegs in the log uprights. On the shelves were many small leather pouches. He resolved not to look into the pouches; they were none of his business. The owner of this house had rescued him. He would not dishonor himself and violate his host's hospitality. He checked his clothes. They were dirty, but at least they were dry. He couldn't find his hat anywhere. He dressed quickly and looked for his belt and dagger, which he found hanging from a peg by the door. He strapped on the belt and slid the dagger into the frog on the belt. His stomach growled with hunger, but the fullness of his bladder was a more pressing issue.

He walked to the rough plank door, slid the wooden latch to the side, and pushed it open. The drizzle of the previous night had stopped, but the sky remained overcast. Mist hovered thickly above the forest floor. The trees and undergrowth looked as if they sprang directly from the shifting fog and not the soil beneath. The air was chill and moisture still dripped from leaf and branch. There was a trail of sorts, leading away from the hut both to the left and to the right. Because of the cloud cover, it was impossible to see the sun, so he had no way of knowing what direction they headed. It would be impossible to get his bearings until the sky cleared.

His overtaxed bladder was threatening to empty itself immediately, and he did not want to offend his host and savior by sullying his doorstep with urine. He picked the right hand branch of the path and began to hurry down it, hoping to find a privy. If not, any convenient shrub would do. When he could stand it no more, he walked a few steps off the path and relieved himself against the roots of a dogwood bush, the damp green leaves, brushed against the backs of his hands as he completed his task. He heard the faint sound of running water ahead of him, undoubtedly a stream.

As he was finishing, he heard a noise in the brush behind him. He turned just in time to see three shaggy shapes emerge from the mist and the bracken. Three gray wolves, legs obscured by the mist stalked silently toward him. He thanked the gods that his bladder was already empty, as he reached for his belt knife, to defend himself from the beasts. He drew it and stood ready for an attack that didn't come. Instead, they fixed their baleful yellow eyes on him and began to close in slowly. His fear escalated into panic.

With his heart pounding against his breastbone, like his father's hammer on red-hot iron, fresh from the forge, he began to back away from the three great animals. He wanted to put some distance between himself and these wolves. He might still be a meal to the beasts regardless of his effort, but he wanted a fighting chance. He began backing away slowly, knife in hand.

They fanned out to either side, as if to flank him, but he kept retreating toward the sound of the stream. The way they had positioned themselves, kept him from fleeing back to the hut. He tried to keep them all in sight, in case one suddenly tried to pounce on him. He had seen what wolves had done to one of his father's sheep several winters ago, and grisly memories of that scene replayed themselves in his mind.

Laakea and Aelfric had heard the sheep, bleating in panic, outside in the darkness. He and his father had rushed out with lanterns to find the cause of the commotion. They were too late to save the ewe that the wolves had already attacked, but they had managed to frighten the predators off, before they made off with the animal. The wolves were gray shadows at the edges of his father's lantern light. Those shadows had eyes that glowed malevolent and red, as they reflected the light of the lamps back at him. It still chilled his heart when he remembered.

The wolves did not have time to finish the animal off before Aelfric had driven them off. It lay in the snow bleating in panic and pain with its flanks torn. It bled from red slashes at its hocks, where the wolves had torn out the muscles in the backs of its legs. Hamstrung, his father had called it. It only had the use of its front legs as it bleated, and tried to escape. It left bloody stripes in the snow as it dragged itself forward, clawing at the frozen earth with its front hooves. He had vomited, while his father pulled out his dagger and slit the ewe's throat, to finish the job the wolves had begun. The warm blood spurted out and melted a large crimson pool in the snow, before the sheep finally stopped twitching, to lie still, and silent. His father had used the snow to wash the red blood off his hands and knife, before he sent Laakea back inside. There was fresh mutton for the next few days, but Laakea could not bring himself to eat it.

It was not difficult to imagine himself, with the backs of his legs slashed, lying as helpless as that bleating sheep. He imagined them closing on him, to rip out his throat and tear out his entrails. He tried to shake off the image as he continued to back away toward the stream. The ground began to slope sharply away behind him. His footing became precarious, but he dared not look back and lose sight of the dangerous predators in front of him. They continued to advance toward him.

Suddenly his heel caught on an exposed root. He lost his balance. His backward momentum, coupled with the steep slope, continued to carry him backward. He rolled head over heels down the stream bank to the gravelly edge of the stream. Running water had sliced away the earth to reveal rocks and roots that dug into his flesh as he tumbled down the bank.

When he finally came to a stop, on his back, at the water's edge, his knife and his breath were both gone. He stared at the brightening sky and tried to force his lungs to work again. Finally, he managed to scramble to his feet. He frantically looked around for his dagger. Fortunately, the fog that was evident at the top of the slope, did not linger here where the sun had already warmed the rocks of the streambed. He spotted it a short distance up the slope. The wolves were not in sight. He could retrieve it if he was quick enough.

As he was about to scramble towards his weapon, all three wolves crested the lip of the bank and began padding downhill toward him. Their eyes were feral and fell in the morning light. He knew he could never run far enough or fast enough to evade them. They were lean and muscular animals, narrow and nasty, built for power and incredible endurance. He was faint with hunger and could never hope to outrun them, nor could he defend himself without his weapon.

Time slowed as he watched them come closer. An unusual calm settled upon him as he began to notice details that he had missed before. There were minute differences between the wolves. One was larger than the other two and he seemed to be the leader. When the animals reached the place where his knife lay among the stones, the largest wolf stopped to sniff it while the others stood by his sides. Laakea closed his eyes and waited for the end to come.

Afraid to look, he listened for movement. Hearing rustling to each side and slightly behind him, he turned his head and slowly opened one eye. The two smaller wolves had walked around him to the creek where they now stood and lapped up water, as if he wasn't there. The biggest one was not with them. He heard a metallic click in front of him. He quickly opened his other eye and turned his head, back in the direction of his lost knife. The wolf lay on the rounded stones of the streambed, watching him, from only a few feet away.

When Laakea had closed his eyes, his knife was well beyond his reach. Now his knife lay at his feet. He only needed to bend down to retrieve it. Had the big wolf set it there before it backed off to watch? There could be no other explanation. He slowly squatted to pick it up keeping his eyes on the animal. Cautiously, he reached down and grasped his blade, when the animal made no move to attack him; he slid it back into the frog on his belt.

Why were they behaving like this?

Everything he knew about wolves, told him he should be well on his way through their digestive tract. The wolf rose, stretched, dog like and padded past him to the stream to join the other two. His fur almost brushed Laakea's leg, while he stood frozen in disbelief. The smaller wolves had finished drinking already. They obviously had no fear of him. They would have already attacked him if they had intended to harm him.

He grew calmer and he remembered that he too was thirsty. He had been on his way to find the stream, moments before they had appeared out of the forest, like ghosts in a dream. They had herded him to this spot. He buried his fear and resurrected his courage, turned, and walked the remaining distance to the water's edge, where he knelt and drank his fill, while all three wolves stood watch.

When he had finished drinking, the wolves began to trot downstream, along the rocky bank. He felt relief watching them go, but they didn't go, they stopped, as if waiting for him to follow. When he did not move, the leader trotted a short way back toward him, looked him in the eyes for a few moments, and cocked his head to the side, as if asking a question. In a few moments, he turned and trotted back to where his two companions waited. He stopped again, looking over his shoulder at Laakea. The leader cocked his head again as if he was issuing another invitation. They were waiting for him to follow.

His curiosity finally won out over his fear. He felt foolish, but he decided to follow them for a while. He wanted to know where they would lead him. His mother had told him stories of animal spirit guides leading heroes in the distant past. He was not willing to believe he was a hero, nor was he willing to believe the old fairy tales were true, but this was so very like one of his mother's stories, it was uncanny. He could not help wondering if the gods had sent them to teach him something. Therefore, with his curiosity piqued, he walked along the stream to where they waited for him. He joined the pack, walking toward the bend that hid the downstream portion of the gully from his view.

Once he had committed to follow them, the three animals trotted downstream. They had not gone more than ten paces past the bend, when he spotted a man kneeling by the creek, filling a large pot with water. He wanted to shout out to draw the man's attention, but he was afraid of what the wolves might do if he startled them. The wolves continued to trot forward, as if they either did not notice the kneeling man or were leading him toward the stranger.

The man finished filling his container with water. He straightened up, then sat down on a large boulder, and pulled out a pipe, which he lit. He puffed on his pipe, sending up clouds of fragrant smoke that the breeze carried to Laakea's nostrils.

They were not more than twenty paces away now. The wolves were definitely heading straight for the man, who still had his back turned toward them. He appeared engrossed in watching the sunrise, where the clouds were beginning to break up.

The sound of running water hid any noise made by wolves' silent approach. The boy, however, made a lot of noise as his feet slipped and skidded in the gravel of the streambed. In spite of the racket Laakea was making, they managed to get quite close before his crunching footsteps finally caused the man to turn his head. When the stranger looked at the boy and the wolves he got up slowly, there was no panic in his eyes.

The stranger waved, smiled, and called out loudly enough for Laakea to hear him over the sound of the running water.

"Hallo, I am called Rehaak. It's good to see you awake. I see you found your clothing, and I see you have also met The Boys." He pointed at the animals. "I was just coming to get water for tea while you slept. I thought we could wash your clothes later if you would like. How did you find me here? I did not see you coming down the path."

"Well met Rehaak, I am Laakea. As to the path, I guess you'd say I found a short cut," the boy replied with a smirk. "I owe you thanks for your hospitality, though I have to say your wolves made a frightening welcoming committee."

"You are welcome, but they are not my wolves: though perhaps I am their man. They occasionally watch me from the edge of the forest. They have adopted me after a fashion, but they have never come as close to me, as they sit to you right now." He pointed to the animals again, who were sitting just out of the boy's reach in a semicircle in front of him. "They must like you. Come let us return to my hut. We will brew some tea and get you something to eat. You are no doubt, hungry."

The path Rehaak had mentioned was in plain sight now. It led up the bank and into the forest. Laakea sized the man up as he gestured for them to go. He guessed that Rehaak was about thirty, greenish skin and emerald eyes like all the folk he knew, from the village near his home. He was slightly less than his own height, but spare and stringy. Aelfric, Laakea's father, had told him that men of this physical type had great endurance in combat. "Large muscles make for great power," he had said. "But in a long battle watch for the lean, wiry warrior. He will outlast the bigger man more often than not." Nearly everything his father taught him had some relationship to combat.

Rehaak's face was lean under his full, dark beard and thick black brows. His eyes were large, deeply set on either side of a sharp hooked nose. It was a pleasant face, but his eyes were penetrating. They were eyes that could look into a man's soul. Laakea certainly felt exposed as he looked into them. The wolves fell in behind them, as they began to walk.

Rehaak carried no weapons that Laakea could see. Over the usual gray homespun breaches, and belted tunic he wore a blood red linen robe that opened in the front. It was cloak length, but had belled sleeves, that ended just below the middle of his forearms. Someone had embroidered the edges with a border of green vine leaves. Laakea wondered about the significance of this decoration, but he was not sure that it was polite to ask, so he started with something he thought would be safer.

"Where did you, or rather how did you find me?" Laakea asked.

"You almost found me. I had gone to use the privy last night; actually, I suppose it was nearer to dawn by then. I left the door of my hut open so I could find my way back in the dark. When I was walking back down the trail to the hut, I tripped over you. You were lying, face down in the path. At first, I was not sure if you were still alive. It was brutally cold and very wet last night. It took some doing, but I managed to get you inside my hut, by dragging you by the wrists."

"I suppose that explains this lump," Laakea said, as he rubbed the tender spot on the back of his head. "I suspect your open door was the light I saw in the darkness. The gods were good to me."

"Well — *one* was anyway," Rehaak said, and smiled in a way that made Laakea wonder what he meant by the remark.

Laakea would have liked to ask about its significance, but he dared not look into those green eyes for any length of time. He felt that if he did the man would ferret out his shameful secret. He decided that it was not a risk worth taking, until he knew the man much better. There would be other ways to find out what he needed to know.

"I was alone. I am afraid I was not able to be as gentle as I would have liked, on your behalf." Rehaak smiled again, but this time his smile was just a smile.

"Well, I thank you anyway. I owe you a life debt. My parents taught me that a man always repays his debts."

"Where are you from lad, you do not look like you are from around here?

"Actually, I am lost," the boy replied. "I lived with my father, the blacksmith."

"I was not aware there was a smith in New Hope" Rehaak replied.

"New Hope? Where is that? We lived near the village of Dun Dale, North West of the village about a half days walk," Laakea said, being scrupulously honest.

"Ah, I see, Dun Dale is a long way, or so I hear, many days journey. What has brought you so far south?

"As I said, I got lost." Laakea evaded.

"But your parents must be worried about you. Surely they will wonder where you are and will search for you." Rehaak ventured. When Laakea declined to comment he added, "You are not Abrhaani, are you?"

"No, we are Eniila, but I know only a little about our people. My parents raised me here in Khel Braah. I have never been anywhere else, nor have I met any others of my race, save for my family, of course."

"There is so much bad blood between our peoples. I am not surprised that you were the only ones; in fact, I am surprised that there were of you at all. I did not think that there were any Eniila on Kel Braah. Have you ever considered going back?"

"Going back where?"

"Back among your people the Eniila, of course, on the other side of the Syn Gersuul, in Baradon."

"I have never really thought of them as my people. This land is the only one I know, so it is difficult for me to imagine going elsewhere. My parents taught me Abrhaani customs and manners. The language is mostly the same as the language of the Eniila, though we have differences in pronunciation. I have no way to cross the Syn, for I hear it is wide and deep. I have never seen it myself; to know if what I have been told is true."

"So, now young sir, you have set out to explore the world, is that it?" Rehaak asked after noting that the boy had spoken of his parents in the past tense.

"After a manner of speaking you have the right of it," said Laakea, shading the truth.

When Rehaak did not respond immediately, he added defensively, "I have enough knowledge to make my own way in the world. My parents taught me their trades and skills, so I can make a living whether it is here or elsewhere."

Rehaak ignored the statement and asked, "As you said you were lost. What will you do now that you are found again?"

Laakea did not know how to answer Rehaak's question, without revealing more than he was comfortable with about himself, especially to someone he had just met. He was normally open and honest, but circumstances had changed him. He could feel his face and ears burn with shame, as he remembered how he had cursed his father, and dishonored himself. A lump rose in his throat.

When he did not answer, Rehaak stopped walking. He turned to look at Laakea, who would not make eye contact, and said. "It's all right lad, I had no wish to pry. I overstepped myself. I understand that most people have things they would rather not discuss with nosy strangers that they have just met. Everyone, including me, has their share of things they would rather not have exposed to the entire world."

Laakea did not reply. He was still trying to get rid of the lump in his throat. His face and ears felt ready to burst into flame. The tears that were threatening to flow from his eyes would never contain enough water to extinguish the fire of his shame. He stood looking at the ground, unsure of what to do next. He was unable to move or make a sound. If the earth had suddenly opened up, to swallow him, he would have been very grateful to escape this man's penetrating eyes.

Rehaak gently broke the uncomfortable silence for him, "Let's get you fed and cleaned up anyway."

Rehaak had just given him a way out. Not knowing what else to do he looked up and sneaked a glance at Rehaak's face. He was surprised to see tears in Rehaak's eyes. It made him wonder about the source of Rehaak's pain. He wondered if he could trust this stranger. Would Rehaak understand and accept him as he was?

They both turned back to the path in silence. They walked the rest of the way to the hut without speaking another word. Laakea looked back. The wolves, who had been padding along behind them, had vanished into the forest. He matched his stride to the dark stranger beside him, and wondered how much of his story he should reveal.

He needed to tell someone, but at the same time, he was fearful that Rehaak would condemn and shun him, if he knew what Laakea had done. The shelter and friendship, that Rehaak had offered, was more than he could expect. In spite of his fears, he could not help feeling that he had found his way to the right place. Now that he had a place of refuge, he was fearful of losing it.

"Will Rehaak still let me stay, once he learns what kind of person he has rescued from a cold and well deserved death?" he wondered silently.

There was only one way to know for sure. He would have to tell Rehaak the truth. He hoped that he could summon the courage to humiliate himself further than he already had.

CHAPTER 9: A LESSON IN TRUST

The winding trail they had been following quickly brought them back to the hut. Rehaak opened the door and said with a wide smile and a slight bow, "Please be welcome in my home."

"This is the formal greeting of the Abrhaani people to a guest."

"Thank you for your generous gift of hospitality," the boy replied, which was the correct formal response.

Rehaak smiled and gestured for him to enter. Once they were both inside, he set his chair in front of the fire and indicated that Laakea should sit. He waited until the boy seated himself, before he turned to add more wood to the fire.

"Who taught you the customs of our people?" Rehaak queried, while busying himself with preparations for breakfast.

"My mother taught me what she knew of your manners and customs. She said it was a sign of respect to behave well."

Once Rehaak had filled the large copper pot with water, he set it close to the flames to boil; he turned to face the boy again. He knew that the formal phrases they had been using with each other had given them a social framework to interact, and it had created a more relaxed atmosphere. Laakea would now know what was coming next, and what Rehaak expected of him. It was less intimidating to talk once they had rules for their conversation.

"She was right to say so, young sir," he said, looking into Laakea's eyes. The boy looked away after a moment as if he could not bear to hold Rehaak's gaze. "Do you have other family besides your parents?"

"No, there is only my father and me. My mother died several years ago," he said, without visible emotion. "Do you have family, Rehaak?"

"Yes, but alas, I have not seen them for many years. I have been travelling extensively."

"You must miss them."

"Honestly, I have not even thought about them for quite a while now. My life is very different from theirs, and there has been little opportunity for contact. I have been busy with other things."

"I suppose that is the way it is, once one has grown and has left home," said Laakea, trying to sound wise.

Laakea seemed more relaxed now. Since the conversation was flowing nicely, Rehaak changed direction.

"We have other matters to discuss, if I may be blunt. I imagine you are wondering if you may shelter here with me for a time, and how long it would be before you wear out your welcome."

The boy stared mutely at the floor again and nodded his head in agreement.

While getting the water from the stream, Rehaak had been thinking about his options regarding Laakea.

He needed to know what to do with the boy. His first idea was to return the boy to his own people. However, once he had seen the way the boy had reacted to his earlier questions, he had quickly discarded that idea. Something or someone had driven him out into the cold night. He was just a lad, one of The Creator's beings, who needed help. Rehaak decided to bide his time and gather more information from the boy. Rehaak was sure that he could draw Laakea out. He could sense that the youngster had a strong need to tell his story to someone.

Rehaak had some reservations about inviting the boy to stay. The reservations were more with himself than Laakea. He was not sure he could cope with having Laakea underfoot, because he had been alone for such a long time. He was not well equipped to entertain guests at his hut. Isil had been his only guest thus far, and never for more than one night.

He had plenty of time to decide the proper course of action. There was no need to rush into a decision he would later regret. Although he was still sorting through his own inner conflicts regarding his faith, he was beginning to believe again. He remembered his prayer to his God, just before finding Laakea lying in the path. The Creator might have a purpose in their meeting. Rehaak was short of motivation and needed guidance desperately, but time was the one resource he had in plenty. Time and patience would undoubtedly be the key to unlocking the secrets Laakea carried. The world was full of mysteries and secrets and this chance meeting could well be another one of them.

His curiosity was piqued, and something he had read back in the city was prickling at the back of his mind. He thought he might have to risk eventually going back to Narragansett to consult the texts at the scriptorium. Something about an Eniila — a warrior — he couldn't quite remember.

Rehaak pushed the idea aside and went on, "I sense that you have nowhere to go just now, so I invite you to stay as long as you want. I have limited resources, as you can see for yourself, but you may share all that I have, and you are welcome to it."

The lad remained silent, as if searching for the proper polite response. Laakea raised his head and met Rehaak's eyes for a moment, but quickly looked down again without saying a word.

"This is not a formal offer made out of custom or duty, so there is no formal answer required. It is just one man, offering help to another man. You do not even need to answer right now. You may have other options you wish to pursue. If you do, may the blessings of the Creator be upon you. I wish you a safe journey. However, if you do need my help, it is freely given, with no expectation of repayment."

"We will have breakfast soon. I wanted to give you time to think about your answer. I also want to set your mind at ease, so that you do not worry needlessly. Worry inhibits learning, and we both will have much to learn from each other, if you accept my offer."

Having said what he felt he needed to say, Rehaak rose and went over to the shelves on the wall, where the boy had seen the leather pouches earlier. He selected a few and carried them to the table. There were dried fruits and grains that Rehaak put in the small copper cook pot he had brought to the table.

"I am about to prepare a meal of dried fruits and boiled grains for us," Rehaak explained. "It is my favorite morning meal. I hope you like it."

Laakea could now see what the pouches contained. Once his curiosity had been satisfied regarding the contents of the pouches, he remained seated, deep in thought, staring into the flames of the hearth. Though his body was immobile, his mind leaped and bounded like a rock tumbling down a steep slope. He was having a hard time sorting through his feelings. On the one hand, he felt safe here. It felt right to stay. Rehaak had offered him more than he could have hoped for and certainly more than he had any right to expect.

Laakea also owed Rehaak a life debt, and if he stayed, he might find a way to discharge that debt. It was the honorable thing to do. On the other hand, the man made him nervous, despite the fact that he acted kind and generous. What bothered Laakea the most about Rehaak were his eyes.

"When he looks at me, he can see into my soul," he said, in and internal monologue. He was starting to have second thoughts about his earlier decision to tell Rehaak the truth.

I know, by the questions he asks, and the things he says, that he knows what I am thinking. He will be able to see my disgrace. What will happen then? I have nowhere else to go, but how can I stay when he has powers like that? He is probably a sorcerer or perhaps something worse."

Laakea's thoughts tumbled over each other down the steep slope to the brink of despair. He managed to stop just short of the edge. Finally, he fought off his doubts, and summoned the courage to speak, but before he could tell Rehaak that he intended to accept his offer, Rehaak spoke.

"I suppose I will need to go to the village soon to get some supplies since I am not used to having guests," Rehaak said quietly, sensing Laakea's answer.

Laakea felt his still shaky resolve begin to waver again. Rehaak had once again anticipated his reply.

"How did he know?"

He looked away nervously, and stared intently at the fire while trying to control his rising panic.

"I should run while I have the chance. This man is definitely a sorcerer."

He wanted to get up, but he could not rise from the chair. One part of him wanted to run screaming like a little girl, out the door and back into the forest. Perhaps fear held him there or maybe something deeper and stronger than fear. He was no longer sure of anything. Part of him knew that there was great tenderness in the man at the fire. That tenderness called out to him to stay. A voice inside, like the golden voice he had heard in the dark forest told him he should stay in spite of his fear.

It said, *"This is a place of safety, where you can learn and grow in peace."*

He summoned his courage again, just as Rehaak looked up from the pot he was stirring. Their eyes met briefly.

"I thank you for your offer of hospitality. I will stay as long as you'll allow, and the gods will it," he said, making the decision final by giving voice to it.

"There, I have given my word and now I cannot do otherwise and retain my honor."

Laakea found it strange that honor and duty still held importance for him, even after he had miserably failed in both honor and duty to his father. Perhaps, there was still something worth redeeming in him.

Rehaak smiled at him, as he straightened and stretched. He walked over to the table to get the wooden cup for his tea. With cup in hand, he took some herbs from a pouch and put them into a cup before he filled it with boiling water. He set the cup on the mantel to steep, while he went back to stirring the pot that contained their breakfast. Neither of them spoke for a long time, but the silence appeared more comfortable to the boy now that he had made his decision.

Laakea grew calm. He was at peace with his decision to stay. He hoped that his host would not come to regret the offer of hospitality, and he hoped that he could somehow repay his *Life Debt* to Rehaak.

"Breakfast is ready. Come to the table." Rehaak said as he scooped a steaming mound of porridge into each bowl.

The boy set the chair at the table and sat down. Steam rose from the bowl in front of him carrying the fragrance into the air. It smelled delicious. His stomach rumbled in eager anticipation. He waited in customary politeness for Rehaak to begin eating, but instead of starting to eat, the man raised his hands upward as he stood by the table and began to sing.

> *Creator of all, the stones and sky,*
> *Our thanks we sing to you on high.*
> *We take your gifts that you provide.*
> *Your power graciously bestow,*
> *On all your creatures here below.*
> *Our thanks we give, our strength and guide.*

With that done, he nodded to the boy, then sat down and began to eat.

After the first spoonful, Laakea found it difficult to pace himself. It was the best food he had ever tasted. He had eaten nothing but berries and mushrooms for five days. He supposed that even charcoal would taste good, after a fast like that. Even on a feast day his mother's cooking was never as good as these grains boiled with dried fruit. He finished the bowl in moments, and although his stomach cried out for more, his honor would not allow him to ask for another helping. Rehaak smiled at him again.

"I had forgotten the way a youngster can eat. Thank you for the reminder. Tomorrow I will make a larger portion for you."

Again, the man had divined his thoughts. It was still unsettling, but Laakea was growing accustomed to the occurrence. What made the difference was the man's demeanor. Rehaak spoke with gentle understanding in his voice, and did not seem threatening. Laakea was surprised to realize that he was more at ease with this stranger than he had been with his own father, especially in the weeks before he fled his home. He summoned up his courage and asked the question that had been bothering him since the first look into the man's dark-green eyes.

"How do you always know what I'm thinking?"

Rehaak's eyes lit up and he began to smile, "There is much," he paused to swallow, "Much I have to tell you."

Laakea waited expectantly, imagining some deep revelation.

"I believe our two races may be very different from each other."

"I already know our peoples are very different, the Abrhaani are generally short, sturdy, with greenish skin and eyes. We Eniila are fair, and tall," Laakea said, with all the arrogance and certainty of youth.

"That is certainly true, but I believe there is far more to the differences than simply outward appearances," Rehaak paused again to collect his thoughts.

"Please explain that." Laakea said a bit more sharply than he had intended. He felt that Rehaak had just belittled his knowledge and he tried to control his temper.

"I meant no offense," Rehaak apologized as he responded to the tone. "It's just that you give me more credit than is my due."

He began again.

"I do not always know what you are thinking young sir. You may believe it is true and sometimes it seems that way to you. I must tell you that I can tell a great deal by looking at your face and your posture. I can tell more by trying to put myself in your position, and imagine what you must be feeling by your posture or by your facial expressions. I must also admit that there are times when I can sense strong emotion, when I am near people, but I do not truly know what they are thinking. It is more of an educated guess."

"This ability is something that comes easily for most of my race, more easily for me I suppose. I would have believed that it was common to all humankind, but if you know nothing about it, the Abrhaani alone may have this ability. I will explain much more to you in good time, if you are willing to listen and to learn."

"I have work that I need to complete today. If you would help me with my tasks, and if you are interested in learning, I shall teach you as much as you are able to comprehend. You might say it like this; if you are hungry for learning, I shall feed you as much as you can swallow, my young friend." Rehaak smiled at the simile.

"I will work for you gladly. I owe you at least that much to help pay my life debt to you." Laakea tried to hide the impact Rehaak's words created in his heart. This Abrhaani man had just called him friend. He had never had a friend before. Until recently, he had his parents, but no one, none of the villagers or their families had ever called him friend.

"Then let us begin by cleaning up these pots and dishes. We will cut some fire wood, prepare things for our meals, and make a place for you to sleep for the night, unless you wish to sleep on the hearth again."

When the boy nodded in agreement, Rehaak did not draw attention to the fact that Laakea had just successfully completed his first lesson, a lesson called trust.

CHAPTER 10: HISTORY LESSON

After they had cleaned up their breakfast leavings, they started work. Rehaak used a bow saw to cut up dead trees into short lengths. He set Laakea the task of splitting the blocks into segments for firewood. He wanted to see how the boy dealt with hard labor. It was another way of taking the lad's measure.

"There is honor even in the most mundane task done well," was one of his father's axioms. Having a youngster around reminded Rehaak of things he had forgotten from his own youth."

Laakea worked steadily without complaining. He suspected that Rehaak was watching to see how he handled the hard work he had been given. He was determined to prove himself worthy to his host.

Rehaak had saved his life, so he owed him his best effort. He decided to work until he could continue no longer. He swung the axe in high arcs splitting the wood cleanly and with precision. It felt good to be doing something useful. He set a steady rhythm, one that he knew he could maintain. When the pile of split wood grew large enough, he gathered the pieces in his arms, and piled them neatly and carefully in the woodshed attached to the hut.

After several hours, both men had worked up a considerable sweat. Rehaak found it difficult to keep up with the young axe-man. They switched tasks. After several more hours, Rehaak felt completely spent. He could not match Laakea's physical strength or stamina, in spite of all the physical work he was used to doing. He felt the boy had proven himself, more than sufficiently capable in physical labor, and he could see that Laakea took pride in his workmanship. Nothing the boy did spoke of carelessness. Even when he stacked the wood, he did it with precision and care.

It was time to test his wits. He began with questions as they switched tasks again.

"How did your parents come to live here so far from their people?"

"They wouldn't tell me very much, except to say that they came on a ship that your people used for carrying trade goods to Baradon, the Eniila homeland. At some point, they left the ship and came ashore in a small boat by themselves."

"Did they bring anything with them?"

"Yes, they did. They carried their supplies and provisions inland, in several trips."

"That must have been difficult. Tell me, what did they live in?"

"My father built a house, a smithy, and a smelter in the valley where we live — where we lived. I think that might have been before your people came to this part of Kel Braah and built the village at Dun Dale, but I am not sure."

"What was life like for you and your family?"

"When people learned that my father was a blacksmith, they came to him for help, since they had no other smith nearby. His tools and implements always outlasted and outperformed anything that the villagers could get from the city, and at far less cost."

"My parents didn't go to the village often except to trade. Sometimes they took me with them. My mother stayed home with me, when I was younger but once I grew older, they took me along. I helped my parents with their work or did my own chores. In addition to all that, there were endless hours of combat practice."

"Ah, the endless round of daily work. I have noticed the same thing, since I came to live here." He said before he went back to sawing the log he was working on.

Rehaak sawed the rest of the way through the log and watched as the block he had just cut rolled to the side.

"Where does the iron your father worked come from? Did he mine for it?"

"No, he worked what he called bog iron. That's iron that's been deposited by the action of water in a bog. The bog had dried up, but the iron and peat remain. My father built our house near the bog, to be close to the iron. He refined the iron to make it useable for tools and other items."

"I see," said Rehaak.

"You said that you were going to teach me what you know, not ask me what I know," Laakea said, after a pause.

"There is more to learning than an exchange of information and learning is never just information going in one direction. I need to determine what you already know, so I may teach you new things. Repetition would bore you, and waste both your time and mine. I have been a scholar for most of my life. I have studied much and I love knowledge. You grace me by allowing me to learn about you and your family's customs."

Rehaak felt things were going well so far. By starting with commonplace topics, he had patterned the youngster to answer his questions, and build a greater level of trust. He was continuing to build upon the thin layer of trust already established between them. Soon he could move to deeper issues.

"All right then," Laakea nodded.

"You spoke of gods earlier. What do you know of the gods?" Rehaak asked.

"My mother taught me that there are many gods. The god of growing things, — the god of mining and metal craft — the gods of war and death."

"So there are many gods?"

"Yes. That is what I have been taught."

"What do you know of mankind?"

"I know that there are two races, different from each other in size and appearance."

"Please explain what more you know of those differences."

"The Eniila understand metal-craft, weapon-craft, war-craft, and herding better than your people. Your people understand fisher craft, art, writing, and stone craft better. Your people have written language, which we don't. Storytellers or bards pass on all our knowledge verbally. Your people have books to do that. I know that your people landed on the shores of Baradon and built great cities, before my father's people drove them back onto this island. I know that my father played an important part in the battles that drove your people out, but I don't know what that was. Beyond that, I know little.

"What did your parents teach you by way of a trade?"

"My parents taught me their own trades, smithing, weapon craft, fletching, and the craft of the bowyer."

"You have told me how we are different, but how are we the same?"

"We are all men. We speak the same language."

"What if I were to tell you that there is a third race of men?"

"If there is, I've never heard of them."

"And what if I were to tell you there was only one God, not many gods?"

"So, what my mother taught me — is false?" said the boy defensively.

Rehaak sensed that something was setting him on edge concerning his mother. He knew that she had died several years earlier, but did not know why or how that had happened. The boy was plainly quite fond of her and still obviously missed her. He considered how to approach the things the boy must know, without offending him further.

This was going to be more difficult than he had anticipated. The boy hardly knew Rehaak but he was expecting him to take his word for things. It wasn't going to work that way. The boy needed to know that Rehaak could be trusted to tell him the truth. For that to happen, Rehaak needed to show the boy who he was, faults, and all.

For the first time in years, he would have to let someone get closer to him than made him comfortable. That was not something he wanted to do. He hadn't shared very much with Isil, and she was closer to him than anyone had been for decades. It was ironic. If the lad were going to trust him, he would have to trust the lad first. He set the saw to the log once more, starting another cut.

He smiled inwardly, because he had just told Laakea that learning was more than information passing in one direction. He was mildly amused that his words were coming back to haunt him, so quickly. Ironically, Rehaak would have to learn trust, before he could teach it to Laakea.

Laakea turned back to the wood, picked up the axe and began to attack another block from the pile, turning it into kindling, one blow at a time. Rehaak had maligned his mother's teaching. Rehaak's silence seemed to say that he thought Laakea was an ignorant churl. Rehaak's sudden silence provoked him. He knew that anger was beginning to get the better of him again, but he didn't want Rehaak to see how angry he was.

This sudden cessation of speech, from the otherwise talkative man, caused Laakea to remember his father's sullen silences followed by outbursts of anger. He began to suspect that this man was not so much different from his father.

Just when he had given up expecting Rehaak to speak, the man cleared his throat. Laakea turned to look at him. The resentment and mistrust smoldering behind his eyes, faded with Rehaak's next words.

"You have told me about yourself. It is my turn to share. Trust does not come easily to me. I have not shared this with any other person, since it causes me shame. Now I will tell you my own story," he said, and even Laakea could feel his reluctance.

CHAPTER 11: TAKING CHANCES

"I do not remember much before I was your age, so I will begin my story there."

"I came from a family of farmers, who were wealthy land owners at one time. Now they are just farmers, although it is still a very large farm by Abrhaani standards. My father wanted me to take over the management of our land, since I was the eldest son, but I never cared much about running a farm. I was more interested in books and learning.

I was curious about everything. I think I nearly drove everyone crazy wanting to know how things worked, and why things worked as they did. Even then, I wanted to know the history of everything. I think I was a great disappointment to my parents. They were very practical people, and if they could not see a practical purpose for knowledge, they saw no point in gaining it. The knowledge I sought was not going to make the corn grow taller or it's kernels fuller, so it had no value.

"Abrhaani families are typically large; mine was no exception, with five boys and one girl. My younger brothers and my sister appeared content to follow in our parents footsteps. Around the time I left home, my oldest brother was getting a good grasp of how to run our farm.

He was the son who made my father happy. My father always said, I had a wild heart and I would never be happy in one place. I knew he favored my brother because of it. Father knew by then, that at least one of his son's would amount to something, and would be able to look after him when he grew old. My other brothers seemed much the same."

"My sister — I think she was fourteen summers in the year I left — already had suitors lining up at the door to vie for her hand. She and my mother cried when I left. I think my father was just relieved to see me go. At least he would not have to put up with my endless questions, nor would he have to watch me fritter away my life, on what he considered useless and foolish fancies."

"The younger sibs did not seem to care much, one way or the other. I think they were too young to comprehend that I was leaving forever. The oldest wished me well. We had always been close. Although he did not share my curiosity, he always took an interest in what I had discovered. I believe he looked up to me and respected me. He is the one I miss the most. He gave me my staff as a going away present."

"To defend yourself, wherever your wild heart leads you," he said, as he handed it to me and said goodbye.

"I have not seen any of them since that day and to an Abrhaani that is a shameful admission. Family ties are supposed to be strong and eternal, even extending into the afterlife. I have broken those bonds and brought shame on my house and myself by forsaking my family, but that is not the worst of my story. However, I believe that is enough information about my family. Now I must tell you what set me on the road that I am on today."

"We lived in a house much larger than this hut. It had two floors with several rooms on each floor. The upper floor contained a large storage loft, which had a door, with a stairway leading up into it. The doorway to that loft was in my bedroom. My first and clearest childhood memory is a dream."

"In my dream, I suddenly awaken from sleep, to find that there is a light shining under the door to the storage loft. I know that there should be no one up there at that time of night. I thought that someone must have forgotten to put out the lamps. I was afraid that the lamps might start the house afire. I also know that my father would be displeased at the waste of lamp oil. I went to the doorway, intending to climb the stairs and put out the light."

"Once I have the door opened and have begun to ascend the stair, I look up. Standing at the top of the stair, is a being so dark and malevolent that I cannot describe it. In truth, I cannot even see it clearly, because of the darkness of its nature. It is pure evil, so black that it seems to absorb light itself."

"Once I have seen this Being, it holds my gaze, like chains bind a man to a dungeon wall. I cannot look away. I cannot run to escape. I know that this Being has come to devour my soul and destroy me. My mouth opens to scream, but no sound comes forth. I try to turn and run away but my body will not obey me. I stand rooted in place like a tree. This evil thing approaches me intent on my destruction, and I am powerless to escape. I know that if it lays a hand on me I am lost, lost forever. This dark being has trapped me, inside my unresponsive body."

"With that thought, I realize that although my body will not respond to my wishes, I am still free to think and reason. This only intensifies the terror, because I am aware of both the danger, and my powerlessness to prevent my own destruction. In my spirit, I begin to groan in desperation 'God save me.' Notice, I did not say, 'gods save me.' When that cry issued from my spirit, the creature of utter blackness and pure evil, dissolved like mist in the sunlight and I awoke sweating, shaking, and crying out in fear."

"I had that dream many times, over the next few years, and each time I cried out for God to save me, the dark being would vanish, and I would awaken. It became easier over the years to know what to do when the dream took hold. I wish I could tell you, that knowledge caused the fear grew less, but the terror of the encounters never lessened, in spite of knowing that I needed only to cry out to the One God to save me. I feared that the One might not arrive in time, or that I might not be able to summon the ability to call on Him quickly enough."

"My family, like your parents, believed in many gods, but I began to question them about the One God, who had no name, but had enough power to rescue me instantly from such a dire and potent evil. No one knew anything about him. Years went by, but I never stopped searching."

"So your life is based on a dream, a childhood nightmare? I mean no offense Rehaak, but that sounds rather foolish," the boy said.

"Perhaps it does sound foolish, but hear the end of the tale before judging it."

"I began to search farther and farther from my home. I went to the towns that had libraries near my home first. I began to find references to one god, The Creator, only in the most ancient texts available to me. All newer records contained no hint of Him at all.

There were also references to a book, The Chronicles of Aarda, or The Aetheriad, and a god, called The Faithful One, or The Creator. This book is the oldest of our records, dating back to the creation of the world.

I also found references to beings called the Aethera and the Nethera. The stories mentioned them as beings of great power, which either helped or destroyed humankind. As I studied, I learned that men had sometimes allied themselves with the Aethera for good purposes, so it seemed to me that the Aethera were good. Sometimes the people attempted to placate the beings called the Nethera by offerings, in order to avoid destruction."

"Ah, this is why you asked me about the gods!" Laakea exclaimed. "So you think that these Aethera and Nethera, they're the gods we worship now?"

"I see learning has begun," Rehaak smiled, "since you begin to question. The beginning of all learning lies in the questions we ask. Just remember that the shape of the question sometimes predetermines the answer."

Laakea looked puzzled, but he said nothing.

"If you do not ask the proper question, or enough questions, you will only learn part of what you must know. The fullness of the answer will escape you. For example, to answer your question we need to ask a further question. It is this: What constitutes divinity?"

"That's easy!" Laakea answered confidently.

"Then answer the question wise youth." Rehaak smiled, sagely.

"Power. Only a god has enough power to make anything that they desire happen, and happen exactly the way they desire."

"You have correctly discerned that power is composed of two parts. The first part is, power, physical force, or strength. The second is control, and influence; the ability to use strength to control and influence the outcome of events and processes.

Think carefully for a moment. No doubt power and control are godlike attributes but does having great power and influence truly make one a god?

Laakea looked like deep in thought for a while before Rehaak answered.

"I cannot even begin to imagine a powerless god, but having power, and control does not mean that you are a god. If that were true, then all kings of the earth could be gods, because of the power and control they exert over their kingdoms. They have power, but only within their sphere of influence. Your father would have been a god, because he controlled your life in the beginning. Was he a god?"

"No, he's a man — I used to think — never mind. His power was limited. Now that I think about it, even the power of kings has limits. So a god must have unlimited power. That's the answer."

"I think that is only part of the answer. One might also be tempted to say that those who can see the future might be gods, or those that are creative are gods. Though all these qualities are godlike and godly, they too are possessed in limited quantities by created beings. Many people you will meet have some of such qualities, and they are not divine. People live and they are powerless in some situations. They see the future and can do nothing to alter it. They die and their power fades with them into the dust, so they are not gods. The perishable nature of all created beings is a clue to the nature of the Divine."

"Are you saying that longevity is the key?"

"In a way. Listen carefully. I believe that divinity consists of the attributes we have talked about so far. A true god has all these qualities without limit and without end —longevity — as you call it, is the one thing that is the true essence of divinity."

"The one thing?" asked Laakea.

"To be truly divine one must be uncreated and immortal."

"What's that mean? How can destroying something or someone make it a god?"

"I did not say destroyed, I said uncreated, meaning without precedent. A true God is someone who has always existed, someone who had no creator, no father, or progenitor. A true god is one who is eternal, everlasting, without a beginning and without an end, or in your words, has longevity. Someone who just is, who always was, and always will be. God has no starting point or maker, and no ending point or destroyer. He is eternal, all powerful; creative, and yet uncreated."

"That's a lot to think about."

"Yes I know, and I have spent years of study coming to this conclusion. It would be wrong for me to expect anyone else to get there faster."

"If you're right," said the boy. "Then no created being has the right to be called god."

"Exactly."

"So. The Aethera and the Nethera — are they created beings or are they gods?"

"The fact that there are many of these beings indicates that they are created. It is unlikely that there are many uncreated beings. To my way of thinking, there can be only one uncaused cause, one Creator of creation. It makes sense to me, if to no one else. If there were many gods, creation would be torn apart by their competing wills and motives."

"So, if they're created beings, they're not gods!"

"That is my assumption."

"If they have a beginning — they must also have an ending. Can they be destroyed then?"

"Since they have a beginning point, it is logical to assume that they can also have an ending point. I believe that you may have discerned correctly. Although,

I have never given it much consideration, you have raised a good question, one that begs for more research."

Rehaak continued, "Mankind has been helped by the Aethera, but has suffered much from the Nethera. If man could destroy the Nethera, then it might be possible that mankind can be free of their attacks. If humankind, as weak as we are by comparison to the Nethera, can destroy them, one might ask, why the Aethera have not destroyed them. One might also ask why The Creator has not done so. Why did He create them, since they seem to be at war with the rest of his creation? Why does he allow them to continue their destructive actions?"

"You ask so many questions, Rehaak. Don't you risk going mad?"

"You may be right in this. I may be already mad and there are some that would agree that I am, but I must continue to ask, and I fear now you must seek answers as well."

"Neither the Aethera nor the Nethera seem to have been very active in recent records, but your questions have caused me to ask why that is true. Are they gone from Aarda or only from our knowledge? Are they no longer working in the affairs of men, or are they merely hiding their involvement? He paused for a second.

"A third possibility exists, which has just occurred to me. We may simply have grown too dull to perceive their activity. We have lost much knowledge through the wars we have fought. We have even lost an entire race of men, the Sokai. It is entirely possible that we have lost the ability to perceive spiritual activity. You have asked questions, for which I have no answers yet. Your questions have given me more questions of my own. Learning and perhaps madness has begun now for both of us."

"Where can we find answers to these questions Rehaak?"

"In the Scriptorium, in Narragansett, I have found some clues, but I am now forbidden to enter the city on pain of death," he said sadly. "Hopefully there are other ways, as yet unknown to us, which may be revealed by The Creator."

He reflected for a moment before he brightened. "Since you have said that *we* need to find the answers, am I to assume that you are making yourself a participant in this quest?"

"I suppose I am," said the boy. "My father always told me that a man needs to have a purpose in life, if he is to amount to anything. He must dedicate his life to accomplish something larger than his own desires. I believe it may be my purpose to help you. I can't read so I can't help you with your research, but I can work hard and my father trained me as a fighting man. Those skills may be of use to you. Why else has fate brought us together?"

"Not fate young sir, I begin to see the sense of what my friend Isil has been saying to me. I see the hand of The Creator at work, but his purposes remain a mystery."

"So, what do we do next Rehaak?"

"We continue as we are I suppose, until more is revealed. Isil is much better at this than I am. I wish she were here now, but it will be many weeks until she returns."

"You wouldn't happen to have a bow to hunt with would you?" said Laakea, changing the subject.

"No. Why do you ask?"

"I'd feel more comfortable if I could contribute more to my upkeep. If you had one, I could hunt to supply us with meat. If I had the wood I could even make one."

"Wood we have aplenty young sir, but what kind do you need?"

"Odom wood's ideal, but the wood need only be sound, free of knots, and resilient, and I'd need strong fibers for a bow string, steel for the arrowheads, and feathers for fletching."

"I think we can find most of what you need here or nearby, with the exception of the steel," Rehaak interrupted.

"I'll start right away then," the boy said, excitedly. "A flat bow would probably be the fastest, if the wood has been properly seasoned.

Rehaak listened as the youngster planned aloud. It was good to see him brighten by taking an interest in something that he cared about, so passionately. Rehaak found that he genuinely liked the industrious lad. He was so eager to please. Unless things changed drastically, he was almost certain that they would get along well enough to share the hut. It was good to have someone to talk with and someone to share ideas and insights. Rehaak felt strangely lighter since confessing some of his shameful past to the boy. Trust apparently had its own unique rewards.

They spent the rest of the day finding suitable supplies for the bow and the arrow shafts. Laakea was busy with his project and seemed far happier than he had been. He had still not shared what had caused him to leave his home, but Rehaak had given had a place to belong and plans that excited him. He had also given him new ideas and concepts to roll about in his mind. Rehaak hoped that made Laakea's problems, seem remote and unimportant for now.

CHAPTER 12: FINDING A WAY

The days passed quickly, as the bow took shape under the blade and the sanding stone the boy used to tiller it. For the arrows, they split wood from a knot free, straight grained block and sanded them smooth and round. They found stout raven feathers for the vanes. Laakea carved bone to form the nocks and mounted them to the shafts with hide glue. The fibers they used to fasten vanes to the shafts came from a trip back to the grassy plain. They gathered enough dry grass to make not only a bowstring, but also a good quantity of rope and other cordage. By the time the boy had his bow ready, Rehaak had fashioned a hammock, made from more of the grass fibers, for the youngster to sleep in.

Over the course of several tendays, a deeper level of trust grew between the two men. They often laughed and bantered together as they worked. As the work on the bow had progressed, Rehaak noticed the boy growing quieter. Laakea had practiced archery with sharpened bone arrowheads on the arrows. Rehaak had to admit the lad was amazingly quick and accurate with the weapon. Even with only bone tips, the bow was a formidable weapon in his skilled hands. They would need to trade for the steel arrowheads in Dun Dale, since there were none available in New Hope. It was a long way to go, but Laakea was adamant that he needed arrowheads made of steel.

Rehaak held off leaving as long as he could, because he sensed that Laakea found the idea of going to Dun Dale difficult. Finally, he could postpone the trip no longer. They needed more than arrowheads now. With the two of them living in the hut together, supplies were running low. Rehaak brought up the subject as gently as he could, giving Laakea several days of notice. On the morning he had planned to set off, he rose early and prepared for the trip.

"We have more work to do before we leave for the village today. I will need to gather my medicines and bundle up some herbs to trade. If you would finish stacking the rest of the wood, we will be on our way after lunch," he told Laakea.

Laakea nodded in agreement and headed for the woodpile without saying anything, but he looked more morose than ever. He had barely spoken in the last two days.

"Is there something wrong young man?" Rehaak asked.

Laakea stopped and turned to face Rehaak. The struggle he was having inside was plainly visible on his face and in his posture. He did not answer immediately. Rehaak could see he wanted to speak but was afraid of something.

"You don't have to tell me anything if you don't want to," Rehaak said gently.

"No, I want to tell — I just — I don't — I don't want you to drive me away."

"You think you have done something horrible, is that it?"

"Yes."

"And you think that if I know your shameful secret, whatever that is, that you will not be welcome here anymore?"

"Yes."

"Have you ever wondered why I live here alone?"

"No, but what's that have to do —?"

"Because my boy, everyone has a past. Everyone's past contains shameful secrets; things that they would rather keep hidden. My past is why I am here alone, and your reason for being here alone is probably similar. If I reject you, I will have to reject myself as well, or be a hypocrite. I am not prepared to add that sin to the already significant tally against me." Rehaak sat down determinedly on a block of wood and waited looking up at the boy.

Laakea pulled up a block of his own and sat down in front of Rehaak looking very serious. "We have to go to the village for arrowheads, I know that." he said, and stopped, as if that was enough explanation.

"Forgive my thick skull but I don't see how that is a traumatic experience. You've been to the vill before, haven't you?"

"Yes, but that was before —"

Laakea struggled to keep his emotions in check. If there were no arrowheads for trade in Dun Dale, it would force him to go trade with his father for them. How could he tell Rehaak that his father would most likely kill him on sight, in order to satisfy his *Blood Debt* against him? Amazingly, it wasn't that he feared death; it was that he feared the shame of facing his father more.

Rehaak watched and waited patiently for the boy to continue, remembering his own history. Seeing Laakea struggling with his past was like looking in a mirror. He carried his own load of shame, so he could easily identify with the boy.

Laakea drew a deep breath and began again, "I've cursed and dishonored my father, he blurted." That's a very serious offense to my people. It's an offense worthy of death, so it's called a *Blood Debt* by the Eniila. My father could collect payment at any time and no one would have any right to interfere."

"Forgive my interruption but, by collecting payment, you mean to say your father would kill you?"

"Yes."

"That sounds barbaric!"

"It's one of the customs of my father's people. They put a very high value on honor. If a man sullies another man's honor, the injured party has the right to exact vengeance for the slight. Wrongdoers face trial by combat; because we believe that the god's judge the case through combat." He paused for a moment before adding, "We have phrases like, 'vindication in victory.' I have done far more than impugn my father's honor. I have cursed him to his face. To fulfill the requirements of justice, we must now do battle, to the death."

"Now I know why the Eniila are constantly fighting with each other," Rehaak said in surprise. "So, you don't want to go because your father might see you and kill you? You told me he hardly ever goes to the village, so the chances that he will see you are remote."

"Not exactly."

"Well what — exactly is the problem then?"

"If there are no arrowheads available in the village, and most likely there aren't, because the Abrhaani don't use bows or other edged weapons, we'll have to go to the forge to get them from him directly — or wait around until he comes in to trade."

"Ah, but I could go alone if that is the problem. He would not have to know you were even alive. It has been many tendays since your arrival here. He may think you have perished."

"I want to go along, to make sure you get what I want — but if the village folk see me and tell my father I am with you; it could be as dangerous for you as it would be for me, even if he is not there."

"Draw a picture instead, that way I can still get what you want without you risking your life."

"You don't know the way to my father's forge Rehaak, and to my knowledge, none of the villagers do either. My father is very," he struggled to find the diplomatic word, "secretive."

"Well then, I will go alone anyway, and if there are no arrowheads available, and your father is not present, I will return with my own supplies. No one will be any the wiser about your location. While I am there, I can make some inquiries about your father. I can ask when he is expected, so that I can return to town later and fetch what you need."

"Alright then, I suppose I can wait that long."

Rehaak gathered the supplies he needed to take with him on the walk to Dun Dale and back. He left immediately after the midday meal.

The walk was uneventful, until he reached Beren's Ford.

Everything looked peaceful enough, perhaps too peaceful. He noticed the lack of birdsong first, just before he felt the wrenching wrongness of evil again. The feeling intensified, as he grew closer to the mill, just upstream from the ford.

He had decided not to make a call on the miller. The mill was on the way to New Hope. He would have to pass by it and use the ford to reach the road to Dun

Dale. It was a good place to stop for a rest. The miller and his wife had four young children. What with childhood illnesses, and accidents, they had called on him frequently, for his healing expertise. They were more nearly Rehaak's friends than most of the people who lived in town. Today he was in a hurry, so he did not plan to stop, but as he was about to pass the mill he noticed that there was no one in sight.

The mill wheel was turning as water ran under it in the millrace channel. Usually the children played outside if their parents were at work in the mill. When the force of the water was driving the gears and pulleys, it was far too dangerous inside the mill for rambunctious youngsters. It was much too early for supper, so the children should be about somewhere. He could usually hear them long before he saw them. They were a boisterous brood.

Every step he took closer to the ford intensified his sense of dread. He called out hoping for a response. As he did, the miller's wife burst out of the door of the millhouse. She had three of her four children in tow.

"Go's save us!" she shrieked. "Come and elp, my Gillam's bin 'tackd by summat." She raced across the grass toward him, reminding him of a mother hen, flapping and clucking in alarm. The children followed close behind, like little chicks. "Ee's in t'house. Come quick."

Rehaak ran as quickly as he could to the door of the stone millhouse that served as both a place of business and a dwelling. He never knew how they could sleep with the millwheel constantly making noise, both day and night.

Ee's on t'bed sir," she struggled to catch her breath. "Is t'ere ought y'can do fer 'im?"

Rehaak walked to the bed where her oldest son Gillam lay. It took a few moments for his eyes to adjust to the gloom inside the building. The boy lay still on his small cot. If Rehaak had not known it was Gillam, he would not have recognized the form on the bed at all.

He would not even have recognized it as human. The only thing he knew beyond any doubt was that this was far beyond his ability to heal. He tried to run his hands over the boy's skin to check for injuries. The skin was dry as parchment and grey as ashes. The skin and the flesh beneath flaked away like ash, under his touch.

Something terrible had happened here, something beyond his ability to understand, let alone repair. The child was already dead. The sense of wrongness and evil he had felt earlier was so intense that his stomach began to heave. He ran outside and vomited on the grass.

After he had cleaned himself up, he turned to the woman sobbing softly as she stood in the doorway. She stared at the figure in the bed with a look of absolute desolation in her eyes. Her three remaining children clustered around her, hugging her legs. They sought protection and comfort, like chicks huddling under a hen's wings, until danger passed. A moment of terror had altered their world. Suddenly their safe and friendly little home had become a frightening and dangerous place.

"It was too late madam," he said compassionately. "Even if I had come earlier, I doubt if I could have done anything to help him. This is something unknown to me or to my arts."

At that answer, she began to wail despondently, and soon the younger children joined her in a chorus of grief. Rehaak fished through his pack for Elam root, which had sedative properties. He found it and shooed the four of them into the millhouse again, where he started making the infusion. He planned to dose them all with it, before he tried to find out what had happened. While it was boiling, he wrapped the boy's body in the

143

bedclothes and carried it outside. This prompted another chorus of grief from the family.

The lightness of his burden surprised him. He had played with the boy about a tenday ago, on his last trip to New Hope. Gillam had been a sturdy lad, but now even his bones had no mass to them. They felt light and hollow as a bird's bones. He had no substance left to him at all.

His trip to Dun Dale would have to wait until he could find out what had happened to this child. Once he had them calmed down, he hoped he could find out the cause of the boy's death.

He dug a shallow grave for the bundle he carried in his arms. There was no need to go deeper. No predator would want to disturb Gillam's body. There was nothing of value left in it. It was a burned out husk, like a cinder from his fireplace. It was already starting to crumble into dust when he set Gillam reverently in the hole he had made. He gently covered him with fresh cut sod.

What would he tell the Miller when he returned from the village? How could he explain this catastrophic loss?

CHAPTER 13: EVIL INCARNATE

When Rehaak returned to the house, Riata, the miller's wife, was already busy preparing the evening meal as if nothing was wrong. Rehaak knew it was her way of coping with her grief. It was routine. It made the house and the world seem normal again, but it was an illusion. Nothing would ever be normal again, for this family, or for Rehaak after seeing what had happened to the boisterous, exuberant Gillam.

By evening, the miller returned from town, where he had gone to trade. His world flipped upside down, when his grieving wife greeted him at the door with the awful news that one of his children had gone onto the next life. There was another short bout of hysteria before Rehaak managed to get them calm enough to share their stories. Rehaak hoped that Laakea would be all right and not worry because of this delay. He felt a strong need to hear what had happened to Gillam before he returned, or continued his journey. They had planned for the round trip to take six days in all. This was going to add another day.

On the other hand, he could always take the short walk home tonight to tell the boy. He finally decided that it would be better if Laakea knew about the incident and the need to change their plan.

He listened as the family told their stories. He pieced the various narratives together, as they rambled through the story and struggled with their grief at the same time. What he heard was more unsettling than he would allow the miller's family to know. His vision and his nightmares were coming to life horribly, here in this quiet backwater.

The children had been playing together along the stream bank when they had noticed an unusual dark shape in the water of the ford. At first, they had thought it was some debris, which had washed downstream and snagged on something in the streambed. As they approached it from the bank, it moved. It rose up from the stream and advanced toward them. They described the smell of death and decay that emanated from the creature. It caused suffocating fear that paralyzed them. They knew it meant to harm them, but they were powerless to do anything to stop it or avoid it.

They were unable to flee, although they all knew its touch meant death. When it got close enough, it reached out with one of its black claw-like appendages trying to touch them. Finally, young Gillam managed to overcome his fear. Pushing the younger ones ahead of him, he drove them back toward the hut, as they fled for their lives. His action released the hold of terror on their tongues, as well as their limbs, and all four ran screaming in terror toward their home.

They had not been fast enough to make it to safety. Gillam had shielded his younger siblings with his body by running behind them, keeping his body between the appalling evil and the younger children. When the little ones were almost to the door of the hut, the sinister, entity reached out with its dark, misshapen claws and grasped him by the neck as he ran. It picked him up off the ground as if he were fluff in the wind. The little ones had not stopped to look back to see what was happening, but the Miller's wife had heard their shrieks of terror, as they fled toward home. She had come to the door in time to gather the little ones in her arms, just as the thing had grabbed Gillam. At that point, she froze in terror just as her children had.

She described what she saw with detached calm, as if it were some story she had heard from a neighbor. She said that she had watched helplessly as the "beastie" sucked the life out of her son. It fastened what looked like its mouth over her son's, in a twisted parody of a kiss. Gillam had seemed to shrink and grow ashen, as the creature clutched him in its repulsive embrace.

She watched helplessly as he writhed and twisted in agony. The thing enfolded the form of her oldest child and continued to feed on him, until he stopped moving. Fear and disbelief had paralyzed her, like her children, until she eventually managed to scream out "God save us." The creature had looked up at her for a moment. It made a sound somewhat between a shriek and a hiss, as if frustrated from its intentions.

Darkness roiled about the figure like mist, making its form indistinct, and difficult to see. Unmitigated hatred shone from its glowing, crimson eyes. It had even made so bold as to move toward her for a moment, threatening her as its next victim. Then, as if it changed its mind, it turned and began to move away from her before it disappeared, like mist in the morning sun.

When it had left, she had gathered the desiccated remains of her child in her arms and carried him into the hut. She tucked him into bed fearing the worst, but hoping that he could make a recovery. Only a moment later, she heard Rehaak call out from the road.

By the time Rehaak saw the boy, there was little else he could do except bury his scant remains. Rehaak collected his thoughts for a moment while the family members strove to master their emotions.

"Wat think y'on't," the miller, Gael asked, in bewilderment, as his wife sat silently beside him. She appeared drained and drawn, as the sorrow of her loss finally penetrated her heart.

Rehaak chose his words carefully. "I have not encountered this type of being before sir, except in my nightmares," he said solemnly.

"Wat mean y'by at?" asked the miller still bewildered. "Wat manner o' creechur be it?"

"What I mean Gael — I am not sure, except that I have only met creatures like this in my own childhood nightmares," he said, remembering his own young heart pounding in fear, in the middle of the night. The memory alone was enough to make him shiver and sweat, as he sat with the miller and the remaining members of his family.

"I never expected to see or even hear of such things walking in the waking world."

"Kin we do summat to stop it cumin back 'en?"

"I wish I knew."

"Be ere sum'ere we kin go to get away 'en?"

"I fear there is a time of great trial coming upon mankind. If what I suspect is true, we will be lucky if any of us survive." Rehaak could not withhold his tale any longer.

He told his whole story, leaving nothing out. These people needed to know what type of forces were against them. He cast caution aside as he started his story. In a passionate torrent of words, he told them of his own horror-filled childhood dreams. He told them of his search for knowledge, and the vision The Creator had given him, about the battle to come. He told them about the Faithful One's command, that people turn to him for protection from the desolation that was about to overtake them all.

"Likely it was your cry to the one God that drove the 'beastie,' as you named it, off madam, as it did for me in my dreams. It may also be that having feasted on the life of your son it was sated and saw no reason to harm anyone else. I have no sure way of knowing what the true explanation is. What I do know is that these things are pure evil. That should be obvious enough from the evidence we have now. I believe they may be the Nethera. Have you heard of them in the legends?"

The terror evident in their eyes told him all he needed to know. Whatever else they knew he did not ask, they knew the legends and they were terrified enough already.

Trembling with fear, they swore they would do whatever The Creator asked from henceforth. Unfortunately, when they asked him what the Faithful One wanted of them, he had no answer. He told them to talk to Isil when she was passing through next. He trusted her experience when it came to these matters, more than he did his own. He told them to worship no other gods, to call out to The Creator if they had need, and to listen in case he demanded anything of them in return.

He had his first true converts.

Finally, he was having some success at carrying out his divine commission, but the success felt hollow, built as it was, on the foundation of their personal tragedy and loss.

He needed to get back to his hut to inform Laakea of the change in schedule, though the miller and his wife implored him to stay the night. They were not willing that he leave the safety of their house to venture out in the darkness, with unknown creatures of evil intent prowling about. He knew mere walls of stone could never keep such a creature at bay, if it intended to harm them. It was a tempting offer nevertheless. The prospect of a long walk back to the hut, in the growing twilight, with living nightmares lurking in the deepening shadows, gave him chills, just contemplating it.

If the Nethera were attacking, here in this backwater, who knew where they would strike next. He explained that he had a houseguest that he was worried about, and parted company with the Millers. He was truly worried about Laakea being alone. He liked the boy. The idea of Laakea sharing Gillam's fate sent chills down the back of his neck. He wanted to protect him, if possible.

He didn't know how he would face one of these creatures, or what he could do to combat them if one attacked him. He hoped that invoking the name of the Creator would be defense enough against them, but was not certain of anything at this point. The only thing he did know was that he would lay down his own life to protect the youngster, just as Gillam had sacrificed himself for his younger siblings. It seemed strange that he should feel this way about, a descendant of one of his people's ancient enemies, a person he barely knew. It defied all logic, and until now, he had believed that he lived and breathed logic.

His thoughts ran in circles as he walked quickly along the trail, with fear growing like an evil weed in his heart. Was this the beginning of what the Faithful One had shown him in his vision? What could he do against such powerful and malevolent forces? He was only one man. It was not fair that The Creator should ask this of him. The task before him felt more overwhelming now than ever, and he still had no clear direction or instruction on how to accomplish any of it. Now, he must journey home in the dark while his fears threatened to suffocate him. He was terrified for the first time in recent memory.

As he began his journey into the darkening forest, every shadow menaced him. Every tree and shrub concealed a hideous peril. For the first time in his adult life, Rehaak was afraid of the dark. Apprehension reduced him to a small boy again, cringing from the night sounds, ready to run from the shadows. He was a man now, not a little child, and this was worse than his boyhood nightmares, because he knew the menace was real. There was no chance to wake up and realize it was just a dream.

There was nowhere he could run, nowhere that he could be safe, ever again. Evil might not strike tonight, but he knew it would and could strike, and not just at night, but also in broad daylight. He had laid the evidence of that horrific reality to rest, under a large tree by the mill. He had marked the grave with a circle of stones.

As he picked his way cautiously down the trail, he was as nervous as a mouse in a room full of snakes. His neck and shoulders knotted with tension before he got twenty paces into the forest. He flinched in fear, when unexpected noises came from the undergrowth on either side of the trail. It was going to be a long walk home tonight, alone, in the dark.

K. R. Schultz

CHAPTER 14: HOME ALONE

Laakea spent the afternoon fighting off attacks from a ravening pack of what ifs. What if his father was not at the market? What if he *was* at the market? What if something happened to Rehaak on his journey? What if he left the hut and went after him?

His friend was not due back for six more days. Thoughts bubbled and rolled around in his head until he was certain that his brain would boil and explode within his skull long before Rehaak returned.

Finally, he decided to see if he could find some steel somewhere around the clearing. Perhaps the previous owners had left some bits and pieces behind. If he could find small scraps of metal, he could cold-forge arrowheads from them. He didn't need much and he knew Rehaak wouldn't have looked for metals at all. Laakea knew that his friend was only interested in the plants and growing things. Rehaak might have missed something that would be useful. Laakea's father had told him many times, that his people had a natural affinity for metals, especially iron. They could find iron where others failed, and once found they could shape it to their needs. Perhaps iron would call him to itself today.

"Iron's in our blood, son," he had always said. "Learn to find it and work it and it'll never let you down. Wood'll rot, stone'll shatter, and people will stab you in

152

the back. Iron will cleave wood and break stone. With iron's help, you can defeat those who oppose you. Iron may rust but if you know its secrets, and treat it with respect, it'll never fail you. Be true to iron and it'll never be false to you. Iron's stubborn like the Eniila, but the flame and the forge, the hammer and the anvil, are your friends to help you bend iron to your will and your imagination."

He began his search near the hut, and then widened his search to include the outbuildings. It helped distract him from the worries that had been plaguing him. He finally gave up, after hours of fruitless searching. There was no metal of any kind lying about the clearing. He might as well give up his fruitless search and begin preparing his evening meal.

He rummaged around in the hut until he found the ingredients he wanted. As he prepared a cooking fire, he discovered a loose stone that covered a niche at the side of the fireplace. It was obviously a hiding place built by the hut's original owners. Inside the alcove, he discovered a bundle wrapped in oilskins. Curious, about what was inside, he unwrapped the bundle. He was surprised to find three blades of excellent quality. He had a queer feeling of dread, when handling them, but brushed the feelings aside. These could serve his needs very well.

Rehaak had told him about the men who attacked him and about how the wolves had protected him. He had neglected to mention that he had kept the men's weapons. Rehaak must have forgotten about them. Perhaps he had no idea that Laakea could make his own arrowheads from these extraordinary weapons. He supposed it was his own fault for not telling the older man that he could cold-forge arrowheads himself. He had only told Rehaak to buy some arrowheads.

153

Laakea inspected his discovery with the practiced eye of a journeyman blacksmith. They were good blades, of excellent, although strangely colored, polished metal, hard enough to hold a good edge, and yet flexible enough not to shatter when struck. They had a guard welded to the tang and leather wrapped wooden handle.

They measured about two spans in length. For an average Abrhaani, they would qualify as a short sword, but to him they were merely exceptionally long daggers. The blades were sharp on both sides, nothing unusual in that. What was unusual was the color of the metal. Laakea had never seen metal this color before.

The weapons were virtually identical. What made them uncanny was that they carried an inscription or runes of some sort on the blades. The smith had somehow worked the pattern right into the molten metal. Whoever created these blades, was a master of smith craft. This was beyond Laakea's skill or even the skill of his father.

What would common brigands be doing with even a single weapon of this quality? Even more puzzling, why would all three have identical blades? Common robbers would most likely have a mixture of weaponry of differing quality, rather than three identical high quality blades like these. Robbers were opportunists who would collect their weapons wherever and however they could. They would certainly take weapons from people they robbed, upgrading as opportunities arose. This was something else that Rehaak would not have stopped to consider.

Another issue puzzling Laakea was their level of uniformity. He knew how difficult it was to produce identical items from steel. It was a costly endeavor because of the time taken to make each item identical. Items forged approximately the same were common enough but every hammer stroke, every cut of the file brought a certain amount of randomness into the process. It was not that hard to bring things to approximate similarity, but for this level of exactitude, a smith would have to be phenomenally fastidious in his work and measurements. All the time and effort added cost to the implement that he fashioned. These weapons should have cost incredible amounts.

These thoughts unsettled him. What was this all about? Common brigands would not be able to afford such weapons and anyone who owned such blades would be more than able to hire protection from thieves.

He would have to question Rehaak more closely when he returned from the village. He turned the blade he was holding, trying to make out the inscription in the gray-green metal. The unknown smith had subtly worked the design into the metal during the forging of the blade with remarkable skill and patience; pattern welding his father called it. Laakea did not have the skill with letters that Rehaak had, so it was unlikely he would be able to read the symbols, even if they didn't seem to swim about within the metal as they did. He wondered if Rehaak had examined the blades closely. He probably just tucked them away and forgot about them.

In his hand, he held an enigma that might divulge clues as important to the quest, as the book that Rehaak sought. He may not be able to read books, but the story written in the metal was one he could comprehend. The implications of what he read in these blades troubled him immensely.

He suddenly realized that the light was beginning to fade, and he had not started supper as he had planned. He set about preparing a rabbit with what little skill he had in the culinary arts. While his hands were busy, his mind kept turning over the questions that the blades posed for him. He wondered if Rehaak would mind giving him the blades to work with.

He could easily make enough points for his entire supply of arrows from the steel of the guard and the tang of one handle. The steel looked soft enough to cold forge. He could reshape the blades into something else, if he had access to his father's forge and time to work it. He had learned a great deal from his father about forging weapons.

A powerful inner force drew Laakea to want to create weapons, although they had only made agricultural and logging tools. The principals of working iron were the same, no matter what purpose the tools served. Weapons were just a different sort of tool, his father had reminded him, whenever he wanted to cut corners with any mundane work.

"Think of the plowshare as a sword to carve the earth, son. If the plow fails, so does the planting. Lives hang in the balance just as they do on the battlefield or the arena of justice," his father's voice echoed in his head. "Use the same care for every item no matter who it's intended for, or how plain its purpose."

His father had been as assiduous in training him in the manufacture of weapons, as in their use. He had told Laakea daily that his skill with the hammer and the blade would someday save his life. According to Eniila customs, anyone might need to defend his honor or his veracity in a trial by combat at any time. The Eniila way was to let the gods judge the rightness of the cause by granting victory or defeat. His father often said cynically, that the gods appeared to favor the more skilled and better armed. Only rarely had he seen an inferior warrior win in combat. He drilled his son as though his life depended on it, because that is exactly what it would come down to in a challenge with another Eniila.

Laakea failed to see the point back then, since they were the only Eniila for thousands of leagues and the Abrhaani who lived around them were peaceful farmers. His father insisted that he persevere, saying, "You never know what lies ahead on the road of your life son, or who, or what you will meet on the twists and turns of it. Prepare for every possibility, and let the gods take care of the rest. That's the way to live. Anything else is just the way to die."

He looked out the window ending his reverie. The light was almost completely gone. For no apparent reason he began to feel uneasy about Rehaak, as he sat down to eat his meal before it got cold. Worry began to gnaw at him as he gnawed the bones of the rabbit he had charred for his supper.

He finished eating. There was still no relief from his apprehension, so he decided to take a walk outside just a short way down the trail to the village. He stuck two of the knives he had found in his belt as a precaution.

It was a warm clear night with the gibbous moon hanging overhead, illuminating everything. The warm weather, now that summer was almost here, made it a beautiful night for a walk. Shadowy leaves etched in silver moonlight glistened and fluttered in the night breeze.

He had little trouble seeing where he was going once his eyes became accustomed to the moonlight. The night blooming flowers filled the air around him with scent and the night creatures made their familiar sounds as he walked along. He had walked the full distance to the main trail to the village. As he made his way along the path, he began to feel foolish about his earlier anxiety. Suddenly, the night creatures became silent all at once.

The hair on his arms and neck stood on end, as if chilled by a frigid breeze. He stopped to listen, but could not hear any sound at all. He had never understood the saying, "The silence was deafening," until that moment. It was so quiet he felt like he had suddenly lost the ability to hear. He withdrew the blades from his belt and began to move cautiously from shadow to shadow along the wagon trail, scarcely daring to breathe for fear of missing a sound. His time spent stalking and hunting game with his father, had prepared him to move as silently as one of the shadows, among the trees. Suddenly, in the distance, he heard sounds, scuffling, and grunting, faint cries of pain and effort. He ran silently along the track not knowing what he would find ahead of him and hoping he would not be too late.

He rounded one last corner and saw a man fighting off several attackers. It was Rehaak. Laakea was almost within striking distance when Rehaak felled one of the men with his staff. Before his friend could recover from delivering the blow, one of the men struck Rehaak on the side of his head. Laakea saw Rehaak collapse on top of his fallen opponent. Laakea felt anger rise up in him at the injustice of what was happening. This was wrong, all wrong; they would pay, and pay dearly for their affront to all that was right. He bellowed a battle cry and cast himself into the melee like a cyclone of retribution. The first to fall was the man who had just struck Rehaak down and who was preparing to deliver the killing stroke with his knife.

Rage erupted within him; white-hot fury suffused his limbs with pure power. Electricity crackled along his nerves, and strength sizzled through his sinews. Around him, everything began to slow. Time flowed at a slower rate than his mind could process. He found it was incredibly easy to perform this slow motion dance of death. He could see the blows coming, anticipate their delivery, and formulate a response long before their blades actually approached him. His body moved at almost the same speed as his mind. He had ample time, to block, parry, thrust, and slash with deadly effect. He planned all his moves well in advance of their execution. He choreographed the sequences in his mind with cold efficiency. He taunted them with false openings in his guard that lured them into traps. He dealt with each new threat as it came. He felt no pain and no remorse.

His mind was the calm in the eye of the storm, while around him his limbs dealt death and disaster to his enemies. His movements were nearly automatic, his body and reflexes conditioned by the long hours of practice his father had forced upon him; his strength and speed augmented by the fury that boiled within him. The long knives in his hands were scythes mowing flesh like ripe grain. He turned, and whirled. He watched detached and calm. He struck out and thrust his weapons through openings in their defenses.

He counted them down. Four men left standing, three left, then two, then one.

He paused long enough to see his opponent's eyes widen in terror as the fellow realized that he was alone and that he faced certain death. Laakea saw his own reflection in the man's eyes. The image chilled him to the bone.

His opponent stared in shock, but he didn't have time to beg for mercy. He didn't have time to flee for his life. Justice, in the form of a boy with bloodstained blades in his hands, overtook him and justice meted out his death sentence. Justice crossed its arms and with a double cross-hand blow sliced the large arteries on either side of his neck simultaneously. In that moment, his life ended, though he remained standing. Laakea's blood spattered face was the last thing his final opponent saw.

Laakea's fierce eyes penetrated his soul and passed judgment on him as his vision faded.

Laakea watched him, as light and life drained from the other man's eyes. He fell slowly to the ground and twitched out the last movements his body would make on Aarda.

The world began to speed up, catching Laakea off guard leaving him dizzy and weak. He came back to himself and realized what had happened. He was no longer a spectator watching his actions from outside himself. His newly re-inhabited joints and sinews ached, sweat stung in his minor cuts, and his eyes. Tired, weak, and shaken, he barely recognized the furious thing that he had been. The whole skirmish had taken less time than it would have taken him to skin a rabbit, but he felt like a lifetime had passed. He was glad that he survived, but the reality of what he had just done; hit him like a collapsing building.

"I have taken life," he said aloud, his voice shaking. "I have met one of the berserkers from my father's tales and it's me."

Nausea followed the revelation; repulsed by what he had done he vomited his supper onto the forest floor beside the bodies of the men whose lives he had taken. He had killed, not just once but many times in just one night. He knew that he would never be the same person again. He was no longer innocent. With the loss of his innocence, he realized how precious a commodity it was. Water could remove the blood from his hands, but nothing could ever remove the bloodstains from his soul. He had turned a corner on the road of his life and there was no way to go back. He had killed and his only consolation was the idea, that he did it to save a friend and to right a wrong.

With his guts emptied of the supper he had prepared earlier; he began to look for Rehaak's body among the slain. He found his friend at the center of the circle of destruction, lying sprawled across the body of one of his attackers.

"At least I can give him a decent burial back at the clearing. The others can rot on the forest floor," he fumed.

He decided to return later to collect what he could from the dead. The spoils of combat were his right, but they were insufficient reimbursement for what he had lost tonight.

He rolled Rehaak's body out of the pool of blood that glistened darkly in the moonlight, where it gathered under his head. There was a sizable gash to the side of Rehaak's head where his assailant's weapon struck him to the ground, but he had no other injuries. One unlucky blow had felled him.

As he hoisted his friend from the ground, Rehaak moaned in pain.

He's alive!

The notion filled Laakea with a sense of urgency and renewed his strength. He knew that he must get Rehaak to the hut before he bled to death from the head wound. He ran with Rehaak bouncing across his shoulders. It seemed like it took hours to get back to the hut though it took very little time at all. Once inside he swiftly put wood on the fire he had banked earlier and brought the candle so he could examine the wound properly.

The wound was bloody, but not life threatening. A glancing blow had sheared a flap of Rehaak's scalp loose from his head. It now dangled loosely from the white bone of his unbroken skull. Laakea got a cloth and water from the bucket at the door and hurried to clean up the wound before Rehaak regained consciousness. He cleaned the wound thoroughly, the way his mother had taught him. He positioned the flap as best he could and bandaged it tightly to hold it in place.

"I have done all I can Creator. You will have to look after him now," he said, surprising himself by praying to a god that he knew very little about, a god he had not heard or believed in only days ago. "I must sleep now my friend. I am sorry Rehaak, for not being capable of more."

He collapsed in exhaustion on the earthen floor in front of the hearth and fell instantly into a dreamless sleep, while shaggy four legged shadows patrolled outside in the moonlight.

CHAPTER 15: AT THE SEA

In the fog gray morning, Aelfric stood on the rocky shore, looking out across the choppy water. The cold wind made his joints ache, as he strained to see the far shore of the inlet. It had been many years since he had been back to this spot. The world was younger then, filled with promise and possibility. A new life had once beckoned him from just beyond the horizon. He supposed that the world had not really changed, but he certainly had.

It was long ago; he was young then, full of ideas and ideals. She had come with him, and loved him, in spite of his foolhardy dream of starting a new life. That dream was now as dead as she was. Sixteen years had changed everything. He was only twenty-six when he had come here, looking for a new life, now he was forty-two, and he felt old. She was dead and gone. The hot flame of her life and her love for him had grown cold even in his memory. Now his son had left too, leaving him alone, in unremitting solitude.

He knew he'd been a fool. He should have talked to the boy and explained the past. Instead, he had withheld information about his own past, and the history of their people, to keep his son from finding out the truth. He had only the best of intentions. Aelfric wanted to protect his son from that history, in the hope that he would not have to repeat it. All he had wanted was to spare his son from hurt. All his son had wanted was information. All Aelfric had given them both was pain.

In spite of abandoning a warrior's life himself, he had trained his son in the arts of war, praying to every god he could name; that his son would never need to use the skills he taught, but aware of the inevitable reality of the need for those skills.

War and weapons making were all he really knew, so he had imparted those skills to the boy on the practice field and in the forge. He taught him to live by the Warrior Code that had ruled his life and the life of every other Eniila for countless generations. Maybe he did it because he lacked imagination. Perhaps he could not envision any other way. He knew, however, that someday the boy would have to return to Baradon, to find a suitable wife, if for no other reason. He would not allow his son to marry an Abrhaani girl. It was inconceivable that an Abrhaani girl could accept his son as a husband. Laakea would have to go to Baradon eventually, if he still lived.

Aelfric had felt that when he came to Khel Braah, that he could escape his fate. He wanted to believe that a man could escape who he was, but fate had delivered the death stroke to his belief when Shelhera died.

He supposed he had known it all along, but was just too stubborn to admit defeat. Yes, his son would need to go to Baradon eventually. In Baradon, his son would need all the skills he had been taught and more. If Aelfric had not left Baradon— perhaps, she would still be alive — perhaps, his son would be an important person — perhaps —.

Unlike his forge in the homeland, he made no stores of weapons in this land. Instead, he and his son had made plowshares and pruning hooks, tools and tack.

They shod mithun and tempered tools, but the blacksmithing skills were the same. Their work was in demand because the settlers around them had never learned to work iron. It was a long way to the city, or even to the town of New Hope, where they could trade for steel tools, and the tools were costly because of the distance they had to be transported. Smithing was a way to make a living here and his skills were in high demand. If he was not popular or well accepted in the community, his work was.

The villagers needed him, so they tolerated him and his family. It had taken years to win that tolerance. The Abrhaani were always suspicious of him, and he had to admit that given the history of their two peoples, they had good reasons. They did not know why he had forsaken his people or why he fled here to escape his obligations. He had enough of war and conquest, a belly full of suffering and sacrifice. He had grown tired of the petty feuds and the bickering that was rampant among his people. He also had enough of politics and betrayal.

He wanted a new start and so he took the chance as it came and Shelhera was willing to come with him. They had set out, to the land of their enemies, with only what they could carry on their strong, young backs. The Eniila had slaughtered the Abrhaani because they had trespassed on Eniila lands. They enslaved the passive and pathetic Abrhaani that remained when their cities fell.

They had captured many Abrhaani in the battles for the coastal cities. Aelfric, himself, had given the order to have them removed to the interior of Baradon where they now served as slaves in the mines, and manufactories. He had not foreseen the massacre that took place at E'shook. Perhaps, in part, he had come here to make restitution for those acts. He could not live with that shame any longer, but that too had failed.

It was no easy task to convince a renegade Abrhaani captain to give them passage to Kel Braah, but enough gold had salved the man's conscience, and clinched the deal. They sailed across the Syn Gersuul to the southeastern side of the island. The captain assured him that there were only a few people living nearby. They would pose no threat to him and Shelhera. At last, he would have the freedom he craved, a life he could fashion with his own hands and skills, without the interference of others of his kind. Between the two of them, they had the skills they needed to make a successful life away from the intrigues that plagued him in Baradon.

He spent many days exploring, until he found a place that looked like a promising location for a home. He remembered how he had built his first camp by a small stream. When he found the bog nearby, he praised the gods for bringing him near to iron that he knew he could refine. With his smithing skills and Shelhera's agricultural knowledge, they could make a good life for themselves and their children, when children came. They could build a legacy for their children here, away from the infighting and intrigues of Baradon.

They began to build their new home, in the isolated valley, in the hills near the coast. She had gotten pregnant soon after the house was completed. It was not an easy time for her, or for him. When the time came for her to deliver, she had almost died. He remembered being very frightened for the first time in his life. Nothing he had experienced on the battlefield had shaken him as much as the near loss of his beloved wife.

When it was over, he had a son. She recovered slowly but never truly regained her strength. They had many happy years as the boy grew up, but she had been unable to conceive again. Years passed as their son grew, strong and tall like his father. Then suddenly, she contracted the wasting disease, and she began to grow frail and weak. It took three years for her to die. She drew her last ragged breath while he held her in his arms one night. When the end came, he was ashamed of the relief he felt, that it was finally over.

As the days passed after her death, he missed her presence. He spent silent days going through the motions of his life without any feeling at all. His house, his forge, and even his son gave him no comfort. Now that she was gone, all he had built had been for nothing. He was a ragged collage of raw nerves and guilt. The boy had asked so many questions about the past. He could have explained things to him then, but his grief over her death was fresh and raw. It had gripped him like a vise between its opposing jaws of pain and loneliness.

Looking back on those days, he saw that he had been silent when he should've communicated, and he had spoken when he should've held this peace. When he had spoken, or rather when he had shouted, it was out of his pain and anger. His bitterness at his loss had driven the boy out and he would probably not see him again. He prayed for his son's safety and he longed for his presence, but he felt both prayer and longing were wasted efforts. He knew he had provoked the boy with his anger, and he had frightened him when he picked up the firewood, while raging at him. The things he said had hurt the lad, and the boy had retaliated by soundly cursing him. Although the boy had dishonored him, he did not want to collect the *Blood Debt;* he only wanted his son back, safe. In a perverse way, he was proud of the boy for standing up to him. That had taken courage.

He had tried to track the boy the morning after he had left. The trail had ended where the rain had washed away the signs and he could do nothing more. He supposed he could inquire about the boy, at the village, but he was far too proud to parade his failure as a father in front of Abrhaani villagers. There was nothing to indicate that the boy's life had ended, but neither was there any way to find him. Unless Laakea returned of his own accord, he and his son would never reunite. He would wait.

He waited, for two tendays, lighting a lamp in the window every night, hoping for his son's return. He would have given his right arm to take back the words he had spoken that night, and to have the boy safe with him again. He spent long nights pacing the floor of their empty house, his thoughts whirling, in rapid, vicious circles. His loneliness intensified with each passing day, until he was certain that he would go mad from it.

Finally, when he could stand it no longer, he turned the sheep loose from their pen to fend for themselves. He made the journey to this beach where he and his wife had come ashore so long ago. It had taken him three days to reach the place where he now stood. Aelfric had arrived at dusk the previous night and made camp.

He was not certain why he had returned to his landing spot. He looked around, perhaps expecting her to arrive on the boat again.

"What foolishness," he thought.

In his mind, he could see her jumping out of the boat into the water again. She was laughing, as they reached the shore, standing in the thigh-high surf. He wanted to recall the good things that had happened, along with the bad. Their life together had truly begun here, on this beach. He understood now that it was a pilgrimage of sorts.

Once the boat grounded, they had unloaded the supplies, and hauled the empty boat further up the beach toward a grove of trees to hide it in case anyone should come looking. Later he had come back to turn it upside down on some large deadwood logs to preserve it from decay. Not that he had planned to use it, but it irked him to waste anything. Under it, he had stored his weapons wrapped in oilskins, and sealed in a brass chest. He swore never to come back and never to take up the sword again. He wandered aimlessly, remembering, until he found himself at the grove again.

The trees were larger. Underbrush had grown back where he'd cut it a way to hide the boat. Pushing his way through the thick growth, he located the hull.

The exposed surface of the logs had rotted away to mossy mush, but the boat itself looked fine, if somewhat weathered. Its builders had tarred it to help prevent rot and the tar had worked well enough. He flipped it up on its side. It was still a sturdy little craft though he knew very little about the sea and the craft that sailed on it. The oars had rotted away so he would have to make new ones.

There, under the boat, inside the brass chest, lay the oiled skins that wrapped his sword and his war bow. He felt like he was looking into a tomb as he did an inventory of the items. The bow was bone and untouched by the weather, but the bowstring was gone. Rust pitted the sword in some spots where the oil had not completely protected it from the humidity in the air. He could restore and sharpen it. Arrow shafts and heads were intact, but the vanes had loosened on every arrow. The quiver was intact. Looking back, he felt foolish having left these implements of war here. It was such a pointless gesture.

"A man cannot escape his destiny or his past," he growled. "These weapons look like I feel, rusty, tattered, and moldy."

He picked his blade up and swung in a few practice arcs. The sword felt the same, but he felt different. There was stiffness in his hands and joints. He had gotten old without noticing the passage of time.

He sat in the bracken and wept, finally mourning his losses, succumbing to the grief that had held him prisoner for so long. In time, grief gave way to anger. As the sun began to burn the back of his neck, rage began to burn in his heart.

Cursing, he rose, snatched up his sword again, and began to hack away at the thick brush. He slashed and hacked around him as if the forest was his enemy and he was in the thick of battle once more. He could actually see ghostly faces as if his old foes stood before him passing judgment on him once more, telling him what he could and could not do. They had no right! He attempted to hew down his memories along with the vegetation.

In an hour, he was exhausted, but he had unintentionally cleared a passageway through the brush to the beach. It was wide enough to pull the boat through and launch it if he wanted. He suddenly realized that was exactly what he wanted. He wanted to escape the last sixteen years. He sought peace from memories of her. He wanted to run away from all that reminded him of his pain. To hell with the son who had dishonored and discarded him! To hell with these pensive, passive Abrhaani! He would go back to civilization, back to the land of his birth. He would make them all pay for their treachery. A man could not escape his destiny, but perhaps he could reclaim it.

He rested on the grassy bank that overlooked the beach, listening to the breakers and the cries of the gulls. Rage and grief had both burned out. Calm settled on him like a warm blanket. Yes, he would go back, but not now, not today. He had work to complete before he loaded the boat and left the island forever.

In the morning, he started the long walk back to the forge. He had settled things in his mind by the time he got home. He would return to Harthang, the city of his birth. He had spent sixteen years away and he had never been back.

Once he got a reading on the political climate in Baradon, and if he found his brother alive, he would settle his grudge with him and take back what was his, by right. He had fought for it, suffered, and bled for it. It was his. Aelfric was sure that once the people knew that he had returned they would follow him again, as they had before. The people would follow him even if their Lords would not. He had scores to settle that were over a decade old. They had treated him like a dog. It was time for the dog to bite the hands that had beaten him, time to bite — hard.

He believed that he had left that life behind forever after he had met Shelhera, but now she was gone and Laakea was lost. He had nothing to hold him here in his self-imposed exile. The anger he had held in check for so long now, seemed to boil to the surface easily. It felt good to be angry, it felt good to plot revenge, and he was sure it would feel even better when he could get his hands around his treacherous, false-hearted brother's neck, and strangle him until his eyes bulged and glazed in death.

The ghostly faces returned, their voices blending into a savage roar. "The King is dead. Long live the King! Long live King Aelfric!" Aelfric looked as deeply into their eyes as any mortal man could stand, but could not discern whether they felt joy or anger at the prospect of his return to the throne. He was beyond caring in any case.

CHAPTER 16: AFTERMATH

The sun was high in the treetops, when Rehaak's groans of pain awakened Laakea from his deep sleep. Laakea walked over to the bed to check on his friend, who only stirred slightly, as he tucked the blanket in around him. Rehaak's lips and mouth were parched, and he was a little feverish. Laakea brought him water and managed to get the semiconscious man to swallow some.

"You have a hard head my friend, and it's a good thing too, otherwise I'd be sticking you on a pile of firewood and lighting it with a torch to send you to the afterlife," Laakea said, not expecting an answer, as he lowered Rehaak's head back onto the bed.

"I'll need to get more water soon, but first I'll go get the spoils left behind on the trail last night," he said knowing that Rehaak was not able to hear his explanation.

Laakea was not looking forward to seeing the carnage in daylight as he headed back to the site of the previous night's battle. It was bad enough in the moonlight. He felt he needed to go back and treat their bodies with whatever honor he could. They may have been scoundrels and cowards, but he never to never become like them.

He had decided to gather their weapons, and at least cover their corpses with something to keep the scavengers away. This was in keeping with the customs of the Abrhaani. He had no time for proper Abrhaani burials nor would he cremate them like his people, the Eniila did. He hoped he could find clues about who they were and why they had attacked Rehaak last night.

It was easy to find the battle site. The carrion birds were already circling overhead. They were evidence that the forest was trying to cleanse itself of the stains of violence, without his help. The trip did not take long, but the sun was hot in the sky when he arrived. The heat made his grisly task even more unpleasant. He had to chase off the scavengers, before he pulled the bodies into the forest and covered the remains with brush and debris. He was glad he had not eaten breakfast. The smells of death and decay brought on fresh waves of nausea. By the time he was done, it was nearing late afternoon. He was tired from his exertions. If he had eaten before he left, he would have had more energy, but he didn't want to repeat the experience of emptying his gut like the previous night.

He did not find many clues about the identity of the dead men. He noticed one significant thing, although he did not know what it meant. Each of the men bore tattoos across their chests and shoulders. He would not have noticed except that when he dragged the first one off the trail by his heels, the brigand's shirt slid up over his head revealing the markings. This prompted Laakea to check the rest. They too had similar markings. Each one was slightly different, but they all had certain elements in common. They obviously belonged to some type of secret society, or an assassin's guild, but beyond that Laakea could decipher nothing of the meaning of the marks. He could only guess that someone had hired them to attack Rehaak, or that their organization carried some sort of grudge against his friend.

When he had done all he could for the bodies, he scooped up their scant belongings. He could sort through the stuff back at the hut and try to make more sense of it there. His head was spinning and he was too hungry to think clearly now. He did notice, however, that he had gained six more long knives, exactly like the ones still stashed back in the hut. These were his lawful spoils, so he could do what he willed with them. He would have more than enough metal to cold forge arrowheads for all his arrows.

When he had everything bundled so he could easily carry it, he headed back to care for his friend. He arrived just in time to see Rehaak slump back onto the bed with a groan.

"How're you feeling?" he asked.

"Like a big boulder fell on my head. What happened?"

"You don't remember?"

"Nothing after leaving the Miller's."

"You were attacked on the trail by six men. One of them knocked a chunk out of the side of your head, just as I arrived."

"What were you doing out there? I told you to stay."

"If I'd listened to you — you'd be dead!"

"Good point, but try not to make it so loudly please. I have a headache."

"That ache is in a head you're lucky to still have, I'd say," Laakea said, with a grin, relieved that his friend was beginning to recover.

"Did you drive them off then?"

Laakea paused before answering. "Sort of; I drove them into the next life — I killed them." He flushed with shame at the memory.

"Six men? You're just a lad! Ah, my head."

"Stay calm and don't shout. I imagine its worse when you shout than when I do."

"You are right — it is. But you killed all six?"

"Just five really, you killed one before they split your head open. You need to rest. I'll get you some more water and put it by the bed. We can talk later."

"Taking a man's life is not as easy in real life, as it was in hero's tales. You will need time to heal from the psychic wounds arising from killing other men." Rehaak advised, as he lay back down on the bed.

Laakea watched as his friend closed his eyes and gritted his teeth against the pain.

"Do you need something for the pain? He asked

Rehaak managed to instruct Laakea in the preparation of some herb tea. Once the tea took effect, he drifted off to sleep again.

After Laakea was sure that Rehaak was asleep, he went to get something to eat. He was ravenous. He had eaten neither breakfast nor lunch and it was almost evening now. He was beginning to feel nearly as weak as his wounded friend did. He knew little about the healing arts, but it brought him a measure of joy to see the tea he had brewed bring relief to his friend.

As he went through the belongings that he had taken from the bodies this morning, Laakea reassessed the events of the previous night. Although he tried hard to find something that made sense of the assault in the forest, he found no additional clues to why the men had attacked his host. When Laakea had first come to live with Rehaak, he had told Laakea the story of the previous attack, by men, bearing identical weapons. There was obviously some sort of conspiracy against Rehaak, but who would want a scholar dead and why?

Scholars were unlikely targets for assassinations from all accounts he had heard. Laakea could not rule out the possibility that this particular scholar might still have other shameful secrets that could provoke a lethal response from someone. A powerful person or organization was coordinating these efforts, but who could have that much power, and enough malice toward Rehaak, to use that power in this deadly way?

He would have to be vigilant in case further attacks occurred, and he would need better weaponry than what he had now. The pattern of the attacks indicated an escalation in force, since more men were involved each time. He would need to go to see his father. He needed his father's help to forge the tools to combat this threat, or barring that, he needed to manufacture his own, but he needed a good forge and the proper tools to do it.

His father had told him that it was time for him to do his journeyman project at the forge, but his departure had indefinitely postponed it. His final test of skill was to make a sword, since swords were the most difficult tools to master. The dimensions of a blade and its handle needed precise attention to make a weapon that handled properly in combat conditions.

He had enough excellent raw materials now, with all the long knives he had gathered. He could cold forge all the arrowheads he needed right here, with metal he already had on hand, but what he wanted were swords. It might cost him his life to obtain entry to his father's forge, but he needed access and he needed it quickly.

He made up his mind in an instant. As soon as Rehaak could travel, they would go to his father's house. He would find a way to convince his father that this man needed their help; even if it killed him, in fact, his death would be one way to ensure that Aelfric helped Rehaak.

The custom of *Blood Debt* was a two edged weapon. If one man killed another in a dispute, *The Code* required that the winner take on the obligations and responsibilities of the loser. It was common practice for duelists to disclose debts and obligations before the struggle began, so that each combatant knew in advance, what his new responsibilities would entail.

It was a way to balance the scales of Eniila society, and make sure that no one issued challenges frivolously. It tended to weed out the bullies. The cost of defeat was death, a high cost indeed, but so was the cost of victory when the winner had to assume the responsibilities of feeding and caring for another man's family, or paying his debts. It was common practice for those facing possible challenges to borrow huge amounts of money, to discourage anyone from issuing challenges against them. Shrewish wives had much the same effect according to his father, as did large families, or indigent relatives. The rich childless man with a pretty, sweet-tempered wife, on the other hand was likely to need all the battle skills he could muster.

Laakea could swear a *Sword Oath* to Rehaak. That way, the Warrior Code would compel his father to help Rehaak, as though Aelfric had sworn to help the Scholar by the words of his own mouth. Rehaak would get the help he needed, regardless of the outcome of the meeting with his father. If Aelfric killed Laakea in combat, *The Code* would force him to assume Laakea's obligations to Rehaak. The only issue that stood in the way was Rehaak's ability to travel to the forge. *Blood Debt* obligations needed a witness to finalize them. Laakea's witness to the oath would be Rehaak, the man to whom he would give his word.

He began making the arrowheads from some of the guards and tangs of the long knives while Rehaak slept and recovered.

He worked quickly and efficiently. In five days, he had enough for all the shafts he prepared and fletched earlier. He knew that if he worked by lamplight tonight, he could fix the broad-heads to the shafts and sharpen them before he went to sleep.

Laakea got up to go inside and check on Rehaak, as he had done periodically throughout each day. He found Rehaak sitting at the table eating and drinking. Laakea was certain that his friend was beginning to look much better, though Laakea noticed that Rehaak winced occasionally as he chewed on a crust of bread.

"How're you feeling?" he asked the injured man. "Are you remembering any more of that night?"

"I am not sure."

"Why don't you tell me what happened from the time you left until you got back, it may help sort things out for you."

Rehaak smiled at the boy, "That is a wise suggestion. I was not aware that you had gained so much wisdom."

"I have learned far more than I had wanted to know, since the night I came to your aid."

Rehaak let the comment pass, and nodded before saying, "Very well, I will tell you what I remember, but you must fill in whatever blanks you can, up to the time I awoke here at the hut."

Laakea agreed with a nod. Knowing he would have to share the events of that night made him apprehensive, but he had given his word and he would just have to believe that Rehaak would not reject him because of his actions. They had been down a similar road before. That knowledge made Laakea somewhat more comfortable, but only somewhat. After all, everyone had limits when it came to tolerance.

Evidence of his wild blood lust just might be the final sticking point for the tolerant man with the bandaged head. It was one thing to live with a coward, but it was another thing entirely to live with a homicidal maniac. He considered telling just the facts of the incident and leaving out the emotion, but he knew Rehaak would sense what he was holding back. He might as well just reveal it all, and let Rehaak sort out his response for himself.

He resolved to live with the consequences no matter how it turned out. It was a warrior's choice and it was *The Warrior's Way*. If Rehaak would stand with Laakea in spite of this new revelation, then he was a true friend. Laakea suspected that they would soon face many more perils. If they stayed friends, they would face those hazards together. Laakea decided it was time to stop running from his fears.

His battle with the five assassins had changed this about him too. He had seen a side of himself he did not like; a side that frightened him, but he was harder and stronger now, like iron quenched in brine after being forged. The Creator had heated him in the forge of battle and quenched him in blood. He would flex and not shatter. The iron in his blood, that his father had mentioned, was now the kind of steel that would stand the test of adversity, strong enough and hard enough to deal a killing blow, but still flexible enough to withstand hardship.

CHAPTER 17: CHANGES

Laakea listened carefully to the story. Rehaak was able to remember everything, until the time he left the Miller's house. Everything after that was a blank. Laakea asked questions but nothing more of Rehaak's memories returned.

"What do you think the creature was, Rehaak?"

"I think it was a Nethera, an evil spirit, one of the Dark Ones."

"Can spirits take on a physical form? How's that possible?"

"I wish I knew. The universe runs by rules that none of us fully comprehend."

"If they were in a physical form wouldn't they be subject to physical laws just as we are?"

"I suppose they would, but this thing turned into mist and vanished almost immediately after it drained the boy of life. We still know so little." He shook his head in frustration and fell silent.

Laakea knew it was his turn to speak. He approached it with trepidation. He started with the facts leading to his departure from the hut, and explained why he had left the safety of the hut against Rehaak's instructions to the contrary. He recounted the facts as he remembered them, but shied away from the feelings that had upset him. He needed to know two things.

First, he needed to know if Rehaak would fear him as some sort of insane bloodthirsty barbarian, or if he would accept this too, as part of Laakea's identity. Secondly, he needed to know if Rehaak knew anything about the bloodlust that had overwhelmed him just before the battle. Rehaak listened quietly without commenting or asking questions.

Laakea paused for a second to collect his thoughts, and to gather his courage.

"Rehaak there's something troubling me about the battle and I'm not sure how to tell you."

"Go ahead lad. I sensed that something happened in your heart. What was it?"

"It was what I felt while in the battle — no — I remember now — it came upon me just before."

"Go ahead."

"I was so angry."

What were you angry about?" Rehaak asked softly.

"I was angry that six men should attack you without warning or provocation. The odds were in their favor and yet they chose the darkness to beset you. Rage rose up in me at the injustice and I just wanted to avenge the wrong they were doing to you."

"Was there more?"

Yes, when the anger took hold of me everything seemed to move very slowly. All I could think about was killing them. I planned the quickest and easiest way to do it. I felt no pain, no shame, and no pity. I stood outside myself, watching, as if it was someone else doing the killing. Someone else was wearing my body like clothing, while I merely watched. At the same time, I was very sure that what was happening was right. It left no room for doubt, but now I have so many doubts and questions that I don't know what to do with them all. I feel like an evil monster."

"Are you afraid that this may happen again without warning?"

"Yes. What happens if this bloodlust suddenly overtakes me and I hurt someone who is innocent or someone I care about?"

"I am willing to risk it." Rehaak smiled warmly and continued, "From what you have told me, I doubt that you would injure a friend. It seems that the anger you had was only directed at evil doers."

"But, it felt like I was out of control!"

"No, not out of control — being controlled."

"But by what or by whom?"

"There may be a proper explanation for this 'bloodlust,' as you call it, in some of the old texts. It may even be part of The Creator's design for your race; something that He placed there for his own purposes."

"Are you sure? I prayed to Him you know — when you were wounded."

"The Creator? You believe?" Rehaak asked. *"Had he recruited another follower for The Faithful One?"*

"I guess I do."

"Now, what makes you think that you are an evil monster?"

"I felt no remorse."

"Pardon me for asking, but what is it you are feeling right now, if it is not remorse?"

Laakea looked dumbfounded by the question for a few moments. "Yes now I do, but then I didn't."

"I am glad that you felt none for them at the time, because if you had, most likely neither of us would have survived to feel anything. I suspect you would not have been able to survive that encounter, if you had not done what you did. I know that *I* would not have survived it without your aid. In any case, I am also glad that you feel remorse now, because that tells me that your conscience is intact. You are no monster. If you were, you would still feel no guilt or shame at what you did."

"How do you know for sure?"

"I have experienced the same feelings, when I had to take a life to defend myself. I still experience those feelings every time, although not nearly as powerfully as at first."

"You do?"

"Yes, I do and from what you tell me, your father trained you to be a skilled warrior. Your training saved both our lives. Let us leave it at that for now."

"Alright, but why do these men keep attacking you?"

"I don't know, but they attacked Isil the first time. I just went to help her."

"Are you sure? Has anyone attacked Isil before or since that time?

"No."

"Alright then. Are you sure, they weren't waiting for you on the road? They only attacked once you were present. Isn't it possible that they were after *you*, not Isil?"

"Then why did I feel such an urgent need to catch up with her, to help her?"

"If you had been later on the trail they would have caught you alone. Do you think you could have handled them by yourself?

"No."

"Perhaps you needed Isil's protection, and not Isil who needed yours." Rehaak made no response, so Laakea continued, "It occurs to me, that for a learned man, you are sometimes a little thick headed."

Rehaak looked as if he was about to protest, but Laakea continued on.

"Please don't look so offended. That thick head saved your life last night anyway," Laakea grinned, impishly.

Rehaak scowled at him and said, "This is a possibility I never seriously considered, although Isil has suggested a similar explanation earlier. She was more tactful in the suggestion, but you have come to the same conclusion on your own, without all the information that Isil and I had. It must be true.

"I suppose pride has prevented me from seeing it. I believed I was being Isil's valiant rescuer, but now I find that the reverse might be true."

The irony forced a smile from Rehaak.

"Isil saved my life. To be correct, Isil and her mithun, Hort, saved my life. I am incurring many debts to people for saving me. I remember that I had assistance in every encounter with the knife-wielding assassins. Isil and the mithun, then the wolves, and now you, Laakea."

"That reminds me that I have not seen the wolves at all lately. I used to see them frequently, until the day they brought you to meet me, at the river. They seem to have vanished like river mist in the warm sun. Perhaps there were just too many people hanging about now, for the wolves to feel comfortable staying near the hut, or perhaps they feel that I no longer needed them."

"Ignore all that — if you are correct, what is the purpose for the attacks? Why would these men want to kill me?" he asked Laakea.

"I don't know — yet, but I will tell you these are no ordinary brigands. Why didn't you tell me about the knives you had stashed in the niche at the back of the hearth?"

"I expect I just did not think of it. The weapons made me feel so uncomfortable whenever I handled them, that I suppose I just put them out of my mind."

"I am almost a journeyman blacksmith. I can tell you that the knives they carry are not the weapons of brigands. They are finely crafted weapons, too expensive for a common thief. The metal in them is something I have not seen before; likewise, the runes crafted into the blades are unfamiliar to me. These are uncommon weapons and they would never be in the hands of common criminals. Then there is the matter of the tattoos. Did you notice if the others bore marks across their chests and shoulders?"

"I don't remember. We did not look at the bodies very carefully."

"There are larger forces at play here. Someone is directing these men in their attacks, someone with a lot of power, money, and influence. That someone is trying to make the attacks look like common crimes, but there is nothing common about the men or their weapons. You have a powerful enemy, Rehaak. Someone wants you dead and will spare no effort to see that his desires are accomplished."

"What can I do?" Rehaak asked, trying to quell the rising tide of panic in his heart. "I should be safe out here in the back end of creation."

"There are many places for you to hide, but unfortunately that also means there are many places that your enemies can hide. There is also a better chance to hide the crime out here where there are fewer eyes to see."

K. R. Schultz

"So I have a very powerful enemy. That is not a comforting thought."

"No, it isn't, but each time you were attacked, you received help from some unlikely and unexpected sources. That should tell you that you also have a very powerful friend."

"Your father taught you much wisdom, my young friend."

"I am just beginning to realize that myself," Laakea admitted, smiling softly. He grew serious and stiffly formal as he spoke his next words.

"I will join with you in your quest Rehaak. I swear *Sword Oath* to you, to defend you and protect you. I call on The Creator this day, to witness this oath, to bind me to it in life, and to strengthen me in it until death. Do you accept my oath to you?"

Laakea bowed low as he completed the formula his father had taught him. The name of his charge, the work undertaken, the name of the god he followed, the duration of the oath, all were included. He was now sword sworn to Rehaak. He would be faithful in his oath, or he would perish trying to fulfill it. He only needed to take care of two more bits of business. First, his father, and second his journeyman smithing project. He already could see in his mind, the swords he planned to forge for himself, as he waited for Rehaak to respond.

Laakea's seriousness when he spoke the oath and the words he had used seemed to unsettle Rehaak.

"No one has ever wanted to go with me before. I have never really had a friend before. Loyalty to the death is something that I cannot understand. I have always gone wherever the wind blew me and I have always been loyal only to myself. No one has ever promised, nor have I ever promised, that kind of loyalty to anyone. That kind of commitment is literally beyond my comprehension."

186

"If that isn't friendship, I will never understand the meaning of the word. I am not sure I want the responsibility engendered by that level of commitment from someone, especially someone as young as you are. Neither of us knows what lies ahead."

Tears threatened to spill out of his eyes, as the full impact of Laakea's generosity and the depth of his friendship dawned on him.

He responded, "I accept your gift of friendship and swear loyalty to you as well." It was all he managed to get out before his voice broke. They were now bonded, as companions, adventurers, and brothers.

""You should look at the blades to see if you can decipher the runes on them." Laakea said, relaxing out of his formal posture. "I hope they provide you some clues, since I can't decipher them. We also need to do one other thing, once you are well enough, my friend,"

"What is that?"

"I need to see my father and settle things between us."

"But what if he challenges you to trial by combat?"

"We'll worry about that if it becomes a problem. If possible, I'd like to make peace with my father. If it's not possible then I'll submit myself to trial by combat, as is our custom. If I lose my trial, my *Sword Oath* will bind my father to you and he'll have to watch over you just as I would."

The change in Laakea's attitude stunned Rehaak. A man stood before him now, a man and a warrior. He could see the resolve in the youngster's eyes and the conviction in his heart. Rehaak sensed that his young friend was now a powerful force for good.

Rehaak did not feel he could change Laakea's mind on this topic, so he only asked, "Is that all?"

"I need access to my father's forge to complete my journeyman project."

"Why is that important? I see the need for you to leave on the best terms possible with your father. No man should venture into danger without making peace with those he loves."

Laakea found Rehaak's choice of words sounded strange to him. It had been many moons since he had felt any love for his father, or felt that his father loved him. As the words came from Rehaak's mouth, Laakea discovered that the love he had previously held for his father was still there undiminished, just hidden under his hurt and anger. He kept his thoughts to himself and said.

"For one thing, I'll make weapons that'll help me keep us both from getting killed. That will be my journeyman project. I now have all the metal I need. I'll forge the weapons used against us, into ones that I can use to protect us. For the other, I'm not sure why this is so important, but I just feel that it is vital that I finish my apprenticeship."

"I see, and when do we start this journey, sword brother?"

"As soon as I think you are well enough to travel."

"Oh ho! So now you are a healer, in addition to your other gifts," laughed Rehaak. "Soon your head will be so large you won't be able to get in and out of the doorway!"

"Don't worry my friend; it won't get so big that I can't still carry you when you're leaking blood all over yourself from the scrapes you get yourself into. We won't hang around this smelly hut you seem so fond of one minute longer than necessary. I feel we need to hurry. I sense a storm coming and we need to prepare quickly. By the way, is there another weapon you can use besides that staff of yours? Something that will take out an opponent, before he gets close enough to club you up the side of that thick skull of yours?"

"I can use a sling if need be. When I was a boy, I used to be quite good with one," he said, with pride.

"Very well, I shall make you a sling while you are healing. Now get some rest. If you can manage it, perhaps you can decipher the runes on the blades."

"Yes mother," Rehaak quipped, with mock humility, as Laakea left the hut to find material for Rehaak's new weapon.

CHAPTER 18: INVESTITURE

Several more days passed before they were ready to travel. Rehaak tried in vain to decipher the runes on the blades, but they seemed to shift and change before his eyes, just as they had for Laakea. At first, he suspected that it might be a complication from his head wound, but when he was able to read other writings, he dismissed that idea. The blades were ensorcelled in some way. The meaning of the markings slipped out of his grasp, whenever he felt that he was beginning to make sense of them. Trying to read the runes was like trying to wrestle with snakes coated in oil.

Rehaak practiced with the sling when he could, and was regaining some of the proficiency he had as a youngster. Laakea added to his collection of arrows. They planned to leave a message about their mission for Isil, with the Millers, since Rehaak expected her any day now. Rehaak was saddened that they had to leave before she returned, but Laakea would tolerate no more delays. Rehaak would have liked the boy to meet his only other friend, but he resigned himself to knowing that it could happen later. Their friendship had grown and deepened during his convalescence.

After what they had already experienced, the journey to the forge was anticlimactic. For Rehaak it was just a long boring hike through the forest in the summer heat. The biting insects buzzed around them looking to snatch a quick meal from his veins, if the opportunity presented itself. As they drew close to the valley where Laakea had been born, the boy grew stoic and silent.

Rehaak knew him well enough to detect the tension, hidden behind the quiet exterior. He tried his best to distract the young man from what might lie ahead, by telling humorous accounts of his travels. Laakea spoke little, smiled rarely, and stayed focused on whatever inner dialogue he was having. He was behaving like a condemned man approaching his executioner. Rehaak was not surprised, since he might indeed die at his father's hand in combat. In spite of his earlier confidence about that meeting, Rehaak was detecting some minor cracks in Laakea's resolve.

They had stopped at the Miller's house first, to see how they were faring, and see if they were recovering from the encounter with the Nethera. The couple insisted that they stay for supper, then, because it was late, offered them places to sleep.

Laakea had never met the Miller's and their children before. He explained that he had never seen the inner workings of any family other than his own, until now.

"It's marvelous, the way they deal with their children. The children play games I have never heard of. My childhood had little to do with games and play, and everything to do with work and combat training."

Rehaak silently nodded as his young friend felt the poverty of his upbringing in new and painful ways that night. Laakea endured it without comment and seemingly without anger at the lack.

Rehaak valued the years Laakea had spent learning weapons skills. He knew that he would need to use all those skills, to stay alive, in the face of an ominous unknown threat.

K. R. Schultz

***

It was still early morning, when they reached the lip of the valley overlooking his old home. Laakea felt positively grim.

"This is a beautiful place," said Rehaak, attempting without success, to lift Laakea's mood. "Small wonder your father picked this location."

"I doubt if he picked it for its beauty. This is where the iron is, and there were enough trees to make the charcoal he needed," Laakea answered.

Rehaak's comment was not without effect on him. Laakea looked down into the valley with new eyes, as if seeing it for the first time. The cool air caressed the leaves of the trees like a lover's hand. Sunlight made them sparkle like gems, glowing incandescent green. The aspens and fruit trees moved like dancers, swaying to the rhythm of a song in the air. Pines and firs stood back, dark and brooding like old men too stiff to join in the dance, but longing to participate in the action. The faint jittering at the ends of their branches betrayed their desire and excitement.

Sunlight lit the tops of the clouds with swirls of pastel colors piled high, on dark gray bottoms. Grass, glowed, with the energy of the dawn, waking from its nightly rest, it took its first breath of a new day. A day filled with promise, possibility, and excitement. The air was sweet, thick, loaded with enough fragrances to cast a haze of blue on the distant hills. The few birds already awake sang to encourage the others.

He listened to the birdsong believing that he understood their language for the first time in his life. Pale golden sunlight filtered through the branches, as the dim, damp morning light began to find its way to the forest floor, gaining strength and heat, as the sun climbed higher in the sky.

Trees gravid with fruit, branches bent low, seemed to say, "Here, taste, see what I have for you, this is my offering, take from me, pluck from my plenty. Let the juice run from your lips, and your chin. Run sticky and skipping, as you greet this day with me. The Creator has given me this gift, and I want to share my joy with you, for your profit and pleasure. Relieve me of my bountiful burden. Take from me my blessing."

Suddenly he understood that his familiar home was a place of mystery and marvels. Everything came together and he understood the working of all the parts deep inside. He knew in that moment, that it was his duty and his privilege to protect all of this. Everything he looked at appeared imbued with divine significance and goodness. He could almost hear the golden voice speaking through this revelation.

"Yes this is your calling and your privilege. Protect the weak, preserve the land, fight injustice, and serve me always."

It was good. It was good from the highest cloud, all the way down to bedrock and everywhere in between. He was part of it, and yet set apart, consecrated as its guardian. Joy flowed into him in a torrent that made him weep. It filled him, and when he could no longer contain it, it ran out through his eyes as tears. How had he missed the wonder of the place, where he had lived for all of his fifteen years? How could he say no to the call, now that he saw the beauty and rightness of what lay around him?

His heart was full. He had found his life's work; or rather, it had found him. He knew his purpose and his lips whispered the response that welled up from within his spirit.

"Yes," he answered, knowing that the task was far too large for him.

"Yes," he answered, knowing that it may cost him his life.

"Yes," he said for a final time. He felt the full weight of the burden fall squarely across his youthful shoulders.

He was a man now with a man's duties. His commitment, freely given, bound him with the same force as his *Sword Oath* to Rehaak. He had never heard of anyone pledging a *Sword Oath* to an entire world before — no not the world. He suddenly understood who had been speaking to him. The person he thought of as the Golden Voice was Rehaak's Faithful One, The Creator. He had sworn his *Sword Oath* to The Creator of the world.

He wasn't even sure if it was possible to do such a thing, but that was what he felt compelled to do, and that was indeed what he had just done. The idea was staggering. He was stricken with panic. What in all of Aarda have I done? I must be mad!

He was suddenly conscious of Rehaak's eyes watching him, and he felt his face redden in embarrassment. He had never wanted witnesses to his emotions, but since he and Rehaak had become friends, he found it easier than he had before. Still, the red flush spread across his neck and face, in spite of his trust in the man beside him. Perhaps he should tell Rehaak what had just happened. The moment when he could have broached the subject slipped away, when Rehaak began to speak.

"It is a beautiful place to live," Rehaak said, breaking the silence. "It is even more beautiful than my little spot of paradise. I wonder if either of us will ever see these places again, once we have set out on our quest."

Laakea made no answer as he looked back across the valley that had been his home.

"Perhaps the time to tell of this oath is not now," he thought. "Possibly that time will never come."

He had made his vow silently to The Creator. He didn't want Rehaak to think he was getting grandiose views of his own importance. No, he would keep silent. It was better that way.

As he looked out across the valley, he sensed something was out of place. At first, he could not define what it was, but when he looked a second time, he noticed things missing from the scene he remembered. There was no smoke coming from the bloomery, or the forge where his father refined and worked the iron, nor was there smoke from further up the valley, among the trees, where the house stood. Something was wrong. His father should have at least started the fire in the forge by this time of day.

Where were the sheep that should have been in the pen? He wasn't sure whether to be relieved or frightened by the absence of the fires and the animals. Laakea bit his lip, and fought down his feeling of unease. He hitched up his pack that contained the long knives that they had brought with them, and started down into the valley. He set a rapid pace with Rehaak hard on his heels.

CHAPTER 19: ALMOST HOME

Rehaak noticed the change in the lad. Laakea had certainly gone through a vast range of emotion this morning. In mere moments, he had gone from grim, to joyous, and now he appeared worried, though perhaps not about himself. Rehaak followed him down the trail, his hair blowing back in the breeze. It felt good to be without the bandage he had worn for most of the last two tendays. It would have made his head itch like hell in this heat.

He had developed a minor infection in the cut on his scalp early on. All the hair on the triangular patch had fallen out, before the flap of skin healed back into place. Overall, Laakea had done a remarkable job of putting him back together. The hair was starting to grow back again, but it was coming in white, not the raven wing black of the hair around it. Laakea had taken to calling him Spot, and Rehaak thought it was funny, so he didn't object. If that was the worst he had received in his encounter with six assassins, he considered himself very lucky. He kept his thoughts to himself, as he followed his rescuer into the valley, toward an uncertain welcome.

The character of the valley changed as they drew closer to Aelfric's forge. Aelfric had stripped and burned the large trees from the land around the forge for charcoal. Small plants, saplings and bracken grew up to

196

replace the fallen giants, but it would be centuries before the young growth attained the stature of the trees further up-slope.

The changes in Laakea puzzled Rehaak, but he said nothing to the boy. It was as much out of respect for the youngster's present state of mind, as for his own lack of breath. He was having trouble keeping up to Laakea's long purposeful strides. That difficulty was a function, both of the length of the boy's legs, and Rehaak's weakness, caused by his long days of convalescence. He swore the boy had grown a span in height, since they had met, and he was filling out that large frame with muscle to match it. He was already a head taller than Rehaak, who was large for his people and Laakea was still growing.

Once they drew a little nearer to the forge, Rehaak understood the lack of trees. Aelfric had cut them down and burned them to make charcoal for the forge and the bloomery. Blackened char pits dotted the valley floor. Ash and soot lay in patches among the new growth. Rehaak suspected that the black mound near the center of the destruction must be the bloomery. It stood like a malignancy in the center of a circle of devastation. Unused charcoal lay in a large heap nearby.

This ravaged land was where Laakea had grown up. Rehaak wondered how it had affected the boy's psyche. To Laakea this devastation would have been normal, since he would have known nothing else. Rehaak felt nauseated by the ruin around him. Even Abrhaani loggers like Raamya and his sons only used dead and dying trees. They would not leave a swath of damage like this in their wake.

Laakea picked his way cautiously through the clearing, scanning ahead for any sign of danger. His senses strained to see, hear, and smell danger before it waylaid them. He noticed things that had changed in the months since he had been gone. As they edged toward the forge, nothing moved other than a few birds fluttering from bush to bush and the occasional small animal, startled from cover by their presence. He noticed that the clearing smelled of smoke and soot. He had lived here all his life and had never noticed the smell before. Perhaps his home had not changed so much after all. Perhaps he was the one who had changed.

The tension eased slightly when they arrived at the forge to find it deserted. There was no one at the house either. Aelfric had deserted it as well. There was no sign anyone had been there in many days.

"See," said Rehaak quietly. "There was no reason for you to worry at all."

"There is still plenty of reason to worry. Just because he is not here now does not mean he won't come back and when he does, it will mean trouble for both of us. But more importantly, it means I have a lot of work to do," replied Laakea, peevishly. He secretly worried about his father's well being. The lack of livestock indicated that some drastic unknown change had taken place here.

"Well, if it's all right with you young sir, I shall see what your father has left to eat in the house. I swear I am as hungry as a bear in springtime. Oh — and where are those sheep you mentioned? I saw a vegetable garden over there too." He waved in the direction of the house. "Unless of course, you need my help to prepare the forge."

"No go ahead, just stay nearby, I will only need your help to work the bellows, once I have the fire going in the forge. At least Pa left enough charcoal for the task ahead. When you're through stuffing yourself, could you draw water from the well and fill this slack tub to quench the blade once I have shaped it?" He thought the last statement might be a trifle optimistic. It could be days before he had shaped the blades enough that they would need to be tempered.

"Yes sir!" Rehaak saluted smartly and turned, toward the house in the best imitation of a soldier on duty he could muster.

Laakea knew he was trying to lighten the mood, but found it difficult to enjoy Rehaak's levity with so many things on his mind. The prospect of making weapons for himself, lacking his father's guidance was daunting enough, without the possibility of a trial by combat looming over his head, at the same time.

He set the nine weapons on the ledge of the forge and began to gather fuel for the forge. Though there was plenty of the material stockpiled around the clearing, it took him quite a while to gather it into the forge-house. The sun was already beginning to sink below the treetops before he felt he that had enough charcoal for a decent fire. It was familiar work and it brought memories of better times flooding back into his mind.

He suddenly realized he had not seen Rehaak in several hours and fear began to gnaw at the back of his mind. He picked up two of the long knives from the forge. He had not seen or heard any evidence of a disturbance, but Rehaak always found trouble no matter where he went.

"Damn you Spot, I told you to stay close. Where in all the hells have you gone?" he muttered as he headed for the house.

There was no sign of his friend outside his former home. He was reluctant to call out lest his call draw unwanted attention to them. He knew it was irrational but he couldn't help himself. Finally, after checking outside thoroughly, he opened the door of the house and peered inside. There was no sign of his missing companion in the main room. He paused to look around.

It felt strange to revisit the building where he had spent so much of his life. He knew it had only been a few months since his departure, but things had changed. This was no longer his home. Devoid of his parent's presence, it seemed smaller and colder than he remembered it. He realized again, how much he missed his mother. Tears had just begun to well up in his eyes when he heard noises coming from the room where he used to sleep.

He cautiously approached his doorway. He tore aside the blankets that hung in the doorway. Knives in hand, he leapt through the opening, tense and ready for combat. Rehaak was snoring blissfully in his old bed.

"Damn — Spot!" he swore, when he saw the source of the noise.

At the sound of Laakea's shout, Rehaak lurched into a seated position, completely befuddled, trying to get his eyes to focus and to remember where he was.

"Get out of my bed and get some water like I asked!"

"You don't have to shout, I fell asleep, but I am not deaf — at least not yet."

"We have so much work to do. This is no time to sleep!" As soon as the words were out of his mouth, Laakea regretted saying them.

The look on Rehaak's face displayed the deep hurt caused by Laakea's angry outburst, but he didn't respond in kind. He got out of the bed, left the room, and went outside, leaving Laakea dithering over what to do next. He knew Rehaak was still weak from his wounds and needed more rest. Abrhaani did not seem to heal as fast as Eniila. He was sure his words; had hurt his friend. He seemed to have a special talent for hurting people, just like his father. He couldn't take it back so he supposed he would just have to live with the consequences. If Rehaak wanted to disown him, that was his right. He would be free of his *Sword Oath* to him and that would be that. He followed Rehaak out into the yard.

They both began working, without saying anything else to each other. By the time they finished preparing, it became obvious that it was far too late in the day to even light the forge, much less begin the forging. Laakea was not sure how long it would take to forge the swords he wanted, but he knew they would be there for several days, perhaps longer.

Once Rehaak had filled the tub with water, he walked over to where Laakea was fussing with the charcoal on the forge and laid his hand on the boy's shoulder. He began to speak even before Laakea had the opportunity to turn to face him.

"I know that you are worried, about the forging, about your father, and just recently you were worried about my safety. I know that's why you were short tempered and that you did not intend to be so harsh. I also know that I should have told you where I was going or what I was doing." He stopped speaking and waited for the boy to respond.

Laakea looked into Rehaak's eyes without responding. He had understood that Rehaak could sense what he was feeling and put it into words far better than he could himself. It had always disturbed him before, but now he accepted it without the usual feelings of discomfort. He had always felt uncomfortable looking into Rehaak's eyes because he was sure the man was able to read his thoughts, but right now, he was grateful that he had not needed to put his feelings into words. Rehaak had done him a great service and he acknowledged it by looking steadily into his friend's eyes for the first time.

Rehaak was the one who broke the silence and looked away.

"It is almost dark. We should make ourselves something to eat and get some rest. We can start your project in the morning, at first light, if you like. I do not think your father will return here. Call me foolish if you want, but I believe he is gone forever."

"You may be right, the sheep are gone too, and he would've left them if he intended to come back."

"Pity, they would have made for some good eating."

"You always think about your stomach, Spot. It's a wonder you are not as big as a mithun, but I think you are right about my father." Laakea smiled, for the first time all day.

"Let's eat then." Rehaak turned and walked to the house with Laakea behind him.

Once they had finished their meal, they sat by the hearth. Rehaak smoked his pipe while quietly staring into the flames of the fire.

"Rehaak, I am very sorry for the way I treated you today," Laakea began.

"I thought we already dealt with that."

"I know you did, but I still needed to say it. I don't know how to control myself sometimes, and my anger gets the better of me. As a matter of fact, that's how I ended up disgracing myself and dishonoring my father, and that's why I still worry about the *bloodlust*."

"Everyone makes mistakes boy."

"I know that, but then we have to pay the price for those mistakes, don't we?"

"I suppose that is true, but sometimes people may choose k'harsa, instead of justice."

"I have never heard of this k'harsa."

"Well — suppose you had done me wrong."

"Like today?"

"No, today we were both wrong. I should have helped, instead of having a nap and causing you to worry about me. I mean — for example, if you had stolen something from me. What would your code require of you?

"That's easy; you'd bring accusation against me. I'd deny the accusation and then we'd fight to the death to demonstrate who was telling the truth."

"And that would be justice as far as your people are concerned?"

"Yes."

"But if you stole from me and afterward you killed me in combat, you would have then stolen not only my goods, but also my life. How is that justice?

"The gods decide the outcome, they determine what's just, according to their will."

Rehaak shook his head sadly, unsure of how to explain the concept of k'harsa to the youngster. Obviously, the word had no meaning for Laakea. "Could the Eniila have forgotten this word altogether?"

"What if I decided not to accuse you of theft? What if I decided, to make a gift to you, of the thing you had taken from me?"

"Only someone who was a coward, or afraid to do battle, would do that."

Rehaak refined the analogy, "Alright, how about this. Suppose I knew beyond any doubt, that you had stolen from me and I knew with equal certainty, that I could easily defeat you in combat. Suppose that knowing these two facts, I still chose not to fight, but instead chose to allow you to keep what you had stolen."

"That's crazy! Why'd anyone choose to do that?"

"It was my property; can I not choose to do whatever I wish with it?"

"Yes, but why —?"

"When you can answer that question, you will know the meaning of the word k'harsa."

"Aaah! You make my head hurt with all your riddles. Why don't you just answer the question?"

"If I do that, you will never truly understand the answer."

"And how'll that be different than right now?" snapped Laakea in frustration. "I'm going to sleep. He rose and stomped into his bedroom, leaving Rehaak alone in front of the dying fire.

CHAPTER 20: SEAPORT

It had been almost two full tendays of hard marching, since he had lost the boat and some of his gear, to the rocks and the surf, but he had managed to struggle ashore with his weapons and his pack. Aelfric was almost at his goal. He could see the outlines of the masts in the harbor against the silver morning light. The ocean reflected light from the sky, like a sheet of beaten metal stretching toward the horizon. He could just make out the darker blues and purples of the opposite shore. Silhouettes of the distant mountains of his homeland, their indigo edges delineated against the bright background of the sky, cast their hazy outlines at the very edge of his sight.

Blue gray morning had come, with the air moist and misty around him. It wasn't cold, but the light breeze, combined with the damp air, gave the day an edge that fit well with the sharp shadows of morning. A hot breakfast would be a comfort, if he could get a fire lit. There was plenty of wood but it was not easy to light, being damp from the spray and impregnated with salt.

The gravel of the beach slid and grated under his feet, crunching with every step, slowing him down, and tiring him. It was still easier going here than thrashing through the thick brush further from the shoreline with his gear and the heavy pack strapped to his back. There were no thorny branches here to tear at his face and hands, and no obstacles hidden in the bracken to snare his tired feet.

After several unsuccessful attempts to light a fire, he gave up. He pulled some jerked meat from his pouch and began to chew it, as he continued his long slog toward the harbor. He had seen very few people along the way. Not many hazarded the rocks and gravelly beaches of this side of Kel Braah. Those he had encountered gave him a wide berth. They knew instinctively that he was dangerous and deadly both in body and in spirit. His resolve had hardened to a brittle crystalline edge. He was going home, home to bloodshed and mayhem, home to vengeance and violence. Now all he needed was a ship to take him across Syn Gersuul. That was why he was here.

With luck, that ship was waiting for him there. He could feel it in his bones. His will propelled him forward, overruling his tired legs. He strode onward for the better part of two hours, lost in his own thoughts. He was striding down the street to the wharf, before he even realized he had arrived in the town. The townspeople regarded him warily from the doors of their shops, and peered at him from around the corners of the squared stone buildings.

He walked alone among hundreds of them, but they were still afraid of him. Sixteen or so years of living among them had altered his viewpoint slightly. That was an understatement.

He had come to realize that the Abrhaani, for all their shortcomings were a far more tolerant people than his own race. They were far more kind and understanding than even the members of the *Brotherhood*, the Eniila Holy Men, who guarded their cities of refuge. That tolerance and understanding was, in a way, their greatest strength, but it was also their greatest weakness. They needed some backbone put in them, as far as he was concerned.

He smiled a grim smile inwardly. He imagined how he must look to them now, no longer the quiet village smith. Now he was a strange warrior, armed and lethal. He was huge, battle scarred, as hard and unrelenting as the metal of the sword that hung across his back, or swift and deadly as the bow in his hand. He was the embodiment of their nightmares, come to pay a visit in the bright morning. Death had come to visit the port of Aeron Suul. It stalked through the main street of their beloved village and it wore Aelfric's scarred face.

On the fields of battle, before he had come to live among them, he had faced thousands of their little soldiers in countless skirmishes. He had mowed them as a scythe mows grass. He did not fear them, not then, and certainly not now. He had killed better men than these on his way to a real battle and would possibly do so again, later he hoped rather than sooner. The score that he intended to settle was not with them but with his own kind.

He rounded the corner that led him out onto the wharf, as he disdainfully turned his back on them. He strode confidently down the center of the wharf, as he walked past crates of cargo, smelling the salt and freshly caught fish in the air. He ignored the dockworkers and deckhands, who stopped to stare. Many of the villagers had never seen anyone like him before, but these men surely had. He ignored the ships that were obviously unloading goods and came to a stop in front of a newer looking ship, where men were loading trade goods into its hold. He had no more time to waste. Sixteen years had passed him by in a heartbeat, and all he had to show for it was an empty ache in his heart, where cold anger and bitter vengeance had taken the place of his wife and son.

He halted. Work stopped. Deckhands stared.

He waited for a second before fixing his gaze on the Abrhaani deckhand nearest him.

"Where is the master of this vessel?" he boomed.

He noticed that although the man looked ready to dash away, he stood his ground. He also noticed a crowd growing around him. If he let them get up enough nerve, they might try to overwhelm him with their numbers. He had no doubt that some of these men had fought his kind before and some of them might even have an old score to settle with him as a representative of his race. If they attacked him, he was not sure he would be willing to pay the cost of that encounter. It was best to press on quickly before tempers flared and the situation got out of control.

"I said," he thundered, loud enough for all those assembled to hear clearly. "Where is the master of this vessel? I wish to book passage to Baradon."

"I will take you to him sir," the deckhand answered, with a steady voice. His courage, obviously bolstered by the growing number of other Abrhaani hovering around the blonde, battle scarred giant, who stood shouting at him.

"Be so good as to follow me please." With that said, he walked past Aelfric toward the village, back the way he had just come.

The crowd on the wharf parted to let the two men through, and Aelfric could hear the murmur of their voices, as they talked in hushed tones among themselves. He knew he wasn't out of danger yet, but at least he was getting somewhere. If they intended to ambush him in an alley, they would be at a disadvantage. Their numbers would be ineffective against his strength in a confined space.

He was almost sure that he had won this battle of wits by sheer audacity. Then he saw a bowman scramble onto a roof. The archer cocked and aimed his crossbow squarely at Aelfric's chest. Aelfric pretended not to see, but he tensed for the release of the arrow. An arrow flies faster than a thrown weapon. He prayed that the fool would release his bolt too soon; at a long range, he should have time enough to swat it aside, if he hadn't gotten too old and soft.

Each step he took brought him closer to his potential assassin. Each step reduced his chances for survival, but he pressed on, behind the man leading the way. He considered using his guide as a shield, but the man was too far ahead and he was too large a target for it to work properly. His tension grew with each step. This bowman knew his craft. It was one of his own axioms. "Be sure of your target for the first shot or you may not have time for a second."

He walked on trying to exude a confidence that he did not feel. "Tell that fool on the roof to put up his weapon before I climb up there and feed it to him, splinter by splinter," he growled to his guide, hoping to defuse the situation. "I have no wish to begin a fracas but I swear I will end it, and it will end badly for you, if it is forced upon me.

His guide turned to look back at him. Seeing the resolve in Aelfric's eyes, he shouted to the bowman. "Put up yur weapon yuh ass, unless yuh're trying to get the lot o' us killed. If 'e wanted tuh do us harm he would'a done it long a'fore now, an 'e would'na come alone."

The bowman hesitated, and then lowered his crossbow. Aelfric almost sighed in relief. Instead, he bowed to the bowman with a flourish. The bowman nodded his acknowledgement and began to descend the far side of the sloped roof. Once he had disappeared below the peak, Aelfric breathed a sigh of relief. With that bit of bother safely concluded, he focused his attention on the street in front of him once more. This village was far different from the one near his farm. The Abrhaani here made their houses and shops from squared blocks of stone, not timbers like the ones he was accustomed to seeing.

Sod, not wooden shingles covered the gently sloping roofs. Each house had the usual Abrhaani garden planted with herbs and vegetables of various kinds. He could see few trees of any size nearby, but there were plenty of squarish broken stones along the shoreline. The materials at hand must have dictated the methods of construction.

His Abrhaani guide turned down a side street and walked a few paces, before he stopped in front of a small shop with a brightly painted sign. Aelfric could not read the characters on the sign, but the pictogram indicated that it was some sort of trading establishment.

"Duh master's in here," his guide pointed to the door.

"I suspect you had best go first and give me an introduction."

"I reckon yuh be right. He might think we bin invaded if yuh was tuh go first," his guide smiled sagely, and went through the dark doorway, into the shop."

Aelfric had to duck to get through the doorway, which the Abrhaani had built for their smaller bodies. The average Abrhaani stood just about chest height to Aelfric. Very few stood as tall as his broad shoulders.

Shelves and crates lined the walls, organized in neat rows in the dimly lit interior of the shop. Trade goods of all kinds lay on display on the tops of the crates and boxes. In the far end of the shop, a curtain hung across the door to the back room or office. There were voices coming from the room behind it.

"Duh master be in duh back sir, I'll fetch him out fer yuh."

Aelfric stood at ease among the crates and trade goods near the entrance. He chose the position for two reasons. First, he did not want to appear to intrude and offer insult to the Abrhaani, second he wanted to be able to get out quickly if negotiations went badly. He stood sideways to both doors, so that he could see both in his peripheral vision. He did not have long to wait. The conversation in the back room ended as his guide entered and when the curtains parted again. A large Abrhaani man emerged followed by his guide and another Abrhaani of similar build.

The men approached slowly through the semi gloom of the shop and stopped just outside of arm's length. The large man in the lead looked carefully at Aelfric for a moment and started to grin.

"It's been a long spell since I laid eyes on yuh. Last time we met yuh offered me a King's ransom tuh bring yuh tuh the south. I warn't sure yuh would survive the boat ride tuh the shore let alone be standin in front o' me again now — what — fifteen or so years on? An' where's dat woman o'yours.

"My compliments to you captain Harmish. It is good to see you again after — sixteen years. I would have believed that you'd have drowned long ago in that leaky tub you used to sail," he said, avoiding the question about Shelhera.

"Well as it so happens, dat ship did sink some years back. But I warn't on it at the time," he laughed. His rough voice sounded more like a seal barking than a laugh. "I sold it tuh another unfortunate fella and bought me a fine new ship. With what yuh gave me as yer fare, and what I got fer d'other, as a down payment." He smiled again and held out his arm in greeting.

The two men clasped each other at the elbow in the common formal greeting.

"I have need of your services again captain, to bear me in the opposite direction this time. Unfortunately, I cannot pay you as much for this crossing. I have only a small purse of gold and some fine silver for trade."

"Should I ask why yuh be wantin tuh go back now, or am I better not knowin, like duh last time?

"Let's just say I want to go home to pay my respects to my family, shall we?

"Nuff said. Yuh can keep yer gold but how much silver duh yuh have."

"I have a half hundred weight in my pack, that I carried with me."

"How far have yuh come?"

"It was three tendays ago I left my house with all that you see on me."

"So yuh was on duh road thirty days luggin dat great heavy sword, and a half a hundred weight o' silver, and provisions? I'm surprised yuh be still standin. I imagine yuh set a good pace too — with dem long legs o' yourn."

"I suppose I did well enough for and old man, but part of my journey was by boat."

"By boat! Who'd a brung yuh by boat?"

"No one. I came alone."

"Well den, where's dis boat o yourn?"

"I lost it twenty days back in a squall. I never claimed to be a seaman and I guess that loss proves that I am not one. It broke apart on the rocks, so I walked the rest of the way. My house was not far from the village called Dun Dale. It's a three-day walk from the town of New Hope. Do you know of it?"

"Gods man! Does I know of it? I trade for lumber from dere for our shipyard. It takes near tuh two months tuh get dere! And yuh done it in twenty days loaded like a pack beast!"

"You might say I took a short cut, and it was nearer to thirty days."

"An I might not say shortcut either. Climbin over all dem rocks and through dat gravel, dat'd not be a shortcut I'd be takin, old man or young, with or without a hundred weight of gear strapped to my back. But enough o' dis jawin, we got a bargain tuh strike about a fare tuh Baradon."

"I wish to leave immediately and the price is whatever you name sir."

"Well den we be leavin with duh tide dis evening, and because of duh luck yuh brung me after duh last trip, yuh can keep yer silver too. I could'a just as easy bin on dat ol boat o' mine had yuh not paid so 'ansomly fer duh last trip. I reckon I owes yuh dat much at least, fer causin duh gods tuh favor me summat."

"I'll have no truck with the gods, if it please you Harmish," Aelfric growled. "They have done me no favors."

"Well be dat as it may, dey seems to have truck with yuh, whether yuh likes it or not. So get tuh the Sea Witch, and stow yer gear. Hermad here," he pointed to the guide. "Will show yuh where. We leaves in about three hours. Yuh might want tuh stop and get a good feed afore we leaves — or maybe not — as I recollects yuh warn't able tuh keep it down on duh last trip. Maybe it'd just be a waste o' good vittles." He grinned broadly at Aelfric, still obviously amused that such a powerful warrior had succumbed so horribly to seasickness on his previous voyage.

Aelfric nodded, glumly acknowledging the fact that his stomach had not been up to the challenge of the pitching waves. Privately, he hoped that this trip would not be a repeat of that ghastly experience. He was a man

213

of the earth and preferred good solid ground beneath his feet. The constant rolling and heaving of the Syn Gersuul, under the ship, had been a source of nearly unbearable discomfort for him and Shelhera. Their infirmity had provided the sailors with hours of amusement. He decided to pass on the food and head directly for the ship. He had no wish to repeat the episodes of retching and heaving, while hanging over the rail of the ship. He hoped it would be better on an empty stomach.

"Duh *Witch* has another passenger besides yerself. He be a fine gentleman from Narragansett, headed east, just like yer lordship."

"Oh, I tend to keep my own company."

"Kinda hard tuh do dat on shipboard. It's close quarters my friend."

Aelfric was not pleased at the prospect of sharing the voyage with some dandy from the big city, although he did wonder what business an Abrhaani gentleman would have in Baradon. He began to head for the door, with Hermad in tow.

"Just take me to the ship Hermad, and show me where to bunk and where to stow my gear," he said with finality.

CHAPTER 21: THE FORGING

Laakea and Rehaak rose early to the sound of birdsong in their ears. The sky was beginning to pale in the east. Rehaak started a fire, and began to prepare breakfast. He had learned that it was better if he did the cooking rather than Laakea. Rehaak told the boy that the food he cooked was just barely over the thin line, between edible and carrion. Blacksmith cooking, as Rehaak named it, at its finest far too often resembled the charcoal that fueled the forge.

Whatever skills his parents had imparted to their offspring, did not include the culinary arts. Perhaps they lacked the skill, so they could not pass on something they never possessed. It was a challenge for Rehaak to cook in this kitchen, where finding the ingredients even for breakfast was an adventure. He decided that he preferred that test to the trial of trying to choke Laakea's cooking down, or the even greater ordeal of trying to keep it down.

Laakea went straight to the forge and lit the charcoal. He began to get the tools and implements he would need to reforge the blades they had collected from the dead assassins. He knew it would take considerable time just to weld the blades together, let alone make serviceable swords from them.

Laakea had decided to make two swords instead, of one. It was his first time making something as complex as a sword. If they were both serviceable weapons it would be wonderful, but Laakea only expected one to any good. He remembered all the theory his father had taught him, but theory and reality were often very different things. He fully expected that the first weapon would be a practice run. If he got them both right, it would be nothing short of miraculous. He put two of the long knives in the coals to preheat, when Rehaak called him to breakfast.

The heat would drive the moisture out of the metal, so when he came back to do the welding he would have to spend less time bringing them up to welding temperature. He would need Rehaak's help to work the bellows for that. He hoped that his friend had recovered sufficient strength to keep the charcoal hot enough. The grey-green metal of the knives was unfamiliar to him, but he suspected it was going to take high heat to get the stuff to weld decently. It was going to be a long day for both of them.

After breakfast, they began to work. Laakea showed Rehaak how to work the bellows properly and bring the metal up to temperature. Rehaak caught on quickly. It was a simple task, which required little skill but a lot of stamina. Once Laakea had taken the white hot metal from the fire to the anvil, Rehaak took a break from pumping the bellows. Laakea began the long process of welding the two knives into one solid piece of metal, by pounding and folding them on the anvil. Rehaak slipped off to get drinking water. He suspected they were both going to need a lot of water, in the heat of the forge.

With the first few hammer strokes, Laakea began to realize, the process of welding the blades together to form a new one, was not going well. Though he had no way to explain what was wrong, he knew something was different about the metal he was working. The outer layer of the blades was unlike any steel he had ever worked. It proved to be much harder than the underlying metal. It would not bond to the other blade at all. The blades reacted to his blows strangely. The outer coating stretched and deformed around the softer core metal, like water skins filled with mud. The runes worked into the metal of the blades, stretched and distorted, but little else seemed to be happening.

The longer he kept at it the more aggravated he became. His hammer blows became the vehicles of his frustration, until he was no longer trying to work the metal at all, but rather he was punishing it for not obeying his will. He was so absorbed in attacking the metal with his hammer, that he did not notice Rehaak return to the forge, and stand silently watching his progress, or rather the lack of it.

Finally, when he had exhausted himself he picked up the still glowing metal and threw it back into the forge.

Rehaak, seeing the anger in the boy's actions, went back to the bellows and began pumping them to bring the charcoal back up to heat.

"Never mind," Laakea snarled. "It's useless." Sweat poured off him, and his clothes were soaked.

"There is something wrong, either with me, or the metal and I don't know how to make it right."

"Yes," replied Rehaak, wrinkling up his nose. "There is definitely something wrong with you. You smell very much like a corpse left out in the sun for — oh, are those carrion birds I see gathering in that tree over there." He smiled and pointed out toward the forest. "I think they smell a potential meal."

Rehaak's words broke Laakea's foul mood.

"Are you so sure it's not you they smell, you old manure pile?"

K. R. Schultz

"Wait," Rehaak pretended to smell his armpits. "(*Sniff*) No — (*Sniff*) not me — must be you."

At this, they both began to laugh, pushing each other around the forge, until they both found themselves outside in the sunlight. The cool breeze felt good to Laakea. He had not realized how hot it was inside the forge shelter. It was approaching midday and it felt good to take a break after the morning's exertions.

"I am hungry," Rehaak announced.

"You're always hungry," Laakea countered.

"But I am still recovering from my wounds. I need sustenance to complete my healing."

"If you aren't recovered soon, the land will be stripped bare." Laakea waved his arms in the air at the vultures that Rehaak's imagination had conjured up earlier. "Fly away, poor little carrion eaters! Flee! Flee for your lives lest you be devoured along with the rest, you poor defenseless beasts!"

They both broke out into laughter again. Laakea was tired, and at least as hungry as Rehaak. He decided he would attempt to solve the riddle of the blades after lunch.

"Let's eat. We can continue this later," he pointed in the direction of the smithy.

The afternoon came and went. The only change was that Laakea was more tired and frustrated than before. All he had to show for his exertions were two misshapen masses of metal not the one smooth bar he wanted. He could barely lift his arms. He knew he should feel irritated and angry because of the lack of progress, but he had no energy left to spend on those emotions.

The metal coating one blade refused to bond to the metal of another. It was as if the stuff had a memory and a will and refused to take any shape, other than the one it originally held. Laakea knew that was impossible, because the stuff could not have sprung from the earth fully formed. Someone had worked it to make it what it now was. Someone had imposed his will on it to form it into the knives.

Rehaak was equally exhausted, and after they had washed up and had supper the two men sat before the fire, while Laakea explained his problem with the forging to him.

"Ah," intoned Rehaak solemnly. He nodded his head as he listened to Laakea pour out his frustration.

"Do you understand?" asked Laakea as he finished his explanation.

"I understand that you are working with two different materials, and I understand that one of them refuses to allow you to shape it, but I am afraid that much of what you are telling me is outside of my understanding. There are some words you use that I, regrettably, do not comprehend at all."

"Oh."

"I suspect that what I feel now is akin to what you felt listening to me try to explain the concept of k'harsa. We speak the same language at its roots, but there are words and concepts integral to each of our races that have no equivalents in the other's language and culture. What on Aarda must the Sokai be like, if they still live? Meeting the Sokai — that would be an interesting experience," Rehaak mused aloud, as his attention began to wander again.

Laakea had held out a faint hope, that his friend might have some insight, which would make the problem go away. When nothing useful was forthcoming, he sat quietly, ruminating over the problems he was facing, and weighing the options he had left if he was unsuccessful. He needed to resolve this puzzle, or they would have to continue with what resources they had in hand.

He hated to admit defeat but he was not sure how much time they could afford to waste, while he tried to resolve his dilemma at the forge. He was glad that he had only committed two of the blades to his project. Seven unspoiled blades remained, a small arsenal, and more than he could use, but he wanted the extra reach, that longer weapons would give him. He still felt strongly that he needed to complete his apprenticeship by forging the weapons he envisioned. He felt sure that there was more at stake in the forging than simply creating new and better weapons.

The two misshapen pieces at the forge upset him, but they presented him with a challenge that intrigued and excited him as well. He had enough charcoal to make many more attempts; he would keep at it until the supply ran out. If he could not master the metal by then, they would move on without new weapons. He had made his decision and he was willing to live with it. That was the Eniila way, make a choice and be willing to live with the consequences.

"What cannot be overcome must be endured," he muttered another of his father's aphorisms.

In the morning, they began again, though their muscles ached from the exertion of the previous day. The next several days went much the same. Finally, at the end of the fourteenth day Laakea decided that if he could not get the metal to bond, he would work from the tip to the tang to see if he could force the core of steel out of the hard metal sheath that held it. He thought that he might be able to save that metal and forge a decent weapon from it alone. In spite of his obsession with the project, he knew that they eventually must give up, if he did not succeed soon.

The difficult work was hardening both men. They fell into bed exhausted each night, only to rise the next day to begin again. Their unrelenting exertions blunted even Rehaak's sense of humor. It was not like him to keep a punishing pace like this for so long, but he did not want Laakea to feel alone in his quest. He would work until he dropped, if necessary. He owed the lad his life, and he found the work easier each day. Even he could see that they could not continue for too much longer. Charcoal would eventually run out, and he doubted that Laakea would spend the time and energy to make any more.

The changes in his body amazed him. He had become stronger than he had ever been before, although he was still a weakling compared to Laakea. His muscles had become only slightly larger, although he was much harder and leaner. He had not gained size like his young partner, who had gotten positively gigantic from his continued exertions at the forge. The discipline that Laakea exhibited was new to him. He admired the young man for it. The idea struck him like Laakea's hammer, that there was plenty of welding going on in this place. It was just unfortunate that it was not metal-to-metal. They worked as a team now, welded together by the constant pounding of their work in the smithy. These were his thoughts, as he sweated and strained through the long days. Suddenly, Laakea paused his hammering and let out a whoop of triumph.

"What happened Rehaak asked?"

"The minute I squeezed the last of the softer metal out of its sheath, the skin appeared to work easier."

"I take it that is a good thing?"

"It's a very good thing. Perhaps I can work the outer layer into one sheet, wrap it around the core, and weld it on the opposite edge, just like sewing up a wineskin. As long as I tried to work the two metals while they were together, it was impossible, but now that I have them separated, I may be able work them like normal steel. I don't know what it is but this outer metal is not steel."

"The outer metal is hard and light while the inner steel is heavy and flexible. It adds mass to the blade and helps to absorb shock. The outside was strong and tough, sharp, but it might be brittle. It's too early to tell yet. Without the soft center to stabilize it, the blade might have shattered on impact. The center, though resilient, would never hold a proper edge. The outer metal alone would not have enough weight to cleave armor or bone properly.

"Does it have to be heavy to do that?" asked Rehaak. "It would seem to me that a lighter blade would be easier to wield, and that should make it better."

"Well, it takes as much force to stop a blade as it does to swing it in the first place. Have you ever noticed how a heavy axe splits woods easier than a light one?"

"Yes, actually I have noticed that."

"It's the same with weapons. A light weapon may be easy to wield, but when it encounters a dense object in its path, it will bounce off unless its user is able to swing it very fast. A heavier weapon will cut through with a slower swing, but it requires more strength to move it quickly. That makes it awkward to use for defense. The balance of the blade is another issue that needs to be taken into account."

"There are also similar tradeoffs with hard or soft metals. Hard metal will usually hold an edge well, but it may chip or shatter. Soft metal will not shatter easily but it will also not hold an edge well. It is always a balancing act. More carbon means harder steel, but harder steel may not be the best steel for your purpose."

"As a smith works the steel, he actually works the carbon out of the steel making it less brittle and hard, until its right for his purposes. Most people believe that the opposite is true but that is a myth. There is another myth that quenching a sword in blood makes it better than quenching it in water."

"What on earth is carbon? And how does it get into —," As he was speaking, he noticed Laakea beginning to work up another long explanation. "Never mind — don't even bother trying to explain it to me. I used to think we spoke the same language, but now I'm not so sure."

"I may have to work both metals separately, before I can work them together."

"You know," responded Rehaak; "I was just thinking similar thoughts about you and me."

"What d'you mean?"

"Before we met, The Creator shaped us separately through our experiences. Now through our work together he has welded us —. It was just one of many stray notions."

Laakea let the comment slide. He was preoccupied with the forging, and had long since given up expecting a straightforward answer, when Rehaak was in one of his philosophical moods.

Laakea's optimism quickly faded, as his renewed efforts failed to produce results. The strange metal remained spectacularly stubborn as it resisted his will again. In moments, he went from exuberance to despair as the obstinate stuff mocked his efforts. In a fit of loathing, he picked up the hot metal with his tongs and threw it into a corner. The metal caused the moisture in the dirt floor of the forge to steam as it lay there, cooling slowly. He threw down his tools, while muttering, "That's it. I give up."

Laakea had no sooner spoken the words, than they heard noises outside. Both men looked at each other and reached for the weapons available to them. Rehaak grasped a stout piece of wood to use as a club, while Laakea picked up a pair of heavy steel tongs in one hand and held his hammer in the other. With no more than a glance at each other, they took positions on either side of the open door of the smithy. Shirtless and sweating they stood waiting, tense but calm, ready to deal with whatever came through the open doorway.

Nothing came through the doorway, except the sound of a gravelly voice.

"What is dat horrible stench I smells from in dere? Pee — eeuw —! Smells like a barrel chock full o' unwashed arseholes tuh me!"

"Isil? Is that you out there? Rehaak grinned at Laakea and dropped his makeshift club.

"Yup. Come out here and air yerself out, so's we ken talk proper. Cause dere ain't no way I'm comin in dere. Dat place smells wors'n a stink-cats backside. Don't yuh wash no more?"

Rehaak stepped out into the bright sunlight with Laakea behind him. Isil looked them both over appraisingly.

"I sees yuh got yerself a new hairdo huh? And who be dis strappin lad with yuh?" She grinned at the young giant beside him, feasting her eyes on the rippling, sweat soaked muscles of his chest and arms.

"I sees yuh has gained a lot o' muscle Rehaak. Yuh no longer looks like duh pallid scholar I imagines yuh was afore settin out on duh road. Yuh has taken tuh shavin too I sees. If I had not read your note, tuh come here I might have passed yuh by on duh street and not known yuh at all."

"Isil, allow me to introduce my protector and savior Laakea."

Laakea bowed to the older woman and said. "Pleased to make your acquaintance Ma'am. Rehaak has told me about your adventures with him."

Isil acknowledged his greeting, by flashing her famous smile at him.

"Well now that we have the formalities out of the way, let us pause to get to know each other better. I think a meal is in order, do you not agree?" Rehaak looked hopefully at Laakea.

Laakea shrugged helplessly; there was no point in arguing with Rehaak. He was tired and hungry too. It would be impolite to try to continue to work in the forge with Isil just arrived. His mother had taught him better manners than that.

He was ready to abandon the whole project now anyway. Why should he torture himself any longer? They all made their way over to the house where Isil and Rehaak began to work together to prepare some food. Laakea protested that since it was his house, as a proper host, he should rightfully be the one preparing the meal.

Rehaak laughed and said, "If it is a proper host you want to be, you had best not be poisoning the guests with the stuff you cook and call food."

"You're lucky I am a proper host, or I'd part your hair with a blade, like your six friends did that night."

Isil laughed at the easy banter that passed between the two men. The bond between them was plainly obvious through it.

"Yuh two sound like an old married couple, but never mind dat. What happened since I wuz last at yer hut Rehaak? Who gave yuh duh new hairstyle, not dat I find it unattractive," she teased.

Rehaak started by telling her about the miller's son, and followed with the story of his second encounter with the knife-wielding assassins. Laakea filled in the blanks where necessary, adding his own comments along the way. Once Rehaak had finished his story, Laakea took up the narrative, where Rehaak's memory was still sketchy. He ended with his conclusions about the origin and purpose of the attacks.

"Yuh see? I'm not duh only one what thinks yer duh target o' dis nonsense."

"Good," Laakea grinned. "Maybe two of us can get the idea through his thick skull, since he wouldn't listen to just me."

"Well, I still don't see why anyone would expend this much energy to pay someone to kill me," Rehaak countered.

"Neither do I — yet. Are you sure there isn't something you've forgotten?'

"Yup, be dere somethin you ain't tellin us bout yer past den? I got my own ideas bout duh source o' dis trouble but we best know everythin, just in case."

"What do you mean? Your own ideas?" asked Rehaak.

"I'll be tellin yuh directly, but answer duh question first."

"I have already examined my memory. For all my misdeeds and failures, I can think of nothing that should earn me the kind of malevolent intentions that hound me now.

"No jealous husbands, nor cheated business partners? Stuff o' that sort'll earn yuh grief fer sure."

"Yes, if you want our help, Rehaak you'll have to tell us your whole story, so we know what we're up against and can prepare for it."

Rehaak felt trapped and outnumbered. One part of him wanted to come clean with his two friends, but another part of him wanted to keep his secrets. It was like his dreams of being naked and trying to hide coming to life. He got up to leave. He wanted to run far and fast as he headed for the doorway. He needed fresh air to clear his head, at least that is what he wanted to believe. He recognized that it was a convenient lie, but he was not going to stay, in spite of that knowledge.

"Stop where you are," Laakea commanded, in a voice that rang with irresistible authority.

Rehaak stopped, compelled by the power of that voice, unable to move any farther towards the door. He looked helplessly at Isil, and found her similarly paralyzed. He managed to turn his head far enough to see Laakea. The boy looked almost as stunned as he and Isil. Once the compulsion wore off, they all stood quietly looking at one another. Laakea spoke first.

"What just happened?"

"I dunno. You did it, whatever it was. I'd 'spect yuh tuh know what yuh did?"

"Yes. It was your voice Laakea, but there was power in it that stopped me, as if I had run into the wall of a house. Are you sure your parents never mentioned this ability to you?"

"No! I'm sure I'd remember if they had."

"I think we be needin to just sit a spell and talk dis over," said Isil. "I think we gotta all lay everythin out in duh open. Dere's too much goin on dat we don't know 'bout."

"Fine. I'll go first," said Laakea, still feeling emboldened and strengthened by the aftereffects of the power that had surged up within him moments ago. He felt like he could face almost any peril or hazard and overcome it.

Rehaak was astonished at the uncharacteristic boldness the lad was displaying and envied him his courage. "No," he said sheepishly. "I should go first since I have only been partially honest with both of you from the beginning."

"Yuh got no monopoly on secrets dere, friend, but yuh can go first if yuh likes. But, I believes I should be duh first so's I can splain what I thinks is happenin, and you can be next. Duh lad can go last, as he's likely not tuh have accumulated duh history we has."

"It's all right by me," said Laakea. "Just as long as we can get on with it and get it over with. Rehaak already knows everything about me anyway."

He looked at both Rehaak and Isil in turn, as he spoke, "So, no more secrets then."

CHAPTER 22: ISIL'S STORY

"Yuh mightn't like what yer bout tuh hear, but before I says anythin else, I wants yuh tuh know dat I be cumin with yuh. If'n yuh'll have me. Dat's why I'm here. I be done with the freight business. I gave up my monopoly with duh court."

"What did you do with your wagon and your mithun? You told me they wouldn't go anywhere without you," Rehaak interrupted.

"I sold duh wagon and doh it just about broke muh heart tuh let em go, I put duh beasts out to roam and fend fer demselves. Found a right beautiful pasture fer em too. Dey wuz duh best team I ever had, but dey wuz almost past duh age where dey could pull fer much longer anyway. I would'a needed tuh replace em in a year or two, so I retired em early.

"You mean you have given up everything you had to come on this fool's errand with us? Why?"

"I reckon yuh'd best listen tuh my story den, and stop interruptin me every couple o' sentences."

"Yes, please go on Isil. Just ignore him. It's what I always do." Laakea grinned impishly at Rehaak.

Rehaak slapped the big lad on the back of the head with his open hand, as the boy turned to look back at Isil, with feigned impatience.

"Yer both are impossible! I got a good mind tuh thrash yuh both and leave now. Dis is too serious fer such foolishness."

"We're sorry Isil," Rehaak said, finally looking contrite. Laakea nodded his agreement, as they both fell silent.

Isil took a deep breath, as if preparing to lift something heavy, and looked both of them in the eyes before beginning.

"When I wuz a youngster I had duh usual upbringin, I s'pose, My Ma and Pa taught me tuh raise draft mithun. Dey wuz herdsmen demselves. I s'pose dat explains why I ended up with four of 'em and duh wagon. But, dat's only duh beginning and duh end of duh story. In between is where muh real story lies.

When I wuz not much older'n you Laakea, I got tuh feelin like dere wuz too much o' life I wuz missin, livin out dere in duh back o' beyond with muh family and only duh livestock tuh keep us company. Many o' duh folk what used tuh live round our parts had either died or moved on tuh better things, so we wuz out dere almost alone. I wuz restless and fretted about what I should be doin with muh life. Believe it or not, I wuz quite a looker when I wuz younger." she said, and smiled again.

Laakea nodded solemnly and whispered to Rehaak, "I can identify easily with isolation, but I'm having a little trouble imagining Isil as either beautiful or young."

Rehaak nodded understandingly but remained silent."

Isil continued, ignoring the byplay. "Well, when I wuz about ready tuh start climbin out o' my skin from sheer boredom, dis handsome young fella came ridin by on a big animal, a horse, he called it. I never seen such a beast before."

"I have read that they were once numerous in Aarda in ancient times. There seem to be very few left now. Almost all of them that remain are in Baradon. I imagine because they were used in combat, that many must have perished in the wars," interjected Rehaak.

Isil ignored the interruption, and continued, "Muh parents always tol' me dey hoped I would have a better life dan dey did. Duh life of duh herdsmen of duh eastern plain ain't much of a life. I would'a thought dey'd be right happy about muh prospects with dis young fella, but fer some reason, dey just didn' like him. Yuh could tell right off he had money and had seen tings I never even dreamed of. It wuz like heaven, just listenin tuh his tales. I wuz right taken with him from duh get go."

"Muh parents didn' want me tuh have nothin tuh do with him, but I wuz headstrong, and tuh me he wuz a dream come true. When he asked me tuh come with him, I threw muh clothes in a sack, and snuck out tuh go with him, once muh parents wuz a sleepin. Dis fella promised tuh take me away from dat life, and he did it, right enough, but it didn't turn out at all duh way I expected."

"We traveled around a lot in duh beginnin. He had meetins with odd folk all over Khel Braah and he took me along. Eventually, we ended up at his home in duh city of Narragansett. It wuz big and beautiful. It wuz a palace as far as a country girl wuz concerned, and I wuz living out a dream. Fancy people and fancy clothes, parties all day and night. He wuz a good man den, or leastways I thought he wuz."

"He wuz involved in a lot o' different business ventures. I found out later dat some wuz above board, and some wuzn't, but I never knew duh difference, jus' bein duh stupid farm girl I wuz. In duh beginnin, he treated me jus' like a princess outen a storybook. Den I got pregnant with our child. Things began tuh go off track. Eventually he seemed tuh grow tired o' me, called me coarse and unrefined, 'cause I didn't talk and behave like duh big city folks in his social circle. Duh little farm girl didn't fit wit his image as a mover and shaker among duh high and mighty of Narragansett. I tried tuh change tuh please him but it wuz never enough fer him."

"He started disappearin fer days at a time, an I never knew when he would show up, or even if he would show up. I wuz lonely and scared when I wuz by myself, but I wuz even more lonely and scared when he wuz dere with us — little Eyhan our son and me. He had changed intuh someone I didn' recognize any more. I wanted tuh go home but he tol' me dat he would never allow it. Duh boy wuz his, he said, and he would never let me leave with him."

"I didn' realize it at duh time but he wuz in with a real bad bunch o' sick fellas. Anyhow, things began tuh go downhill from dat point on. He tol' me bout dese fellas, his friends, he called dem. He tol' me," her accent disappeared as she mimicked her former husband's voice:

"These men have a lot of powerful friends. They can help us get what we want and make life comfortable for us. Don't you want more for our son than what we have now?"

"He tol' me dis more dan once, so I went along wit' it hopin for duh best, but fearin duh worst. No woman wants tuh believe her man is bad."

"Sometime after dat, I realized he was goin to duh temple late at night. I hoped dat it would do him some good. I thought bein religious might turn him 'round. I didn't know it den, but duh temple in Narragansett is not built for duh worship o' duh Creator. When he invited me tuh come with him one night, I realized his religiosity wuz not a good thing."

"Dey wuz not worshipin duh Creator like muh Ma and Pa and muh Granthers. Dey wuz doin evil things in duh dark o' night. Killin and torturin animals and such. Blood sacrifices to duh Dark Ones. It made me sick, tuh see creatures bein treated like dat, and it wuz even worse when duh Dark Ones started appearin in duh middle of dese ceremonies. Dey wuz enough tuh make a body crawl right outta dere skin."

"Den tings took an even worse turn, when he began tuh ask me tuh do things dat wuz jus not right. Dey wanted tuh use my blood for dere offerings at duh temple. When I refused, muh husband began tuh beat me, tuh try tuh make me do worse things dan jus bleedin."

Rehaak looked as if he had something to say on the topic before he decided to resist the urge to speak.

Laakea was too engrossed in the story for him to consider interrupting.

"Finally, I couldn't take no more; I packed up young Eyhan and ran back tuh muh folks. Leastways, I tried tuh do it. By duh time I wuz most of duh way home, muh man and his friends caught up with me on duh trail. I figured dey would fetch me back to duh city, or jes' take Eyhan away from me and leave me alone, but dey had other plans."

"Dey came with me to duh farm where muh parents still wuz livin. And when we got dere, dey tied me to a tree in front of duh house and left me dere, while dey went in and dragged my poor Ma and Pa outside where I could see em."

Isil paused for a moment, as tears began to roll down her leathery cheeks. Rehaak and Laakea watched and waited for her to begin again, although it looked like she might not be able to continue her story.

She rallied and began again.

"Muh husband wuz holding our little'un, while his friends wuz pullin muh folks out of duh house. I watched him real careful, hopin he would put a stop to

233

what wuz goin on. Eventually he turned his head tuh look at me. I don't know if I can rightly explain what I saw in his eyes right den, but I could see dere wuz no hope o' any rescue in dem."

"I hope tuh never see nuthin like dat again. His eyes wuz all dark. Nuthin livin could look through eyes like dat. Duh look wuz pure evil wickedness. Den he smiled at me. It wuz duh smile he use tuh give me when we first met. It wuz duh smile dat won my heart, leastways dat's how it looked on duh outside, but when yuh saw duh eyes, yuh knew duh smile wuz evil too. I had tuh look away 'cause I thought I wuz gonna get sick tuh my stomach. When I did, I heard muh son scream. I had tuh look back in dat direction. He wuz twistin Eyhan's arm, just tuh hurt him so he would yell and get me a lookin his way again."

"By dis time, his partners had driven stakes in duh ground and tied muh parents nekid and spread-eagled between dem."

She paused again, as if to gather strength.

"You don't need to go on," Rehaak said softly. "I think we can see where this is going."

"No! I need tuh tell someone. Besides dis is important. I couldn't seem tuh remember most of it before, but now it's come back tuh me and dere is somethin yuh got tuh know," she said angrily, as Laakea sat quietly by Rehaak's side.

"Alright, go on then." Rehaak said. Laakea nodded in silent agreement.

"Anyway, like I wuz sayin, dey had muh folks staked out on duh ground. They started chantin some kind o' ritual, and dey started dancing around wavin long knives," her voice trailed off.

"Wait," Laakea interrupted. "Were the knives like the ones we got off the men, who attacked Rehaak?"

"Exactly duh same, from what I could see."

Rehaak blanched at her reply but said nothing.

"So your husband, what did you say his name was?" Laakea asked.

"I didn't, cause I vowed never tuh say his name again, but he wuz called Voerkett." She spat on the floor after saying the name, as if it had brought a vile taste to her mouth.

"So your husband, Voerkett," Laakea went on. "He was part of a group of people following the Dark Ones, and these knives are part of their religious ceremonies.

"Dey use em tuh make sacrifices tuh duh Dark Ones. From what muh husband tol' me, duh sacrifices give power tuh duh Dark Ones. When dey is strong enough, dey'll take physical form an walk among men again. Muh husband tol' me dat when dis happens, dey would give dere followers duh power and ability tuh rule Aarda with em. Dat's what him and his friends wuz after from duh beginnin, and dey claimed tuh be gettin closer tuh it wit' every sacrifice. Dey called the Dark One dey served Ashd'eravaak. Dey said when he came with his army, dat dey would take back all duh lands from duh Eniila, and make dem pay fer what dey done tuh duh Abrhaani."

She looked apologetically at Laakea, waiting for any sign of offense taken.

"How many of them are there?" Rehaak asked, finally ending his silence and breaking into the conversation.

"I can't rightly say, dis wuz more'n ten years back and Voerkett," she spat on the floor again, "claimed dey wuz gainin followers every day. I suspect dat duh travellin we done, when we wuz first together, was him settin up a network o' dese people."

"So they have been preparing for over ten years and are planning a war with the Eniila?" Laakea questioned.

"Oh it be wors'n dat, lad. Dey also be tryin tuh wipe out all those who follows duh Ol' Way too, and near as I can tell, duh three of us, an now duh Millers be duh only ones left anyway."

"What's the Old Way?" Laakea looked puzzled.

"The Old Way is what Isil's people called believing in and following The Creator, or The Faithful One," Rehaak explained to Laakea.

"How do you know they are trying to destroy those who follow The Creator Isil?"

"Because on duh day I wuz tellin yuh bout. Duh day when dey skinned my folks alive while I watched! Duh day when dey cut muh baby's throat as an offerin tuh Ashd'eravaak while I watched!"

Her words came out in a rush, as if the answer should be self-evident to the two men.

"I'm sorry Isil, but if they intend to wipe out The Creator's followers — I don't understand, do you?" said Laakea, while looking at Rehaak.

He paused while Isil tried to control her emotions, and Rehaak just looked puzzled.

They sat silently for a few moments more, while Isil struggled vainly to get a handle on her feelings and proceed with her explanation. She had been able to contain her emotions for a while, but was sobbing violently now, as though some inner floodgate of sorrow had finally burst. Her grief poured out in a deluge from the reservoir of her heart. Hearing her own story, spoken aloud for the first time, in her own voice had broken it free and it swept her along in its powerful current.

"This is something I don't understand either, Laakea. If they were trying to get rid of all the followers of the Old Way —" Rehaak struggled to balance the volume of his words so that the youngster could hear him above Isil's sobbing, but still not disrupt her grieving.

"I know," he replied, matching Rehaak's tone. "Why'd they let her live? If she's a follower of the Old Way, they should have killed her too."

Isil stopped sobbing as he was speaking. He spoke those words into that momentary silence. She looked up at the two men leaning toward each other in conversation, her grief suddenly overcome by another stronger emotion. She hung her head as her face flushed, under the overall darkness of her complexion. Both men turned to look at her, in response to her sudden silence, realizing that she had overheard their discussion. It was their turn to be embarrassed.

"I can answer dat for yuh," she said. Her eyes never left the floor in front of her while she spoke softly. "Dey made me one of dem."

"What!" both men blurted simultaneously, and then fell silent, waiting for an explanation.

"Dey made me one of dem," she repeated, finally looking up from the floor, with anger blazing in her dark eyes, as if the answer was plain to any but the dullest person in Aarda.

"I'm sorry Isil. I do not see how they could do that."

She took a deep breath, as if she prepared to lift something tremendously heavy.

"Duh oath," she paused. "Dey made me forswear duh Old Way, and made me swear allegiance tuh Ashd'eravaak. A blood oath." She lowered her eyes to the floor again, speaking softly into her own chest.

"How did they compel you to do that?"

237

"By tellin me dey were gonna murder muh baby if I didn' do what dey said." The men could feel her anger beginning to rise again, as she spoke.

"How's that possible? Didn't you just tell us that they cut his throat while you were forced to watch?"

"Dey made me swear duh oath first, and den Voerkett tol' me dat great power demands great sacrifices, and we should be willin tuh offer duh greatest sacrifice he could think of, duh life of our son, so he killed Eyhan right dere himself — right in front of me. He drained duh life out of our baby right dere and laughed at me duh whole time he done it," she snarled.

Rehaak and Laakea exchanged glances, before she began again.

"Ashd'eravaak came, and touched me den — touched muh face just for a moment. I felt his power, as he drained life from me. I thought he had stole muh soul. Dey cut me loose den and said dey had anudder use for me, a use dat would seal my covenant with Ashd'eravaak.

Dey took turns ruttin on me, and I let dem cause I didn' feel nuthin anymore. It wuz like muh soul withered away inside me, and I wuz just an empty husk. When I first saw muh own face, once I got home, I looked exactly like I felt. I wuz no longer young or pretty, but as yuh sees me now."

"I know it is impolite to ask a lady her age," Rehaak began reluctantly. "But I have to ask. How old are you?"

"It's a fair question I s'ppose. I have seen thirty seven summers."

"She's not much older than you, Rehaak!" Laakea said, in astonishment.

"Ashd'eravaak did it when he touched me. He stole muh life and he took muh innocence. Dat leaves me with you and duh lad, trying tuh make amends for what I done."

"I don't understand why you feel you need to make amends for anything," Laakea said gently. "It appears to me that you were a victim not —" he struggled to find the words.

"Yes." Rehaak jumped into the silence. "Your oath was made under duress, and they violated the terms of the oath when they killed your son, in spite of their promise to save him if you followed Ashd'eravaak. An oath like that is not binding."

"But still and all, I submitted tuh dere vile uses and I still feel unclean. I didn't try tuh resist." Isil said sadly, looking at the floor again. "I don' know if I'll ever feel clean again, but at least I'm free of dere power now."

"I don't see how you had any choice, Isil. They raped you."

Laakea rose from his seat, walked over to the older woman and knelt beside her. He wrapped his arms awkwardly around her, while Rehaak watched without comment. He had never seen Laakea offer physical comfort to anyone before. He waited a moment before joining the youngster in embracing Isil. Before long, all three of them were weeping freely together for her loss. She had emboldened them both to share their common frailty with each other, because of her honest confession.

"Dere's just one more thing tuh tell. I thought dere wuz none left till I met yuh Rehaak. I cried when yuh sang your song o' thanksgiving over dat first meal we shared, because — dat day — somethin in my heart broke. I began tuh remember all duh stuff I had forgotten, not just duh bad stuff I done told yuh, but good stuff too. Stuff muh folks used tuh tell me about duh Creator. It wuz like I came alive again, after bein dead for so many years. Dat's duh real reason I am here tuh join yuh. I am alive again and I wants tuh make it right with duh Creator."

Rehaak looked at Isil, as they still held her in their embrace. She was looking into his eyes with tears streaming down her face.

"I'm free, and you wuz duh one what done it for me. I got muh soul back. Yuh set me free with your song, so dey got no more power over me, but dey wants power over all of Khel Braah. As long as dere is followers of duh Creator here, dey can't have duh power dey wants fer some reason. Dey can't, til all of us be dead, or turned tuh duh worship o' duh Dark Ones. We be a threat tuh dere plans."

"Do you know what it is we do that prevents them from taking over Aarda?" Rehaak asked, as she and Laakea broke their embrace.

"I don' know if'n it's what we do, or if'n it's who we are, or what we are dat does it." She said.

"I don't understand Isil," said Laakea, as he moved back to his seat.

"Neither does I," she replied.

"I think we better find out soon, before they send a larger force against us. So far, we have been dealing with small groups, almost like raiding parties. If they can find us and track us long enough, they may be able to mount a force large enough that we cannot resist. We have been lucky that there have been no survivors, from the encounters, to send word back about our location." Laakea said, deep concern showing on his face.

Rehaak and Isil looked at each other and shuddered, as if the room had suddenly grown colder.

"What is wrong with the two of you?" Laakea asked noticing their strange behavior.

"Dere wuz survivors Laakea, two of dem from duh first fight Rehaak and I had on duh trail, did he not tell yuh bout dat."

"Yes he told me, but he never said anything about survivors."

"I did not think it was important. How was I to know?"

"We have to move quickly then, before they locate us here. It's too late to go tonight, and I will not go anywhere without proper preparation, so we may as well hear your story now Rehaak," said Laakea. "Then I shall tell mine. I still think it's important to have as much information as we can, before going on."

CHAPTER 23: REHAAK'S STORY

While Rehaak prepared to tell his story, they all sat silently for a while, digesting the information that Isil had given them.

Rehaak found that he was calmer than he expected, given the fact that he was about to expose all his shortcomings to the only two people in the world he cared about, or for that matter, cared about him. Both had saved his life at least once. He owed them a decent explanation, since they were willing to risk everything for him; they needed to know just what kind of man he was. After hearing Isil's story, he felt he could do no less than be as brutally honest as she had been. Perhaps once they knew everything, they would forget about joining him on the quest that had devoured so many years of his life, and now threatened to kill them all.

"Well," he began. "I will start in the middle as well, with just a few bits of preamble to anchor it in time."

"Once I became convinced of the reality of The Creator, I realized that there were things missing in our tales and histories. I began my search for clues that would lead me to greater knowledge of The Creator. I left my father's house. I wandered for years throughout the west of Kel Braah. I followed trails spoken of in lore and written in legend, to places lost to the knowledge of men. I haunted barren places that had been great cities long ago. I prowled forgotten ruins, covered over by dust and fallen into decay millennia ago. I wandered cracked and cratered streets that had not heard the sound of human footsteps in a hundred generations or more. I saw wonders and marvels that men have not seen in a thousand years, all crumbling into dust and decay."

"I struggled to decipher fragments of drawings and writings on stone and parchment until I thought I would go mad, or blind, or both. There were times when I spent a week trying to decipher some half-discernable scrawls that ended up reading something like "For a good time see —."

"I tried to understand the form and function of incredible machinery, abandoned and left to rust. I lived in caves and makeshift shelters or in whatever habitation the ancient places afforded. I was obsessed with knowledge. I read all the books I could find in any of the remaining libraries, as I scoured the ancient dwelling places for information. I questioned the oldest inhabitants of the places I visited. It was miraculous, that I managed to find so much, but it was all fruitless."

"What did you do for supplies?" Laakea interrupted.

"I had some money given to me by my family. At first, it was enough, but when it ran out, I did whatever work was available to me. I often ate what I could find. I discovered that I had a gift for healing. That sometimes stood me in good stead with the people in the regions I visited. That, however, is only the beginning of the story. Through my explorations, I found out several things; first, that men were far more numerous in the distant past than we are now; second, we had knowledge and technology far beyond our present imaginings. All that knowledge has been lost for many generations. Third, that all the races of mankind had once, long ago lived together in peace, for millennia."

He paused for effect, "That cooperation dissolved into mistrust, then degenerated into outright warfare. That war went on for centuries, and finally ended in the complete separation of our three races. The Eniila and the Abrhaani stayed close enough to continue to skirmish from time to time, until just recently, when we finally stopped fighting. The Sokai disappeared entirely when the rift between the races occurred. No one has heard from them or seen them in many generations. They might have perished in the wars, although there is no record of them involved in the fighting."

"I needed to get more information from the oldest documents, and for that I needed the Scriptorium in Narragansett. All the librarians at all the places I had visited told me that if I was going to find what I wanted it would most likely be in the city."

"I travelled to Narragansett with a caravan and when I arrived, I headed straight for the Scriptorium. When I got there, the sheer volume of the material available for my research shocked me. Imagine seeing stacks of scrolls, manuscripts, and bound volumes filling enormous rooms. What I needed may have been there but it was like trying to find a single pearl dropped at the bottom of the Syn Gersuul."

"It was nearly impossible to find anything. I sorted through as much as I could. Fortunately, their method of keeping similar types of documents together worked in my favor. I was looking for the oldest documents I could find. Some delightful soul had stored all the oldest parchments in a room by themselves. It seems that very few people wanted to bother with the most ancient writings. It was widely believed that those writings were mere legends with no basis in reality.

They had fallen out of fashion and many were crumbling into dust. It was an enormous task, but I managed to find some material that corroborated my theories and I found several works that mentioned an even older volume. A book called the Aetheriad, also known as the Chronicles of Aarda. Then I ran into a dead end. There were some clues about its contents, but only the vaguest hints of where it had been at the time of the writer, and nothing about where I might find it now. That, however, is still only the background information."

"The real story, as Isil put it, is this," he paused to gather strength.

"The real story is — that I abandoned the Faithfull One and the quest he had given me. Isil, you were coerced into renouncing him, but I left the path freely of my own will. I bear the full blame for my own sins."

Isil and Laakea sat quietly without comment watching their friend confess. They could detect the shame in his tone and expressions, and decided not to compound his shame by adding their comments. They waited politely for Rehaak to pick up the threads of his story and continue.

"The problem, I suppose, was that I became famous. I had nothing for so long, that having the ability to own things and live well was something I craved. People began to seek me out for my wisdom and they paid me for my counsel. Soon I was becoming wealthy and well known. Powerful men sought my council and beautiful women sought my company. Money flowed through my fingers like water flows through rocks in a streambed. I spent my nights in drinking and debauchery and my days counseling those who had money to pay for my services. Selfishness and greed took root in my heart.

I no longer cared about the truth. I cared nothing for people or their problems. All I cared about was what they were willing to pay and what I could acquire with that wealth."

"I tried to deceive myself that I was important and that the things I did were significant too; after all, I was helping people. I knew it was all hollow. I knew that I should continue my search for proof of The Creator's existence and that I should share my knowledge of Him with others. I had trapped myself in a prison without walls, a prison created by my sloth, my greed, and my own need to feel important."

"Soon I began to tell people what they wanted to hear instead of the truth, and lost my credibility with everyone. I could feel it all slipping away from me."

"Then in the midst of all the debauchery and deceit, The Creator proved why people have named him Faithful One. In spite of my abandoning Him, He spoke to me and gave me a message for our people. My job was to warn them of the destruction threatening to overtake all Aarda, unless they began to seek Him and follow Him once more. He alone has the power to protect us from the holocaust that is on its way."

"Because I had squandered the currency of my respect and integrity, no one believed me. When they could tolerate my ranting no longer, they exiled me from Narragansett. Once again, I failed The Creator."

"In anger and frustration, I renounced The Creator and vowed never to have anything to do with him again. I headed south toward New Hope, which was where I was going when you found me on the trail, Isil. The time I spent in the forest house would have probably gone on forever had you not turned up, Laakea. So once again, external circumstances thwarted my slothfulness. It is a pattern in my life, that I do nothing unless driven to it. I am like an undisciplined beast that some herdsman must goad into action. Are you both so sure that you want to be part of my madness?"

"It would seem to me that it's more important than ever that we join you," Laakea said softly. "If the Faithful One won't let you give up your mission, it must be very important."

Rehaak shook his head slowly from side to side as if he wanted to deny the statement, but he was simply unable to believe that they would still want to join him.

"If Isil and I are what it takes to keep you on track, and fulfill the plan of The Creator, then so be it. I have sworn *Sword Oath* to you and it cannot be discharged short of death, be it either yours or mine."

"But how can you be sure that I won't desert you when things get difficult, like I have so many times before. I am unreliable, unscrupulous, and undisciplined. I do not even trust myself, why should you trust me?"

"I'd say yuh got it all backwards, friend. It's not you we be trustin, but duh Creator. He be duh one what is moving you — no — all of us, along like driftwood in duh current. He will get yuh — get us where we all needs tuh be. If yuh ain't figured dat out yet, yuh be a whole lot dumber dan we gives yuh credit for. We all got our faults. I don't s'pose yuh be any different dan duh rest of us. We take yuh as yuh are just like yuh done for us. Right lad?"

"That's right Rehaak, you didn't ask a lot of questions when I came to live with you. You accepted me as I was, without knowing anything about me, or my past. The least we can do for you, is accept you in the same way."

"Yes, but now you know what a fraud I am."

"And we don't pay it no mind either," Isil snorted.

"That's all fine to say, Laakea, except my life did not depend on what you did or did not do. I was relatively safe. There was no cost to me other than some hospitality and —"

"You can still say that after what you seen me capable of?" interrupted Laakea, his anger rising within. "Stepping into a *Blood Debt* between my father and me could have easily cost you your life! You did not know what you were getting into with either of us. I could still fail you. I could have left you to die at the hands of those assassins. I could easily have killed you many times over myself! "

"But you did not — and proved that you are an honorable man while I am a deceitful, shiftless, oath breaker!" Rehaak protested.

"You had no way of knowing that, when you took me in. You are who you are, and I am a cold-blooded killer! So what!" Laakea almost shouted

Isil could feel the heat of both their tempers rising, as she moved to stand between the two men. She looked from one to the other and quietly said, "Yes, yuh both be right, and I am a whore used by duh followers of Ashd'eravaak, yet we appears tuh be duh ones duh Creator has picked fer dis job. If yuh wants tuh argue with anybody, argue with him."

"But Isil," Rehaak protested. "We are not even sure what The Creator wants from us."

"I say we continue as we have, and trust that he is not called the Faithful One without cause." Laakea argued, forcefully. "Things are becoming clearer as we go along. We need to move quickly but there is no need to panic just yet. My father used to say that, just because the outcome of a battle is not clear, is no reason to stop fighting, in fact, if you stop fighting, you will certainly lose. We must fight or die."

"More like fight *and* die! What can the three of us hope to accomplish, when there may be hundreds, even thousands of the Dark Ones' followers by now," Rehaak interrupted.

"We have more information now than we've ever had before. The fact that we are encountering opposition shows that we're on the right path. Besides, I doubt that all of them are trying to kill us. They must be busy with other plots as well."

"I do not want to be responsible for the deaths of my friends! You said it yourself, Laakea, eventually we will encounter forces that we are not powerful enough to overcome!"

"First of all, we ain't dead yet, and I fer one intends tuh be summat hard tuh kill. Second, we chose dis of our own accord, so yuh ain't responsible fer nuthin as I sees it. Third, we got tuh believe dat the One who brought us tugedder can keep us from harm if dat's what He wants. Yuh may not believe dis, but I know for a fact dat dere are tings wors'n death."

"I won't accept any more of your excuses. As soon as I finish my weapons, we will go on with the search for your book, though it takes us through the gates of death itself. Now tell us what you know about its location."

Rehaak sat quietly, humbled by the depth of acceptance shown by his two companions. They were far better friends than he deserved. In all his wanderings and searching he had been alone. Now he had comrades to stand beside him, but at the same time, he felt the responsibility of that friendship. If he failed them, it could well cost them their lives. That was something he could not accept. The choice that faced him tore him apart.

On the one hand, he could take up his search again. He would have help and companionship. He knew that their friendship was the thing he treasured most. Of all the things he had ever gained in his life, their friendship had a value higher than all the knowledge in all the books he had read.

On the other hand, the people who were ready to stand by him could well perish in service of his quest. There were no guarantees that his search would be successful. It was too much to ask of them to risk their lives on such a perilous venture, but any way he looked at it, he was going to lose their friendship.

He told himself that if they separated, they would be harder to find as individuals than they were as a group. As long as any of them were alive, the Dark Ones could not have Khel Braah. To spare them, and for the safety of Khel Braah, he decided that he would slip away from them at the earliest opportunity. He would continue, but he would continue alone.

"I will have to consult my notes," he lied. "But first let Laakea tell you his story, by then it will be late. It will give us all a chance to sleep on what we have heard and shared." He hoped that he hid his deception well enough to fool them.

Isil and Laakea shared a look but said nothing further about the issue.

CHAPTER 24: LAAKEA'S STORY

"I cannot start in the middle, like the two of you," Laakea began, "I'm only old enough to have a beginning."

Although my parents raised me here on Kel Braah, my father and mother were both of the Eniila race. You already know that. I know that they came here to escape something that happened back in Baradon, their homeland. Neither of them would tell me much of what caused them to flee here to the land of our ancestral enemies. I have no idea how my father knew it would be safe enough to come, settle here and live among the Abrhaani.

"I suspect he knew that we tends tuh tolerate most tings dat don't directly threaten us lad. One lone man and his woman weren't hardly no threat. Mebbe dat's duh reason."

"Yes, that's possible but — why? What was so bad in Baradon that he wanted to live isolated from his people? Never mind, I will ask him that question, if I see him again and survive the encounter."

"Survive seein yer Pa? Are yuh sayin yer own Pa wants tuh kill yuh lad?" Isil asked incredulously.

"He may not want to, but *The Code* requires it."

251

"What kinda nonsense is dis lad?"

Rehaak smiled, remembering his own incredulity, at the harshness of Eniila customs and laws, when Laakea had first told him of them. "Now who is interrupting every sentence, Isil?" he chided.

She gave him an evil glare before she turned to focus on Laakea again. "Sorry, go on laddy," she mumbled contritely.

"I am sorry too Isil, I have trouble keeping my story going in a straight line, but I will try to keep on track. It's alright if you ask questions when you don't understand, isn't it Rehaak?" he said, mimicking Isil's earlier glare. "You are the one who keeps telling me that questions are the beginning of knowledge."

Rehaak looked at the floor in mock humility. "I consider myself duly chastened."

"Both my parents were accomplished weapons masters, both in their use and in their making. My father was a smith, before he became a war leader among our people. He led our people in the wars that drove the Abrhaani out of Baradon and back to Kel Braah. From the time I was old enough to hold a small wooden sword, he trained me as a warrior in thought and action. Every day we spent hours in drills and practice. He said it was needful that I be an accomplished fighter, if I was ever to be a true son of his and a true Eniila. I trained with sword, axe, spear, and bow daily.

I can remember days when he would make me drill with only one hand, the other he tied behind me. The next day he would bind the opposite arm and repeat the drills, until I could fight with either hand. He said that it was important because I never knew if I might lose a hand or an arm in battle. The limb might grow back but not quickly enough to save me."

"Eniila limbs grow back?" Rehaak interjected in amazement.

"Hush now, Rehaak, yuh can discuss dat later. Let duh lad talk."

"Did yer Da not jus leave yuh be a child, lad?

"Oh no, Isil, I had time for play, and stories in the evenings, I spent some days helping my mother in the gardens, listening to her sing. She had the most beautiful voice."

He fell silent as he could feel tears beginning again at her memory. He swallowed hard to keep them from overflowing onto his cheeks. Isil pretended not to notice, as he struggled to control his feelings. She did not want to cause him further embarrassment, so she sat silently, while waiting for him to continue. Although his voice was threatening to crack and give away his vulnerability, he finally mastered his emotions and began again.

"My mother died three years ago of a wasting illness. After that, my father was never the same. He grew hard and cold. Each day he became more unreasonable and impossible to please. Finally, one night, we got into a huge dispute. I dishonored him and I cursed him to his face." Laakea stopped short, as if that was all that he needed to say.

Isil looked at him in puzzlement, and when he didn't respond, she looked at Rehaak to see if he could give her some hint of what the boy had meant. He simply shrugged and pointed with his chin in Laakea's direction, as if to say, "Ask him."

"Parents and young'uns bin scrappin as long as dere's bin families, I reckon. Den dey forgets about it and goes on livin, dat's what families does."

"Not Eniila families, not if the child is male and not once the child is old enough to be accountable for his actions. You don't understand, Isil!"

"Yuh be dead right bout dat young'un. How about yuh 'splain it tuh me den?"

"Honor is everything to an Eniila. We vigorously defend our honor. Once an Eniila boy becomes a man, he has to live according to the *Warrior Code*. It is Eniila law. He is accountable for all his words and actions, which means if he causes insult, injury or commits crimes of any kind he must face trial."

"I am followin yuh so far lad, we have laws, and magistrates, tuh decide duh guilt and punishment of criminals too yuh know. We're not barbarians."

Rehaak had a hard time holding his tongue, as he sat listening to their exchange, but he knew that he had better let the boy finish his own story, without interference or support from him. Isil, obviously, was having the same difficulties that he had when comprehending Eniila culture. He too felt that they were incredibly barbaric, when he first began to learn of their customs, from Laakea.

"Not a magistrate, or a court, Isil, *Trial by Combat*. The injured or insulted party has the right to require that the person at fault pay a *Blood Debt*, to avenge his honor. The person who was offended, challenges the wrongdoer to combat. The outcome of the combat determines who is wrong and who is right, that way the loser pays with his life-blood. The combat may take place either immediately or at the whim of the injured party. *Trial by Combat* determines guilt or innocence. Combat is to the death."

"Dat's barbaric! How can dat be justice? Duh strongest would always be takin from duh weakest."

"You have some good reasons to say that. My father often said, 'Though the gods decide the outcome of the combat, they seem to favor the better armed or better prepared.' That's why he said it was so important for me to learn to fight well. There are several *Cities of Refuge*, for those who can't or won't fight."

Rehaak could hold back no longer. "They seem to have other ways of curbing excesses too Isil. For example, the winner has to assume the loser's obligations to family or creditors. I don't pretend to understand it all either, but let him continue."

"Fine, but I still think it's a stupid arrangement," she harrumphed. "Go ahead and finish."

"Oh yes and there are hired *Avengers* too," said Laakea.

"You never told me about them, or did you?" asked Rehaak. "Sorry, never mind, just go on with your story. We can talk about that later too."

"I not only insulted my father, I cursed him." He spoke slowly, as if speaking to a small child.

"Because of my disrespect to him, he had the right to require *Trial by Combat* according to *The Code*. I knew that I could never defeat him. The gods would never allow me to win, both because he is a better fighter than I am, and because I am in the wrong. I fled like a coward, because I was in the wrong and I knew it. I ran from my fate and from justice. That makes me both a coward and a fugitive. If I could make it to a *City of Refuge,* I could live out my life there, but presently I have no way of getting to one. They lie across the Syn Gersuul in Baradon. So, unless and until I can find a *City of Refuge*, my father can attack me and kill me at any time, or he could hire an *Avenger* to do it for him."

"Seems tuh me dat runnin away be more an act o' common sense dan cowardice, tuh muh way o' thinkin. Why couldn't he have just extended k'harsa tuh yuh?"

Laakea ignored her interruption. He didn't want to get side tracked into the murky definition of that term again, so he continued. "As things stand now, according to *The Code*, any Eniila designated by my father as his *Avenger*, can challenge and kill me on sight with no penalty, unless I can find my way to one of the *Cities of*

Refuge. Once I enter that city I can never leave it, unless I become a member of *The Brotherhood*."

Laakea looked to Rehaak for assistance with the explanation, since it didn't seem to be getting through to Isil.

"Your explanation is just fine lad. She understands what you told her, but she does not believe it is any way for civilized people to settle their differences."

Indignation finally overcame her, and her words spilled out, like water boiling out of a pot left on the fire. "Blamed right! Lot o' nonsense is what it is! Parents killin dere children, 'specially after all duh grief o' bearin em and raisin em." She finished abruptly before giving a final exasperated look at Laakea and fell silent.

"Well, that's just the way it is." Laakea replied defensively. "If I see my father, he has a right — no — duty, to test me on the field of honor according to *The Code*. Only the strongest are fit to live."

"And where is he now?" she asked to no one in particular.

"I don't know," both men responded simultaneously.

"So he could come bustin in here and start hackin away at yuh, at any moment?

"That is exactly true, Isil," Rehaak interrupted, "but if it is any comfort to you, I believe he has gone off somewhere else. I do not know where or why. It is just a feeling I have and I hope with all my heart that it is the truth. I know the way the youngster handles himself in a battle. Although he is still young and inexperienced, he is unbelievably deadly. His father is a much more seasoned warrior than Laakea. None of us either individually or even together could defeat a warrior the likes of his father."

"Den why are we still hangin around here like duh stink on shit?"

"Because I want to complete the weapons I need, to protect Rehaak's sorry backside, from the assassins."

"Well why we are just sittin around tellin yarns den? Git tuh work, both o' yuh!"

"That's part of the problem, Isil. One of the metals is special in some way, and I can't work it like regular steel."

"Well use regular steel den and stop messin about!"

"I would if I had enough steel," Laakea growled, with a mixture of anger and embarrassment."

"Oh," she said.

"Exactly," Rehaak said. "But I feel there is more to gain from the riddle of this stuff than simply better weapons.

Laakea nodded in agreement. "If I can master the secret of this metal, I feel I will learn something important to our future survival."

"Or it may just be an exercise in character building for us both," Rehaak interrupted with a smile. "Look how we have already changed through the process."

"Yup, I noticed dat right off," Isil positively leered at the men. "I likes muh men all hot and sweaty with big muscles, but maybe yuh been tryin tuh use duh wrong methods on dis stuff. I mean if'n it ain't steel mebbe yuh should stop trying tuh work it like steel"

Laakea shot out of his seat as if he had been jabbed in the backside with red hot metal from the forge. "Of course! Why didn't I think of it? I'm and idiot."

"What an incredible revelation, I knew *that* long ago," jibed Rehaak. "But what are you talking about?"

"She's right Rehaak; I've been going about this all wrong. I just remembered a song my father sang at the forge. *Ehlbringa*, they called it. Stronger than steel, light as feathers, the color of old sea ice. He said the ancients worked it, before *The Sundering*. No one has seen it in centuries. Its source was deep in the roots of the mountains. He learned a song from his father. He told me it was a work song passed along from father to son. My father had never seen *Ehlbringa*, nor had his father, but his father's father claimed that our family worked the metal in times past, though he had never seen it either. His Grandpa claimed that our ancient ancestors were the greatest smiths and warriors ever to walk the face of Aarda."

"And I would bet they were fifteen feet tall, had eyes like molten lava, and ate whole mithun for breakfast, uncooked, of course." Rehaak joked.

"Yuh'd figure that a man chasin a lost book across duh entire world, fer most o' his life'd be a bit more tolerant of others people's legends, wouldn't yuh lad?" Laakea and Isil both glared at Rehaak. He stopped smirking and fell silent.

"I am sorry, but I have never found any evidence in the manuscripts about this metal, this *Ehlbringa*."

"Dat don't mean it ain't so. What was important tuh his people mightn't a bin considered important tuh ours. Maybe our great scholars should' a bin more thorough in what dey included in dere writin's. What dey thought was important den, mightn't be important now. Times change."

"Yuh said it yerself; we lost too much from duh ol' days. I be thinkin dat mebbe dey weren't as thorough as dey should'a bin. Or mebbe yuh should'a bin more thorough in yer research. Yuh ain't found duh location of duh Aetheriad yet by all yer searchin, either has yuh Mr.

Scholar, but does dat make yuh think it ain't real?" Isil said indignantly.

"No, you are right. I have not seen every document ever written, or perhaps it, like the Aetheriad, is lost entirely."

"Another idea occurs to me. I may have not asked the proper questions because I did not know that such a thing exists. I have discovered that though we speak the same language, we have words that we use that Laakea does not understand. For example, he does not understand the meaning of k'harsa." Rehaak replied, suitably chastened by Isil's tirade.

"I'm not surprised he doesn't understand dat word, duh way his people live, dere is none of it among 'em, or in 'em," Isil interrupted.

"It is not all one sided. He has words that I don't understand either. That is correct, is it not Laakea?"

"Umm — I guess so. I wasn't really listening to you."

"Probably duh wisest choice, in dis case, young'un," Isil needled.

"I am trying to remember the words to that song, the only song my father ever taught me, called; *The Song of the Smith*. It's strange in a way, because my father usually never sang. My mother was the one who sang and my father never did, except for this one song. I'm almost certain that the words will tell me how to work the metal of the blades, if I can understand their meaning."

"Can yuh sing it to us den lad?"

"Good idea," Rehaak chimed in. "I don't think I have ever heard you sing yet. Not even hum or whistle."

"I'm not sure my voice is equal to the task but I will sing it for you if you both promise not to laugh."

"Go ahead lad."

Laakea took a deep breath and began to sing. It was more of a chant than a song. He was a little hesitant at first, but then gained confidence as he went along. A fine baritone had replaced his boyish soprano. It was a man's voice singing a man's song.

Blacksmith, fireborn, fierce and able,
Selvyn stands at Hyrim's table,
He drains the flask giv'n by the King.
Takes Ehlbringa he is given,
That from Aarda's heart was riven,
He gives his promise to the King.

He alone has heard the call,
Come to stand in Hyrim's hall.
He stands alone before the King
Feather light like sea ice it shone.
Steel, such strength could never own
He will work it for the King.

Fire burns within his blood,
He needs no charcoal or no wood,
Weapons he promises the King.
Master of the forge and flame,
He calls the metal by its name,
His will forms weapons for the King.

None before him had the skill,
To bend Ehlbringa to their will,
For the armies of the King.
Takes the fire in his hands,

Forms the metal where he stands,
In the presence of the King.

Those who want to work the same,
Must not fear the heat or flame,
Must only fear its maker.
Call the metal by its name,
Stretch the hand and hold the flame,
Sing out to the maker.

Draw the fire deep inside,
Mould Ehlbringa thin or wide,
Calling on the maker.
Seek the shape within the mind.
Fingers form, the flame's design
Sons of the great maker.

Sons who never fear the flame,
Sons who bear the maker's name,
Never shall they falter.
Those who quail must bear the loss,
Fire will require a cost,
At his flaming altar.

Isil and Rehaak listened carefully as he sang. Rehaak had an almost irresistible urge to join him in his song although he knew neither the words nor the melody, but he thought that his own song of thanksgiving might well mesh with the young man's singing. He finally dismissed it as foolish fancy and concentrated on the words and melody just as Laakea finished his song.

"Well dat was entertainin fer sure, but I don't see how dat's gonna help yuh at all. A body can't take fire in his hands and sing tuh cold metal tuh make it do what he wants. Sounds like plain foolishness tuh me."

"Perhaps you're right Isil. However, sometimes people write things as metaphors and symbols of what is real. We're all too tired now to think clearly. Let us sleep on it and maybe a new day and fresh minds will help us understand what the bard was trying to say in the song."

Laakea yawned and stretched. He headed for his bedroom leaving Isil and Rehaak sitting and staring into the embers of the fire in the stone hearth. He was tired, and filled with excitement at the same time. He could not tell his friends how he felt in case this turned out to be a dead end, just like his previous efforts to forge the misshapen metal that still lay on the smithy floor. He was the first in many generations of his people to have *Ehlbringa*, the sea-ice metal, available to him. The first in many generations to hold it in his hands, and perhaps, he hoped, the first to rediscover the secret of its working.

"I wonder if the "Maker" mentioned in the song is the Eniila name for The Creator?" Rehaak mused to Isil, as Laakea left and headed off to bed.

CHAPTER 25: MEETINGS OF FATE

The eyes of the Abrhaani seamen followed Aelfric, as he began his climb up the gangway. He ignored the hatred and distrust in their eyes. He had sixteen years to get used to being alone among men who loathed him. Aelfric strode up the narrow gangplank and stopped at the top just long enough for Hermad to direct him to his berth. Once that errand was completed, the seaman left the ship again.

When Aelfric found his place below, he stowed his gear beneath his hammock, lashing it in place, as Hermad had instructed him. There was no sign of the additional passenger the captain had booked to share the cabin. He could see the other man's gear stored below the additional hammock. The "fine gentleman" as the captain had called him, had brought a significant amount of personal belongings with him. The size of that pile was strong evidence of his fellow passenger's high status.

He stretched out in the hammock, waiting for sleep to overtake him. Although he was tired, his mind was too busy with plans and possibilities to allow him to sleep immediately.

The small window of the cabin allowed very little light into the cramped quarters. It was now just past noon. Slivers of sunlight, reflected from the water outside, played across the beams and planks of the deck above his head. He ignored the noises of the deck hands and stevedores at work, as he considered his options. Once he arrived in Baradon, he could pursue two possible courses.

He had only two options in mind now, although with careful consideration, other possibilities might become obvious. The first and most direct option was to march boldly up to the front gate of the capital city, announce his identity, and challenge his brother to single combat. It was not an elegant option, but it was direct, effective in dispatching his brother, but rather short sighted in the long term. No matter what pleasure he would derive from personally killing Aelrin, he would have to rid himself of all of Aelrin's fellow conspirators afterward.

If he did not deal with them immediately, he faced having them push him out of power later, either by force or by subterfuge. The process of dealing with them individually, could take a long time and wear him out. It was not an optimal solution.

Another thing troubled him about this option. Although he had practiced daily with his son, he had spent the last sixteen years far from the fields of combat, as a father and a husband, not as a fighting man. Aelrin had probably been fighting constantly in one way or another, trying to hold on to the kingdom he had stolen from him. He would be a difficult opponent to kill in single combat. It never entered Aelfric's mind that Aelrin might have already died, either in some trivial duel, or by an assassin's hand. If his twin brother were dead, he felt that he would sense it somehow. No — Aelrin must still be alive.

Aelfric knew he had a month or more of sailing time to practice and drill, while aboard the Sea Witch. Practicing on board would present it own difficulties because of the limited space on deck. He had not practiced his combat skills, since the night that Laakea had fled from the force of his anger. In three ten-days he could toughen up and hone his skills. If at the end of the voyage, he still felt that he was not up to the challenge, he could spend some of his silver on lodgings and lie low until he felt ready, or he could opt for plan number two.

Plan two would take longer. He would have to find enough people sympathetic to his cause, raise a force, and begin a civil war. Hiring mercenaries would not get the job done, for two reasons. First, he didn't have enough silver to hire warriors for a large army, and second, he never trusted mercenaries. They had a nasty habit of switching sides, if one's opponents offered them a richer purse. He would need to win the people's affection. They would be loyal to the death, if they followed someone they loved and respected. That was the kind of army he needed, not a pack of money-grubbing mercenaries.

The effects of plan two, would reach much farther, and be more satisfying in the end. It would prove to everyone, including himself, that he still had the necessary charisma to be the supreme leader of the Eniila. In many ways, it appealed to him more, if the people put his brother's head on a pike for him. It would be the ultimate vindication that he was the true king. It would prove Aelrin was only a pretender to the throne.

Plan two would also resolve his other concern. He could deal with all the plotters who had helped Aelrin achieve power, simultaneously. A purge of the elite would do wonders for his morale and the morale of the people. A coup would deal quickly and effectively with all potential challenges to his position. It would provide him with enough security to allow him to consolidate his hold on power. He smiled at the notion.

The most difficult part would be the beginning. He needed to recruit a force large enough to stand a chance at unseating Aelrin and his co-conspirators. Building up an army that large, without attracting Aelrin's attention too early, would be very difficult. He could let the problem remain unresolved for the time being. He couldn't solve everything immediately. He would face those troubles when and if they arose. For now, he needed some rest. He closed his eyes and drifted off to sleep.

***

Aelfric woke to the sound of movement in the cabin. Sunlight was streaming directly into the small window of the room. He guessed that it must be evening, if the sun was already that low in the sky. The illumination showed that his fellow passenger had arrived and was putting the final touches on securing his abundant belongings. The newcomer was an average sized man, by Abrhaani standards, with aristocratic bearing and excellent clothing. When he turned toward Aelfric and straightened up, the light revealed his features. Aelfric imagined that Abrhaani women would find the fellow quite attractive.

Noticing that Aelfric was awake, he apologized.

"I am sorry if I woke you, I meant no harm sir," he smiled obsequiously, "but we are about to get underway so I wanted to ensure that my belongings would not get tossed about if we hit rough water."

"No harm done." Aelfric replied. "I wanted to wake up just before we got underway in any case."

"I am travelling to Baradon on business," the man volunteered, trying to make conversation.

Aelfric sat up in his hammock without comment. He had to slouch to avoid hitting his head on the ceiling beams. He slipped out of the hammock carefully and stood hunched over, getting ready to go up on deck where he would not feel so claustrophobic. in the cramped quarters of the cabin.

"My you are a big one," the man began. "In my line of work I could use someone like you. If you want a job, I would be only too happy to employ you."

Aelfric ignored the man and made his way up onto the deck. He stood watching as the seamen cast off their lines and pushed off from the dock. Though he had been to sea once before, all that water beneath the hull still made him uneasy. The sooner he got solid ground beneath his feet again, the happier he would be. It had given him a certain sense of relief, when he had lost the small boat on the rocks. Although his load was heavy, and the way was hard, he preferred to struggle on land, walking, with forces he knew he could control.

The seamen trimmed the sails and the Sea Witch got underway, He watched them, as they worked busily to get the trim right and set the rudder, but all Aelfric saw was a flurry of activity that meant nothing to him. The helmsman bellowed out commands and the sailors appeared to carry them out, as far as Aelfric could tell. The words they used were meaningless to him. He had no choice but to put his fate in their hands and hope for the best. It was either that or jump overboard and try to make his way back to shore. As they drew farther from shore, that option looked less appealing with each passing moment.

As he was contemplating whether he should chance the leap overboard, his cabin mate strolled topside and leaned over the rail beside him.

"Excuse me for not doing so earlier, but I just realized that I had neglected to introduce myself properly. People call me Kett." He stood and waited silently for Aelfric to respond.

Aelfric smiled wryly, while looking the man over from head to toe. "Well I can call you Ketty," he said deliberately using the diminutive, "and Ketty when you call me, you can call me Al."

"That's better, Al." Kett responded, deliberately ignoring the slight. "As I said before, I am travelling to Baradon on business. When I say that, people usually ask me, what kind of business?" He paused, waiting long moments for Aelfric to respond.

Once he saw that Aelfric did not intend to ask he continued, "Good, I see that you are a man who can keep knowledge to himself, and his nose well out of the affairs of others. I am impressed."

"I am overjoyed that I can so easily make you happy little man," Aelfric responded in a sarcastic tone. "You will undoubtedly have a very enjoyable voyage, if you are so easily impressed. Now cease your chatter and leave me in peace."

"I shall, in due time, my large and abrasive shipmate, but first let me tell you what I see in you. I shall tell your fortune as it were, for no charge, of course."

"I have no need of a fortune teller."

"I beg to differ. You will have need of far more than a fortune teller before your journey home is over, and you will see why once I begin."

Aelfric turned to glare at the man. *"What is this fop playing at?"* he wondered.

When he looked into the man's eyes, he saw, a hardness that almost matched his own, masked behind that over-eager smile and attractive face. That look intrigued him more than any offer of fortune telling ever could. He decided to listen to what this Abrhaani chiseler had to say.

"Go on then. Tell me what you think you know."

"In you I see a veteran warrior, who has suffered many reversals of fortune. Some setbacks happened long ago and some much more recently. You are a man accustomed to power and authority, yet here you are booking passage back to your homeland with no possessions. I see a man who burns with passion for a mission that is at best, desperate and at worst, hopeless. I see a proud, noble man, brought low by twists of fate, and the treachery of those who were close to him. You have run far to try to escape your destiny. You have squandered your youth in that flight from fate, but your true destiny still lies ahead of you. How am I doing so far?"

"Anyone with a half a brain, and eyes in his head could discern as much as you have. For that matter, someone who has had a short talk with our good captain could do as much or better. Harmish could supply you with most of the same information. It is a good story, as far as it goes. Tell me charlatan, what destiny lies before me? Impress me with that and I shall hear you out. If you cannot foretell that, then be gone, and trouble me no more. I warn you, I am not as easily impressed as you seem to be."

Aelfric tried to stare the man down but Kett would not flinch. Kett's eyes seemed to glow in the setting sun, as he prepared to answer the challenge.

Kett answered so softly Aelfric had to strain to hear the words, above the sounds of the wind, the waves, and the creaking of the ship.

"The rule of Baradon — in your hands." Kett said, "Or more properly, the rule of Baradon returned to your hands — King Aelfric — if you are still strong enough for the challenge."

With that said, Kett turned and went below, without uttering another word, leaving Aelfric standing alone at the railing, gazing across the empty ocean as the sun sank below the horizon, and darkness fell.

CHAPTER 26: THE FORGE OF THE MAKER

Laakea pondered Rehaak's idea that his *Maker* or Rehaak's *Creator* was the same person. A maker and a creator did the same things. The Golden Voice that had called him when he was feeling desperate and hopeless could well be The Creator. Did The Creator only speak in desperate and hopeless situations? Did those conditions motivate the Creator to speak, or was The Creator somehow constrained to speak only then? Did only desperate people cry out for help, or were they the only ones willing to listen? Laakea had no sure answer to the questions.

"In any case, Maker, Creator, Golden Voice, whatever you are called, I am willing for you to speak. I need your help. Your people need your help. Please tell me what to do," he prayed quietly.

He stripped off his clothing and slid into bed, locked his fingers behind his head, and stared up at the ceiling, waiting. No matter how hard he strained to hear, the golden voice of The Creator did not speak to him. All he heard were the sounds of Rehaak snoring softly in front of the hearth, and the night breeze in the trees, outside his window. He finally fell asleep with *The Song of the Smith* repeating incessantly in his head.

Suddenly he found himself standing alone on a great plain of fire. Multicolored flames rose like grass around his feet. He knew he should be in agony from the heat, but the flames did not burn his skin, in fact, he drew energy from the tongues of fire licking his body. The plain of flames stretched as far as he could see in every direction. He began to stroll casually through the fire, feeling the flames brushing against his bare legs. He had nothing to fear from these flames. He had never felt so powerful or alive before. Energy suffused his entire body as the flames climbed higher and danced across his skin to a sort of music. He reveled in the feeling. It was intoxicating and invigorating.

Everything was orderly, different types of flames with diverse colors and varied heights were scattered in random patterns, as far as he could see in any direction. It took a few moments for the patterns to register on his brain. It reminded him of something he had seen before. This place was — a garden! It was a garden of fire. The grass and shrubs and even the flowers of Aarda had their counterparts here in different colors and forms of flame. Unlike any gardens he had seen before, this one was not static. Constantly changing designs danced across the surface of the plain. The fire was a living thing reforming as if directed by some form of intelligence.

He began to walk wherever his eyes led him. He couldn't see any source of fuel, nothing that could support this endless burning. If it had a source that sustained it, he could not perceive it. This was too far beyond his limited experience to comprehend.

"Where did this all come from?" he asked aloud though no one was there to answer. "What is this place?"

"Welcome, youngling," said a deep voice, off to his right. "Welcome to the forge of The Maker. Welcome to the high altar of The Creator."

Laakea turned and looked to see who was speaking. A human form made entirely of flame smiled at him. The being stood to one side of a shrub made up of blue and gold incandescence. It beckoned him to come closer.

"Do not be afraid. You may call me Selvyn. It is not my name but it is my function for this time and it is a name that holds meaning for you."

"Selvyn, from The Song of the Smith?"

"Yes."

"What can you tell me about the metal, *Ehlbringa*? How do I call it by name, like in the song? How can I work it?"

"Alas, I cannot answer your questions for you; you must find the answers for yourself."

"But, why not? Why bother bringing me here, if there is no point to it?"

"I did not bring you. Your coming is your own doing, and the will of the one who made us both. There is a point, as you put it, and there are answers, but you must come to them on your own, just as you came here on your own. You have everything you need around you to learn what you must. Open the eyes of your heart and understand the place where the Eniila were made."

"Faugh! You are as bad as Rehaak, with his damned riddles."

"Your companion is wise. He has tried to teach you how to learn and how to think. He has not tried to teach you what to learn and what to think. Remember, youngster, what you told your companions; that only the strongest are fit to live. You must learn the language of the fire. You must prove your strength.

There is a cost to learning, but an even higher cost to remain ignorant. You must learn to control the fire of your anger, and master the tools that the Maker gave you. If you do not succeed, you will perish here. "

"But if you don't teach me how will I learn it? There is no one else who knows the way. The secrets of working *Ehlbringa* have been lost for generations."

"You are here. The knowledge you seek is here. The Maker has heard your request. Surrender yourself to Him. Surrender to His holy fire, and you shall be as no one since Selvyn, who I represent."

"He came here too. He was the only person in his generation who learned the secrets of this place. He was the last of your people able to work the *Ehlbringa*. He learned here and grew stronger. If you fail, you shall perish. If you succeed, the power you wield shall be unlike anything in the living memory of your kind."

"But if I have so much power, and misuse it —"

"You have spoken truth. There is a risk. To his disgrace, Selvyn also found this to be true," said the figure, as if he could say more about the subject, but was constrained not to speak of it.

"I am not able to discern good from evil." Laakea began to tremble as though he was cold.

"All men have the ability to judge between good and evil. Discernment is not the root of humankind's problem. The tribulations men face arise from a different origin. If you find the root of a problem then you have also found the solution to it. Remember what your companions have taught you. Farewell."

With those words, the figure turned, and faded, or merged into the forest of flame. Laakea was not sure which was true.

"Come back!" Laakea shouted after him, angrily.

There was no response. He was alone again. The garden of fire still flickered and flared all around him.

The flames sang their own songs, as they danced in place. It was as if the flame being that had called itself Selvyn had never existed or Laakea had only imagined him.

Laakea sat down disconsolately among the flame flowers as they burned around him. He turned everything over in his mind as he idly stared at one flame flower that was particularly beautiful. This was as frustrating as his talks with Rehaak.

What did the fiery figure mean about the ability to discern between good and evil not being the root of humankind's problems? How could he find the answers to his questions here, when all he had were more questions, no answers?

Rehaak had told him that questions were the beginning of all knowledge. Is that what the flame creature had tried to tell him, when it said he was being taught how to learn, not what to learn? He had so many questions already, that he would undoubtedly be the wisest man in all Aarda, if he could find only a small portion of the answers to them.

"I cannot judge between right and wrong. That is nonsense," he said aloud, beginning a dialogue with himself.

"Wait a moment. That is not a question. That is a statement of belief, but is it true?"

His mind began working methodically on the problem. He finally decided that it was not really the truth. He found that speaking aloud helped him articulate his thoughts more clearly. Vocalizing his ideas lent form and substance to them, so that he could work them like metal from a forge.

"Is this why we Eniila have no written language?" he wondered. *"Are we verbal people for a purpose?"* He realized that he was becoming

sidetracked. He forced himself back to his quest for the origin of evil.

"I can tell the difference between what is right and what is wrong. Sometimes I decide to do what is wrong in spite of knowing better."

"Why do I do wrong?"

Memories cascaded across his mind as he recollected the things he had done in the past that he knew were wrong.

"I do wrong because I want something. Aha! Desire is what makes me — no wait — desire is not always bad. I can desire good things, as easily as evil things. Desire, in itself, is neither good nor bad. It's when I want — I want —. Wait!"

He leapt up to his feet and danced among the flames.

"I want. —- Now I understand," he sang out, as he danced. "I do wrong when I want something so badly that I don't care about the consequences of my actions on those around me. That's when I do wrong. That is selfishness. Selfishness is the root of all my wrongdoing and the root of all the problems of mankind.

Selflessness is what my companions have taught me, by their actions and by their words. They put the needs of others first consistently, motivated by respect, honor, and love."

The flames rose higher and danced, celebrating with him at the revelation.

"So if I care as much for others as I do for myself, I will not do evil. On the other hand, if I care more about myself and my own wants, than I do about others and their needs, then I do nothing but evil. Wait till I tell Rehaak!"

"Now, what about the other problems?"

"Is it right to take life, if I care about others? Is it ever right to kill another person?"

He paused and reflected silently before he began to speak aloud again.

"If I had not killed those men, they would have killed my friend. If I had not taken action, they would have been able to carry out their selfish, evil intentions toward him. I opposed those evil intentions. If they had succeeded, then evil would have won. I intervened. I had no time to reason with them. They would not have listened, even if I had tried. They were determined to do evil. What I did was justice according to *The Code*. If we allow evil to continue unchecked, all creation will be laid to waste. That is exactly what we are trying to prevent. I have sworn to protect the weak and the innocent. I have taken an oath to oppose wickedness, even if I must take the lives of those who do intentionally do evil to accomplish it."

Once again, the flames danced and celebrated with him in his newfound wisdom.

"Alright, where am I? Selvyn said this was the forge of the Maker. So why am I here? Why do we put metal in the forge? To heat it, so we can form it to our purposes."

"If that is true, The Creator has brought me to his forge to reshape me. Very well then, come flame; heat me until the Maker can shape me."

He stooped and scooped handfuls of flame, as if he were gathering a bouquet of wildflowers for his mother. As he gathered armfuls of flame, he suddenly saw a flaming forge standing before him, like an altar to the gods. He was sure it had not been there a moment ago.

"No, he corrected himself, not to the gods — to the One God. The only God. An altar to the Maker."

He walked over to inspect this new thing. Standing before the forge was an anvil and a pile of metal waiting like an incomplete offering. The two misshapen masses of stuff he had been trying, without success, to forge, lay near the anvil where he had left them. They were incomplete implements. He had been trying to make something from them before, but he could not remember what it was just now.

Seven more pieces were twisted and ugly parodies of offerings. They reeked of evil, and the flames swarmed over them as if trying to devour them, or at least prevent them from wreaking havoc.

"What would you have me make for you, my Lord Maker?"

"Make Truth for me," the words drifted into his mind.

He realized that he still held flameflowers in his left hand as he reached out with his right to take up the first two lumps of metal that he had already tried to work into a sword. He looked intently at them before he set them down on the anvil. He caressed the metal with his fingers while whispering — truth. He repeated the word continuously. The repetition took the form of a melody, as he continued to caress the metal with his fingers. The flameflowers in his left hand began to creep across his body to the metal, joining his fingers in the caress. The metal of his two failures slowly joined and reformed. He could see into the metal. Crystalline structures, like tiny jewels, vibrated in time to his chanting and realigned into new configurations within the metal. They linked up in orderly formations, as he continued chanting. Soon Truth was complete.

He held Truth in his hand. It was perfect. It had two very sharp edges. It was complete in its beauty, but it was alone. Without truth, there could be no — something more was needed.

"What else shall I make Lord Creator? He whispered in reverential awe?"

"Fashion Justice for me."

Laakea recognized the Voice now, as the melodic golden words entered his mind.

"You shall be called Justice, he chanted as he set Truth aside, to pick up two of the twisted offerings that lay beside the anvil. He repeated the process of caressing the metal on the anvil, stroking it lovingly, and singing softly. The tune was slightly different, but once again, he could see into the metal. He saw the perversion of the pure metal. He saw how the previous smith had twisted it into a form that served evil, but as he sang, his song grew in power and intensity. He crushed evil from the metal with his hands. He drove it out with his song.

The crystals aligned into a slightly different pattern from the first sword, a pattern called Justice. Soon Justice lay before him. It was both beautiful and terrible at the same time. It had two sharp edges just like Truth, and he knew that Justice could not exist without Truth. He knew that Truth demanded Justice.

"Is there anything more beautiful than Truth and Justice," he thought.

"Righteousness," the voice whispered to him. *"For without Righteousness, Truth and Justice can still be twisted and perverted."*

He grasped the rest of pieces of metal from the pile and began to sing a bold new melody to them, as he ran his hands across their surfaces. They flowed together as he worked the evil out of their shaping. Wickedness was becoming righteousness on the anvil of his will, beaten into shape by the hammer of his song. Righteousness was good and it was strong. It was a defense against evil.

He hardly noticed that the flameflowers had been almost completely absorbed into his skin. Then,

279

almost before he realized that he had begun, Righteousness lay complete in front of him. He held it tightly to his body; it fit him well, covered his chest, and protected his heart. This too he set aside, feeling suddenly tired and spent.

"Is there aught else I can make for you my Lord Maker?"

"It is enough for now. Rest, lest your labors overcome you. Depart in peace my champion."

Laakea knelt on one knee before the anvil with his head bowed before his Maker. The flames coruscating over his body subsided, but he was at peace. He was too tired to rise, but he knew he must leave this place before the fire consumed him completely. He had no strength, not enough even to lift his tired head. He struggled to stand, but fell facedown instead. Velvet darkness enfolded him into its quiet heart.

Then, suddenly, the darkness was no longer silent. Voices were calling him away from the darkness and back to the light. They called his name, drawing him back from the forge of the Maker. He wanted to stay but he knew they needed him. It was time to leave, but it was such a long journey. He was so weary. He wasn't sure if he could make the trip. Suddenly he felt gentle hands lifting him. They would help him return. He thanked the Creator for sending them, because he knew his own strength was not enough to make the journey alone.

From far away a voice, rough edged, but filled with compassion sang out. It was a beacon of light in the darkness. It filled him with courage and strength. He fought to follow the sound back to Aarda, where they needed him more than ever.

CHAPTER 27: RECOVERY

It had been three days since Isil and Rehaak had found Laakea naked and unconscious at the forge. They had carried him back to the house and laid him on his bed. Isil tended him and sang to him, day and night, as he burned with fever. Neither of them had seen anything like this before. Laakea had not moved at all in three long days of waiting. He made no sound other than his breathing, which was labored. Not even his eyelids had twitched. They kept an anxious watch over him and bathed him with moist cloths to keep his temperature down.

"Are yuh sure yuh can't do something more fer him, Rehaak?" said Isil, her voice filled with concern. It was the morning of the fourth day of Laakea's coma.

"I have done all I know how to do. I have no idea what happened to him that night. I am reluctant to give him anything for two reasons; first, I doubt if he can swallow, second, I do not know what has caused this. I would only be guessing what to give him. If I guess wrong, it could kill him, since he is so weak. I feel as helpless as you do. I know nothing else we can do to break the fever. He is in the Creator's hands now. Whether he lives or dies is up to God."

"Why didn't we hear him working duh forge? We should'a heard him banging on duh anvil while he made doze swords and dat breastplate, shouldn't we?"

Rehaak shrugged, "That is just one more thing I can't explain. If he ever wakes again we will have to ask him, but for now we can only observe him and make him comfortable." Rehaak walked from the room, while Isil continued to stand watch over her young friend's motionless form.

She was exhausted and needed rest herself, but she refused to leave his bedside. She knew Rehaak had done everything in his power to help Laakea, but she was frustrated that she could not do more to help.

"We needs yuh back laddy. Yuh got yer weapons — but dey be useless if dere be no one tuh wield em," she said hoping he could hear her.

Although they brimmed with hot moist tears, her eyes felt like she had sand trapped under her eyelids. If her son had lived, he would have been almost Laakea's age. Her friend was a brave, strong lad. That was as much as any mother could ask from a son. She decided to close her eyes for a bit, while she waited. She leaned forward to rest her head on the bed beside Laakea. It was going to be another long day. She felt like an eggshell in an empty nest, with all the hatchlings fledged and flown, fragile, empty, and alone.

Sorrow rose to the surface of her thoughts like sulphurous bubbles from the depths of a swamp. In response to her despair, she poured out her heart to The Creator.

"I feels so lost and helpless. I know I've only just met Laakea, but I already loves him like he wuz muh own boy Eyhan. If yuh be takin him now dat be your right. He belongs tuh you, but what'll I do?

How can yuh 'spect me tuh continue, if I loses dis boy too? Muh life'll be like water poured ontuh dry ground, absorbed without even a damp spot tuh prove dat I wuz ever here. I done lived without direction, or purpose, or meaning tuh muh life, fer too long now. I gave up everythin tuh join dese men on dis journey, and if yuh takes him now — if it be over, I'll just drift through duh world again til duh frigid fingers o' death reaches out tuh claw me out of it."

"It used tuh be easy, clear what I should be doin next. But now, dat all seems like wasted time. Meals made, cleaning done, mithun tended, freight hauled from one place tuh duh next. Is dat all muh life amounts tuh? Is muh life jest a list o' tasks completed, with tally marks beside each one? I wants more'n dat. I wants muh life tuh amount tuh somethin. I needs tuh make a difference. I needs tuh be somebody."

"I used tuh be somebody, tuh someone once't. I had folk what cared about me. I needs dis here young'un tuh live, cause tuh him I'm somebody." Please don't be takin dat away now dat I got it again." Consciousness slipped away from her, and she finally slept.

She awoke to a hand stroking her hair, as bright morning light streamed through the window. She bolted upright to see Laakea looking at her. He looked pale and drawn but he was awake at last! She grasped his hand in both of her calloused palms. It felt cool to her touch. His fever had broken.

"Creator, be praised!" she shouted, and without thinking, she threw herself on Laakea, enfolding him in a hug that threatened to squeeze the remaining life out of him.

"Isil," he panted. "Let me go before you smother me."

"Sorry laddy." She released him, embarrassed by her thoughtlessness, but flooded with relief that he was alive. Rehaak raced into the room and skidded to a halt beside her.

"You are back," He said, relief showing, in his voice.

"Spot, your keen grasp of the obvious never ceases to amaze me."

Laakea's weak grin was like a balm to Rehaak's heart. He would never admit it to Isil, but he had been deeply concerned that Laakea would die from his unknown affliction. That concern had only intensified his desire to flee at the first opportunity. He had only stayed because he felt responsible for the boy's condition. Although he didn't know what had caused the problem, or what to do about it, he did not want Laakea to perish because he lacked medical care.

"And your sense of humor is still as bad as ever," he responded, smiling back.

"Stop it, duh pair o' yuh," Isil said sternly, though there was the hint of a smile at the corners of her mouth. "Is dat duh best yuh can do fer someone who has laid at duh gates o' death dese past five days and nights? Rehaak, get dis young man some vittles, afore he wastes away completely."

"Yes mistress," he mocked.

"It is good to have you back Laakea. While you have been sick, she has been an unbearable tyrant. I need your help to deliver me from the scourge of her incessant demands."

Isil rose from her chair threateningly, and raised her hand as if to cuff Rehaak.

"See what I mean," he said, as he scampered from the room, in mock terror. "Please don't beat me anymore. I promise I will be good from now on."

"I will show you all the bruises later Laakea."

Laakea chuckled at Rehaak's antics. Although he was as wobbly as a newborn lamb, he managed, with Isil's help, to get out of bed. After he had dressed himself, gone to the privy and washed, he hauled his exhausted body to the dining table. While he sat waiting for breakfast, he drank mug after mug of water trying to quench his nearly insatiable thirst.

"I had an interesting dream while I was asleep," he said, as they all sat down together. Isil and Rehaak looked knowingly at one another, but remained silent as Laakea related his experiences in the Garden of Flame.

Neither Rehaak nor Isil interrupted his story. He told Rehaak what he had discovered about selfishness being the source of the problems that plagued mankind. Rehaak nodded in solemn agreement.

When Laakea finished his story, Rehaak rose from the table. "Stay here with Isil, I need to get something," he said, and left the house.

"What's going on Isil?"

"Yuh'll see in a bit I imagine."

Within moments, Rehaak returned with a large bundle wrapped in oiled skins. It clanked when he set it on the table in front of Laakea without any comment.

"What's this? A present for me?"

"It is a present. I was hoping you could tell me how you got it, but I think you just did," Rehaak said cryptically.

Laakea unwrapped the package. He recognized the objects inside as soon as he saw them.

"How is this possible? Did I make these?" he asked, as he looked at the shiny objects in front of him.

The *Ehlbringa* was different now, not just in its shape, but it looked brighter, almost translucent. There were runes scripted near the guards of the swords. He knew they meant Truth and Justice. He also knew the rune worked into the center of the breastplate meant Righteousness. They shone strangely, as if light trapped within them, was trying to escape. The perfectly

285

balanced swords had just the right weight. The breastplate was thin and light as thistle down. He could wear it padded under a shirt, and no one would notice it. He had no doubt that it would withstand most blows directed against its wearer.

"I had hoped that you could answer that question for us." Rehaak began.

"Now that we have heard your dream experience, I think I understand. It was not just a dream. These items were beside you when we found you, on the floor of the forge. You were burning with fever and as still as a corpse. You must have made them while you slept, though I sincerely doubt that you were experiencing anything we would call sleep at the time. You were at the forge of the Maker. The journey and the forging of these things almost destroyed you in the process.

"I reckon. Dat splains duh fever too," Isil added, nodding sagely. "Yuh was in duh forge o' duh Creator and it took yuh a while tuh cool down again."

"Well then, I suppose we can continue with your quest Rehaak. Now I have the tools I need to protect you —well almost. I still need to wrap the sword grips with rawhide and attach binding straps for the breastplate, but that won't take long.

"Yuh still needs tuh rest laddy. Dat took a lot out o' yuh, forgin dem things. Yuh almost died doin it,"

"I suppose you're right Isil, but Rehaak tells me, and I have seen it for myself. We Eniila heal much faster than you Abrhaani heal. It won't be long before I'm back to normal.

"That's right Isil, but he'll eat a mountain of food to do it." Rehaak added before falling silent.

Laakea noticed Rehaak sitting, pensive and troubled.

"What's wrong, Spot?" he asked.

"Oh — nothing, just thinking," he answered.

"It's not really a lie," Rehaak convinced himself. I am just thinking that this quest has cost everyone too much already. I must leave soon, before someone dies on my account."

"At least we know the meaning behind your father's song," he said smoothly, changing the subject. "Do you think he ever managed to do what you have just done?"

"No, I don't. For one thing, he never had any of the *Ehlbringa* to work with. As far as he was concerned, it was a work song, a ballad, set to the rhythm of hammer blows on the anvil. He said that no one since Selvyn had been able to work with *Ehlbringa*."

"I just had an idea. I could be one of Selvyn's descendants! My mother used to recite her genealogy to me. Someone named Selvyn was in the list, more than ten generations ago."

Laakea paused in his recollection. His face solemn, he spoke again, "But that leaves me with an uncomfortable conclusion about the assassin's blades."

"What conclusion?" asked Rehaak?

"The flame creature said Selvyn was the last of my kind to work with *Ehlbringa*. If Selvyn was the last of my kind to work this metal, then who made those knives? If that is true then Selvyn himself must have made them. That is the only explanation."

"Why is dat important?" asked Isil.

"Because, Selvyn is a hero of the Eniila people. How could a hero do such wickedness? Those weapons radiated evil, they were twisted creations, wrought to serve the darkness; designed to take life for the Dark Ones. "

K. R. Schultz

"Is dat why dey gave us duh creeps tuh handle 'em den?"

"Probably. I wonder what happened to Selvyn that caused him to turn away from the light and create those perversions of his craft. I remember something the flame being told me, when I said that I might misuse power, if I received it."

"What did it say?" asked Rehaak, looking puzzled.

"He said, 'You have spoken truth. To his disgrace, Selvyn also found this to be true '."

"It must be difficult to believe that a hero of your race followed the Dark Ones," said Rehaak.

Laakea did not answer as he began, rewrapping the breastplate and the two swords. He knew that this metal would never rust, but they were holy items, so he wrapped them with reverence. He wondered how Selvyn could have managed to twist *Ehlbringa* to serve the evil purposes of the Dark Ones. Why would he have even wanted to do such a thing? He shuddered at the thought of so much power bent to the service of evil, even as he rejoiced that he had such fine weapons to protect his friends.

"I already have rawhide for the grips. I will have them wrapped before tomorrow," he said finally.

"Yuh best take it easy young'un," Isil cautioned.

"Wrapping the grips won't take a lot of strength or energy, Isil," he said, as he rose from the table. He lifted the lid of a trunk near the kitchen and rummaged through it. "See, here it is. I can start right now."

He brought the rawhide strips to the table, and got a bowl from the kitchen. Isil can you get me some water to soak this leather? I will wrap it around the hilts while it is still wet and when it shrinks it will remain tight on the grip."

She left to fetch the water. Isil had notice the change in Rehaak's mood. It troubled her but she said nothing to Laakea. She did not want to bother him with her worries just yet. He needed time to heal, although after the meal and copious amounts of water, he already looked considerably better than he had earlier. Her cooking was good, but not that good. Laakea must be right when he said that Eniila bodies healed faster than Abrhaani bodies. The change looked nothing short of miraculous to her.

Rehaak rose and began to clear away the dishes and cleanup the breakfast leftovers. He worked silently, periodically looking at Laakea over his shoulder, while he worked.

Laakea had taken the swords out of their wrappings again and sat contemplating the work he had done, five nights ago.

"Rehaak, can you go to the village soon? I will need some heavy leather strapping for the breastplate. I already have buckles, my father and I made hundreds of them, and there are still some left."

"I shall leave first thing tomorrow morning to see the tanner. You shall have the finest and strongest leather he can supply."

The day passed quickly, as they all found work, to keep them busy. By nightfall, Laakea had completed wrapping the sword grips.

***

The following morning they were all up at sunrise. When they ate breakfast together Laakea looked as fit as he ever had. He tried to ask Rehaak for details about the next step in his quest for the Aetheriad, but Rehaak gave him the impression that he wanted to avoid the issue. Finally, Laakea gave up and went out to the forge to find some buckles for fastening his breastplate.

Rehaak got up and began to gather his things preparing to leave for the village.

"Yuh best not lollygag." Isil chided.

"I shall hurry as if my life depended on it — because it does," he answered, and left the house, closing the door behind him. "Farewell friends," he whispered.

Rehaak struggled to keep his emotions at bay, as he parted from his friends for what he knew was the final time. He felt it was better to leave now before anything awful happened to them. He convinced himself that fate had constructed the twists and turns of his life and he made himself believe that circumstances beyond his control forced him onto paths he would not have chosen. He wanted to escape from fate's unwelcome demands on his life again.

Laakea and Isil were the only two people he truly cared for. It was the only way to protect his brave friends. His heart felt like a shard of stone in his chest as he walked swiftly away from the house and forge.

The strong bonds that bound him to Isil and Laakea waged silent warfare with his resolve. Although his feet still led him away, his heart kept turning back to Isil and Laakea. He began to waver in his decision.

Perhaps he would go to the village and get the leather after all. He still had all day, before he had to decide whether to go back to Laakea's house or not. His mind was in utter turmoil, as he repeatedly made and unmade his decision to abandon his friends forever. He followed the trail leading to the Dun Dale road. For most of its length, it ran beside a stream. He was so busy with his own thoughts, that he did not notice that silent shadows tracked him.

CHAPTER 28: A NEW OPTION

Rehaak hurried along the road toward the village of Dun Dale, lost in a morass of conflicting thoughts. He noticed a man ahead of him heading in the same direction. He gradually gained on the fellow who was obviously not a local. The man was dressed in fine clothing, only slightly travel worn. This was definitely no one from the village, or from anywhere nearby. It was not often that outsiders came to the village, especially not outsiders wearing expensive clothing.

Rehaak's curiosity took over. He just had to know why this man was strolling along the road to Dun Dale. No one important ever went to Dun Dale, or even knew Dun Dale existed. He put on a burst of speed to catch up to the man more rapidly. The fellow ahead sensed his intention. He stopped and turned to watch Rehaak's approach.

"Hallo!" he called out to Rehaak with a smile.

"Well met, friend." Rehaak responded. "Are you on the way to the town of New Hope?

"No, I am on the way to Dun Dale. Have I taken a wrong turn?"

"No this is indeed the way to Dun Dale. You have made no mistake. Though I suspected that perhaps you were lost, since I barely know of the place myself and I am quite familiar with these parts."

"Dun Dale is indeed, my goal, as it has been all the weary way from Narragansett. I would relish some company, if you have a mind to walk with me." I fear the trees are beginning to close in on me, in this deserted place. These open spaces without people about tend to give me the shivers. I fear his is no fit place for one accustomed to city life."

"I have no objection to your kind offer sir." Rehaak paused, wondering if he should give his name to the fellow since he was obviously a nobleman from the city that had exiled him.

The stranger broke the silence. "My name is Dreyenar Asanudain," he said, using the second name as was customary with the nobility. "Call me Drey. I have come on a tour of inspection."

Drey did not say what he was inspecting, nor did he mention who had sent him all this way without escort. The omission set off warnings in Rehaak's mind. Nobles would not wander about the countryside without a retinue of some sort. Rehaak decided in that moment to use a false name. He felt it was better to err on the side of caution when approaching this stranger.

"My name is Melnrun noble sir," he lied.

"I can tell by your speech that you are a man of some breeding yourself, unless I am badly mistaken," said Drey. He paused for a moment looking into Rehaak's eyes, as if to gauge his veracity.

"Not of breeding, good noble-sir, but I am a man of some education. That result having been caused by the inclination of overly ambitious parents." He lied again.

"Ah, I suppose that all parents have that inclination to a greater or lesser extent. It is natural, is it not, for parents to want better for their children than what they, themselves have received at the hands of the gods? Let us continue our conversation along the way, if you would be so kind as to accompany me."

"With a good will, sir. Lead on." Rehaak replied.

"No doubt you are wondering about my retinue or rather my lack thereof."

"I admit the thought had crossed my mind. It is — unusual for one of the gentry, such as yourself, to journey this far without companions."

"Ah yes, they all deserted me along the way when we were set upon by brigands. They left me to fend for myself. I should have taken my own men, instead of hired mercenaries for the journey. I will not repeat that error again, Melnrun," he nodded trying to look ruefully at Rehaak.

Rehaak felt that he sensed falsehood in the statements but could not be sure.

"What is it that brings you so far from the capital, if I may be so bold as to enquire?"

"You may indeed ask, but I am afraid that I am not at liberty to expound my reasons. How did you come to find yourself out here, in the back of beyond, Mel? May I call you Mel? Or do you prefer Melnrun?"

"Mel is fine. I grew tired of the city and I chose this direction on a whim and it has suited me well enough until now."

"Ah, do I detect the winds of change tugging at your cloak once more? Do you seek new adventures to satisfy your soul, my friend?"

"You might well say that, Drey. I have travelled extensively most of my life and perhaps it is only habit that calls me on, but I do believe it may be time for me to move along once more."

"Wonderful!" Dreyenar gushed. "I am in need of companions. Perhaps you would consider joining me.

Our meeting may have divine significance. We may accrue some mutual benefit from journeying together."

"I must first ask a question." Rehaak hesitated. "Where are you bound?"

If this fellow were heading back to the city, it would mean trouble for him. Perhaps the Creator had provided Drey as an avenue to protect Laakea and Isil from their foolhardy commitment to him. They would be free from the need to carry on the quest once he was out of the picture. He felt relatively certain they could then live safely anonymous lives.

"I am bound to meet my master, who is undertaking a voyage to Baradon. Once I have overseen his interests in this region, I shall journey southward along the coast, to the port of Aeron Suul. We shall be too late to meet my master, but we will seek passage to Baradon and meet him there."

"That sounds well enough to me, I accept your offer," Rehaak said confidently, but in the back of his mind, something did not sit well.

There was a niggling doubt about Drey and his mysterious master. Perhaps Rehaak felt pangs of conscience about betraying the trust that Laakea and Isil had in him. He determinedly shrugged it off and the feeling abated. They continued their conversation as they walked towards the village together.

Once they reached the village, Drey excused himself to attend a meeting on behalf of his master. He left Rehaak alone to wander about aimlessly. Rehaak finally decided to stop at the inn for a pint of beer and a joint of mutton. He sat alone at a table in a dark corner of the Dancing Dog, as the decrepit inn was named. It was his custom lately to remain inconspicuous, when in a town on business.

As he sat trying to enjoy his meal and his beer, four men entered the establishment and made their way to a table across the room from him. All four men were heavily cloaked and hooded, in spite of the midday heat. The sense of uneasiness that he had been feeling all day intensified, as the men ordered food and drink. He tried to shrink further into the shadows in his corner. He had chosen a table well away from the window and door. In hindsight, he wished that he had picked a spot nearer the door, so that he might slip unnoticed from the inn, but it was too late for that now.

A sinister cloud hung over the fellows across the room. The innkeeper seemed to sense it too as he brought the men their beer. Once Aert, the innkeeper, had set down the tankards, he hurried off quickly. It appeared that he wanted to get as far from that table as possible. He slipped over to Rehaak's table to see if he wanted anything more.

"Have they been here before?" Rehaak asked softly with a nod of his head in the direction of the newcomers.

"Aye, dey has." Aert whispered his response. "And dey gives me duh shivers jus lookin at em. Dey be up to no good. Anyone can tell dat right off. Why does yuh ask?"

"I may have met them before, or some like them."

"And yuh survived tuh tell about it? Consider yerself lucky den. I hear dey be assassins, but who dey'd want tuh assassinate in dese parts is beyond muh reckoning. Dey'll be gone soon enough, thank duh gods. Dey never stays long."

Rehaak breathed a sigh of relief at Aert's last statement. He had been considering making a run for it, but if they were going to leave soon, he would just wait them out. He sank lower in his seat and pulled his hat down over his eyes, trying to become one with the shadows. He nervously checked to make sure that his staff was still leaning against the wall beside him and felt the reassuring weight of the knife in his belt. His sling would do him no good at such close quarters.

Once he had steadied his nerves, he cupped his tankard in both hands like a determined drunk, lowered his head and surreptitiously watched the men. Time passed at a snail's pace, as he waited for the men to finish their meal and leave. Rehaak drank very slowly watching the strangers from under the brim of his hat. Tension built. Just as he felt that he could no longer stand the strain, the door to the inn opened and Drey walked in.

Drey looked around, waiting for his eyes to adjust to the gloomy interior of the inn. Just as Rehaak was about to beckon to him, Drey walked over to the table occupied by the four forbidding strangers. They shared a handclasp and he sat down with them. Rehaak could not hear what they were saying but he could tell by the way they all moved in to huddle over the table, that they were sharing something very private. He could also tell by the way that they held themselves, that they considered Dreyenar an authority figure among them.

The innkeeper brought a tankard to Drey and asked for his order, which he declined. They had stopped talking when Aert approached and did not begin speaking again until he departed. They were definitely plotting together.

Rehaak's desperation had reached a high pitch by the time Aert returned with another tankard of ale for him. Rehaak had not asked for another. It would have been his third, and that was two more than was usual for him. When Aert set the tankard on the table, he paused and leaned down to whisper to Rehaak.

"I knows who yuh are, Rehaak and dey be looking fer yuh. I knows dey thinks muh wits is dull, and dat may be, but muh ear is sharp as any. I owes yuh fer duh cure o' my little'uns, when dey got duh fever last winter."

Rehaak began to say that he knew nothing of this cure or the village, but Aert signaled him to silence.

"I knows yuh don't know nuthin bout us, but muh cousin what lives in New Hope; he got duh potion from yuh and sent it on tuh us. Follow me an I can repay muh debt tuh yuh right now. If'n yuh waits much longer, it might be too late."

Rehaak rose casually without attracting the attention of the men conspiring at the far end of the room. He followed Aert into his living quarters, attached to the rear of the inn. They made their way quickly and quietly through the kitchen. Aert hushed his wife and children as they tried to greet Rehaak, and whisked him out the back door to the woodshed.

When they reached the shed Aert said, "I wouldn't stay hereabouts now if'n I was you. Rumor has it dey got Raamya's boys lookin fer yuh too. Dey bin out tuh yer place and found it empty. His son Mato's bin askin fer yuh all over duh place, but none likes him and none would tell him anythin even if dey knew sumthin, which dey doesn't —leastwise not yet."

"I must get some leather for a friend before I leave town. Is it safe for me to do that?" Rehaak said as he realized his only option left, lay in fulfilling his original mission.

"Not unless it be more important dan yer life. Tell yuh what — I'll send one o" duh young'uns tuh fetch what yuh need and you just hunker down here in duh shed until dark. Den we can get yuh on yer way without no fuss and bother."

"Thank you for your aid Aert. Here is some gold for the leather."

"Never mind dat foolishness. Duh tanner owes yuh fer yer healin potions too. He'll be more dan willin

297

tuh give yuh what is necessary once't we explain it tuh him. We are all beholden tuh yuh in one way or anudder."

"Don't any of us want yuh tuh come tuh no harm. Cept fer dat skunk Raamya or his boys maybe, and I doubt even he'd wish yuh duh kind o' misery dat is sittin, an waitin back inside. Most of us'd rather eat our own slops dan help him and his kind agin yuh. Now you just lay low and we'll take care of everythin fer yuh."

With that said, Aert turned and went back inside the inn. Within moments, his youngest daughter Breisha, slipped out the door past the woodshed toward the alley. She was as silent as the gathering shadows, as she stopped, to offer an encouraging smile, and a wink at Rehaak hiding among the hearth logs.

Rehaak was surprised at the respect the village folk apparently had for him. He had never been to Dun Dale before. He had no idea, that they knew of him or held him in such high regard that they were willing to risk their lives to help save his. He had unknowingly helped heal them for almost three years and had never charged them for his cures. They felt obligated to him for his remedies. Everywhere he went lately, people were risking their lives on his behalf. Was there no escape from other people's devotion to him?

It was very different in Narragansett. In the city, in the midst of abundance, everyone was out to grasp whatever they could for themselves. Here, out on the edge of barbarism, where everything was in short supply, small acts of kindness and care abounded. It was perplexing to say the least.

As he waited, he turned over recent events in his mind. He was certainly glad that he had not given Drey his real name. He was also glad, that over the last three years his appearance had changed so radically.

He had taken to shaving his beard like Laakea, he had put on several pounds of muscle from hard work, and now thanks to the previous assassination attempt; he had a striking strip of white in his hair. He supposed that anyone who did not know him well would be unable to recognize him.

Now he knew beyond any doubt that Laakea and Isil were right about his enemies. He had somehow angered a very powerful man. That man had sent a young nobleman out to find him, along with several groups of assassins. He was no longer safe here, nor was he safe anywhere else, if that man's influence extended all the way to Baradon.

What was happening in Baradon? He knew that curiosity was getting the better of him again, but he wanted to know what plans Drey's master was plotting in the Eniila homeland. He wanted to know, more now than ever, what had happened to Aelfric, Laakea's father. He wanted to know what had happened to Voerkett, Isil's husband. It might almost be worth the risk to pretend that he was Melnrun and travel along with Drey until he got some answers.

When he left for the village this morning, he had planned to leave his companions behind, to spare them certain death at the hands of assassins. Previously simple choices were now life and death decisions, and not for himself alone. He wondered how many times people made decisions in their lives, that could mean the difference between life and death; never knowing that their lives, and the lives of those they loved, hung on those choices. Life and death hung on the toss of a coin and people chose without perceiving the danger.

The consequences of most of his choices had seemed so innocuous and unimportant, when he made them. Many of those had landed him in serious trouble. He had no difficulty making choices when he believed that nothing rode on the outcome, but now that he knew the wrong decision could be disastrous, he felt incapacitated. This morning he had decided to abandon his companions. Later in the morning, Drey offered him a way out and he had taken the bait, without getting so deeply hooked that he could not wriggle free.

He needed more information, but for every answer, he received three more questions. It was nearly intolerable, but he now knew one thing with certainty. Those choices he had made earlier today, had led him to this predicament, where he sat dithering in a woodshed. Ironically, he had only one sure choice left. He could not risk discovery by travelling with Drey. He must return to the forge and then continue to look for answers with Laakea and Isil.

They needed to go back to Narragansett, to find more information from the Scriptorium. Something he had read somewhere was still haunting his memory like an ancient ghost. It had something to do with Baradon, of that he was certain. Drey had unintentionally given him a clue, when he mentioned his master's trip to the Eniila homeland. Quite possibly Baradon held the answers he needed to save Aarda from the ravages of the Nethera. Baradon was the only place he had not searched for the Aetheriad. His conversation with Drey had convinced him that he had been looking in the wrong place.

It would be risky to go to Narragansett, even more hazardous to go to Baradon. The Eniila did not like Abrhaani interlopers, but perhaps with Laakea in their party they could pass Laakea off as a young Eniila lordling with his two Abrhaani slaves. Their meeting had not been an accident. It just might work. In fact, it might work better than trying to get into Narragansett.

CHAPTER 29: TRUMPET CALL

Eideron awoke, uneasy, troubled by his dreams. He could not remember the details of what he dreamt, but his rest had been disturbed for weeks now. Something unusual was happening. He just wished he knew what it was. He rose as usual and began getting ready for his day.

He was an old man. His curly white hair rose like a silvery halo around the weathered ocher of his wrinkled face. Thoughts spun in his head like dust caught in the desert winds outside their protected valley. He felt trapped here in the moment between darkness and dawn. The burden of leadership felt particularly heavy on his old shoulders this morning. How could he lead his people, when he did not know which way to go himself? He supposed that he was an expression, in miniature, of the rest of his beloved Sokai people.

The Sokai had lived here protected — no not quite the right word — isolated from the rest of humankind. In times long passed, the Sokai had feared that the madness of the Abrhaani and the Eniila would taint them, so they had fled here to Abalon.

Perhaps, because of their long years of isolation, the Sokai had succumbed to their own peculiar form of madness. The Synod was due to meet today, to begin another of their endless debates. The discussion invariably centered around what activities and actions comprised purity and sanctity. He was tired of the internal strife, but couldn't find a way out of the endless rounds of point, counterpoint, debate and discussion. That perpetual wrangling, ultimately led nowhere, except to censure new, useful insights, into the direction his people should pursue.

"Perhaps we need to leave this valley," he said quietly, not truly believing that he ever would. This was his birthplace and it would likely be his tomb. His wife's final resting place was here. Fierra's bones lay in the crypt along with at least ten generations of their forebears. He was old now; too old to travel the barren wastes; too old to go looking for the Abrhaani and the Eniila. If only he was younger —.

"We have become like insects trapped in amber. Perfectly preserved, and permanently incapacitated, by the very nature of our preservation," he mumbled.

Eideron smiled. He liked the analogy. He might just use it in the Synod, if the opportunity presented itself. He knew he was not alone in his feelings of unease. Several of the other Synod members had confided similar misgivings, arising from their own dreams or feelings. Something was definitely brewing outside their protected haven, but whatever it was, was unclear. Even if it became clear, they would still face months of debate and wrangling, before deciding what to do about the situation.

He doubted whether the present Speaker would ever approve of any action, unless she saw proof that the world was ending, directly beneath her ornamented council chair. She was a good woman, trying to preserve all that was right and good. She was — they all were — trying to maintain purity of thought and deed, but she seemed too rooted in place; too bound to the past, to move forward.

Maybe that wasn't entirely accurate. Perhaps she and the entire Synod weren't looking far enough into the past. None of them looked beyond the time when the Sokai had arrived in this valley. They had built a comfortable life for themselves here. Comfortable lives were all they wanted nowadays.

The Sokai needed to look back much farther in time, back to the time before the Sundering. They needed to look far enough back to see what the Creator had fashioned them to be, instead of merely continuing to exist as they were now, a blind, self centered people. He could feel a familiar passion rising within himself.

The Creator meant them to be the Seers and the Speakers for all humankind, and yet for the last thousand years they had been talking to no one but themselves. They were like doddering old fools muttering into their beards in their own rooms, while nobody listened. Nobody was there to listen, because they never left their valley, nor did they ever invite anyone in.

There was only one problem. How would he convince the Synod to act? Even if he could make them believe the need for action — who would go — how many would go and where would they go? It made his head ache just thinking about the decades of discussion that would cause.

Fortunately, a crashing sound in the kitchen interrupted his ruminations. He smiled to himself and called out.

"Simea, is breakfast ready?"

"Yes master Eideron, I was trying to be quiet, but I dropped a plate. I am sorry to disturb you."

"Do not fret youngster. I was awake and shall be out as soon as I am decently dressed."

He listened for more sounds of catastrophe in the kitchen. When there weren't any, he assumed his young apprentice had left. Lately it seemed like the lad had grown half a span every tenday and thumbs had replaced all his fingers. He was constantly tripping and stumbling about the place. Nothing breakable was safe in his presence.

He was a good lad, with an eager mind and a willing heart, and he often perceived what others, including Eideron missed. Yes, the lad showed promise. Even at the cost of the shattered crockery, he was worth having around.

Eideron finished dressing and went into the kitchen where breakfast and a silent apprentice both stood waiting at the low wooden table.

"Is there something else I can do master?"

"No lad I think that you have done enough damage already," he smiled at Simea, to soften the sting of his caustic humor, expecting the lad to bow and leave as he usually did. Instead, the youngster continued to stand at the table, looking like a trapped animal, uncertain of his fate, but powerless to prevent it.

"Don't worry about the plate Simea, it can be replaced."

Since he had already absolved him for the broken dish, Eideron expected the boy to leave him to enjoy his breakfast alone, as he settled onto his cushion. Instead of leaving, Simea continued to hover over his reclining master, looking more hopelessly trapped by the second.

Eideron pretended not to notice the boy or his discomfort and began to eat. He would wait it out, to see if the lad had the nerve to speak. He derived a twisted pleasure from making his apprentices uncomfortable. He justified it by saying that it built character, His friend, Himish, believed it was purely a streak of perversity in his nature.

Simea was the fifth apprentice the Synod had assigned to him. He was the fifth to undergo Eideron's efforts at building character in him. The Creator knew that all the others had been characters, by the time Eideron finished with them. As far as Eideron was concerned, anyone headed into the Holy Orders needed a backbone, and a good stiff one at that. He had a hard time suppressing a smile at the memories of those young men formerly in his service. He sadly noted that he had already outlived two of his former charges.

"Master," Simea began tentatively.

Eideron pretended not to hear. He continued to scoop up his breakfast and pretend to chew thoughtfully. Simea reminded Eideron of a fish, as he repeatedly opened and closed his mouth, while he fidgeted and blushed. For a moment Eideron thought Simea was about to turn tail and run, but eventually he mastered himself and began again.

"Excuse me, Master."

Well, Eideron thought, at least this time he was polite. He looked up at the boy with a stare calculated to throw panic into him.

"If you are going to interrupt my breakfast by jigging about like that, it had better be important," he pointed his spoon at the boy, as if it were a weapon.

"Well, out with it! I don't have all day you know!" he feigned impatience, knowing that it would make it even more difficult for the lad to continue. "Well — spit out whatever seems stuck in your craw."

"Master, I have a question for you, I know you are busy, but there is this girl," he began in a rush, and then stopped as Eideron interrupted.

"If you have questions about girls you had best ask one of the other Masters, one who is not so old, or at least one whose wife has not been dead for so many summers."

Eideron had a hard time keeping a straight face now. So it was a girl that had Simea tied in knots. He vaguely remembered his own feelings when he had first met his wife Fierra, but the boy broke into his reverie, wringing his hands and stammering.

"No sir — it's — it's not what you think." He picked up speed as the words began to come. "It's my friend Aibhera. She lives below us on our street. We have been playmates since birth and we talk a lot about things. Things like dreams, and your work in the Holy Order," he paused for breath.

The word dreams caught Eideron's attention. He listened, suddenly and silently attentive.

"We have been dreaming of things lately. We are dreaming the same dreams — both of us," he paused, as if waiting for encouragement from the older man.

"Continue." It came out as a command, although Eideron did not intend it to sound quite so harsh. Simea had finely focused the older man's attention at last.

"At first we dreamed of a dark cloud obscuring the sun. Darkening the sky in the west and moving towards our valley. It was a growing, glowering darkness, threatening the peace of Abalon. We dreamt of death and disaster occurring throughout Aarda. It was heading in our direction like a giant wave." He paused again.

"Well nightmares are not uncommon lad, but usually they are not dreamed in tandem."

"I know that sir, but there is more. Now we dream about three strangers, in the midst of the darkness. These three stand alone. The darkness tries to overcome them, but it has not been able to defeat them yet."

"The one is young like me but different, tall as a tree, fair as grain at harvest. These people are riddles we cannot solve. He has fled his home only to find it. He is a fearsome warrior with mighty arms, yet he doubts his own strength. The hand of The Creator is heavy upon him, but he fears and does not understand his own calling. He is called Judgment or Justice or some such thing."

"The second is older, olive skinned, dark, and doubting. He is shorter of stature and weaker in his sinews, but mighty in healing and lore. He does not comprehend his full power, nor does he understand the magnitude of the call of his destiny. He is alone in the midst of his friends. He is weak of will, yet powerful in compassion, but the Maker is strong upon him as well. His name is Healing and Truth."

"The last is old, but young at the same time. She is jade skinned like the second. She has seen much, endured much. She has remained whole, although she has been broken to pieces. Her insight holds them all together now, though she feels frail and foolish. Her name is Wisdom and Compassion."

"They are seeking something that was lost long ago. They have attracted the attention of the Dark Ones, who now seek to destroy them. The Nethera have attempted to silence them, but they have been unsuccessful. The Dark Ones are trying to keep their work secret, but the actions of these three may force them to reveal themselves, and their works. The Dark Ones are not ready to move openly yet, but when they do it may be too late for anyone to withstand them. The Three are a light in the darkness and a beacon of truth. The darkness seeks to snuff it out."

"We do not understand what this means. Is it possible what we have dreamed is true?" He stopped, waiting for a response from his master and mentor.

Eideron sat silently pondering the information, as the boy stood by impatiently, shifting from foot to foot. Finally he spoke.

"How long have you both been having these dreams?"

"It has been several months since we first started dreaming about the approaching darkness, but it has only been a few nights since the first of the dreams about the three, who stand alone against it. We felt it best to tell you, as soon as these new dreams started."

"I will need to meet your friend — Aibhera, was it?"

"Yes Master, I will fetch her straightaway," He began a frantic dash toward the door.

"Hold! There is no need for such haste! If it has waited several months, it can surely wait a few more hours. We are far from being certain what we must do, and even if we intervene, it would take us a long time to reach them, since we are far into what they would call, the Eastern Wastes."

"I must also attend a meeting of the Synod this morning. Have you forgotten?"

"Sorry, Master. When shall I fetch her then?

"Bring her for the evening meal. We can dine together. Now be off with you, and let me finish my breakfast in peace."

"Yes master." Simea bowed and scurried off. He narrowly avoided breaking a vase filled with crystalline flowers, which was set near the doorway.

Eideron's breakfast was anything but peaceful, after the boy left. Thoughts chased one another through his head with uncontrollable rapidity. The boy had given him a meal much larger than the food in front of him. In spite of his inner turmoil, he managed to finish his breakfast.

He hurried off to his meeting, still mulling over the possibilities that Simea had set before him. He scowled up at the sun, as he realized that he would now be abnormally late for his meeting. He usually liked to take his time and watch the wind-riders soar across the caldera. He had never flown one of the gliders but he liked to imagine the freedom they must feel while soaring high above the valley floor. He had no inclination or time today for flights of imagination, so he hardly noticed the view from his home, near the lip of the ancient crater.

By the time Eideron arrived in the council chamber most of the Synod members had already taken their seats, on low benches around the perimeter of the room, but the Speaker had not yet convened the assembly. Many members were still busy chatting with each other. A few looked up from their conversations, when Eideron entered. They acknowledged his presence with a nod of greeting. He made his way to his usual place and sat beside his oldest friend, Himish.

"What kept you old friend? You are usually among the first to arrive," Himish questioned softly. "Is anything amiss? You look troubled."

"My apprentice —" he began, but the sound of the Speaker pounding on the dais with her staff of office called the meeting to order and cut off his comment.

"We'll talk later Himish," he whispered.

The meeting dragged on interminably for Eideron. He was only partially aware of the proceedings. A sense of foreboding enveloped his thoughts. Simea and Aibhera's dreams troubled him. When the session finally did end, he dragged Himish off to the side, to explain the source of his distraction.

"Apparently Simea has a young friend and they are dreaming of the Nethera. They are active again. At least that is the way I interpret their dreams.

"What? Both of them? At the same time?"

"Yes, Himish, but keep your voice down. I don't want to stir anything, up until I have a better grasp of what is going on here."

"They dream of a great darkness that is coming our way, and three people who are trying to stand against the tide of destruction. Even more importantly — the three who stand together — are two Abrhaani and one Eniila."

"Eniila and Abrhaani, working together?" Himish looked solemn.

"Yes, you know what that means."

"I know Simea is one of our best, but who is this girl, Eideron? Who's apprentice is she?"

"I know nothing about her at all. I have heard no one mention an apprentice by that name. Simea doesn't talk much about his life outside of the order."

"And when he talks at all, he tends to stammer. I know," Himish smiled. "You really ought to be less intimidating to your apprentices, you know."

"Nonsense. It's good for them. It builds character, but let's not debate that again. I would like a second opinion, though. If you have time, could you come for supper?"

"Of course I can. I could always use a good meal." He patted his small paunch lovingly. "That boy cooks far better meals than anything my wife prepares. You know that well, old friend."

"No doubt, about that. She is a saintly woman devout and dedicated —" Eideron began.

"And unable to properly boil water," Himish interrupted sardonically.

"Undoubtedly one of the reasons I work as hard as I do," said Eideron. "I keep busy, to avoid her persistent invitations to your house for meals."

"On the bright side," Himish countered, "she is prolonging my life by preventing me from overindulging in food, unlike your rotund self," Himish needled.

"You're just jealous."

"Forsooth, you have exposed my inner darkness. Will you report me to the speaker? Will they now ostracize me from this august assembly?"

Both men chuckled together. They had been cronies for decades and they did not have many secrets left between them. In private, they often bantered this way. The speaker would have censured them if she knew, but she didn't, and she never would. Their bond of friendship ran deep, and their trust in each other was hard earned and well deserved.

"Come just before sundown if you can," Eideron said as he turned to leave the hall.

"Both I and my appetite are looking forward to it; I will be there as fast as my skinny old legs can carry me."

CHAPTER 30: AIBHERA

"But why can't I come with you Aibby?" pouted Kyonna.

"Because — you haven't been invited silly." Aibhera pretended that she didn't notice the grimace her younger sister made at her. Kyonna was only one summer younger than Aibhera, but in spite of looking nearly identical, they were as different as night and day. Both had the dark hair, ocher skin, high cheekbones and finely chiseled facial features that were typical of their Sokai ancestry. Both were slightly built, but Aibhera had the edge on her sister in height, although only about a quarter span.

"Simea is my friend too," she protested, reluctant to give up easily, in the face of her older sister's refusal.

"Master Eideron is the one doing the inviting, not Simea, and I doubt if Eideron even knows you exist. I'm sure he didn't know I existed either, until Simea mentioned me to him this morning. Besides, I'm not even sure I want to go. He's — a little scary."

"Nonsense, Aibby, he looks like a nice man. If I meet him, I can show him how wonderful I am."

She produced her most charming smile, made even more charming by the flash of her indigo eyes. Her smile was enchanting. Rather than detracting from her charm, her slightly crooked teeth added more charisma to it. When Kyonna smiled, she was letting you in on a secret that no one else would know. The sun rose with Kyonna's smile. With a demure tilt of her head, she curtsied; her black ringlets partially obscured her face and flashing eyes.

Kyonna was as impetuous and audacious, as Aibhera was stolid and trustworthy. Aibhera supposed that her sister's ability to adapt swiftly and intuitively made Kyonna such a great wind-rider. It took daring, and lightening reflexes, to ride the thermals, while carrying messages and light freight, back and forth across the breadth of their valley. The Synod Council would have assigned her sister a job as a planter by now, if not for Ky's outstanding ability with the gliders. Aibhera supposed that the same would be true of her, if she was not so organized. Her talent had earned her a place to work in the library.

"She is pure trouble," Aibhera thought to herself. *"If she wasn't so beguiling and charming, someone would have throttled her long ago."* There were occasional days when she considered choking Ky herself — right now, for example.

"Eideron is not one of your love crazed beaus, Ky. He's an old man, and a Councilor of the Synod for heaven's sake. I doubt that your flirting will turn his head. Besides, someone has to stay and help Ma with the young ones, when they get back from the crèche."

"But, if he could just see me."

Aibhera suspected that Kyonna would never tell her the real reason she wanted to come along. Aibhera felt that it was dangerous for members of her family to attract attention from the ruling elite. As long as they escaped notice, things ran smoothly for them, but once the Synod got involved in their lives, all hell usually broke loose. Being a nonentity had obvious and definite advantages in their society.

"Enough! You were not invited. It would be rude for you to show up without an invitation, and that's settled! I don't understand why you are showing any interest. What has got you so fired up about this meeting? I don't know why you would want to come anyway."

Aibhera scowled at her sister, who pouted back at her. In spite of what she had just said, she could understand why Ky wanted to come along. It was not every day someone from her family got an invitation, to the house of a notable person, like Master Eideron. In fact, it was not every day that someone from the Liara family got invited anywhere.

"I don't know Aibby," she lied, softening her stance on the issue. "I just want to come with you. You know it's going to involve politics."

"You never wanted any involvement in politics before. Why now?"

"Because politics has never involved a member of my family before." Kyonna decided that this was as close as she would come to declaring her true intentions for wanting to accompany Aibhera.

"You know that's not true." Aibhera let the statement stand on its own, because Kyonna knew the sort of politics that had affected their whole family, not just today, but every day of their lives.

Their mother worked as a planter in the communal farms of their valley. It was drudgework. It was the only work the Synod allowed Riessa. Aibhera was the eldest of four children. She and Ky were the offspring of her mother's first, bonded husband. When he had died, under mysterious circumstances, their mother, Riessa, had taken Leoned as her husband. Conservative members of Sokai society and the Synod frowned on remarriage.

The usual case when one's husband died was either to follow him into the flames of his funeral pyre, if childless. If there were offspring from the first union, the woman usually remained celibate for the rest of her life. Neither of those options suited their spirited mother's style. Instead, she had found herself another man. Riessa and Leoned had produced two more children together. They were much younger than either Kyonna or Aibhera.

Before their father's death, they had held a much higher place in Sokai society. Riessa had been the head librarian in the archives. Aibhera had inherited her mother's abilities. Their father had been a mid-level engineer. That had all changed once Riessa had begun courting their stepfather. Suddenly, Riessa was no longer fit to catalogue and sort records. She was fit only to labor in the fields, and that was all purely political. Suddenly the family found itself having to move out of their higher status home into the slum-like conditions near the base of the caldera, where all the other field hands lived.

Their stepfather was an engineer, as their real father had been. He built and maintained the great wind turbines that provided power for all the devices and pumps that kept the valley running smoothly. They direly needed his abilities with the complex engineering, so in spite of his relationship with the Riessa, he had managed to keep his position. He had moved down-slope to live with them, because the Council had forbidden Riessa and the girls to move higher. It was no small sacrifice for him, but it proved his devotion to Riessa and the girls.

The result of their union had profound implications for the entire family. Nearly everyone shunned Aibhera's mother and her children. They considered her mother a loose woman, and tarred her eldest daughters with the same brush. It did not matter whether or not they were guilty of immoral behavior. Sokai society had already tried them, found them guilty and passed sentence on them all. Aibhera's reaction to this treatment was completely different from Kyonna's response.

Kyonna acted out. Through her outrageous speech and behavior, she relished the role of the temptress. Aibhera compensated by going to equally extravagant lengths to prove everyone wrong. She was the model of propriety and purity in everything she did. Where Kyonna tried to shock everyone in authority, to prove she didn't care what they thought, Aibhera's speech and actions would have been worthy of the most priggish matron of the synod. Despite those differences, both girls had their mother's strong will and determination to succeed in spite of adversity.

Riessa never complained about her treatment. She took it all in stride, and made the most of her life, in spite of her lack of status. She often said, to her daughters, that in some ways her life was even better now than it had been before. She was free of the burden of expectations, that other upper class women were forced to carry. She could do as she pleased, whereas, they had to keep up appearances at all times. Aibhera understood, since she was the one trying to carry that burden of propriety, for the whole family.

Kyonna had young men circling around her, like flies around a pot of honey. Aibhera had few close friends and almost none of them were male. The lone exception to this rule was Simea, Master Eideron's apprentice.

The Synod governed the people of the valley. It drew its members from the ranks of the most learned men and women of the Sokai. They were the elite of Sokai society. Everyone held them in high regard.

Some were revered, and others simply· feared. They literally had the power of life and death over their people. Any decision by the Synod had serious implications for individuals, either for good or for ill. No one wanted conflict with a synod member. Some Councilors could act incredibly petty and vindictive, so the common folk feared them. They held others like Master Eideron, in high esteem, because of his firm, impartial judgments. Master Eideron was one of the most senior men in the Synod.

Since Simea had come to her with the invitation to Master Eideron's' house, Aibhera's mood had oscillated between feeling flattered and flustered. As the time approached for the dinner hour, her emotions skewed decidedly toward the latter. Her parents would arrive soon, bringing the younger sibs back from the communal crèche, where unmarried young women tended the field hand's children, while the planters worked the fields.

The council would not allow Aibhera and her sister to serve at the crèche like many of the other young women. The mothers of the children attending the crèche believed that Aibhera and especially Kyonna might be a negative influence on the younger children. Aibhera's younger siblings went there each morning, in the hope that their attendance, would help mitigate some of their mother's supposed immoral influence.

Simea would be here any moment, to escort her to Eideron's dwelling, high up the east wall of the valley. Aibhera hoped that he would arrive before her parents, so that she would not have to explain herself to her mother. She could leave that to Kyonna, who continued to sulk in their room. At seventeen, Aibhera had ample freedom from her parent's control.

A visit to the upper levels was special. She knew metaphorically that she should be soaring like a Wind-rider. She had flown one of the small gliders with Kyonna only once in the course of her duties. She would never be able to fly like her sister, but that one experience had been exhilarating. All she could think was, *"What will I say to the Master, and what will he think of me?"*

The valley where the Sokai lived was the gigantic caldera of an ancient volcano. They called it Abalon. A spring fed lake, lay in the center of the crater and in the center of the lake, was a small island that the Synod had preserved as a park. The Sokai built their dwellings into the walls of the cliffs surrounding the basin. This valley was their home for centuries. Great hydraulic elevators lifted the crops from the valley floor to the storage caverns, which the Sokai had carved from faces of the cliffs. They had simply converted the caves that already pockmarked the cliff faces for their homes and storehouses. They needed the fertile valley floor for food production, so they built their dwellings in areas that were not arable.

In recent years, Council converted some of the lower dwellings into terraced areas, in order to provide more land to raise crops. The most visible sign of status for anyone was his or her dwelling height above the valley floor.

Aibhera's family lived among the terraces at the base of the escarpment. They were the lowest of the low. Simea's family lived only one level above, yet the Synod had chosen him to train as Master Eideron's apprentice. Some people felt that his selection was a concession to the lower classes. Something to keep the common folk pacified, by making them believe, that they too could attain a higher level of status someday. Aibhera knew it was because her friend was brilliant and spiritually sensitive, He had scored very high in testing, and his abilities alone, were what had won him his position.

Council required testing of all Sokai children, regardless of sex or status at puberty, but the synod had passed over Aibhera for testing. It was another slap in her mother's face by the Synod. Simea had smuggled a copy of the written text of the test to her, although it was supposed to be confidential. She had taken the test herself, in secret, without the knowledge or consent of the Synod. She scored slightly higher than her childhood friend did, but she didn't begrudge Sim his good fortune.

They had been friends virtually since birth. Simea's mother and father had been some of the very few of her mother's old friends, to stand by her when she had remarried. They had stayed close, in spite of the pressure to disown Riessa. It had probably cost them their social status, but they were loyal in spite of it. Nothing would ever stand between her and Simea. She felt certain that they would be friends until death.

She dressed quickly, paying strict attention to what she was doing, but before she felt ready, Simea called out to her from their front door.

"Aibby! Hurry up. We have to get going. It's a long climb to master Eideron's dwelling. We don't want to keep him waiting."

She rearranged her dark ringlets one last time, while looking in the small mirror by the door of their living quarters. She straightened herself up, threw back her shoulders, and took one last look before answering.

"I'm coming!" She hurried to the door where Simea stood waiting. "I hope this is not a mistake Sim, maybe you shouldn't have mentioned it to him."

"I had to, you know I did."

"I suppose so," she sighed. "Do you think we'll get a good night's sleep once we turn this problem over to the Master?"

"I certainly hope so. Let's go. We don't want to keep him waiting and I still have to prepare the meal."

"I can help you with that, and I'll probably break less of his crockery," Aibhera smiled.

"I'm never telling you anything again!" Simea protested. His voice squeaked, as he said it, the way it always did lately, whenever he felt stressed. "I'm just — nervous around him."

"I know. I am afraid that I won't know how to act around him either, but you are with him every day. Surely you must have gotten used to him by now."

"I sometimes feel like he is doing it on purpose Aibby, making me feel uncomfortable, that is. It's like he's either testing me or trying to get rid of me."

"Now why would anyone want to get rid of the smartest, handsomest, young man in the entire valley?" She batted her eyelashes at him and tilted her head in a parody of her younger sister's mannerisms.

"You do that really well," Simea laughed. "But you'll never be able to match Ky."

"I wouldn't want to, I love her to death, but sometimes she is just so —"

"Ky," Simea finished her sentence with a chuckle. "There are no words for what she is, and I love her too. I just wish she wouldn't flounce about the way she does. It makes her look tawdry. "

"I believe that's exactly the look she's aiming for Sim."

"But why? Is she determined to prove herself every bit the hoyden that people think she is? That's not the way she really is you know."

"I know that silly, I'm her sister. She has a big, tender heart. She's so strong, and she sees deeper into people's hearts than anyone I know. I think it's her way of fighting back. She doesn't want them to know how much their disapproval hurts her."

Conversation fell away as the exertion of the climb to the upper levels claimed their breath. They climbed onward, up the sloping roadway, without further comments. They could have taken the tram, but they both preferred walking. It gave them time to experience the bustle of life on the streets and the ramps. They would have had an exquisite view of Abalon from the tram, but it always left them feeling disconnected from the life of the people who lived down below. They reveled in the sights and smells of their home.

As they walked along, both carried their hopes and fears tightly bound within their souls. They had both borne the burden of their dreams for months now. Tonight they carried them to Master Eideron's house. They expected that, they would finally unload that burden on Simea's master. Once they told Master Eideron, he would take it to the Synod, and then the Synod would take the appropriate action. They both believed that once they had finished telling their story, they could go on with their lives as they had before.

They were both wrong.

CHAPTER 31: THE MEETING

Aibhera and Simea were working smoothly together. Preparations for the meal were well under way, when Eideron arrived earlier than usual. Aibhera noticed an immediate change in her friend. The moment that the old man walked into the dwelling, Simea's coordination disappeared. He immediately became ham-fisted and clumsy. However, before he became completely tongue tied, he managed to introduce Aibhera to his mentor.

In complete contrast to her friend, she was completely calm. She sensed that this man would brook no foolishness from anyone. He was someone that she could be comfortable with and respect. His temperament suited her own straightforward, disposition. She also perceived that he was fair minded and gentle underneath his crusty façade.

He was one of those people, who built a hard shell around themselves, to protect their tender hearts. In that way, he was much like her sister Kyonna; perhaps that was why she was not nervous around him. She was used to being with someone who had a similar spirit. She imagined that he had lost many friends through his long life, and that those losses had affected him deeply. He was a man who loved deeply and cared passionately, both for his friends and for his causes. He had built strong, thick walls around his heart, to keep it from being broken repeatedly.

With that in mind, she clearly understood why Simea became so flustered in his presence. She suspected he was right to believe that Eideron was testing him. It would be entirely in keeping with the old man's character, to play the bad-tempered old codger, to see if Simea had the strength to stand up for himself. He would never let people close to him, until they had proved their trustworthiness, beyond any doubt. In spite of the chinks she detected in his armor, he was still an imposing presence, a force that commanded respect and obedience. She understood now why people called him the 'Old Lion of the Synod'. Woe to those unfortunates, who fell prey to his fangs and claws.

Eideron explained that he had returned early, to tell Simea that they would be having another guest this evening. He lingered in the kitchen for a few moments. Aibhera could feel his eyes watching her and Simea as they worked. After a short while, he excused himself and went to his room to prepare for his guest. Aibhera thought it was a good thing he had left, before Simea managed to chop off any of his fingers. He was so nervous around the old man that disaster hovered over him, waiting to pounce.

The two friends worked quickly to complete the extra preparations for the meal. Any further conversation they had was limited to whispers about food preparation. Before long, they heard Eideron's friend Himish arrive. The two old men sat in the parlor talking quietly. Neither of the youngsters could overhear the topic of discussion. When Simea finished fussing over the meal, they brought it out to the dining area.

"Ssssupper is ready Mmmaster," Simea stammered, doubly intimidated by the presence of Eideroñ and his guest."

"Well, let's eat it then," Eideron said gruffly, gesturing for them all to sit down on the cushions around the low table.

As they took their places, Eideron introduced them.

"Himish, this is Aibhera, the young lady that Simea is so fond of."

Aibhera noticed Simea change color like a chameleon, only instead of blending into the surroundings, the head to toe blush only made him more conspicuous.

She bowed her head respectfully to Himish and, responded in an even voice "Pleased to meet you, Councilor Himish."

"Not as pleased as I am to meet a beautiful young woman such as you," he teased. "I am looking forward to hearing what you two youngsters have to tell two old fossils like us."

She smiled to herself, as she thought, *"What a shameless old flirt. I think I like him almost as much as Eideron."*

The meal proceeded with pleasant conversation about the weather and other innocuous topics, until Simea nervously spilled his water. He bolted from the room to get something to soak it up, nearly turning the low table over as he shot up from his seat.

Once he was out of the room Himish said, "I told you that you should try to be less intimidating to your apprentices Eideron. That boy is a nervous as a long tailed cat in a room full of rocking chairs."

"And I told you it builds character. He will need a backbone to stand up to some of the fools we have on the council," Eideron retorted, forgetting for the moment that Aibhera, Simea's friend, and confidant was present.

The grousing of the two old compatriots amused Aibhera. She tried to hide her smile behind her hand. She began to giggle. She choked on the mouthful of food she hadn't managed to swallow yet. She tried to cough gently to dislodge it. Unfortunately, her gag reflex got the better of her.

The resulting explosion sprayed the contents of her mouth across the table hitting both Eideron and Himish and everything in between. Unfortunately, Simea chose that exact moment to re-enter the room. If someone could die of embarrassment, Simea looked like he could accomplish it on the spot.

For a moment, silence sat like a boulder, teetering on the edge of a precipice.

It began with Himish, as a quiver, expanded to Eideron as a snicker, and then exploded into a full-blown belly laugh from both the older men. In moments, they were all laughing uncontrollably.

"That was the best —" Himish gasped, "The best way to end and argument," another gasp, "I have ever seen."

"Yes. You win Aibhera." Eideron struggled to regain his own composure. "I am overcome, by the explosive force, of your persuasive power." He began to guffaw again.

This set them all off again and it was a long while before anyone could draw enough breath to speak.

The atmosphere of the room had changed. It was more congenial than Simea had ever experienced. He suddenly realized, in all the time he had served Eideron, he had never heard his master laugh. Eideron was human too. He was not just a saintly figure, inspiring fear and reverence. He was not just the Lion of the Synod, waiting to devour him for his mistakes. He was a man, a man with a sense of humor and real feelings. An invisible wall between him and his mentor had been broken down. He timidly waited to step into the gap, for fear that it might suddenly close up again and trap him.

Himish was the first to speak. "That, my new, young friend is the best way I have ever seen, to bring my pompous old crony back down to earth. Simea join us at the table, if you please."

Himish invited him to the edge of the gap. Simea stepped through onto new ground. His world had changed in an instant, and he had Aibhera to thank for the transformation.

"Now," began Eideron, "What do you two have to tell us?"

They both told their stories to the older men in a torrent of words, which wound together like water in a stream, as they interrupted and corrected one another, or clarified some point that the other believed was unclear. The tension in the room had evaporated, like morning mist, destroying all the barriers to friendship. Both Himish and Eideron listened intently, without comment. When the youngsters had both finished speaking, Himish looked gravely at Eideron.

"You were right old friend. The Synod needs to hear this very soon. Perhaps at the next meeting if we can get it on the agenda. It appears that the Eniila and the Abrhaani are working together again, which fulfills the old prophecy. This means that it is time for us to rejoin them."

Eideron looked at Aibhera. "Why aren't you apprenticed to someone like Himish or me? It is obvious that you are very gifted. What were your scores in the testing?"

Both young people visibly paled at the questions as if temperature in the room had fallen to near freezing.

"What is wrong with the two of you?"

"The Synod has never tested Aibhera," Simea blurted.

"I detect no falsehood in the statement but —" Himish started.

"Don't try to protect me, Sim," Aibhera cut him off, when it looked like he would start again.

"All right then! Who tested you? Since by the wording of Simea's half-truth someone tested you. Moreover, why didn't we test you? It is compulsory that every youngster is tested at puberty, by Synod law." Eideron's voice rose slightly.

"It's not her fault Master; they denied her for testing."

"Who? Who denied her testing? For what reason?" Eideron's voice rose still more and Simea began to tremble, but Aibhera could see that he wouldn't back down this time, out of loyalty to her.

"Enough! Eideron, calm down!" said Himish. "You need to stop bellowing at them, and listen to what they have to say."

"Aibhera, tell us what happened," Eideron said more calmly, as he took control of his passions once more.

"Simea's essentially, telling the truth. The committee for testing refused to allow me to sit for the test. Simea felt it was unfair and smuggled the test to me so that I could take it after he did."

"What reason did Councilor Herron and his bunch of legalistic nitwits, give for disallowing you to test?"

"They said I was unfit because my mother had remarried"

"What does your mother have to do with it?" it was Himish's turn to raise his voice.

Aibhera continued in spite of the interruption. "My mother had remarried, sir, and they said that I was morally unfit for testing because of it."

"They can't do that!" he spluttered. "The only reason for disallowing testing is for immorality."

"Yes, that was what they said," Simea interjected. "Her mother's immorality prevented Aibhera from undergoing testing."

"What!" Both men nearly shouted, simultaneously.

The youngsters looked at each other, completely baffled by the reaction of the older men. They had expected a scolding, at the very least, for disobeying the direct edict of the Testing Committee. Now they were seeing two men they had only recently begun to trust, both in fits of rage, but neither man was angry with them. It felt like standing in the center of a dust devil. The dust and debris flew all around them, but they were calm and untouched, in its center. It was disconcerting and they were nervous, not knowing what to expect next.

Himish was the first to notice their puzzlement.

"The only reason for disallowing testing is moral failure," he began.

"Have you had any personal moral failure, to your knowledge, or Simea's?" Eideron asked.

"No," they both answered, still puzzled.

"You may *only,* be disallowed for your *own* moral failure, *not* someone else's immorality. There is a *very* good reason for that rule." Eideron spoke slowly and with heavy emphasis.

"As a matter of curiosity," Himish interrupted. "What was your score Aibhera?"

The youngsters began to understand the situation. Apparently, the Testing Committee had overstepped their authority, and Aibhera could serve as an apprentice after all.

"She scored ten points higher than I did," Simea boasted, proudly.

"Those idiots! — Himish, we have sitting before us, the two highest test scores in at least eight generations, and that moron, Herron has disallowed the better of the two from testing!"

"I know. It's no wonder things are going to hell here."

"We have to get her tested immediately; otherwise they will not allow her to testify in the council. This is too important to let those pompous bombasts win. If our interpretation of what Simea and Aibhera told us is true, and I believe it is. They will allow the destruction of Aarda, while we dither and debate. The Abrhaani and the Eniila are fulfilling the prophecy, while we, the supposed protectors of truth, cower here in Abalon, ignoring our responsibilities. The Abrhaani and Eniila are ready and we must join them. They need us. "

"At least some of them seem to have joined forces," Himish qualified.

"Then it's time for us to join those that *are* working together, before it is too late."

"I agree. The Nethera will destroy them without our help. How can they win, when they can't even see what they are fighting against?"

"Or who is on their side."

"I will talk to the ones I trust on Council."

"And I will do the same, I hope it is enough."

"What can we do to help Master?" Simea asked.

"Nothing for now — Aibhera, we will contact you when it is time for your testing. Until then, both of you go back to your duties, and leave this to us."

"I believe it is past my bedtime, so I will be going now," Himish said. "It appears he Bright Host is active again too. We have seen nothing of them since the sundering. That alone is a momentous event."

"Yes it is, momentous indeed," Eideron seconded.

"Simea, see your friend back to her home. I will tend to your chores, myself, tonight. You have both done very well and I am proud of you."

Simea blushed again, as he heard the words of praise from Eideron. Aibhera knew it was not embarrassment this time. He was basking in the warm glow of his mentor's acceptance and approval.

As they left, Eideron began to clear the table. He felt good to do honest work again. He had suffered pampering and coddling long enough, so had the rest of the Sokai. It was time, perhaps long past time, for the Lion of the Synod to roar once more. He doubted that he would get many more opportunities.

CHAPTER 32: VOERKETT

Laakea and Isil spent the day preparing, so that they could leave quickly, when Rehaak returned with Laakea's leather. Isil packed provisions and blankets, while Laakea practiced with his new weapons. He tested their feel and weight. He padded the backside of the breastplate and tied it in place temporarily, with cords instead of the leather straps. By midday, Laakea was satisfied with the weapons and armor. He set everything in order, and added his leather forearm guards to the pile. They had protected him from sparks when he worked in the forge, so he suspected that the heavy leather would do nicely for vambraces.

They expected Rehaak to return in the early evening, so they planned to set out at first light the following day. Isil had prepared another meal for them to share. She was constantly amazed at how much food Laakea needed. He had fully recovered from his ordeal, in the forge of The Creator, but he still ate like there was no bottom to his belly. She supposed that he required more fuel than the average Abrhaani, because of his larger frame and musculature.

"Thank you for cooking again Isil, I don't seem to have the knack of it like you and Rehaak do."

"Dat be a bit o' understatement, methinks, but yer welcome all duh same," Isil teased, though she did not have firsthand knowledge about Laakea's infamous cooking.

"Could you tell me more about your husband, if you don't mind?"

"Sure I'll tell yuh bout him if yuh likes. I got most'a duh hate outta me now. Whaddayuh wanna know?"

"Do you know anything of his history before you met him?"

"Sure, he told me some stuff 'bout how he used tuh live in Baradon. Does dat interest yuh, lad?"

"Yes, very much. Go ahead."

"Apparently, his folk wuz rich merchants. He wuz born an grew up tuh be a strappin lad like yerself in duh port city o' E'shook. Apparently, his folks were important folk in dat city.

"What caused them to leave?"

"Dat's duh story I'm getting to, if yuh keeps yer britches on."

"Sorry," Laakea apologized, taking another bite.

"Duh city was under siege by yer Pa's folk, an duh gates of duh city were about tuh fall. Young Voerkett's folks had put him into a secret room above duh portico, in dere mansion, tuh hide him from duh invaders. He wuz only a small boy, maybe eight or nine summers."

Laakea remembered the name of the city from something his mother had told him. Apparently, his father had led the Eniila forces that took E'shook, and forced the Abrhaani out of Baradon. According to Shelhera, E'shook was the last of the Abrhaani cities in Baradon to fall. It was the Eniila's final victory, for control of Baradon. It forced the Abrhaani out and sent them packing, back to Khel Braah. The victory set the

Eniila free and in control of their own homeland. Laakea's attention shifted back to Isil's story.

"While he was in hidin, he could see duh city below him from duh window of his secret room. He watched as duh Eniila broke down duh city gates and stormed into duh city. Our people fought valiantly, tuh defend dere homes and dere families, but dey was no match for duh bloodthirsty Eniila invaders."

Laakea found it strange to hear the story told from the viewpoint of the other side. He had always imagined the battle, as a glorious uprising of the Eniila people, to repel Abrhaani interlopers. It was strange to hear the Eniila forces described as bloodthirsty invaders, of a peaceful and prosperous city. He felt the urge to correct Isil's account, but he resisted it out of loyalty to her. She had earned the right to keep her opinions, without argument from him, although he knew she was wrong.

"Duh fightin flowed right up to duh house where Voerkett wuz hid, as duh Abrhaani forces fell back to duh center of duh city. The last of duh city's forces made a stand on duh steps of duh house, with Voerkett's father and dere household guard. They withstood several vicious charges from the Eniila warriors. It looked like dey was gonna be able tuh hold on, until duh King of duh Eniila arrived."

"Sorry to interrupt again, but what did he look like?" Laakea asked hungry for more details.

"He wuz an enormous man, with a fearsome look in his eye, covered in duh blood o' his many victims. He wore a great horned helmet an carried a big two-handed sword. Dere wuz a big gash on his left cheek, so dat side o' his face wuz covered in blood. Voerkett told me he looked like, 'a rampaging demon, escaped from hell'."

Isil's description awakened memories in Laakea. He remembered his father's many battle scars. They covered his body and face. He too, had a big scar on his left cheek that glowed like coals when he was angry, but most Eniila bore similar scars.

His father had called his scars, "Evidence of hard lessons learned and bitter memories best forgotten."

Isil went on, "Once he got dere, things changed. He organized duh forces dat had bin skirmishin with the household guard and led duh final assault on the house. He cut through duh defenders' center like a hot knife through butter. His men followed him, fighting dere way up duh blood soaked stairs and over duh bodies o' duh fallen.

Duh household guard surrounded Voerkett's father, tuh try tuh protect him but duh king, an his blood crazed horde, cut dere way through. When duh guards wuz all dead, he made Voerkett's Pa kneel in front o' him, while dey brought out duh servants, duh women, an Voerkett's Ma. He made 'em all kneel beside his Pa, while dey looted duh mansion."

"Once all duh valuables wuz hauled away, duh king turned to Voerkett's Pa, an said, 'This is what you Abrhaani can expect, if you ever set foot in Baradon again. This is our land, not yours and the only way you may remain here is in death or in chains. What is your choice? You may give your answer to my men.' He turned and walked away through duh bodies without waitin for duh answer."

"Voerkett said, dat he would never forget dat face, as long as he lived, an he swore dat he would get vengeance on duh Eniila, an dere king fer what happened dat day."

"Why was he so bitter, when they were allowed to leave?"

"But, dey weren't allowed tuh leave, laddy. Dose bastards stripped and raped duh women; even Voerkett's ma. Dey forced his Pa tuh watch.

Voerkett watched too, from duh window above duh portico. Some o' duh women died from bein raped. Once dey done dere worst tuh duh women, dey cut off Voerkett's Pa's head an stuck it on a spear, tuh parade around duh city like a trophy. Anyone dat survived, dey took away in chains tuh be slaves."

Laakea felt sick. He no longer had the urge to correct her version of the story. He imagined how he would feel, if he had seen his mother raped and his father butchered like an animal, in front of their home. Those images would poison his life forever. Laakea felt sorry for Voerkett, and ashamed of his father's people. There was no honor, and certainly no justice in such behavior. He couldn't bring himself to ask if Voerkett's mother had survived the rape. Isil never mentioned it, perhaps Voerkett had not told her.

Isil continued again, "Once night fell duh Eniila got tuh celebratin dere great victory, with more rapin and burnin. Voerkett slipped out o' his secret room. It took days of hidin in duh sewers, eatin rats, an lizards, an other filth before he found a small yacht anchored offshore. He swam out tuh it and climbed aboard. Duh Eniila don't put much stock in boats, so dey had left all duh boats alone. Most had already sailed away tuh escape duh carnage but dis one's owner had probably waited too long."

"It took him more dan a tenday tuh sail it across duh Syn Gersuul by hisself, tuh Khel Braah. He wuz nearly starved, and he was sick from dehydration, by duh time he got dere. He used tuh wake up with nightmares from it."

CHAPTER 33: DEBATE

After hours of debate, they were no closer to a resolution than they had been at the beginning of the day. What had begun as an orderly meeting had descended into chaos. Amoreya finally managed to call the meeting back to order again, by pounding her staff of office on the dais. The volume of a hundred voices dropped, from the roar of a waterfall to the trickle of a brook. She stared down the few remaining talkers, until she had complete silence.

"On the motion of testing for the girl, Aibhera, we will have a vote," she said firmly. "The vote on whether to allow her to give evidence to the Synod Council will be deferred, pending the outcome of that vote."

"I still feel that there is no need to vote on this matter —" Herron paused to augment the contempt in his voice, "This young — woman —." He looked at Eideron and Himish with deliberate disdain. "The Testing Committee found her unfit, and their judgment should be final. If you overrule them, you set a bad precedent."

"The bad precedent has already been set by the Committee itself, Herron," Eideron interrupted. "Overruling that stupid mistake, would simply be a step in the right direction."

The noise level of the combined voices began to rise again, as people voiced their agreements with either one side or the other.

"Silence! All of you!" Amoreya was one of those women, whose voice could carry across a crowded room, no matter what or who competed with it. "There will be a vote! And it will be now, with no further debate!"

"All in favor!" bellowed the Steward of the Chamber, as he rose out of his seat beside the speaker. He counted the vote and wrote it on his tally sheet.

"Those opposed." He counted again.

"Abstentions." He made the final tally.

Himish and Eideron could see it was going to be a near thing either way. They had not expected it to go like this. They had prepared for weeks, cajoling their friends, as they tried to convince them to right the injustice done to Aibhera. Eideron began to feel like he was out of touch with the Synod, when he realized how influential Herron had become. He cursed himself for not noticing. Herron had been very busy, accumulating favors, while he had been busy, standing on principles. It had now come down to a vote, a vote based on politics versus principles.

"If the Synod has descended to decision making based on nothing more than popularity," he whispered to Himish. "The Sokai are doomed."

Herron and his cronies had done everything in their power to save face. They had slandered Aibhera, and her younger sister, who they claimed was a seductress. They brought several young men forward with testimony about her. Eideron asked how only Kyonna was branded iniquitous, and therefore excluded from testing, when the young men, guilty by their own admission, could still be accepted. He asked what made Herron allow admitted lechers to test, when they had disqualified Aibhera, in spite of no proof of wrongdoing. That had caused a furor, which took quite a while for Amoreya to quell.

They had maligned Simea, for associating with Aibhera and her sister. They alleged that there was impropriety in their relationship, but could not offer any proof of the allegation. They argued that based on those allegations Simea's testimony was also suspect and therefore disallowed as well.

Eideron countered, "If there are witnesses to any moral failure on the part of Simea or Aibhera, where are they? Unsubstantiated claims are not now, nor have they ever been, proof of anything, other than the prejudiced mind of the accuser. If there is any failure here, it is the failure of my colleague and his friends on the Testing Committee, to treat every applicant impartially and fairly, and that failure is glaringly obvious — to anyone who values the truth."

Those comments provoked another uproar, which led Amoreya to pound on the podium with her staff and call for the vote. Now the debate was over and the Steward counted that vote. The murmur of conversations subsided as everyone waited for the result

"This has not gone at all well old friend," Himish whispered.

Eideron nodded in agreement. His mind was already working feverishly on alternative plans. His gut told him they were going to lose this vote.

As the Steward rose and walked to the podium to hand the speaker the tally sheet, the crowd went silent, anticipating the announcement.

"On the motion to allow testing for the girl Aibhera Liara, daughter of Riessa Liara, the motion fails," she said. "The vote is forty five in favor to fifty one against, with four abstentions. The full council was present with no members missing, so quorum was not in doubt."

Herron and his cronies had won, and sensing weakness, they went for the jugular. Herron suggested that Eideron was too partial to his apprentice. He moved that the Synod should have Simea transferred to the tutelage of another Councilor forthwith.

When the debate was over and the smoke finally cleared. That motion had also passed. For the two old men, it was like standing in the path of a rockslide, as it picked up momentum. It swept them away, leaving them dazed and bruised, at the bottom of the slope.

Eideron shook his head sadly. "I fear there is no way to work within this system any longer," he muttered.

The next day brought yet another defeat in the council for Himish and Eideron. The vote in this case, was not even close. The council voted overwhelmingly not to send a delegation to find the people who fought against the Nethera.

Council had disallowed both Aibhera and Simea's testimony, so Eideron and Himish had no witnesses to prove that any threat existed, nor could they prove that the Eniila and Abrhaani were working together. Most devastating of all, was the overwhelming consensus that any expedition outside the valley risked the peace and safety of the Sokai people through exposure to the outside world. The vote had been nearly unanimous on that point.

No matter what else they said, Eideron and Himish knew that this attitude, now so firmly entrenched, would not allow the Sokai to play any role in the protection of Aarda. The Sokai were now a people dedicated to the protection of themselves, and nothing else.

The Sokai had avoided destruction, by fleeing to Abalon, but the victory had cost the loss of The Creator's purposes for their lives. They had lost sight of Aarda's needs and the needs of the Abrhaani, and the Eniila. To them the other two races were not worth saving. The Council believed that since no one knew their location, the Sokai could go on living in peace, and safety, no matter what happened outside Abalon. Eideron knew that was a false hope.

The Council believed that the Sokai could carry on with their lives, and avoid the chaos that threatened to engulf the rest of humankind.

Eideron called them shortsighted fools. He told them that the annihilation of the Abrhaani and the Eniila spelled their own eventual destruction. He further stated that, even if the other two races were not working in concert again, their existence at least served to divert the attention of the Nethera, from searching for the Sokai. If the Eniila and the Abrhaani perished, it was inevitable that the Nethera would find Abalon. When that happened, they would stand, alone and unaided. They could not hold on without the help of the Eniila warriors and Abrhaani healers. They would have no more rocks to crawl under, when that day dawned.

Herron countered Eideron's assertions, by repeating the same refrain, that there was no evidence of a threat, and therefore, without clear evidence, there was no need for action. He denounced Eideron's proposed mission, as lunacy. He said that as long as everyone remained unaware of their presence, there was no threat to their security. He argued vehemently that any expedition outside Abalon, inevitably risked exposing them and their location, thereby putting the entire race at risk, needlessly.

Eideron had done his best to turn them. The Lion of the Synod had roared loud and long, but few would heed his warning. They had defeated Herron's final motion to have Eideron censured. That had been a near thing. Now Himish and Eideron sat together, and commiserated in Eideron's parlor.

"Well, that is that," Himish sighed resignedly, content to lick his figurative wounds.

"That is most definitely not that," growled Eideron.

"What do you mean? There's nothing else to do! If you try anything else, they will vote again to have you censured, and next time they may win!"

"If that is the worst they can do, so be it. My position on council is worthless now anyway. We cannot accomplish anything by trying to work with those ninnies."

"They think we are getting senile —" Himish struggled to pick the correct words. "They have a point."

"Don't tell me you think we are senile too!"

"No — I just want you to acknowledge the fact that they are right about —" he held up his hand to prevent Eideron from exploding in rage again. "Hear me out damn you! They are right in saying that if anyone leaves the valley, we risk exposing the rest."

"Do you think I am stupid, as well as old? I know that as well as they do, but if we do nothing — and this effort of the other races fails, the Dark Ones will swallow us up too. This valley is not immune to attack or discovery. In fact, it is a poorly defensible position."

"How long do you think we will last, once the others are gone and the Nethera are allowed to act unhindered? The wasteland was broad and we have depended on its protection for centuries. If things have changed, it may not be as broad as it was. Aarda may have begun to reclaim it, and therefore we may not be as safe, as we believe we are.

"The truth is — we don't know anything about the outside world anymore. And that is aside from the other problems we face."

"What other problems?"

"Surely, you must have realized by now that we are running out of room and resources here.

"There is plenty of space, they are digging more dwellings into the cliff faces, as we speak, and work is proceeding quite well according to recent reports."

"And what will we feed them? Our land is almost at capacity now. Each generation our population grows larger, while our capacity to produce food shrinks because of that increased population. I estimate that in only two generations, we will need to look for more land outside this valley or face severe famine. If we have a crop failure, perhaps even sooner."

He paused to let that idea sink in.

"Even if we leave water supply out of the equation, we cannot continue as we have done for all these centuries. Our growing population, coupled with our limited resources, will force us to leave here soon and expose our position. If the Eniila and Abrhaani are gone before then, we will face whatever threats out there we find completely alone, and you know as well as I do, that our race has produced damnably few warriors. We have no one that could dispatch one of the Dark Ones. We cannot avoid discovery by remaining hidden we can only postpone it. "

"So what do you mean to do?"

"It is probably best if you do not know, my friend. That way you will not have to share my disgrace."

"No. Tell me what you plan. I might be able to help."

"I can plan nothing for now. First, I need to talk to Aibhera and Simea again. If you still want to know my plan after we have finished, I will give you some more details. Now that they have barred me from further contact with Simea, I need a favor from you. "

***

When Aibhera arrived at Eideron's house, it was already quite dark. She hid in the shadows, while she waited. After a few moments, Simea arrived to join her. Neither of them spoke a word to each other. Eideron had sent a message, via Himish, that they were to come to see him, after sunset, without anyone knowing that they were meeting. Neither of them understood the need for such secrecy. The prospect of meeting again, especially in secret excited them. It added spice and mystery to their otherwise boring evening.

They had come separately, by roundabout routes, making sure that no one was having them watched or followed. They had seen no one so far, so the precautions seemed unnecessary. In a way, it highlighted the arrogance of the Synod. They were sure of themselves and their power. They could not believe that anyone would dare to violate their edicts.

The dwelling was dark, as Eideron had told them it would be. To anyone watching it would appear that Master Eideron had turned in early for a good night's sleep after another disappointing day at Synod meetings. The young people scratched at the door, exactly as Himish had instructed them, and it opened almost immediately. Eideron must have been waiting in the foyer for their arrival.

"Enter. Hurry." He pulled them inside his darkened home. "Come into the pantry in the rear where there are no windows."

When they had negotiated their way through his darkened dwelling into the pantry, Eideron closed the door and lit a lamp. Simea was surprised to see cushions set up in the storage room with a low table on which Eideron placed the lamp.

"Why are we meeting like this Master?"

"I am not your Master anymore Simea, you can stop calling me that. Call me Eideron. The council has judged me as someone without honor. There is no need for you to honor me any longer."

Aibhera began to protest, but Eideron silenced her with a look. "The council shall have its own way. They look after the interests of all the people in this valley, and they shall continue to do so long after we are gone. I will not tolerate disrespect of the Synod. I believe they are mistaken in their recent decisions but that does not mean they do not deserve our respect."

"Very well Mm — Eideron." The words came out with difficulty. The habit of preceding the name with the honorific was deeply ingrained. He had served this man for over two years now, but he had only come to know him in the last few days. Eideron would forever be 'Master' to him, no matter what the council decreed. He was loyal, and right now, he was angry.

"No matter what the Synod says, you shall always have honor in our eyes," he said as he bowed low before Eideron.

"What is your plan?" asked Aibhera, as she also bowed before him. "Since we are meeting in secret like this, you must have some plan. One that you want no one to know about."

"Very perceptive young lady. It's easy to see why you should have been tested along with your friend." There was a bitter edge to his voice.

Eideron settled himself onto one of the cushions and indicated that they should also sit down.

"First, I have some questions to ask you both. If I receive the answers I expect, I will tell you what I have in mind. If you answer otherwise, I will forget the whole idea and this meeting will never have happened. Our lives will go on unchanged."

CHAPTER 34: NO SMALL SECRETS

Silence hung over the small room, as the two youngsters waited for the old man to ask his questions. For the second time in as many days, Simea found that he was no longer afraid of Eideron. This revelation only reinforced his loyalty and respect for the old man. Eideron was no longer a threatening and forbidding presence. He was just a wise old man, with more fire in his spirit than his frail old body could possibly contain.

Aibhera imagined that he was like the grandfather she had never known. She knew how he had fought for her in the Synod. Simea had been present and he had shared the account of the debate with her and her sister. Kyonna had wept bitterly, when she had heard about the ruling. She blamed herself for Aibhera's difficulties. Both Aibhera and Simea had assured her that it was only a maneuver by Herron to divert attention from his own guilt, but she was inconsolable.

Aibhera and Simea respectfully waited for Eideron to speak. The Synod had bent Eideron, but could not break him. They had shunned him and pushed him to the sidelines, but he was still vital in spirit, heart and mind, if not in body.

"Are the two of you still having the same dreams?" he asked.

They nodded.

"If anything the dreams have become more vivid, not less. We now smell and hear what is going on, though the words are muffled and obscure." Aibhera affirmed. "It is as if we are actually there with them now."

"And so you should be," Eideron thought, as he asked, "Are you convinced that what you see there, poses a grave danger to mankind and to Aarda?"

"More now than ever Master Eideron," said Simea, as Aibhera nodded in agreement. "Why are you asking?"

"I ask, because I need to know the depth of your commitment to your visions. Therefore, I must ask you this too. Are you willing to do whatever is necessary, to help those who oppose that threat?"

"Yes Master Eideron," responded Aibhera. She looked at Simea to see if he still agreed. "I believe we are."

"Are you willing to be censured and to become outcasts? Are you willing to never see your families again, and to cross the Wasteland to find the ones you seek?"

"So that is what this is all about," she thought. *"He will send us out to find out what is happening on the outside."*

Once she finally the understood the full cost of the task ahead it tore a hole in her heart. "We will need to think about that sir, we have no experience outside this valley. We know nothing of the outside world."

"Since I too lack that knowledge, I cannot be much help to you," Eideron said, shaking his head sadly.

"Do you intend to send us out there?" asked Aibhera, putting her fear into words. All Sokai children grew up hearing stories of monsters and dangers outside the caldera. Their ancestors had to overcome many perils, before they arrived in the safe haven of Abalon.

"Not exactly, but think hard before you answer. Many lives may depend on your choices. You may discuss the issues now, if you like, or you may do so in private and we when we meet again, you may give me your answer then."

"With each meeting we increase the risk of discovery. We will discuss this now and make our decision now. Do you agree Sim?" Aibhera knew that she had already decided. The visions were too powerful to ignore. She did not want to live with the shame that she done nothing to help the people she saw in her nightly visions.

Simea began. "Aibby, we don't know anything about the outside and we risk exposing our people to discovery, especially if we fail, or are captured."

"I know, and that much responsibility frightens me too, but think about this for a moment. My mother tells me, that the planters all say that we must either stop having children, or find new land for crops outside Abalon. That will risk our exposure too."

"This decision is too big for people as young as we are," Simea protested.

"But Simea, the Creator has given us these visions. No one else knows what we know. Now that the Synod has refused to act, what else can we do? I am terrified of leaving everything behind, but I am equally terrified to do nothing. My head tells me to stay here, but my heart tells me that staying, and doing nothing is an act of cowardice, and worse."

"You are right. I know it in my heart too," he conceded. "We may need them as much as they need us.

If we refuse to aid them, and they perish, there will be no one to come to our aid when we need help."

"Master," Simea began. "We see no other option. We must send a party to aid the Abrhaani and the Eniila, who now fight alone against the darkness. You know that we are afraid, but if you send us, we will go on behalf of our people."

"We know that they will curse us for going, and that we will never be allowed to return. That is, assuming that we survive the attempt," added Aibhera, with a smile, trying to lighten the mood with gallows humor.

"I have listened to you discuss the issues. You covered more ground than the Synod has debated and have come to an entirely different conclusion. You both demonstrate wisdom beyond your years. You are rightly afraid of the consequences of your actions, but you will not flinch from your duty. No Councilor of the Synod could do more. However, I will not send you."

Both young people looked puzzled, when he stopped speaking.

"No, I shall not send you," he repeated. "We shall go together."

Simea looked as if he were about to protest, but Eideron held up his hand, signaling him to keep silent.

"I know I am old. If you say one word about it, I shall beat you senseless. I am still quite confident that I can carry out that threat."

"I may not survive the journey. None of us may survive this journey, but you are too young and inexperienced to undertake this task alone. I still must teach you some things. The Synod has secret knowledge, which may help you in your task, knowledge that I can pass on. You cannot learn it out in the wasteland alone. If I try to teach you here, before we leave, we risk discovery, censure, and imprisonment, or worse. That would end any chance we have to assist the ones we seek."

"I must go with you, in order to complete your training, if for no other reason."

"Besides, what kind of leader would I be, if I were willing to burden you with a load that I refused to bear?" he paused and sighed.

"There is no one else, except Himish. He is almost as old as I am. He is probably more physically able than I am to handle the rigors of the task, but Himish has family responsibilities. I have no one left here. No one will miss me when I am gone. The Lion of the Synod will snarl one last time, but not within a cage devised for him by shortsighted fools."

Both young people looked surprised, when he referred to himself by that nickname.

"Yes, I know what they call me, and I intend to live up to it. A lion is not a house cat. The wilderness is the only fitting place for a lion to die. I am the only logical choice and I will tolerate no argument from Himish, or from either of you. Is that clear?" He said, feeling far less stern than he sounded.

"Yes master," they replied contritely, in unison.

"Now it is well past time for this old man to get some rest."

He put out the lamp and guided them to the door in the darkness.

"Farewell," he whispered. "I will send word to Simea through Himish, when it is time for us to meet again. Come prepared to leave immediately. I am sorry I cannot tell you what to bring, but I don't know what we will need either."

"Creator, guide us all in our preparations," he prayed aloud.

"Try to listen for His voice children, since He alone knows what we need. One more thing, do not meet together, for any reason, before we leave. I suspect that Herron may decide to have us watched at some point. He would like to find an excuse to have me impeached and imprisoned. We need to move very quickly, before anyone suspects anything."

Aibhera and Simea said nothing as they separated to go back to their homes. Aibhera took a different route home than the one she had taken to come to Eideron's clandestine meeting. Her mind raced, as she glided silently down the deserted alleys and pathways toward her home. She was sad that it had come to this, but she was excited to be part of something so dangerous and daring. It amused her, that her younger sister was not a part of this adventure. The creator must have a sense of humor. She had always taken the safe route, while Kyonna had always been the impetuous risk taker.

As she slipped silently through the shadows, she began to feel that someone or something was watching her. At first, she suspected that her participation in the conspiracy had made her skittish, but she heard little noises now and again that did not fit with the normal night sounds. After several more incidents, the feeling that someone was following her was too strong for her to deny.

She wracked her brain for a solution. She could just run home hoping to outdistance whoever shadowed her, or she could try to find out who followed her. If she ran home, she could draw trouble to her house. It did not seem like a good option. Her family had enough trouble, without her bringing more to their door. In spite of the danger, she desperately wanted to see who was following her. Perhaps she could avoid capture and still find out. She remembered a place that might make it possible.

Just around the next corner, a ladder led up to the roof of one of her neighbor's houses. They used the place to dry herbs in the sun. If she was quick enough, she might be able to climb the ladder to the roof. Once whoever shadowed her went past, she could climb back down behind her pursuer. She should be able to see who was following her, as they went by. If her tracker climbed the ladder after her, there was no way to escape from the roof, but she was willing to chance it. She wondered if Simea was having a similar problem.

She sped up suddenly, dashed around the corner and climbed the ladder as quietly as possible. A flurry of little noises on the street below rewarded her caution. She was not imagining things after all. She waited tensely, peering over the parapet of the flat roof, as she waited to catch sight of her stalker. A figure, in a hooded cloak hurried past the ladder, trying to catch sight of her again. She lost sight of the shadowy shape as it rounded a corner and disappeared. She still had no idea who it was. She waited a bit, and stealthily slipped down the ladder, into the shadows of the street below.

She was more cautious now. Her ears strained to pick out unusual sounds from the background noises of the night. She could hear nothing, other than the crickets, and the whirring wings of the occasional moth. Finally, as she neared her own house she saw the hooded figure again. It crept around the side of the residence where her bedroom lay. She crouched low and glided along as silently as she could. She rounded the corner in time to see her pursuer begin to climb into her bedroom window. The moon was low in the sky. She could see the outline of the person attempting to climb through the opening against its bright disk.

The hood caught on the top of the window frame. Aibhera's stealth and patience was finally rewarded with a view of the profile of her mysterious stalker. She ran forward quickly and grasped the cloak, preventing the shadowy figure from climbing all the way through. "Stop! Kyonna!" she whispered as loud as she dared. "What are you doing?"

Her sister jumped with fright and smacked her head on the top of the window frame. She whimpered in pain but did not scream.

"God, Aibby did you have to do that? That hurt." She rubbed her head rapidly where she had banged it on the lintel.

"Serves you right. Why were you following me?"

"I just wanted to know why my incredibly honorable sister was sneaking out, when she was supposed to be in bed."

"Well, what did you discover, nosy brat?"

"Let me go. Let's both get inside before we get caught out here."

"Oh — sorry."

"I'm a lot better at this than you are, you know," Kyonna said, haughtily.

Once they were both safely inside and seated on their beds Aibhera asked, "Alright, Ky, why were you following me?

"I just wanted to know what was happening. You have never snuck out at night before. I have, but you — never. That was strange enough, but instead of going to meet a boy, you went to see that old man Eideron. Too weird. When I saw Simea show up, and I knew you were up to something big. Especially after that huge fracas with the Synod. So what is it? What is going on?"

"I can't tell you that Ky. I want to. God knows I want to, but Eideron told me not to."

"Never mind," she said. "You don't have to tell me."

She stretched out on her bed and turned her face to the wall. Aibhera could feel the resentment in her sister's posture from across the room.

"Don't be like that, Ky, you know that I can't tell you."

"You don't have to tell me," she repeated, with an icy edge to her voice.

Her tone set off alarms inside Aibhera. She knew her sister. It was unusual for Kyonna to let go of something easily. They had always shared everything with each other. They had lived almost independent lives from their mother and stepfather, for the last several years, but they were very close to each other. This secret had come between them and it threatened to break the tight bond they shared. She wanted to grab Kyonna's shoulder, turn her over to see her face. She wanted to tell Kyonna everything. It was tempting, but she resisted.

It was already difficult enough to slip away without any farewells. Ky's unwelcome interference made it much more difficult. Keeping this secret from her sister was the hardest thing she had done, but she knew far worse would be required of her before long.

Soon she would leave forever. She would never see her sister again and Ky wouldn't know where she had gone. She stretched out on her own bed, as she felt the tears make hot trails down her cheeks. She wept silent, bitter tears into her pillow, and surrendered the outcome to the Creator.

CHAPTER 35: NO FAREWELL

An early riser might have noticed three silhouettes against the brightening sky at the lip of the crater. Eideron and his young companions could see nothing but an ocean of blackened sand and rubble, as they looked outward from the lip of the crater.

Aibhera looked back, into the bowl of the caldera, the only home she had ever known. The lush greenery looked out of place in the barren wasteland outside. It looked small from up this high on the rim, a fragile island of green surrounded by an endless blackened desert. She could see the network of canals and fields laid out below her. The orchards and vineyards lay in neat rows fading off into the distance. The grain fields and gardens, at varying stages of maturity, some yellow nearing harvest, others covered in the bright green of new growth formed a patchwork pattern on the valley floor.

There were very few trees, other than the fruit trees and the few small remaining areas of rough parklands. Most of the caldera had held lush forests, when the Sokai first arrived. In the last thousand years, the Sokai had converted the forest to farmland, out of necessity. The absence of trees meant that wooden objects had become treasures among her people. She could see the lake glistening in the distance, but beyond that, everything was blue and hazy, in the moist morning air. It usually took three days to cross the interior of the crater from one side to the other on foot.

Wind riders like her sister, could do it in less than half a day, which was why the windriders carried packages and light freight from one side of the settlement to the other. The thermals around the edges of the crater could lift the gliders high into the sky and across the valley with rapidity that was not possible on foot or by tram. Her stepfather and his friends had invented the trams. They were light baskets that ran on heavy cables suspended above the valley floor. It took a full day to go from one side to the other, but it was much faster and easier than walking.

They desperately needed agricultural land to support the population of the valley. The trams were a blessing because they carried agricultural produce and work crews, as well as other passengers. They had entirely replaced the old road systems. Wind turbines powered the trams, the irrigation pumps and the elevators. Wind powered almost everything except for the things that required heat. Another entirely different system trapped heat from the river of lava that still ran below the surface of the Caldera for that. She and Simea knew very little about the systems that provided the Sokai with levels of comfort unavailable to their refugee ancestors.

She and her companions stood silently, trying to capture what they could in their memories, before they left it behind forever. Eideron finally broke the silence.

"Well, shall we continue? Or, do you both have second thoughts? This is our last chance to turn back."

The three companions turned to face the other side of the slope. From where they stood, they could see the desolate wasteland that stretched to the far horizon. Crossing that expanse had been an arduous trek for those who survived it. It had been a death march for those who did not, and the dead were in the majority.

They had all heard the tales since birth. Probably no more than nine hundred lived through the ordeal of the march through barren, blackened lands that surrounded Abalon. They had brought all the supplies and technology they could carry with them, to make Abalon a place that was fit to live in. The wasteland had not been kind either to them or to their equipment. It had destroyed most of the machines they had brought with them. They had to abandon equipment along the way when there were no longer enough hands to carry it. Stories and songs contained several versions of that march, inextricably woven into the fabric of their culture. Once they had settled in Abalon, no one had left the valley. Eideron, Aibhera and Simea would be the first to abandon its security in almost a thousand years.

Sokai songs and literature told the story of the Time of Sorrows. The epic ballad, The March of the Five Thousand, began with stories of attacks on the Sokai by twisted creatures that prowled the edges of the wasteland they called the Blasted Lands, or nowadays the Western Wasteland. It told how the remaining Sokai beat off those creatures, before they straggled into the heat, of the volcanic rubble field. Thirst and hunger took a continuous toll of their numbers, until less than one thousand Sokai remained to found the colony in Abalon. That song and the legends they had heard, struck fear in each of their hearts, as they looked ahead. They were about to relive that march in reverse and leave their haven forever.

Their numbers had grown since those days. Over forty generations of Sokai had been born and lived out their lives in the caldera. When they died, their bodies had contributed to the fertility of the land. Their bones were later saved and laid to rest in the communal tombs beneath the cliff walls. Almost a million Sokai dwelt in a

K. R. Schultz

fertile area just over sixty miles across and roughly circular in shape. They were about to leave all that history behind, but perhaps they would write a new history for their people, outside that protected circle of green.

Eideron would not have blamed his two young companions for turning back once they saw what lay ahead. If they chose to stay, they could live long and productive lives. He was old. He had less to lose than they did, but the sight of the apparently endless desert before them, had him rethinking his commitment as well.

He wished that they had some of the technology the original five thousand had available to them.

Sokai culture and technology had grown in some areas but atrophied in others. He particularly regretted the loss of land transportation. There had been no way to bring the ancient land speeders down the cliff wall intact, and no reason for their use in Abalon. They had cannibalized them for parts. Nothing remained of them except the memories recorded in the Annals of Abalon. For their return trip across the wasteland, they would walk.

Simea broke the reverie when he answered the question.

"No Master Eideron, but we just wanted one last look. To remember."

"I told you not to call me master."

"But you are our master, our teacher, no matter what the Synod said," Aibhera argued. "You are all we have left of our homes, and our heritage." She began to cry.

"I am sorry. I suppose I need to let it pass. I regret that neither of you were able to say proper goodbyes to your families, but we needed to leave before they mis us. They will come after us if they realize what we have done.

"I don't understand why we couldn't have taken three of the smaller gliders," Simea said.

"For one thing, I could not fly one," Eideron confessed. "The second reason is that they would be missed. They would know we had left with them. Himish will keep them all guessing where we have gone. The missing gliders would be harder for him to explain away. He is quite creative when it comes obfuscating. He says it is one of the most important prerequisites of a good Councilor. You should have heard — oh never mind. That's a story for another time. Shall we descend?"

They picked their way carefully, westward, down the slope of the ancient volcano; down across basalt flows and obsidian outcrops. There was little soil, no organic material at all, only gravel and fine sand between the crevices of the rocks. By the time they reached the base of the cone to relatively flat terrain the full heat of the noonday sun struck them like a hammer. The slight wind brought no relief. It only served to desiccate them further and occasional gusts blew fine dust into their eyes.

"We had best use our water sparingly. We have no way of knowing when and if we will find more," Eideron cautioned.

The two youngsters nodded in agreement. Their thoughts were on the homes they had left and the families they had abandoned, as they trudged on through the heat of the day speaking little, suffering in silence. Their skins were not used to the dryness, nor were their eyes accustomed to the glare of the sun off the bleak landscape. They made slow progress across the ancient lava field. The lava crust was broken and cracked providing uncertain footing. In many places, it had collapsed in on itself in roughly circular craters. Dust had filtered into the cracks and crevices of the rock and scraggy vegetation managed a precarious foothold in those spaces.

Eideron kept up a steady stream of talk, teaching them history. He felt it was important that his two young companions learn as much as possible, before his life ran out. He wanted to initiate them into the secrets of the Synod as soon as possible, but that would require concentration. They would have to stop for that. The uneven footing out on the lava field made that level of concentration nearly impossible. He kept a good pace without complaining. He did not want Aibhera or Simea to see how frail he truly was.

By nightfall, they were footsore, tired and coated in a fine layer of dark colored dust from head to toe. Anyone who looked would have seen three lumps of earth moving along the desert floor. They decided to stop for the night in a large circular depression where the lava had collapsed and crumbled. The air had already cooled noticeably, though the rocks retained much of their daytime heat, which they released slowly. They managed to find enough vegetation to build a small fire in a crevice large enough for them and all their equipment.

Eideron stopped them before they began to prepare the meal. "We have things that I must teach before we go farther. We will eat after the lesson. Think of the meal as a reward for your efforts."

Both Simea and Aibhera groaned inwardly but said nothing. Eideron said it was important, so it must be vital to their survival and their mission.

CHAPTER 36: LESSONS IN THE DESERT

Eideron was exhausted but he began the lesson anyway, as the firelight cast dancing shadows across the rocks behind them.

"I know we are tired, but there are things you must know, and the sooner the better. I must speak to you first about *The Quickening.* The concept of *quickening* is important for you to understand. It is one portion of the secret knowledge of the Synod. This information is given only to those who have proven themselves capable of using the knowledge for good —"

"Is that why all young people are supposed to be tested Master?" asked Aibhera."

"Partially. Testing reveals potential. Both of you scored very high on all areas. The Synod never reveals those scores to the initiates. Since those rules no longer bind us, I will tell you this. Both of your scores were the highest in our recorded history. I tell you this to give you confidence, not to inflate your egos." He said sternly.

"Since there are no others to support you, you will need confidence and daring for the tasks ahead. That is why I tell you now. Once the Synod establishes an individuals' potential, the second phase of training begins."

"What is that?" Aibhera asked.

"The Apprenticeship is the second phase where we try to train gifted students in areas of moral and ethical development. *The Quickening* can pose hazards to both the user and those around them. Power has the capacity to twist and corrupt its user, if they have not been properly trained."

"We understand Master," said Simea, matching his mentor's somber mood. "This is a special circumstance."

"*The Quickening* is the term we use to describe how The Creator endues his creatures with special power when needed. We believe that all that lives and breathes on the face of Aarda exists, because The Creator brought it into being. We also believe that nothing can continue to exist without his sustaining power.

Through the *Quickening,* He pours an extra measure of His power into an individual for a short time. When the Creator quickens us, we become conduits for His purposes in the world.

Each race has their own special ways to receive and direct this power. Individuals within a racial group may have greater or lesser capabilities in any area of gifting. You both demonstrated the highest levels of potential ability. You both appear to have a high level of integrity and moral development. Perhaps you may be able to receive abilities that were lost to our people millennia ago. In any case, that is my fervent hope.

"I suspect that you both have your impressive abilities at this time, because it is part of His plan."

"In recent times, *Quickenings* have almost ceased to occur among our people. I believe it is because we are not working for the good of the other races. We also know that the Creator responds to need, and to prayers of request. He does not respond to selfish and idle requests. He does not display his power just to demonstrate it or flaunt it. He *quickens* people, to carry out his will in Aarda. We experience few quickenings, because we are no longer willing to do what He asks."

"What kinds of things might we expect to happen, Master?"

"That is an excellent question, Aibhera. The dreams that you have already experienced are a type of prophetic *Quickening*. You are able to see things happening, either in the future, or across incredible distances. Sometimes prophecy is foreknowledge, knowing things in advance. At other times, it is the ability to discern between truth and illusion."

"Are there other abilities available to us?"

"Yes, Simea, we believe that the possibilities are virtually limitless, since the Creator's power is immeasurable. For example, there are legends of the Sokai who were able to protect people with shining walls, attack enemies with javelins of light, or travel incredible distances in the blink of an eye."

"If we — Sokai can travel like that, why are we stumbling along through this wasteland, and why did so many die on the way to Abalon, Master?" asked Simea, perplexed.

"Both, are very good questions. We have lost much knowledge over the centuries, but let me begin by explaining what we still know."

"Aarda is only a part of the universe that we can experience, the world of the Aethera is also part of that universe, and both worlds are only a tiny portion of what the Creator has made. Both the Aethera and The Nethera can move at will between Aarda and their world, which I suppose is not so much a world as a separate plane of existence or energy level. Does this make sense to you?"

"Yes, My stepfather, Leoned, is an engineer. He talks about energy states all the time," said Aibhera. "He told me that liquid water and steam are different energy states of water. But he also says that it takes energy to change water into steam."

"That is a perfect analogy, my girl. The natural state of water is liquid. We must heat it to gain enough energy to become steam, or it must loose energy to become ice, which is its solid form. The natural state of humankind is what we experience now. The natural state of the Aethera and the Nethera is the Aetherial form. For us to interact with them, either we must somehow gain energy to reach their level, or they must shed energy, to reach ours."

"How can a shift in energy levels happen?" asked Simea.

"Without the assistance of the Creator, it is not possible for us. He must pour energy into us to do it, just as we must heat water to turn it into steam. Be aware that we risk the destruction of our physical bodies when we operate at that higher level. Our bodies cannot live on the Aetherial plane for long periods. Think of it like this. If you had a piece of sewing thread and a piece of rope and you tried to lift a rock with each of them, which one would break?"

"The thread would break, of course," said Aibhera.

"That is correct. The Creator designed each of His creatures with different capabilities. Each one is able to cope with different levels of energy, or stress. Man is not designed to live for long on the Aetherial plane, nor are the Aethera designed to live at ours."

"The rope can lift light objects, as well as the heavy ones. So, they are like the rope. I understand that, but why not just use the rope for everything?" asked Simea.

"Imagine trying to thread a needle with a rope and stitch up your torn clothing with that rope, Sim." Aibhera interjected.

"Exactly," answered Eideron, pleased at the quickness of the young woman's mind.

"Each of The Creator's beings has a special purpose and function. Apparently, they can discard energy to interact with the physical world. There is a risk for them, that they may become trapped in this world, if they do not have a way of replenishing their energy. Without gaining energy again, they cannot make the transition back to their own energy level. "

"Would that destroy them like it would destroy us to remain in their world?"

"We presume that is true, but we are not entirely certain of it. It would certainly take a lot longer for them to perish in our world, than it would for us to be destroyed by living in theirs. It would be easier for a body designed to exist at a higher energy to live at a lower energy state than the reverse. Remember the rope and thread analogy. The rope can lift lighter objects while the thread will break when attempting heavier ones."

"Is there an energy state below ours, or are we at the lowest level?"

"The Sokai have always believed that Aarda itself, in some sense, is alive. If that is true, that is probably that lowest level."

"Master, tell us how we can travel the way you mentioned, I am already tired of walking," said Simea with a wry smile.

Aibhera elbowed him and gave him a fierce look, as if to tell him to stop.

Eideron laughed at the byplay and continued, "That is just one of many things that I hope you two can manage."

"You two," questioned Aibhera. "Do you mean that we must do this alone?"

"I am afraid that is correct my observant youngster. The attempt would probably kill me. I am too old."

"Pardon me, for saying so Master. I mean no disrespect, but the walk will surely kill you. I can see how this journey wears you out, although you try to hide it from us. Surely travelling instantaneously would be easier on you."

"Creator, preserve us from sharp-eyed children," Eideron said with a sigh, slumping visibly, as he gave up the pretense of strength he had been maintaining. "To answer your earlier question, Simea, it seems that we Sokai can only shift to a place we know or have seen before, and not every Sokai has the ability. Anyway, I never expected to return from this errand of ours."

"Return is not the issue, Master, the survival and success of this mission are," interrupted Aibhera.

"We all do as we must to fulfill the will of Him who made us, dear girl. Our fate is in His hands, not our own. Let us continue, shall we? Without all the interruptions, if you please."

"Yes Master," they both responded.

"Let me quickly cover the *Quickenings* commonly experienced by all three races, but understand that the list is not exhaustive. To recap, the Sokai are quickened for *Prophecy*, *Shifting*, and *Protection*.

Battlefury is the Eniila quickening, as are *Justice*, and *Voice of Command*. The Abrhaani are quickened for *Healing*, *Compassion*, and *Mercy*."

"In addition to their spiritual abilities, the Eniila have great physical power and regenerative capabilities, along with a talent for working and shaping metal. They also have some sort of affinity with fire. We don't completely understand what that affinity allows them to do."

"The Abrhaani understand agriculture, the arts, and healing, they can sense the emotional states of individuals. They have great understanding of water, waterpower, and marine craft, for example fishing and sailing."

"The Sokai are builders and engineers and are able to master the wind. We can see into the Aetherial realm far more easily than the others can, and we can see through the illusions of the Dark Ones. We protect and possess more of the history and lore of Aarda, than the other two races, because we avoided the fighting."

"We suspect that when we escaped to the Eastern wastes, we did so with most of our knowledge intact. That is why the center of our culture is, and has always been, learning and education. We still lost much on the journey to Abalon and in the centuries between, but we probably possess more technology and knowledge than the Abrhaani and the Eniila. It is possible that they have sunk into barbarism."

"There is one more thing that we have lost. It has enormous value to all humankind. It is a book called the Chronicles of Aarda by some, or the Aetheriad by others. An Aethera named Naom'han wrote it. It could provide us with the knowledge we need to stem the dark tide, but that is enough about the book for now. All we truly know about it is that it is not in our possession."

"There is a legend about a faithful remnant of the Eniila who still follow The Creator. Supposedly, one of our ancestors entrusted them with the book, since he believed that only warriors like the Eniila were strong enough to protect the precious volume. It is only a legend, and the book may indeed be lost after all this time. I doubt that he expected millennia to pass before someone needed the book."

"Tomorrow night I will teach you what I know about *Shifting*, which is what we call instantaneous travel between two points. You will need time to prepare, and you will need to concentrate. We are all too tired and hungry for that now. So ends the first lesson."

After eating and drinking, they rolled themselves in their bedrolls. Aibhera fell asleep quickly. Simea spent time memorizing each scrap of stone in the area, for his reference points to attempt to *Shift* the following day. He also left a medallion, a birthday gift from his mother, in a crack in the rock nearby. He felt that it might help him to fix his location better than just the landscape alone. When he was satisfied that he had done enough, he fell asleep.

Neither of the two youngsters awoke, when the old man rose before dawn to feed the fire. He sat down to write on a parchment, before he returned to his bedroll.

At dawn, Aibhera awoke, to the sound of her own teeth chattering. "How can it be so blasted cold," she muttered. "We almost baked during the day and now I am about to freeze to death."

"The March of the Five Thousand records that this effect is common here," Eideron answered, in a muffled voice from inside his blankets.

"I'm sorry to wake you," she began to apologize.

"I was already awake. It's too cold to sleep." Eideron interrupted. "We might as well get started, moving around will help us keep warm."

They woke Simea. The sun had just appeared above the horizon, by the time they had eaten, and packed up their gear.

"Which way are we going?" Simea asked.

"The ancient records indicate that our people took several different routes to get to Abalon. The majority of those who survived came from two parties that came from that direction." He pointed to the horizon opposite the brightening dawn. "I hope that bodes well for our success."

"We estimated that we brought enough water to last us for five or six days." Is there any chance that we will find water before it runs out?" Aibhera asked.

"The last week of the journey was apparently the most difficult. By then, our people were on foot with very little water left. Most of the deaths occurred during that period. There is supposed to be a canyon that we can follow, which may have pools of water we can use. If we can find the canyon we should be fine," Eideron replied.

"And if we can't?" asked Simea.

"In that case we shall have to depend on the mercy of the Creator or your abilities to *Shift*."

"So we have five or six days to either find water or learn to *Shift* — or both?"

"No pressure, right Aibby?"

They set out again in the direction Eideron had chosen, picking their way through the broken lava field and the scrubby brush that grew in the cracks and crevices. The sun was a pitiless burning eye, staring down from a pale blue sky. They stopped to eat at midday, in the shade of a boulder, on the south side of a large depression.

"We are all very tired Master, and it would do us some good to rest here until the heat of the day passes. We are using up the water far too quickly, by exerting ourselves in this heat."

"I agree Sim. We did not get enough sleep last night either, so we should have a nap before we continue. Master Eideron you look worn out."

"I will agree, only if you attempt to *Shift* while I rest. Agreed?" His easy acquiescence emphasized his weakness to the youngsters.

"Yes, that's a good idea," both youngsters agreed. "What do we need to know?"

"First, you must empty your mind. It is not easy. Focus on your breathing. That should help. Then call upon the Creator for help, while holding as much of the image of where you want to go in your mind. That is what I know, although no one has shifted in centuries."

"But Master, we know only one place other than this one, which is Abalon. We can't go back there." The enormity of the task suddenly seemed overwhelming to Aibhera.

"That is true young-one, but if nothing else, that will get you safely home, but you both have told me that your dreams of late are very vivid —"

"You think we can shift to where the others are?" interrupted Simea. "Or I could try for last night's campsite.

"It is possible that you could *Shift* to their location if it is indeed that vividly fixed in your minds, however I think we should try something more modest for a first time, last night's campsite would be enough."

Aibhera already had her eyes closed and was concentrating on a particular rock, that had dug into her back all through the previous night. At the same time, she reached upward with her mind. She had always pictured that the Creator lived above them so it was the natural choice for her. To calm herself, she began to hum a cradlesong she remembered her father singing, when she was very small. It reminded her of home, and as she did; she felt her mind connect to another incredibly ancient and powerful mind. Stately and sad, it spoke to her.

"Be careful little sister. You are lucky it was I, you reached and not one of the Dark Ones. My name is Shel'gharim, of Naom'han's cohort."

She broke the connection, quivering with fear.

"What happened? Aibby, what just happened?" asked Simea in a panic. "You seemed to almost fade out of existence for a moment, and suddenly you were back."

"Describe what happened, please, Aibhera," Eideron coaxed, "as soon as you have strength."

"I reached up like you said and I found someone ancient and powerful. He called himself Shel'gharim. I got frightened and I came back."

"Shel'gharim of Naom'han's cohort?" Eideron asked disbelievingly.

"Yes, that is what he said his name was. Why?"

"He was the Aethera that was given charge of watching over the Sokai in ancient times. He can be a great help to us. You must try again, as soon as you are ready."

"He warned me to be careful. He said that I needed to watch out that I did not encounter any of the Dark Ones," she answered, afraid to try again so soon.

"Very well, we will all rest now and continue our journey when the heat is less. Sleep now, while Simea and I keep watch over you."

Aibhera fell asleep almost instantly and awoke to the sound of Simea and Eideron talking quietly to each other.

"Is it time to continue?" she asked.

"Yes, we were just discussing whether we should wake you. Have a drink and we will be off."

The day continued as it had begun, with them struggling to find a path through the broken crust of the plain. They discussed and dissected Aibhera's experience, as they walked. Simea suggested that he be the next to try. He recapped his plan to *Shift* to the previous night's campsite, where he had left his medallion. When nightfall began to approach, they

371

gathered firewood and found shelter, in yet another of the small craters that dotted the landscape.

Eideron sat quietly by the fire, while Simea and Aibhera prepared the meal. They could tell that the old man had exhausted all of his energy getting them all this far. They whispered together as they worked.

"I don't know which will give out first Aibhera; the Master, or the water."

"I know. Both are depleting faster than I expected. I did not expect to use so much water in so short a time. I thought we had enough for five or six days. Now two days later, we are halfway through our supply."

"We have enough if we turn back now, but if we walk one more day we have no hope of returning."

"Unless — we master *Shifting*. No pressure. Right, Simea." Aibhera jibed.

"None at all. Let's eat. I'll try *Shifting*, while the Master rests. Even if we turned around right now, I don't know if he would survive the return trip. This is much harder on him than he expected. He should have stayed in Abalon and lived out the rest of his life in comfort. It's hard to remember that only last week I was afraid of him. Now I am afraid *for* him."

They ate in silence as Simea tried to prepare for the task ahead.

"After finishing his last bite of food, Eideron broke the silence," You should leave me here and go on alone, taking the supplies with you. You will get farther without me. I am merely using up your resources and slowing you down."

"We can discuss this in the morning once you are rested, Master. Definitely not until I know if I can shift or not."

Eideron did not have the strength to argue with Simea. It showed how exhausted he was.

With that settled, Simea began as Aibhera had described the process to him. He reached up for the Creator and contemplated his medallion, remembering where he had carefully placed it the night before.

Although she was not sure what she should watch for, Aibhera stared at him intently for any signs of distress. Her eyes grew heavy, as she watched the regular rise and fall of his chest. He was no longer the Simea she remembered from childhood.

He was a man now, who was attempting to do what no other man had done in over a millennium. She was more tired than usual after a day of walking. Her short trip into the Aether earlier combined with the day's exertions had tired her more than she had expected.

The Master had warned them not to stay for long. If that short experience had tired her so much, she could only imagine the risk involved in a longer visit. Her eyes drooped for what felt like only a moment. Her head dropped forward onto her chest. A sharp pop jarred her back to wakefulness. She opened her eyes to look at Simea — but he was gone.

CHAPTER 37: LOST IN THE WASTELAND

In the first moments after awakening, Aibhera thought Simea had given up the attempt to *shift* and moved to another location, while she had nodded off to sleep, but after a careful search, it was clear that he was nowhere nearby. She rocked back and forth, by the fire, telling herself to be calm.

"It's going to be alright. He will find his way back."

It became her mantra. With each passing moment, she found it more difficult to convince herself that nothing was wrong. She considered waking Eideron, who still slept in front of the fire, but quickly discarded the idea. What could the old man do about this? Eideron was too exhausted to be much help. Simea would need to find his own way back.

More time passed and Aibhera became frantic. She had to do something. She was certain that without Simea, they could not succeed. She and Eideron would be doomed to die in this wasteland. Finally, in desperation she prepared to search for him the only way that stood any chance of success. She tried to reach Shel'gharim again with her mind, as she had at midday. Her thoughts scattered like clouds before a strong wind and she had no way to control them. The tempest of fear and concern was too strong for her to master. She gave up.

She considered waking Eideron again, but refrained. She decided to try once more before waking the Master. Instinctively she began to hum the tune that her father sang to calm her, when she had bad dreams. She felt the storm inside give way under the influence of the melody. Finally, she reached up and outside of herself once again.

She met Shel'gharim again, but now she was not afraid. This time she could see him, as well as hear him. He was the most beautiful thing Aibhera had ever seen, a huge, ephemeral, being of light that continually changed color and intensity. She could sense a profound power and tranquil dignity emanating from him. If he was only an Aethera, a created being, the Creator must be infinitely more overwhelming. The idea of someone so incredible frightened and humbled her.

"You have returned little sister. For what purpose?"

"I fear my friend is lost. I need your help. He has tried to *Shift* to our last campsite. He has been gone a long time. I fear for his safety. Please help us."

"It has been a thousand of your years, since your kind has ventured here little one, and longer still since any of your kind have tried to use the Aether to journey to and fro. I do not doubt that he is lost. I shall find him and bring him to you, if I am able, brave one. Do not stay here too long, it could cost you your life. Your kind is not strong enough to bear it."

"I know, Master Eideron warned us of the danger, but may I stay a little longer to search with you?"

"This area is unsafe. The region under our guardianship is limited and you are nearly at its

border." He indicated the shadows at the edge of her sight. "Stay here, if you must, and reach out to him as you did to me. That would be the safest way to proceed."

Shel'gharim left so fast that he appeared not to move, but simply shrink and vanish. Without his presence, the area already seemed much darker and the shadowy border was closer than before.

Aibhera began to take note of her surroundings. She floated in air filled with luminous clouds of brilliant colors. The colors were so vibrant the she could hear them as well as see them. Everything around her, including the air itself, pulsed with energy and sang with life. The Aether infused her with energy and she felt more alive than she had ever felt before. How could this be bad for her she wondered? If it were not for Simea's disappearance, she would have liked to stay and learn more. How could a place that energized her like this possibly destroy her?

In the distance, she could see the dark edge of the border Shel'gharim had pointed out. She could see nothing beyond that barrier. The impenetrable darkness attempted to absorb the light and energy of this place. She could sense it tugging at her, trying to absorb her energy as well. She ignored the feeling and focused on what she could see.

She could make out shapes of the land below, semi-transparent and shadowy. She could see Eideron, where he lay and all the places they had stopped along the way, both yesterday and today. She could even see the valley of Abalon. It looked easy to step out of this place and into any of those locations. So this was how the Sokai travelled from place to place. They stepped into the Aetherial realm, and afterward stepped back out again at a different location on the surface of Aarda. She suddenly realized that she could only see places she knew.

She focused on home in her mind, and sang the song from her childhood again and home drew nearer — no — she could not abandon her quest and her friends. She thought of Simea instead and called out to him, but could not sense him anywhere. She reached out to Eideron and watched as the old man roused in his sleep.

"Eideron. Help us find Simea. He is lost," she cried out in desperation. She watched as the old man roused from sleep, and looked around for her and Simea. It was strange to see him casting about below like a shadow flitting across the blackened rocks surrounding their campsite. She desperately needed his help and formed the thought of Eideron standing beside her

Suddenly Eideron was there with her.

"What is going on? Where are we and how did I get here."

"In the Aether. It is somewhere and everywhere at once, it seems. I called you and you came. I can't find Sim. He's not here. It is fascinating. This place fills me with power."

"You brought me? That is unheard of. Be careful that you do not become drunk with power. Remember what I told you about staying too long and about how power can twist one's thoughts. Fire burns and gives warmth but if you stray too close, you will be burned. The log that remains in the fire is consumed, just as you will be if you remain here."

"Have you looked over there in the darkness?' asked Eideron.

"No, Shel'gharim said to stay away from the dark. It marks the boundary of his protection. He does not think it is safe for us to go further. He said to reach out to Simea, instead."

"Just as well. I feel an overpowering evil emanating from it. Let us call out together to Simea."

377

They joined hands and called, their voices floated off into the distance in all directions at once, without any trace of an echo. They alternated between calling and listening. They were about to give up, when Aibhera heard a small cry off in the distance.

"Help me. I am trapped." It was Simea's voice, calling out to them. He was calling out from the darkness.

"I hear him now Eideron, he's trapped in the darkness. We must go there and help him."

Aibhera began to head toward the dark wall. She could not bear to leave Simea trapped and alone in that dark place.

"Stop! Aibhera. I sense nothing but evil from that direction. Do not go there," Eideron shouted, but she was determined to help Simea. Nothing he could say would deter her. As she approached the wall, he raced to catch up to her. "Wait. Do not enter. For the Creator's sake go no farther."

She paused for a moment and turned back to Eideron. "I can see him now, Eideron. We must go after him. He is hurt and cannot get out without help. We must not fail him."

"It is a deception Aibhera. He is not there. If you enter there, you will never return. It is a trick of the Dark Ones. Please believe me," he begged.

"Surely you can see him. Surely, you can see that we must help him. It's hurting him. Don't you care? What kind of heartless man are you?" Indignation rose up inside her, that the man who professed to be their guide and mentor was so insensitive to the suffering of his apprentice. How could he allow cowardice prevent him from effecting Simea`s rescue. Her anger grew into a resolve that no one could overwhelm.

"You are not strong enough to stop me you feeble old fool. I dare you to try." She strode toward the barrier her eyes blazed red and dark shadows began to play across her face.

Eideron stepped between her and the barrier. She knocked him aside with the back of her hand, as if she were swatting an insect. He struggled to get up from where he had landed and grappled with her. She cast him aside again, but this time she turned to follow him.

She picked him up as easily, as if he had been one of her childhood playthings. She threw him in the general direction of the wall of blackness. He fell, and lay still for a moment, before struggling to his feet to face her again.

"Get out of my way old man," she snarled as she stalked toward him like a predatory animal.

"I shall," he said calmly, as he backed toward the blackness behind him. Black tendrils reached out from beyond the wall of darkness, as he approached. They enveloped him sapping the life from him.

"See," he croaked as life drained from his body. "See what they would do to you. Do you believe now?" His voice faded as the last of his strength ebbed and his body turned to ash, falling into a heap.

Shock managed to accomplish what his failing strength had not been able to do. She shook free of the compulsion that had held her captive. She dropped to her knees sobbing and found herself alone among the blackened rocks of their campsite once again. It was her fault Eideron was gone.

Simea was lost. She had allowed the Nethera to become corrupt and deceive her. She had killed Eideron. She was alone with nowhere she could turn for aid. She was doomed. She lay down beside the embers of the fire, exhausted by shame and exertion and slept like a dead woman.

***

She woke to a hand on her shoulder and the sound of Simea's voice. Sunlight blinded her. She sat up. Was she dreaming? She threw her arms around him glad that he felt so real, weeping with both joy and sorrow simultaneously.

"Sim, you're back. Oh, thank you Shel'gharim. Thank you Creator," she blubbered. Now that Simea was back, she allowed herself to feel grief for the loss of Eideron. She cried as she had not cried since the death of her father, years ago. Tears ran down her face onto Simea's shoulder, soaking his clothing.

Simea said nothing at first. He held her, as she shuddered and sobbed against him. Once her crying subsided, he held her out at arm's length to look her in the eye. "I am sorry, Aibhera. I should not have tried to go so far on the first try, but I wanted to get more supplies. I tried to get to Abalon. It was foolish. I ran out of strength and could not make it back on my own. I got help from Shel'gharim."

"I know, I sent him to get you," she interrupted, "but I was foolish also, and my foolishness cost Eideron his life." She shared her shameful failure with Simea until her confession disintegrated into another long bout of wracking sobs. This time, he wept with her.

When they finally regained their composure, they began to break camp in silence. Both felt guilty and ashamed that their combined failures had cost Eideron his life. Neither of them would speak more about it, nor would they blame each other, they blamed themselves alone. As they packed up Eideron's things, they found a folded parchment and a scroll with his belongings. Both were sealed, but he had addressed the parchment to both of them. They opened it with shaking hands, struggling to keep fresh tears at bay, and read:

***

To Simea and Aibhera:

It is time for your initiation into adulthood in the Synod. I feel a mixture of sorrow and pride for you young people. If you are reading this, it means that I will not be able to perform the ceremony that was ancient, at the Time of Sorrows, and even before the Sundering, when all humankind lived and worked together. I had so looked forward to that day.

Tradition requires that the Master perform the ceremony with the apprentice, in front of the entire Sokai Synod. Once complete, initiates should be welcomed into the Synod and honored with a feast. It is a sad day, when one old man and two children are all that is available for this solemn and sacred rite of passage. I regret that we are not even capable of so small a recognition for the two of you.

You are the best and bravest of our race. Farewell. Be strong and courageous in the face of adversity.

You have already accomplished more in your short lives, than I have in my very long one. I am proud of you, beyond anything words could describe.

I knew that I would not survive this mission. I hope I ended well and with dignity. Think kindly of a weak old man, who loved you both as much as if you were my own children.

With Pride,

Eideron.

I have included the map of the route I planned to take. I hope that it guides you better than I was able to.

I want you to know that you can also use your abilities to protect yourselves and others. I pray that you rediscover how to use The Creator's power to do battle and I hope you find the scroll I brought with us useful.

They both began to weep again, but the wellspring of their sorrow was nearly dry. They packed up the rest of their gear, and began to pick their way across the ancient lava flow, in the direction Eideron had chosen for them.

They had seen no sign of any creatures, other than a few insects, so they were astonished when a large shadow passed over them. They ducked and cowered in a crater behind a large rock, before they looked up. After the experiences of the previous night, their first thoughts ran naturally to the ancient stories about predatory beasts, lurking in the lava field.

"It's a Wind-rider, Sim. It's a big glider too."

Aibhera jumped up from behind the rock waving and shouting. "Down here, we're down here."

Simea pulled her back down. "What are you thinking? It could be a scout for the Synod. Eideron said they would follow us if they figured out what we were doing."

"It's not," she said. "Don't you recognize the style? The way she pulls her turns when she banks to maintain just the right amount of lift through the turn. It's Ky. She's followed us."

The glider swooped lower and now Simea could see the pilot. It was indeed Kyonna. Wind was blowing through her hair, and a satisfied smile lit up her face. She banked once more to lose airspeed, before she turned for her final approach. They could see that the big glider was loaded with supplies. Ky swooped down on them, and at the last minute, she pushed the control bar forward causing the glider to stall, with her feet just inches from the ground.

It always amazed Aibhera how she could time that move just right in any weather condition. Aibhera was sure that Kyonna's skill with a glider would allow her to land on a branch like a songbird.

Aibhera and Simea swarmed the younger girl, attempting to hug her, while she was still trying to get out of her harness.

"Get off me you two. Let me get out of my gear, before you properly and humbly thank me for rescuing your sorry tails. Where's the old man? Isn't he going to thank me too?" Seeing how Simea and Aibhera's faces fell at the mention of Eideron she paused. "Something bad happened, right?"

"Eideron is dead." Simea said impassively. He had no strength left to grieve.

She studied them both closely before speaking.

"I am sorry I never got to meet him," Kyonna said embracing both of them, now that she was out of her harness.

"I brought supplies, as you can see. I didn't know how long I was going to have to stay aloft to find you. It is less than I wanted to bring, but it should be enough. By the way, there is a big canyon further west. I could see what looked like water shining in the bottom of it. If we can make it there, we should be all right as far as water is concerned, unless you want to turn back."

"Let me tell you though, that's probably not the best idea. I'd rather face the unknown than what's waiting for you back in Abalon, if you ever decide to return."

"I guess the Synod council is upset." Simea said passively.

"They are so very, very far beyond upset; that upset will never; ever, see the light of day again. They have incited the whole population of the valley against you. Poor councilor Himish is in irons."

"If you two return, they will hang you, draw, and quarter you, then feed you to the crows, but only after they have pissed on you, both figuratively and literally. Its not my idea of a proper welcome home party.

So, my daring darlings, I suggest we grab as much as we can carry, then hustle our sorry little backsides down into that canyon, as fast as our feet will carry us. Let me tell you, the next glider that shows up, will not be carrying any presents that you'll want to receive."

"They're not gonna be too happy with me either, seeing as I stole their best freight glider to come out here looking for you." She began to unhook packages from the glider, then turned and looked at Simea and her sister. "Did I forget to mention the time constraints we are under? Why are you both still just standing around? Move it people!" she shouted.

Ky's yell shook them out of their daze. They jumped into action to help unload the supplies that Kyonna had brought with her. Once they had everything taken off the glider, Kyonna began to disassemble it, stowing the pieces into crevices and cracks in the ancient lava flow.

"Come on; help me with this. If they spot the glider, they will be able to figure out which way we were going. Like I said before, that would not be a good thing."

Once they had hidden everything they could not carry, and did not need, they set a brisk pace in the direction of the canyon.

"At least Eideron's map seems good thus far," Simea, thought.

Kyonna chattered like a small bird, as she led the way across the rubble field. Simea and Aibhera were still too heartbroken to carry on a coherent conversation. Ky filled up the silent spaces with enough words for all of them. They were content to follow, since they were too numb to care or listen, regardless of how comforting Kyonna might have believed her prattling might be.

By nightfall, even Kyonna had no strength left for anything other than walking. They were completely exhausted, but they had managed to find a gully that looked like it might lead, into the canyon. Kyonna decided not to light a fire, because Windriders might spot it.

Although the gliders seldom flew at night, the moon was full and the sky was clear, so it was possible that the Synod Council might be desperate enough to have sent someone to look for them. They shared a cold meal and huddled together for warmth, sharing their bedding. They managed a reasonable night's sleep in spite of everything.

CHAPTER 38: THE STORY IN THE SCROLL

Their footsteps and voices echoed eerily off the rock walls, as night approached. They slowly picked their way through the broken stone and sharp gravel. They had seen no signs of life, but they heard noises among the rocks from time to time. Much of the canyon lay in deep shadows even at midday, when they decided to stop for a meal and a rest.

For three days, the three Sokai youngsters had continued walking down the canyon, following Eideron's map. This part of the journey proved every bit as difficult, as the preceding days. The shade in the canyon was a welcome protection from the heat of the lava plain above, but the footing was still treacherous and the nights were bitterly cold. Had it not been for Kyonna's arrival with supplies, they would have run out of water and food by nightfall. There were pools of water in the canyon, but it looked unsafe to drink.

Once they had eaten, Simea suggested that they open and read the scroll that Eideron had left them, while they rested. As they unrolled it, another note from Eideron fell out.

Aibhera read aloud though her tears blurred the words before her.

***

If you are reading this note before I have read the contents of this scroll to you, I want you to know that this has always been one of my favorite stories. I am not sure why I decided to bring it along, other than the fact that I have always liked it. I hope that you can find something useful in it. It is a condensed version of 'The Book of Songs'. Please take time to read it, if I am gone."

***

Kyonna wrapped her arms around her sister to comfort her and said, "Sim, why don't you go ahead and read the scroll."

He wiped the hot tears from his own cheeks and began to read.

***

The Book of Songs

The One existed, and He was alone in the vast and empty void. He sang forth his songs. The melody flowed out of the abundance of joy in his heart. It filled the darkness with joy.

"It is a good song, but let Us not merely sing. Let us create with our song."

Thus, he became The Creator, as He sang the universe into existence. Its dazzling brilliance glittered and shone in the dark void. He was pleased with His work. He sang to the stars as they gave light to the darkness. Seeking to share further splendor, He sang Aarda into being, that it might be the choice jewel in all creation.

He spoke again, "Let us create living beings to share in our song, and sing with us. He sang and the Aethera came to be. They were beautiful and brilliant, creatures of light and power, shining like the stars of the heavens, but they were living beings, able to sing with

Him, and share His joy. They loved their creator, as they journeyed among the stars, and added their songs to His. The sounds of their harmonies filled the universe with a heavenly chorus, sound and color, song and shape, blindingly beautiful, incredibly intricate. They sang together for uncountable ages in sweetness and harmony.

The Creator gave names to the Aethera and loved them as a father loves his children. He loved them and the beauty of their songs. In time, S'ek'zekaar, one of their number, became unhappy with the song of The Creator. He was no longer content merely to sing harmonies to His tune. He felt a melody of his own growing within, a song of power and purpose. His song beguiled him, until he entertained rebellion against The Creator in his heart.

He began to rejoice in his own strength, for he knew his song would set him free from the control of The Creator, so he began to sing his own song into the universe. The notes were discordant with the song of creation, but the power within them was seductive, and beautiful to him in its own way. Some of the other Aethera became seduced by the melody of S'ek'zekaar, and began to sing this new song with him. Discord arose in the universe and among the Aethera. For the first time, chaos threatened creation.

The Creator heard S'ek'zekaar's song. He stopped singing, to determine where this new song would lead. The absence of The Creator's song filled the universe with an immense, awful emptiness. The Aethera wept in sorrow. The missing melody of The Creator impoverished creation. They tried in vain to make up the difference with their own songs.

Only S'ek'zekaar, who became known as The Defiler, reveled in the absence of The Creator's song. In his heart he said, "Now I can make the universe as I wish. I will be its god and all that exists shall be mine to rule. I shall set them all free as I am free."

The Creator commanded Naom'han, chief of all the Aethera, to summon all the Aethera for a council. He commanded him to make a record of this council, that it might be known for all time and by all creation. In the council, The Defiler, and his followers demanded to be set free, to do as they wished in the universe.

The Creator heard their demands and acceded to them by withdrawing his power from them. From that day forward, they became known as the Nethera or Dark Ones, since they no longer shared the light of The Creator nor did they receive his power. The Aethera loyal to The Creator brought forth a request of their own. They requested help for their work in tending Aarda, since the task was large, and their numbers were reduced by the rebellion among them.

The Creator spoke again, and said, "Let us sing together once more, and bring forth more life. For its song will balance the discord in creation. Let us sing mankind into being. The song took root in Aarda, and so the Abrhaani, the Eniila, and the Sokai came to be.

The Creator gave mankind charge over Aarda to tend it, and care for it. Under their care the earth flourished. He gave the rest of creation to the Aethera to tend. The Aethera were also to help mankind care for Aarda as they could. They were happy in their work, watched over mankind, and helped men to create and sing their own songs.

The three races of mankind began to sing their songs along with the Aethera. Mankind sang a new chant of life upon Aarda, bringing harmony back into the song of Creation. The Creator drew back from Aarda, withholding his presence and stopped singing yet again saying, "The song is yours now, my beloved ones, *to sing as you please. Sing well, for I will return to judge what you create, with your songs, and your lives.*

S'ek'zekaar grew exceedingly angry with mankind, because the songs of men had restored harmony in creation. He changed his song yet again. His anger made his song darker, more ominous and strident, filled with hunger for power, and unbridled selfishness. It was a song of decay and destruction, a song to destroy mankind. Some men became enamored with the song of S'ek'zekaar, and its promise of freedom. They began to desire power for themselves just as he did.

***

"That is all there is," Simea said as he re-rolled the scroll and tied the thong around it once more. "What good is it to us?'

"I was thinking that when I tried to come and get you, I was so worried that I had trouble focusing, until I began to sing. The song calmed me and anchored me."

"It's like—" Kyonna started to interrupt, "Never mind,"

It's like what, Ky?" Simea asked.

"It's not important, go on Aibby."

"What if songs help us get in tune with what we need to do? The song reminded me of home, so it anchored me and allowed me to come back and wake Eideron. Perhaps you might not have gotten lost, if you had done something similar."

"I suppose it's possible," Simea said, thinking hard to remember the process he had used.

"What else did Eideron tell you?" Kyonna quizzed. "What other magic can we do?"

"Not magic Ky. We merely open ourselves to the power of The Creator. We allow his power to flow through us. I want to be cautious though, because I have learned, to my shame and regret, that when we open ourselves to the *Quickening*, we also become susceptible to the influence of the Nethera. That is why the Synod insisted that apprentices were fully trained in moral and ethical development before they were allowed to attempt to use their gifts."

"Ah, I see," Kyonna said.

"Eideron mentioned prophecy, discernment, travel, and protection, but he said that the possibilities were virtually limitless," Aibhera answered.

"What was the song you used Aibby?"

"The one Pa used to sing to us when we were little, Ky, you know it, Aamori's House."

"Oh! I know that one too," Simea added.

"What if that is the purpose of the song? Think of the words. It's all about the things Aamori misses in her house, It lists them all, until she realizes that she misses her family more than all the things combined. It reminded you of familiar things. It focused you on home. It grounded you to our people."

"Hey! What if Dragan's Wall was the same?" Simea interrupted. "It's about building a wall to protect the people."

"Yes, an invisible wall, remember the line, 'to keep the beasts at bay'. If we focused on trying to build an invisible barrier—it might work that way. Let's try it now. We might need it soon. It would be good to test it before we do. Help us Ky."

They began to sing the song, while focusing their thoughts of building a wall of protection around their position. Within seconds a wall of light surrounded them, building in intensity as they continued. Once it was in place, Ky stopped singing. The wall held.

"Stop Aibby, but Sim keep going," she said.

Her sister stopped singing and Simea held the wall alone. The two sisters looked at each other in triumph.

"Remember the chorus about the gate in the wall, Aibby? We always sang it as a round with the song."

"Let's."

The sisters began the second song, the wall shimmered and faded in one place, but suddenly the whole wall winked out.

"Forgive me," Simea said. "I'm just too tired to go on."

"It's ok Sim, besides, it's getting late. We should stay here for the night." Aibhera said.

Night fell like an ax, in the canyon bottom, cutting off all light. There was no moon, and only a tiny strip of stars directly overhead, just endless silent stillness. They prepared their meal by firelight, as they discussed other ancient songs that their parents had taught them, and fell into a deep sleep as soon as they lay down on their bedrolls.

CHAPTER 39: TORTURED SECRETS

Rehaak awoke. He could see nothing, for it was black as tar where he lay. He could not remember where he was or how he had gotten here. He had always hated nighttime. All the Abrhaani avoided darkness, whenever they could. If deprived of sunlight for too long, they tended to weaken and become ill. This was more important to Rehaak than to others of his kind. He was afraid of the dark.

He could smell the soil of a dirt floor beneath him, as he lay on his side. His arms were in an awkward position, his wrists hurt, as did his ankles, and he had an atrocious headache. When he tried to move, he discovered that someone had bound him, hand and foot. Bound and helpless in the dark, his childhood fear of the darkness began to assail him again, but he fought it off determinedly.

Eventually he heard noises. Footsteps approached. A faint glow gradually brightened behind him, until he could make out the rock walls that enclosed him. He was in a cavern. Hands seized him roughly and forced him to sit up.

"Get up — on your feet, the Master wishes to see you now," one of his captors growled, as he untied Rehaak's feet and hands.

Rehaak stood with difficulty. His hands and feet were numb and refused to obey him. They tingled unpleasantly, as the blood and feeling flowed back into them. His captors forced him forward, partially carrying him, until he was finally able to walk without their aid. The floor of the cave was uneven so he stumbled several times, as the two men pushed him ahead. Fortunately, it was a short walk.

The passage ended abruptly in a large gallery lit by torches. Many men knelt there, stripped to the waist, all facing in the same direction. All bore tattoos across their bodies. Rehaak did not count the men, but there were a lot. He looked to see what held their attention. Dreyenar Asanudain, the young nobleman he had met on his way to Dun Dale, stood over an altar fashioned of rough stone. Drey wore a ceremonial cloak. In his hands, he held one of the long knives, with which Rehaak had gained an unwelcome familiarity.

Isil was right, they did use them to offer sacrifices to their gods. On the altar, he saw a lamb. Its legs were bound. Rehaak stumbled again and fell to his knees. This time, neither the irregular footing, nor the sight of the imminent sacrifice caused his fall.

What sapped the strength from his limbs was the entity behind the altar. A creature, from his childhood nightmares, hovered there. The tattooed men worshiped it. He wanted to rise and run, but fear paralyzed him just like in his childhood dreams.

The Dark One loomed over the altar. Its form was total darkness that flowed and shifted, so that his eyes could not focus to see it clearly. It was not black in the way normal things are black, its darkness came from a deeper origin. It was the antithesis of light. Rehaak could sense the hunger within it. Hunger and hatred motivated it, as it anticipated the knife stroke that would end the life of the innocent creature on the altar.

The men in the assembly began to chant, slowly at first, building to a frenzied crescendo of hatred and madness, as they rose in anticipation of the sacrifice. The knife descended in Dreyenar's hands. Blood spurted from the lamb's severed throat. Drey caught the flow in a chalice, and then held it high, while the lamb twitched and grew still. They shouted as though they had accomplished some great victory, instead of killing an innocent creature. The Dark One moaned in ecstasy at the offering. Rehaak sensed that it received more sustenance from the debauchery and the madness of the chanting men, than from the offering on the altar.

It was drawing strength from them, growing in power because it had demeaned and twisted them into parodies of what The Creator had intended. The men did not realize that the creature drew its strength from them, nor did they realize that their participation in this sacrifice weakened them. They mistakenly believed that the lamb was the offering it fed upon, when in reality, their corruption, was the offering that actually made it stronger.

They gathered eagerly, pushing each other to be the first to drink the warm blood of the lamb, as if it were an honor rather than a disgrace. Dreyenar passed the cup to them, after he had wet his own lips. He turned toward Rehaak. Blood still stained his lips. For a moment, his eyes had an unfocussed look to them. He stared at Rehaak for an instant, before he seemed to collect his senses again, and then walk slowly toward him, where he knelt on the floor of the gallery.

The Nethera followed him closely, seeming to rend the air of the room, leaving a void in its wake. Rehaak nearly fainted from the overpowering stench of rotting flesh that emanated from it. He did not know how any man could abide its company without becoming violently ill. Although the Nethera was still halfway across the underground chamber, he was having difficulty keeping his stomach from rebelling. Fortunately, it kept its distance.

"We meet again Rehaak, scholar, troublemaker, and heretic," Dreyenar snidely commented. "It would have been easier on both of us, if you had simply accepted my offer and come with me, instead of making me send some of our disciples to bring you here by force."

Dreyenar's words reminded Rehaak what had happened. He had been hiding in the woodshed of the Dancing Dog until Breisha had brought him the leather straps for Laakea's breastplate. He had hardly exited the shed, before someone had, put a sack over his head, and grabbed his arms from behind. He remembered nothing more until he awoke on the cavern floor. An ache in his temple confirmed his suspicion that they had clubbed him into unconsciousness.

He could not take his eyes away from the Dark One, who loomed only a few feet behind the young nobleman.

"What do you want with me, Dreyenar?" Rehaak asked, though he was not able to look at him.

"We wish to converse with you about the error of your beliefs. My master's master, he nodded toward the evil presence behind him, thought that you would greatly benefit from a display of the reality of his presence. Ashd'eravaak hoped that, through a demonstration of his great power, you would come to serve him as we do. He is after all our rightful master and god."

Rehaak shuddered at the idea of serving the abomination before him, but said nothing.

"Now that we have your attention, we would like to reason with you, in the hope that you might finally see the true path. We wish to free the last remnants of mankind from its bondage to the Nameless One. We will achieve that aim by the reunification of mankind, under the benevolent leadership of Ashd'eravaak and his brethren. They have fought tirelessly for our freedom for countless millennia."

"We seek to bring the Eniila and the Abrhaani together, so that we might enjoy harmony and fruitfulness, as we did in ancient times. Surely, that is a noble goal and one you would be willing to support? Is this not at least in part, what you want for mankind?" He stopped to wait for Rehaak's answer.

"How will you accomplish such an ambitious goal friend Dreyenar?" Rehaak asked, hoping he kept his sarcasm veiled. *"Who was the Nameless One that Drey mentioned?"*

"We will send our brothers gathered here, to spread the good word of our god's return to the lands of men," he said, as he pointed to the men behind him.

The men knelt, chanting softly again, after they had finished drinking the blood from the chalice.

Dreyenar began again. "The first of our apostles have already made inroads in Baradon. As I told you, my master has gone ahead of us to complete some arrangements for the word to be spread further still."

"And if the Eniila will not listen to reason?" Rehaak questioned further.

"Then we shall compel them by every other means at our disposal, friend Rehaak. This mission is far too important to allow a few stubborn, misguided men to frustrate."

"You said 'every other means' — what other means do you plan to employ?"

"Mankind has been ignorant for too long now. What does that matter, as long as we are united and free from the oppression of the Nameless One? "

"You mean The Creator?" Rehaak asked, finally making the connection. "Where does He fit in into all your plans?"

The Nethera hissed and spat, as if water dropped onto hot iron. It glided toward him threateningly. It obviously took issue with his use of The Creator's name.

"He is gone, deserted us, leaving Ashd'eravaak, and his kind in charge of Aarda. They are very few; their strength has nearly run out, because the task is far too large for them alone. That is why they have enlisted our aid to help them accomplish the reunification of the races. We assist them to become strong again, so that we might all benefit from their benevolent aid and leadership."

"Do you not wish for mankind to rediscover the knowledge it lost in the Sundering? Do you, a scholar, not value — even long for such knowledge? Is knowledge not the reason you seek the Aetheriad?" Dreyenar continued.

"Yes I value knowledge greatly," Rehaak replied astonished at how much they knew about him and his desires.

"Then join willingly with us, and all the knowledge you seek and much more will be given to you."

"And, friend Dreyenar, what will such great knowledge cost?"

"It costs you nothing, but your allegiance to our true god, the only god with the power and will to act on our behalf. Ashd'eravaak and his kind require that all men serve them, or they will not have sufficient strength for the task. The followers of The Nameless One, who remain, hinder their efforts on our behalf."

"A true god does not require power from its creations; it supplies power to them instead. What true god would need our pathetic help, Dreyenar? Surely you must see — and smell — that this vile thing you worship is no god," Rehaak spat.

"Tell me Drey, how the few remaining followers of the Creator can be so detrimental to your cause. It would seem that you have far greater numbers than they do. If your god is so powerful should he not be able to triumph over so few."

"Aarda was given to the Nameless One's followers by decree, so as long as one follower remains that decree is in effect and our gods cannot legally exercise complete and proper control over the world, and as a result, chaos continues to reign among us. Now that I have answered your question, join us and rule Aarda with us."

"And if I decline this beneficent offer?" Rehaak asked sarcastically while he thought to himself.

"Aha, At last we come to the meat of their problem. The Creator ceded control to us by divine fiat. That is what has stymied them in their efforts and why they are trying to eradicate the followers of The Creator. I notice he omitted to mention who issued that decree. Perhaps Ashd'eravaak has not seen fit to share this information with them."

Rehaak now knew that only The Creator and true God could issue such a declaration. He kept the information to himself. He was sure he had nothing to gain by pointing out Ashd'eravaak's fundamental weakness to Drey.

"Unfortunately, that cannot be allowed. If you decide foolishly and stubbornly resist, it would put the reunification of Aarda at risk. We shall endeavor to convince you of the nobility and correctness of our path, but if you persist in your rebellion, our relationship will end unpleasantly. You would be very wise to consider accepting our offer."

"Look around you Rehaak; can you not see that this is the best way for us all? We are aware of how many times you have already compromised your so-called principles, for far less benefit. Surely you are not foolish enough to believe that you can resist our methods of persuasion?"

"The one thing I am sure of is this; I cannot abide the stench of your pathetic false god any longer." Rehaak shouted. He spat in the dust of the cave floor to emphasize his disgust.

It was true that he had rebelled against The Creator before, but faced with this choice, with evil so manifestly evident, he would not, could not give in. The consequences of taking this stand would likely cost him his life. He saw no way to escape; however, death had not claimed him yet. Rehaak suddenly understood something Laakea had once said to him.

He quoted it now to his captors, "It is better to die fighting than to live on in the shame of surrender to evil."

"Take him, and teach him the error of his choice," Dreyenar snarled.

Two men rose and dragged Rehaak off into the darkness.

"You will beg for the end to come. You will long for death to embrace you and end your suffering," Dreyenar snarled again, as the men dragged him away.

***

His tormenters took him to new heights and depths of pain. They were masters of their craft. Each time Rehaak lost consciousness; he believed it was the end. Then he would awaken again into an ocean of agony, so deep he believed that he would never break the surface again. He prayed for death to release him from his anguish and proved the truth of Dreyenar's words.

Somehow, the pain did not obliterate his faith. The pain etched his faith deeper into his soul. With every burn, every cut and every stroke of the lash, he reached out to The Faithful One and stood with Him outside his pain, outside his body, watching his tormentors mutilate his helpless flesh, while hearing his own screams.

He knew he would die from the abuse, if it continued much longer, but every man died. Isil would die and eventually Laakea too would die. He could not prevent their demise. He had always considered death a problem. Death was not a problem; it was a solution to the problem.

Life was the problem. The manner of life he should have lived, mattered more than the manner of death he would die. He would rather have come to death nobly doing things he had chosen for himself, but few people had that option. Instead, he faced this humiliating death at the hands of his tormentors. Only death's merciful hands appeared able to resolve his present predicament.

Both his friends had been ready to give up their lives for him, and his quest. Rehaak realized now, that it was their choice, not his to make. In cowardice, he had almost abandoned them to make himself feel better. He had convinced himself that running away was a noble act of self-sacrifice, but he had nearly dishonored their choice and their gift of friendship to him. He had been ready to desert them, but he had come to his senses just before Drey's henchmen captured him. He wished that he could tell them that he had not deserted them.

Rehaak had been running since childhood, running away from all the things he had feared. He had fled from his duty to his family, abandoned his duty to his god, and deserted the only people left who truly loved him. He could run no further. He surrendered himself to death and in the surrender; he finally found peace and freedom.

Every shriek of Rehaak's agony declared, "I will not surrender to evil!

Not this time!"

Eventually they stopped.

Dreyenar had come.

"Bring him to the great hall." We will remove his skin, one piece at a time, as an offering to our god, since he refuses to listen to reason."

Rehaak passed out again to the sound of his own screams, as they peeled his mutilated body from the rack that held him.

CHAPTER 40: AMBUSH

Isil and Laakea were just finishing their evening meal, when the door to the house burst open. Laakea leapt up from the chair, whirled and took up his weapons from the sideboard. In a fraction of an eye blink, he held them to the neck of the breathless villager, who had burst in on them.

"Don't slay me young sir," he panted. "I brings yuh word 'bout yer friend."

"What word?" Laakea snarled.

"Easy, lad," Isil counseled. "Yuh can see he be frightened outta his wits."

"Dat I am. Dat we all are in duh village," the stranger admitted. "I must tell yuh 'bout yer friend. He's bin taken prisoner by some vile men what has been hangin about of late."

Laakea lowered his weapons and listened.

"Tell us what yuh knows. We be mighty interested, if yuh can tell us where dey took him."

"Dat I can, because Aert's little'un spied on em, an followed em to dere lair. Soon as she told us, I came straight here, tuh tell yuh 'bout it, 'cause it near skairt duh liver outta her. She was on an errand tuh get some leather fer him from duh Tanner. She had just given it tuh him, an bid him farewell when she seen dose men take him."

They let the man sit, as he told them of Rehaak's capture. He explained how the men had carried Rehaak to a cave near the waterfall. When he finished his tale, they thanked him for his aid and sent him off, with some food for his family.

Laakea decided that he and Isil should start immediately for the cavern where the men held Rehaak captive. Isil packed some gear and provisions in their packs, while Laakea put on his breastplate, fastening it with some cordage, instead of the leather straps Rehaak was supposed to buy in the village. He felt a twinge of guilt that his friend had been captured while trying to get those items for him.

Once they were ready, they set off at a lope following the directions the villager had given them. It was only a short trip to the falls. The sun was just above the treetops, when they set out. They assumed that they could easily reach the cavern before dark.

When Isil became winded, they slowed to rest along the trail. Four men and a dark shape leapt from the shadows of the forest, and encircled them. Laakea drew both swords from his belt as he could feel the surge of his berserker rage begin to rise again.

"That thing must be a Nethera," he thought.

He killed the first man easily, as the dark shape closed in on him. He managed to disembowel a second man, before the Dark One grasped him from behind.

Laakea lost the use of his muscles, as the Nethera touched him. The creature was sucking the life from him, as he would suck an egg through a hole in its shell. The thing was rending his soul from his body. If he could not break free, he would soon be as empty as that eggshell. The pain was intense, but he was unable to utter a sound. The colors faded from his vision, as

Laakea screamed inwardly and struggled to hold himself together.

As his consciousness began to slip away, the creature spun him around so that he faced it. He had lost sight of Isil and had no idea where she was or whether she still survived. To the best of his knowledge, this was his battle to fight and he was alone in it.

Nothing that had happened to him so far in his life had prepared him for this. Neither his father's drills, nor Rehaak's knowledge, nor Isil's wisdom could help him in this battle. If he lost this fight, there would be no others. He refused to go easily. His spirit rallied and fought back. He clung to consciousness, as he peered over the edge of the precipice into the dark creature's soul. He could feel its joy and pride, at its assumed conquest of him.

He summoned his anger, his outrage at the injustice it did to him and to all creation merely by its continued existence. He held it like a shield about him. He began to see that this was a very different battle than he had ever fought before. This was no contest of skill. Neither was it a contest of will, although his will to live certainly was involved in holding off the creature. He sensed the Nethera's frustration resulting from his unexpected and continued resistance. He knew now that this was a spiritual battle. His will and his anger, as strong as they were, could not hold this hate filled horror at bay forever.

Eventually he would weaken and its power would overwhelm him. It would swallow his soul as it had consumed so many before him. He realized his spirit could not defeat this malevolent being. In the same instant, Laakea also realized that he had not yet plumbed the depths of the resources available to him for this battle. He had not called on the Faithful One to come to his aid. Rehaak and Isil had both told him that The

Creator would respond, if those in need called upon Him. He was in need now, more need than he had ever been in his short life. His shield of righteous anger buckled, but held, as he inwardly formed his prayer.

He was not eloquent; he was desperate. He strained to focus his fear and panic into a single word.

"Help!" he inwardly shouted towards the place where he imagined his God, The Creator lived. He could feel the thought travel upwards like a shaft of light, a beacon of frantic need, streaking up from him into the dark and infinite heavens. He waited, in a place of calm, where before there had been only pain and terror. It was only a moment since his cry, but in that moment, his call had opened up a conduit to the heavens. He began to sense power running back down that channel, like water in a riverbed. It was a trickle at first, but it suddenly grew to a raging torrent, like a dam breaking.

It intensified, until he could see a shining pillar of power extending down to him. It grew in brightness, until it nearly blinded him. If he were seeing it with his physical eyes, he knew he would surely be blind for the rest of his life.

Then suddenly, the power surged brighter still and flowed into his anger. He saw and felt his shield of rage suddenly thicken and flare brighter than the sun. It exploded outward with blinding speed and intensity. There were words in that explosion, melodic words with the power to shatter the mountains and kindle their covering forests into instant flame. The power contained in those words humbled him. He understood their meaning. He had heard the golden voice several times before. He recognized it now, though it had changed subtly. This time it spoke not with love and reassurance to him.

Instead, it spoke out through him with incredible power and a towering anger that dwarfed his own. The voice slammed into the Nethera.

"Let my servant be!"

Its sound threw his attacker back across the clearing, leaving them both stunned. Laakea recovered before the Nethera, since he was the channel of the power and not the target. Color returned to his sight and strength flowed back into his limbs. He recovered one of his swords from where it lay beside him, and advanced toward the dark shape that lay crumpled on the ground. Holy rage burned within him, as he raised his weapon.

"You have overstepped your bounds Dark One, it is time for your wickedness to end," he thundered in a voice that was only partially his own. Both man and weapon glowed with unearthly brightness, as he raised his sword and plunged it into the center of the hideous dark shape. Power flowed through Laakea and engulfed him. He was bright and terrible to the creature of gloom. As the sword pierced the creature, its darkness began to decrease. It turned lighter by degrees, hissing, shrieking and writhing in anguish.

"You are judged guilty and condemned," he said. The demon began to dissolve into a light gray mist.

With the death of the creature, the glow around Laakea began to fade. He felt weak and wobbly. As he sank to his knees, he felt a hand upon his shoulder. Looking up, he saw Isil looking down on him with awe in her eyes. It took some time before either of them spoke.

"I suppose yuh have just answered duh question yuh once asked Rehaak," Isil said with a wry grin on her face.

"What question?"

"Duh one yuh asked him long ago, 'bout if yuh might be able tuh kill dese things. I remembers him askin me if I knew summat about it."

"Ahh, that question," Laakea murmured, as he slipped into unconsciousness, and fell forward onto the grass of the clearing.

Isil knelt beside him, rolled him onto his back, and supported his head in her lap. She checked him over and watched in concern for her young friend, but she knew he was in more capable hands than hers were. Instead, she offered a prayer of thanks to The Creator.

When Isil saw that Laakea's breathing was regular again, and that his heart beat slowly and steadily within his chest, she rose to retrieve their scant belongings and she covered the boy with their blankets. Laakea was too large for her to move without aid, so she left him where he lay. It was becoming harder for her to remember that he was still just a youngster. He was over a full head taller than Rehaak now and seemed as massive as one of the trees that surrounded them.

Once she was sure that he was comfortable, she left him lying there and began to gather wood for a campfire. They would simply have to stay where they were, until Laakea recovered.

Isil was unsure why Laakea had collapsed. It may have been because the encounter with the Nethera had left him weak. However, if that were true, why would he only collapse after he had rallied to slay the thing? There was more to this than she understood, perhaps Rehaak could understand the issue. She cursed her lack of knowledge, as she gathered dead brush for the campfire.

Her mind raced in circles as she returned with deadfall gathered from the edge of the forest. It was obvious now that Rehaak's captors knew they were on their way to rescue him. In fact, they had probably used him as bait to lure them into this ambush. She busied herself setting up camp for the night. She shuddered and tried not to think of what they would face, when they reached the place where they imprisoned Rehaak. She was so busy that she never noticed the eyes watching from among the trees, or the shapes slipping silently among the shadows.

CHAPTER 41: DIRE STRAITS

Morning broke and Laakea awakened to find Isil bent over the campfire preparing a meal for the two of them. Although he was stiff from his battle of the previous day and sore from sleeping on the cold earth overnight, he was surprised to find that he felt fine otherwise.

"Good morning Isil."

"Good mornin tuh yuh as well, lad," she replied. "I suspected food would rouse yuh from yer beauty nap."

"I hope you made plenty, because I'm very hungry for some reason."

"Yer always very hungry for any reason, from what I have seen," she shot back.

"We'd best eat and be off as quickly as possible. I fear that we sprang a trap set for us yesterday by Rehaak's captors. I fear that they used him as bait to lure us into the ambush, and if we don't move fast enough they will kill him, since the ambush failed," Laakea told her

"Yup I been thinkin duh same thing myself, lad."

"I'm sorry, Isil, I should have been more observant. If I had, we might have been able to avoid that bit of unpleasantness."

410

"Nah, look at it dis way, yesterday we whittled down dere numbers summat. Today we'll have less of a problem, because of it."

"I hope you are right, Isil, because I don't know if I can survive another fight like that one. If there are more of those things —" he let the comment hang without finishing the sentence.

Isil said nothing. She shrugged and continued what she had been doing.

They broke camp quickly under the brightening sky and continued on their way. Laakea urged more caution than the previous day, so they moved more slowly. Once they began to hear the sound of the falls ahead of them, they crouched low to avoid making silhouettes that sentries could spot and began to move slowly from one patch of cover to the next. Laakea scanned ahead for guards, as they went. The sound of the rushing water hid any noise that he might have heard, so he had to rely on his eyes and nose.

It was not long before his keen eyes spotted movement near some large rocks along the stream bank. After warning Isil with a hand signal that there were sentries, he took time to observe their routine. He was not about to rush headlong into another ambush.

One of his father's sayings echoed in his head, "The gods don't abide repeated stupidity." He did not intend to push his luck again.

"A wise man learns from his mistakes, if he gets the chance to outlive them," another of his father's aphorisms, sprang to mind.

There were three guards, in cover, among the rocks. They had spread out in a semicircle, well in front of the cave mouth. The interior of the cavern was dark. Laakea could not see more than a few feet inside the opening, so there was no way of telling how far back the cave went, or how many men it held in its depths.

411

He decided to wait until dark, while observing their routines. By dusk, the guards had changed three times. That meant that there were probably more than a dozen men inside the cave. The odds were terrible, unless he could do something to even them up.

Once it was dark, they began to creep toward the sentries. The men had lit a fire to ward off the chill, and four additional men had emerged from the cavern to stand around the flames. The firelight was bad for them and good for Isil and Laakea. It showed Laakea where they were and ruined the sentries' night vision. He smiled to Isil, as he pointed out their respective targets. They took out the two guards on the flanks first. Isil used a rope to choke her objective, while Laakea simply slit the other man's throat. Neither made a sound.

Isil began to work her way toward the last guard, while Laakea nocked an arrow and crept as close as he dared, to the four men gathered at the fire. He stuck four more arrows in the dirt so he could nock, draw and release them quickly. He watched Isil move into position, and as soon as she had throttled the last guard, she began to move toward the fire. She was supposed to act as bait.

He gave her the cue and she began to rustle the bush she hid behind, as a small animal would. The men were talking, but grew silent. Two of them motioned and picked up their weapons. They began to move toward Isil, where she waited. As soon as they were over half way to Isil's hiding place, Laakea picked his first target at the fire and sent an arrow through his throat. The man standing beside him, barely had time to realize what had happened, before his own death caught up with him.

The sentry stared down at his chest, surprised to see two feet of wood ending in black crow feathers sprouting from his ribcage. He managed to cry out before he collapsed. One of the men, heading in Isil's direction, managed to hear his call above the sound of the water and turned to look back.

That act made him Laakea's next victim. When he fell, the remaining sentry turned to see what was happening. Isil made a dash for him swinging her staff, but before she got to him, he too was sprouting a black feathered shaft from his chest. Isil clubbed him for good measure as he dropped to the ground.

Laakea and Isil dragged the bodies into cover, while carefully watching for more men to emerge from the cave. It was nearing midnight, before they began a slow approach to the cave opening. There were lighted torches inside the cavern now, so they could see that there were no other men just inside the entrance.

Once they entered, they began to hear chanting, punctuated by screams.

"That'll mor'n likely be our friend Rehaak joinin in dat sing-along. It sounds like dere still be a whack o' dem crazies though," Isil growled in a low voice.

"Let's fervently hope we whittled them down enough," Laakea added with a grim smile.

It took only moments of following the sound, until they had found the altar room. There were over two dozen men all chanting and dancing frenziedly. Isil made as if to dive into the crowd when she saw Rehaak tied to the stone altar. He bled from many wounds. A man in a dark robe held a knife to his naked skin. Laakea stopped her and removed the last of his arrows from his quiver.

"Me first, greedy, you can have em when I'm done with em. Hold these arrows for me and put one in my hand each time I release," Laakea said, not worrying about the men overhearing his words. The noise inside the chamber was so loud that he almost had to shout, in order for Isil to hear him.

Three men fell to his arrows before anyone noticed. Two more before anyone did anything about it.

413

The next one died with his warning shout still in his throat. Two more fell, as they began their charge and then they were on them.

Laakea threw down his bow. He drew Justice and Truth from his belt. The opening into the cave was narrow enough that only three or four men could come at them at once. Isil and Laakea fought effectively, without wounding each other. They fell back slowly under pressure, trying to make the assassins pay for every inch. Three more fell to Laakea's swords and one to Isil's staff, before she hooked her heel on a rock and went down on her backside.

Laakea saw her fall and moved to protect her. He had been fighting valiantly, using all the skills his father had drilled into him, but the berserker rage that overcame him previously, did not empower him again. The preceding night's battle had drained him too much. He knew that without it, he could never withstand the onslaught of these crazed minions of the Dark Ones.

He rallied what strength he had left and shouted, "Creator, hear us!"

He pushed them back again with a flurry of blows just long enough for Isil to get up, but she limped badly. She had twisted her ankle in the fall.

"Creator, hear us," he bellowed again and this time Isil joined him in shouting.

Their shouts accomplished nothing, except to enrage their attackers to new heights of bloodlust. They shrieked incoherently and pressed Laakea even harder. Isil did what she could as she hobbled backwards, toward the cave entrance.

Laakea felled two more men before a hard blow struck him in the midsection. His breastplate stopped the weapon from disemboweling him, but it knocked the wind out of him. He struggled to breathe, as he fell back further with Isil.

She stood on her good leg and fended off blows for him, until he could breathe again. His arms and hands were getting tired and blood was making the rawhide grips of his swords too slippery to hold. As he blocked a blow from an opponent, he lost his grip on one of them. It flew out of his hand while he felled another with his remaining weapon.

He knew it was only a matter of time now, until they overwhelmed him and got to Isil.

On the positive side, their battle had brought a halt to the activity at the altar, because the screaming had stopped. Either that or Rehaak was dead.

CHAPTER 42: IN THE WASTELAND

Another three days of walking, brought the three Sokai out of the canyon onto a flat rocky plain, dotted by scrub brush.

They were beginning to understand that the ancient nursery songs were meant to focus their concentration and empower them in specific ways. They had time to practice each evening. It seemed that with each practice session that they got stronger, and able to do more. Kyonna suggested that it was like manual labor, that the harder you worked the stronger you got. Aibhera returned to Abalon that morning to fill water bottles from the lake at the center of the Caldera. Fortunately, she had escaped notice.

While Simea and Kyonna had waited on the plain for her to return, they sang as many of the ancient songs as they could remember, with varied and sometimes unexpected results. Once Aibhera returned, they continued on their way, consulting Eideron's map as they went. It did not take very long before they began to realize that the map was virtually useless out here on the plain. A thousand years of wind and rain had completely obliterated all the landmarks mentioned on the map. The world had changed radically, since the Sokai had abandoned their brothers and slipped unnoticed into Abalon.

Walking on the hard flat surface of the plain was far easier physically, but the fact that they no longer had any way to navigate, wore them down far more, than the physical challenges they had previously faced. As tension grew, they began to brood silently as they walked.

Aibhera still felt responsible for Eideron's death. She knew that if she had not succumbed to the influence of the Dark Ones, he probably would still live. She began to imagine that the others blamed her for his death. Shame weighed her down more than the pack on her back. To atone for her perceived failure, she carried the largest portion of the load of provisions and pushed herself harder each day.

Simea felt that he had been responsible for his Master's death. If he had not become lost while trying to do too much, neither Aibhera or Eideron would have had to come looking for him. He knew it was entirely his fault. He was still just the clumsy apprentice, tripping over his own feet. He was inept and incompetent and Eideron should have forbidden him to come along on this mission. In fact, it would probably be better if the two girls continued without him. They might have a better chance than if they had to carry him like a dead weight.

Kyonna noticed the brooding of her sister and her friend, but chose to keep her thoughts to herself. The daylight receded from the plain, as the three companions trudged along through the dusty wasteland. Finally, Kyonna called them to a halt.

"We need to rest,"

"Just a little farther, it's not dark yet Ky." Aibhera said wearily.

K. R. Schultz

"Maybe we should go back and forget the whole thing," Simea said.

"You always want to quit when it gets hard Sim," Aibhera retorted.

"Oh, and you always have to be perfect," Simea snapped back at her.

"Stop it! Both of you! You know we can't go back. The Synod will have us flogged and burned at the stake if we go back! Besides, our dreams—" she stopped short, as both Simea and Aibhera looked at her.

"Yes — *our* — dreams. I've had them too. You don't have to look at me like that. It's all I've dreamt about for months now. The two of you needn't think you're so special, that you're the only ones that had those dreams. I heard you talking about them. I just wanted them to go away— I couldn't talk about it. I had to come too, don't you see— they need us so badly!" Kyonna began to cry.

Simea had never seen Ky cry. Aibhera could not remember the last time her sister had wept. She had not even cried at their father's funeral.

"It will be fine Ky. We're sorry, please don't cry," Simea pleaded.

"Let's stop here for the night then," Aibhera said, as she tried to console her sister.

After a hearty meal and a long talk, the three made peace with each other around the fire and finally dropped off to sleep.

***

The dream rolled in on them like a wave to engulf them in terror. A dark figure loomed in the background. Its baleful crimson eyes stared hatefully into their hearts, while a man in ceremonial robes cut pieces of skin from their bodies. He stopped after each cut to hold up the gory trophies, as an offering to the evil

418

being that hovered in the shadows. The pain and the horror rolled over them, in wave after wave.

The warrior lad and the old woman stood nearby, powerless to help, surrounded, held at bay by vile enemies, who had almost overwhelmed them. Dark rocks surrounded them and gloom closed in on every side.

All three awoke simultaneously to stare at each other with terror in their eyes.

"It's the people from the dreams!"

"It's very bad, they need us right now. We don't have time to wander around anymore."

"Let's do it, but what or who do we focus on?"

"The young warrior, he has always been the clearest for some reason," Kyonna said to Simea and Aibhera as she grabbed both their hands.

Kyonna began first, and Simea and Aibhera quickly joined her. The journey was not like their practice sessions at *shifting*, darkness surrounded them for a moment then a loud bang occurred, as they arrived. Bodies flew in every direction, as the force of their arrival hurled both groups of combatants backward.

"Wall, now!" Simea barked into the sudden silence in the midst of the bedlam of blood and bodies.

CHAPTER 43: RESCUE

Suddenly there was an explosion. Laakea's remaining sword flew from his hand, as the force of the blast threw him and Isil back toward the cave entrance. They both lay stunned, waiting for the end to come. The noise of their attackers was muffled somehow. Isil thought the blast might have deafened them but when she sat up, she saw three, slender ochre-skinned people standing between them and their attackers. The three newcomers were singing. A wall of light blocked the passage between them and the men, who wanted to kill her and Laakea.

Laakea rose, picked up his weapons and wiped the blood off the grips on the thighs of his pants. With swords in hand, he shrugged his shoulders and rolled his neck to get rid of the tension as he stepped toward the three smaller young people, two females and one male holding back the Dark One's followers.

"I don't know how you got here, but thank you for your aid," he said. "I'm ready now. Can you let them through one at a time?"

"I think we can, but it would be better if we all fled," the youngest female replied.

"We will not leave without our friend."

"Where is he?" Kyonna asked.

Laakea could see that the two girls were sisters. They were nearly identical in appearance.

"In there," he pointed in the direction of the altar chamber. "Now let em through one at a time so I can kill them all and retrieve him."

By this time, Isil had hobbled over to join them. "Maybe dey got a better way lad. Did yuh ask em dat?"

"They might not, but I do," the younger sister said with confidence. "By the way, my name is Kyonna." She batted her eyelashes and smiled at Laakea. "This is my sister, Aibhera and our friend Simea."

"Stop flirting Ky, and do whatever you're going to do quickly. Sim and I are getting tired of holding this shield," Aibhera, the older sister said as she stopped singing for a moment.

"Fine, on the count of three, you two drop the shield and let me try this." She turned to Laakea. "And as for you, you big strong handsome thing," She lay her hand on his blood spattered arm, "you get ready, in case this doesn't work."

"Ky —hurry!"

Kyonna knelt on the floor of the passage to pick up two fistfuls of grit and gravel. She motioned for Isil to do the same. "Now on three, throw this stuff up in front of us. Once the shield is down, Sim and Aibby hit the dirt. Otherwise — never mind, just duck and cover. Everybody ready?"

"One, two, three."

Several things happened simultaneously. The glowing shield wall vanished. Simea and Aibhera hugged the floor of the cave. Isil and Kyonna threw the gravel into the air. The gravel and sand started to fall to the floor, then abruptly and violently changed direction. It flew at the men, as though Kyonna had loosed it from a sling. The assassins at the front of the pack lurched

421

forward, as the shield dropped. Some fell dead or bleeding where they had stood, when the stones hit them. The grit and dust blinded others. Those near the back, who remained uninjured, stood stunned by the event.

Before Laakea could move, three large furry bodies hurtled past him into the remains of the crowd. Three wolves snapped and lunged at the remaining men, driving them back into the chamber. The Nethera shrieked and spat in rage, once it saw the wolves.

Once Laakea recovered from his surprise, he joined the mêlée and waded into them swinging with the last of his strength. Isil hobbled along behind him making sure that the wounded would never rise again. Soon only a handful remained.

While the wolves held the remnant at bay, Laakea managed to find his bow and one last arrow. Before Laakea and the rest managed to enter the altar room, the wolves had the last of the men down. Isil finished them off, while Laakea nocked his last arrow and drew it back.

Dreyenar stood over Rehaak's bleeding body with a knife poised for the killing stroke.

"Not one step closer or I kill your friend," he snapped. "He'll make a fine offering to Ashd'eravaak here," he jerked his head in the direction of the Nethera, who hovered behind him. "And then, he'll feast on all your lives as well."

"He best be better at feasting than duh last one we met," Isil crowed defiantly. "Muh large muscular friend ended its foul-smelling life last night with one o' dem nice shiny blades yuh see hangin from his belt."

The wolves snarled menacingly at the Dark One, showing their bright fangs. The Nethera spat and screeched in rage before it dissolved into mist. The overpowering stench in the gallery vanished with it. It left Dreyenar alone standing over Rehaak's helpless body. Drey was so intent on the group facing him that he did not noticed its departure.

"Yer phony god just abandoned yuh," Isil taunted.

Dreyenar turned his head to look back. Laakea loosed his arrow. It took Dreyenar in the throat driving him backwards. The knife fell from his hand, as he lay on his back choking on his own blood.

Isil rushed forward to cut the unconscious Rehaak loose from the altar. "He's chewed up somethin fierce, but I think he'll be all right once we get him mended proper."

The three Sokai stood staring at the wolves in astonishment.

"What's wrong?" Laakea asked.

"It's *them*," Aibhera answered, "The three of the bright host. We saw them watching over you all in our dreams."

"You are talking about the wolves? They have helped us before." Laakea said, shrugging off their comment.

"Those are no ordinary wolves," Simea insisted.

The wolves looked at one another for a moment, then they began to change, growing taller, they stood upright and became three brawny men, wearing silvery armor that looked similar to Laakea's breastplate.

"We are sorry for the need to deceive you and Rehaak, the leader said to Laakea, but it was necessary for our mission. We did not want the Dark Ones aware of our involvement too soon. We must leave you now and return to protect Abalon. The Nethera have discovered its location. Farewell and fear not, we will return when we can." With that said, all three became translucent, and then disappeared.

CHAPTER 44: CONCLUSION

The five companions made their way back to Laakea's house carrying Rehaak. There was a good deal of discussion, as they all told their individual stories along the way.

They reached Laakea's house before midday. Isil and Laakea dressed Rehaak's wounds, as he drifted in and out of consciousness. They put him into Laakea's bed to recover, while Isil stayed to watch over him crooning softly, Laakea returned to talk to the three young Sokai who had seated themselves around the table.

"Thank-you, again friends for your timely arrival."

What is your plan now, Laakea," Simea began. "Our dreams led us here, but we have no sense of what we must do next. Perhaps you could lead us."

"Not I, but once Rehaak recovers I'm nearly positive that we shall make a trip to Baradon, the homeland of my people. You are more than welcome to join us. That wall you put up was more than helpful. It saved our lives."

He looked at Kyonna before continuing. "That trick you did with the pebbles was amazing. Where did you learn to do that?"

Yes where *did* you learn to do that, Ky?" Aibhera echoed.

Haven't you ever wondered how I became the best Windrider ever, sister?"

"I can give things a little push, when I need to. I discovered it by accident. I almost crashed, when I first started on the gliders. I panicked and tried to push myself away from the cliff face. It worked. I push against the ground and it gives me more lift. That's why I could always carry heavier loads with less wind than anyone else could. I just expected that if I pushed very hard on smaller things like the pebbles the things would move instead of me."

"Lucky for us it did," Laakea said admiringly.

"I'm sorry but I find that I am exhausted. I can barely keep my eyes open. I must rest now to recover." Simea apologized.

"I think we all feel the same," Aibhera added. "Channeling the Creator's power as we have done drains our physical bodies. Can we speak more of this tomorrow? Perhaps Rehaak will be well enough to join us."

***

Rehaak could hear the sound of Isil's' voice singing in the distance. She sounded far away. And farther still were the voices of Laakea and the others discussing what they should do next. Rehaak knew that his friends had rescued him from the brink of death. His physical pain was great, but the pain of knowing he had lived in rebellion for too long was greater. It weighed down his soul. He suddenly knew what had been holding him back for so long.

He had never truly trusted the Creator. He had tried to follow Him, without really surrendering to the Faithfull One. He used that name intentionally, because he knew that his halfhearted commitment would no longer be enough. If he were going to continue, he would have to commit everything to his God and serve Him with all his heart.

It seemed that his whole life, to this point, had been one long lesson in building trust. He would have to trust that his God truly was the Faithful One. He had lived long enough, crippled by doubt, to realize that Isil was right when she had said there were things worse than death.

Rehaak heard his followers settling in for the night. It felt strange to think of them as his followers. His heart cried out silently to his God for help, while Isil was still singing healing into his body.

"I need you. I need your help. I am sorry that I never truly trusted you. My heart is hard and I am not fit for your service."

"Do not call what I have set aside for my service unfit. No my son, what you need is my k'harsa. I have called you to lead and you must lead. I have chosen you and I will restore your heart so that you may serve me completely for the first time. I will be your God and you shall lead my people," a gentle voice whispered.

Rehaak wept for joy inside, as a sense of The Creator's love for him filled his heart. With this knowledge and acceptance, he could continue. As long as he knew that his God accepted him, he felt that he could face all the difficulties ahead. His inner conflict had been the most difficult part of his quest and that was behind him now. He finally felt true peace.

He fell asleep to the sound of Isil's singing.

***

The new day found them all well rested. Even Isil had managed to get some sleep. Rehaak was awake too, though he was swathed in bandages from head to toe. He was in remarkably good spirits and insisted in sitting up to take part in the discussion after breakfast.

"Let us share what we know. You have stuck a courageous and decisive blow to the work of the Dark Ones. I owe you all my life, and I am very grateful."

Rehaak nodded to each of them in turn. It was all he could manage without too much pain. As he looked at their faces, he could finally see the love that they held in their hearts for him.

Laakea began, breaking the silence, "I have far more *Ehlbringa* to work with and I intend to make more tools to combat the Dark Ones. We have bought some time to get better prepared for what lies ahead."

"We have seriously hindered the Dark Ones work here in Khel Braah for several reasons. We have provoked them into revealing their actions and acting openly against us. The entire village of Dun Dale is now aware of their plots. I know that does not seem like an important thing, but I expect that word will spread to New Hope and the other towns of the eastern slopes. I never realized how quickly word travels between the settlements out here," Rehaak said fighting against the weakness he still felt.

"Yes, and the Aethera sprang to our aid as well," added Simea. That's no small thing. I suspect that when we worked together that it prompted them to help us, and to reveal themselves and their intentions. They will be powerful allies."

"However, I am concerned that the Nethera have discovered the location of Abalon and our people," he added.

"That might work in our favor. We might be able to convince more of our people to join us in the fight, now that we have proof of what the Nethera are doing. If they are under attack, they just might be forced into action."

"We don't understand all of the implications in the scroll that Eideron left us, but we now possess Eideron's portion of the Book of Songs. We also know that he too suspected that the Aetheriad is in Baradon," Aibhera said.

"And we have made a good beginning in understanding the power contained in the Songs of our people, and the other songs of Aarda. Perhaps Rehaak can use the Book of Songs to encourage people here to follow the Old Way again, right Isil?" Kyonna added.

Isil acknowledged Kyonna's comment with a nod before beginning, "An like I told Laakea, we thinned em out a bunch too. Dey are gonna be a long while collectin more o' dere followers tuh mess with us again, 'specially if dey are workin in Baradon at duh same time. Dey is gonna be spread mighty thin fer a spell."

"The most important thing — we are no longer alone in this struggle," said Rehaak, as he looked out at the faces of the others from behind his bandages. "It is good to know that we will likely find the Aetheriad in Baradon. All our information leads us there."

Rehaak's heart filled with new hope, as he began to summarize the conversation. It was difficult to believe that all his apprehension had evaporated, like water in a pot left too long on the fire.

"We know some of the objectives of the enemy. Our own objective has become much clearer and we have bought time to recover and prepare. We have new friends and allies, with new knowledge and potent weapons available to us. The light is dawning on a new day in Aarda."

"By uniting members of all three races in this conflict, the Aethera have joined our fight. Although we are few in number, we have struck a powerful first blow against the Dark Ones. Those who follow the Nethera are convinced that they are doing what is best for mankind. They are deceived and there may yet be hope for them if we can show them their error."

"We are growing to understand the abilities that The Creator has given us. The Book of Songs has provided more information about the war in the

Aetherial realm and our part in it. I have discovered that The Creator has ceded control of Aarda to us who follow Him. As long as we exist, the Nethera cannot rule it, or destroy it. They can do a great deal of damage to Aarda and to us but they cannot win outright. With the knowledge it contains, we can begin to undo the damage caused by the Song of the Defiler."

"Now it is time to rest, to recuperate and to prepare for war."

Characters

Males

Aelfric: Laakea's father
Aelrin: King of the Eniila
Eideron: Sokai elder
Himish: Sokai elder
Herron: Sokai elder
Laakea: Eniila youth
Leoned: Stepfather of Kyonna and Aibhera
Rehaak: Sage and Healer
Simea: Sokai youth
Dreyenar Asanudain: Voerkett's second in command
Radik: Eldest son of Raamya
Ogun: Middle son of Raamya
Mato: Raamya's youngest Son and follower of the Dark Ones
Aert: Innkeeper of the Dancing Dog in Dun Dale
Voerkett Telmakus: Leader of the Cult of Ashd'eravaak/Isil's husband

Females

Aibhera: Sokai girl
Amoreya: Speaker of the Sokai Synod
Isilakari/Isil: Drover
Kyonna: Aibhera's younger Sister/Windrider
Riessa: Mother of Aibhera and Kyonna
Shelhera: Laakea's mother
Breisha: Aert the innkeeper's youngest daughter
Aamori: See the song Aamori's House
Latonia: Raamya's wife

Nethera Leaders:

S'ek'zekaar: Supreme leader of the Nethera

Ashd'eravaak: Nethera in charge of the Abrhaani
Jesh'zed'haak: Nethera in charge of the Eniila, and
S'enkashaar: Nethera killed by Laakea

Aethera Leaders

Naom'han: Supreme leader of the Aethera
Shel'gharim: Aethera in charge of the Sokai
Sa'khalin, G'haelarin, Sh'imbalaan: Three Aethera who
guarded Rehaak